EIGHT KISSES

EIGHT ALL-NEW TALES OF HANUKKAH
ROMANCE

LORI ANN BAILEY   MINDY KLASKY

ROSE GREY   MICHELLE MARS   JT SILVER

ERIN EISENBERG   LAVINIA KLEIN

LYNNE SILVER

PEABRIDGE
PRESS

Published by Peabridge Press
P.O. Box 42133, Arlington, VA 22204

ISBN 978-1-95018-404-0

100219mkm

CONTENTS

EDITORS' NOTE

A Miracle of Lights…

The story of Hanukkah has been around for over 2,000 years. It is a tale that comes to us from the books of the Maccabees. In the year 168 BC, at the orders of the Syrian king Antiochus Epiphanes, soldiers were sent to Jerusalem to abolish Judaism by outlawing the observance of Shabbat, festivals, circumcision, and Jewish marriages. Jewish people were given the choice to convert or face death as Syrian soldiers set up altars and idols of their Greek gods in the Jewish Temple, renaming it after Zeus. Judah Maccabee led a rebellion against the oppressive forces, winning two major battles and soundly defeating the Syrians.

Centuries later, a story was written in the Talmud about a jar of oil that was used during the rededication of the Temple. It was said to have had only enough oil to provide light for one day, but it miraculously lasted eight nights. Hanukkah means "dedication" and today this holiday reminds Jews to rededicate themselves to keeping Jewish religion, customs, and culture shining bright so it may be passed on to future generations.

Several years ago, some fellow romance writers were discussing books we'd like to read. Several of us had enjoyed the holiday stories that typically are published every December, but we longed to read stories in our own, Jewish, tradition.

We talked about putting together an anthology, but there wasn't enough time to create a quality book before that year's winter holiday season. The next year, we began discussions earlier, but we were stymied by technical challenges related to compiling and distributing one book from multiple writers. The year after that, some of the most interested authors had committed their time to other projects, and the year after *that*...

It would be an exaggeration to say that it took a miracle to pull together this anthology. But we're thrilled that so many authors answered our open call for submissions, making time to contribute such wonderful romantic stories covering a range of time periods, locations, and characters. Our only wish was that the Talmudic jar of oil had lasted for weeks, or even months, so that we could have included all the amazing stories we received.

Please enjoy *Eight Kisses*, our way of passing on the flame and celebrating Jewish heritage.

Mindy Klasky
Lori Ann Bailey
Washington, DC
November 12, 2019

A HIGHLANDER FOR HANUKKAH

LORI ANN BAILEY

AUTHOR'S NOTE

HISTORY IS RIFE WITH RELIGIOUS TENSIONS. IN 1290 JEWS WERE expelled from England. Although allowed to return in 1655 because Cromwell wanted Jewish merchants to transfer their trade routes from Holland to London, they were not allowed to become citizens. The London Society for Promoting Christianity Amongst the Jews officially started in 1809, but was active before that time period. Some of the historical documents regarding the group's misunderstanding of the Jewish faith are appalling. Jews were afforded more freedom in Scotland. On the converse, for hundreds of years throughout Great Britain, Catholics were forced to hide aspects of their beliefs. The strife between Catholics and Protestants even reached into the monarchy and led to revolts, wars, and the loss of many lives. I hope you enjoy "A Highlander for Hanukkah," an interfaith tale of hope, love, and acceptance.

FIRST NIGHT OF HANUKKAH

Edinburgh, Scotland
Saturday, December 14, 1807

SHOSHANA MESSINGER STEADIED HER BREATHING AS THE Highlander bent to retrieve the smoking pistol that had been pointed at her chest only a heartbeat ago. The echo of the thief's feet still pounded across the pavement. But she was safe, thanks to brawny James MacDonald, her father's accountant, who took her arm and hustled her through the door of the shop.

Blood dripped from his brow. She'd occasionally—no, she couldn't fool herself—usually studied the man when he visited her father to discuss his ledgers, but now she had a valid excuse for staring at him so intently.

"You're hurt. Were you shot?" she asked.

"Nae, the bullet struck the stone. But the arse got in a punch." His thick brogue washed over her. Although she'd known the man for four months, it was the first time they'd spoken.

"Come inside and let me look at it."

Before guiding James further inside, she placed her menorah in the stand she'd brought out earlier. It sat outside the door of the

Messinger's Shoe and Clothing Emporium, where she currently resided above the stairs, on the next level with her father. Not a drop of oil had spilled from her treasured heirloom despite her hands that still trembled as if she bounced along in a carriage.

The darkness of December nights crept in early here in Scotland, but there was still some light from the surrounding buildings. She'd return to say the prayer and light the wick after she'd seen to James.

Once inside, she bolted the door.

Her father burst into the room. "What was that noise? What happened?"

"I'll tell you while I check on James's injury. Up the stairs," she ordered both the men as she motioned to the steps.

The criminal might come back, and she wanted the safety of the home that was just now becoming familiar to her. She'd come to live with her father recently due to the death of her grandmother. In London, she'd learned to be wary of the vagrants who had loitered on the streets near her family's shop. She'd presumed the city was safer here in the north, but perhaps she'd assessed her surroundings in haste.

After making their way through the shop, they climbed the back steps into the apartment on the next floor. "Sit," she instructed as she pointed at the table. Both men obeyed as she retrieved a wet cloth.

"What happened, daughter?" Her father's voice shook.

"A brute tried to push his way into the shop. He had a gun." She took a soothing breath, then continued, "But James stopped him."

Her gaze rested on her savior. He had thick blond hair, but what caught her attention was the way his body commanded the whole room, not with his size, but with confidence.

"Did ye recognize the man?" James asked.

"No, I've never seen him." She dabbed at the spot on the Highlander's head and was surprised that her hands were steady. The smell of sandalwood and fresh air reached her nose, and she leaned in, inhaling the masculine scent. The injury appeared to be a small cut that would most likely heal quickly.

"What did he say?" her father asked as she gently caressed the skin under James's injury. The Highlander's flesh was smooth and warm despite the cold, clear evening.

The man flinched, then studied her as if it was the first time he'd seen her. Odd, as she'd been watching him for months, always averting her attention before he could catch her looking.

"He said, 'Get inside and show me where the money is.' Then he pulled a pistol from his jacket and pointed it at me," she told her father.

A shiver ran down her spine. There was no way to convey the menace that had been laced into the words or the desperate cruelty of the brute's terrifying expression. The thief was gone, and her father was already pale with worry. It was probably best not to frighten him further.

"That's when James tackled him."

She smiled at the man who watched her with the bluest of eyes. She'd suspected they were this dark sapphire shade but had never been close enough to see them. They were like the sky just before twilight, a sight she had missed since her youth. She'd not been blessed with the view since going to work in London, and even now she was cloistered in her father's shop in the middle of a city with tall buildings impeding her view.

"Thank heaven you were around." Her father clasped the man on his shoulder.

"Your cut isn't too deep. I think it will heal nicely," she said. She forced herself to take a step back.

"Thank ye." His attention remained locked on her, and the room seemed to tilt. Her chest fluttered. To break the spell, she dashed back to her room to put away her medicinals and bandages. She took her time, making certain her pulse returned to a normal pace before she reemerged into the main room.

Her father and James sat at the table, hunched close, conversing in hushed tones. She straightened her skirts and moved toward them. James glanced at her, and the crease in his brow straightened.

"Will you stay for the meal tonight? I've made more than we can eat." She was indebted to this man who had stopped the burglary and perhaps even saved her life.

The brute's stare still haunted her, and the Highlander's presence provided a calming influence.

"Nae, thank ye. It smells delicious, but I must get home." He stood, his chair scraping backward as he put distance between them. Something had spooked him and it hadn't been the burglar. Had her open stare been alarming?

"I insist you join us tomorrow then." Her father smiled at the man. "Shoshana is making fried cheese, and you have not truly had a pleasurable meal until you've tried it."

"I shouldnae intrude."

"Nonsense, tomorrow, around sundown. I insist." Her father rested his hand on James's shoulder.

The Highlander nodded and they headed downstairs.

Once below in the shop, Shoshana grabbed one of the new matches her father had ordered from Paris, along with the bottle that would ignite the stick.

They walked out into the cold night air.

"Good night." James nodded at her father, then returned his gaze to her.

She smiled. "Thank you and good night."

His regard remained on her a moment longer, then he pivoted, and her father called out to him, "See you tomorrow."

James hurried down the street.

She glanced at her father and nodded, then they recited the Hanukkah blessings.

Blessed are You, Lord our G-d, King of the universe, who has sanctified us with His commandments, and commanded us to kindle the Hanukkah light.

Blessed are You, Lord our G-d, King of the universe, who performed miracles for our forefathers in those days, at this time.

They continued with the blessing reserved for the first night.

Blessed are You, Lord our G-d, King of the universe, who has granted us life, sustained us, and enabled us to reach this occasion.

As she lit the wicks, she added a small silent prayer of thanks that James had been close at hand when the burglar had appeared…a small miracle on the first night of Hanukkah.

~

James MacDonald climbed onto his horse, then touched his temple one last time. Not for the ache, but because Shoshana's soft hand had sent tingles fluttering down his spine. His flesh was still sensitive, and he couldn't stop thinking about her.

If he'd not been passing by David Messinger's shop on the way to the stables, he wouldn't have been there when the arse had threatened the lass. And if the man had gotten her into the shop, both she and her father might be dead now.

Over the last few months, there had been a rash of burglaries, some of which had culminated in murders. The killings had him on edge. One of his own clients had been a victim. He'd not gotten a good look at the man tonight, but the arse's voice and build had been familiar. Of course, he saw hundreds of people a day at the table he owned at the market.

He went to bed that night recalling the slain man whose accounts he'd kept and how a whole family had been eliminated as they slumbered. It reminded him of the short conversation he'd had with David. The man had voiced concerns regarding a few clients he was having trouble collecting debts from, but then Shoshana had come back into the room, and David had told him they'd discuss business another time. James didn't like the emerging thought that perhaps the two were connected.

The next day, back in the city, he stabled his horse and spent all morning at his table, but while he tried to concentrate on the accounting work he was hired to do, he thought of Shoshana and how frightened she must have been. Leaving his assistant in charge, he strolled the short distance to the Messinger's shop.

They had a brisk business, and he had to wait for the lass to finish helping a customer before he walked up and presented her with a package he'd picked up on his way out of the market.

Her eyes, a deep shade of brown, lit. "What's this?"

"Something to say thank ye for tending to my wee cut last night. 'Tis also a present to welcome ye to Scotland." While she'd been here a few months, he'd never had an excuse to speak with the small lass, but now that he did, he wasn't going to miss the opportunity.

As he handed her the bundle, their hands brushed, and he became aware of how smooth her skin was and how she smelled of honey and cinnamon.

She peeled the thin cloth back to expose the treat.

"What is it?" she asked.

"'Tis Scottish shortbread. I would have brought ye lavender so ye would know the warmth and beauty of my homeland, but 'tis no' in season. This was a favorite to our Queen Mary, and I hope ye will enjoy it too."

"I'll save it for after the meal this evening. Will you still be joining us?"

He hoped that was anticipation in her voice.

"Aye, but are ye certain ye wish to have another mouth to feed?" For years, he had been solely responsible for his siblings, and he knew the burden it was to care for others. He now enjoyed his nights alone, but he felt a strange pull toward Shoshana and found himself wanting to spend the evening in her company. Anticipation coursed through him at the thought of seeing her again.

"Yes. I would like for you to join us."

"I will see ye tonight then, but I need to get back to work now."

She nodded.

"I almost forgot. The reason I came was to tell ye and yer father to be careful. Keep yer doors locked at night and be aware of yer surroundings."

"I will."

Satisfied that she'd be vigilant, he smiled and turned to leave.

As he strolled down the street, he found himself studying the faces in the crowds, looking for the man from the previous evening, but no one stood out.

Back at work, the scent of honey from another stall drifted his way, and he thought of Shoshana and the many times he'd seen her when he'd visited David. She seemed so alone, and her father had confided in James of their recent familial loss. He knew what a difficult adjustment this move must have been for her.

A drunkard bumped into a table across from his, and the vendor's wares crashed to the ground. He recognized the lout as one of the men some of his clients lent money to. He would have to warn his associates that they should no longer support the wastrel's habits because he seemed to be losing control. He wondered if the man could be one of the clients who was delinquent in payments to David. But perhaps he was overthinking it. Seeing a gun pointed at Shoshana last night had him on edge and questioning everything he saw.

SECOND NIGHT OF HANUKKAH

Shoshana rushed around the kitchen to be certain she'd have the meal prepared on time. James was kind, and the way he looked at her made her feel important. He could be a friend. She hadn't made any since leaving the world she'd grown up in.

And she wanted to share her customs with him. He was Catholic, but he'd been doing business with her father, so maybe he was open to understanding or at least tolerant of other points of view. With all the English laws aimed at trying to change her heritage and religion, it was refreshing to think she could have a conversation with someone who might not try to sway her.

It wasn't yet dusk when her father crested the stairs with James. The Highlander was a tall man, but most of the men in Scotland towered over her. His gaze met hers and she fought to hide the flush heating her neck.

It was silly to act like a young girl in front of him. She was nearly twenty-one years of age and well past when a lady should be hunting a husband. A family was the last thing she could have with a man who was not the same religion as her, and Jewish men were rare in Scotland and in England, where she'd lived most of her life. She would be foolish to focus too intently on this unavailable man.

Water dripped from his blond hair, giving it a slightly darker hue.

"Is it raining?" she asked.

"Aye. It came on quite sudden."

"It's a good thing you brought the menorah in this morning, Shoshana," her father said.

"Yes. I agree. It's almost time to light it. Should we do that first? James, would you like to join us?"

"Aye. I would be happy to."

They descended the stairs, and James stood by respectfully as she and her father said a brief prayer and lit the wicks in two of the oil wells of the menorah she'd been placed in the window.

"Why did ye have the candelabrum outside last night?" James asked quietly.

"It's a custom we inherited from my grandmother, along with this special menorah," she explained. "It has a stand made for the outdoors, but the weather sometimes interferes."

"'Tis lovely," he said.

His compliment warmed her. The glow of the lights was pleasing, but she knew with each passing night, their brilliance would bring more joy. Perhaps she could find a way to invite him back when all the candles were lit. She'd love to see what he thought of them then.

Back upstairs, the men eased into their seats as she poured wine for each of them. Her father recounted the tale of Hanukkah to James. As she placed their food on the table, she was thrilled to see the Highlander enthralled with the tale of how her people had led a successful rebellion and then rededicated the Second Temple.

"What is this?" James asked as he sampled the meal. His eyes brightened.

"It's a pancake of fried cheese. Do you like it?"

"Aye, I've never had anything like it."

"This is also a tradition from my grandmother, but I have heard in Eastern Europe, people are starting to make them with potatoes too. I may have to try that soon, but I have such fond memories of this recipe."

"My mother used to make the most delicious salmon. Maybe one evening I will bring ye both some. I still have her recipe even if I haven't taken the time to make it recently."

"I would like that," she chimed in.

"I think Shoshana would enjoy Scotland's salmon," said her father.

They finished the meal, and as she cleared the table, she relished the giddy sensation that buzzed through her at the thought of seeing James again.

~

James reclined in his chair, at ease with David, but also trying to avoid openly staring at Shoshana in front of her father. He'd lived alone for two years now, since his youngest sister had married, and he had always looked forward to returning to a quiet home at the end of the day. The responsibilities thrown upon him when he'd been but a lad of fifteen had been tremendous. He'd seen to the care of his siblings, and shortly after he turned twenty-four, he'd struck out on his own.

Shoshana moved around the kitchen with ease, comfortable and content in her surroundings. Her rose-colored gown complimented her golden skin and her dark eyes. Some man would be lucky to have her for a wife one day.

"I've saved this for tonight." The lass turned around with a familiar bundle in her hands, set it on the table, then poured them all a small cup of ale.

Banging rent the air. Shoshana flinched. Perhaps she was still shaken by the incident the previous evening. He was. Seeing a gun aimed at her heart had nearly stopped his.

"I'll see what they want. It's likely just a customer who couldn't get here before we closed," David said and headed down the stairs as Shoshana settled at the table again.

"This is delicious." Her eyes closed for a moment as she savored the buttery treat.

"I can teach ye how to make it." Why had he volunteered to do such a thing? And why had he offered to bring them his mother's salmon?

Since coming to Edinburgh, he'd avoided anything that reminded him of familial responsibility, and one of those things was cooking. He typically purchased something small to eat on his way home. Although, he had been spending less time in his cottage lately, preferring to keep long hours at his worktable and then visiting his account clients in the early evening hours.

"I would like that." She took another bite, then washed it down with the ale. "Have ye always lived in Edinburgh?"

"Nae, I come from the Glencoe, but once my younger sisters all found husbands, I came here to put my talent to use."

"And what is that?"

"Numbers. I've always been good with them."

Her smile was genuine, and he found himself wanting to lean in and tell her more about himself.

"What's it like to have sisters? I always wanted a sibling, but my mother died shortly after I was born."

"They kept me busy, and 'twas a lot of responsibility to see to them, but I enjoy visiting with them now."

Shoshana opened her mouth to ask another question, but her father's steps sounded on the steps.

David said, "There was no one there—most likely someone drinking or a child playing."

"That's odd. It sounded urgent." She shrugged.

She had been correct to assume it. The noise below had set him on edge too, but if there was no one there, it must have been something innocent.

"Yes, but nothing is there. And the rain has stopped. I'm glad you won't have to ride home in it," David said.

He was reluctant to leave the warmth of the Messinger's home and return to his, but it was getting late, and he needed to let them rest and prepare for the next day.

"I should get home while it's clear."

Shoshana's shoulders dipped. Perhaps she was disappointed to see him go. Anticipation flared in his chest. Would she welcome a visit from him again? Could he devise another reason to stop by to see her?

And why did he want to come back? This was what he'd said he never wanted again. Responsibility, others depending on him. He didn't want the burden of a family, so why had he enjoyed this evening?

"Thank ye for the meal and the company. 'Twas lovely."

He stood, and so did the lovely lass across from him. Their gazes met and locked. A sensation akin to the sun warming his face on a bonny spring day hugged him. He didn't want to go, but this wasn't his life. They could be friends; he couldn't give her anything more.

"Thank you for joining us and for the shortbread. It's my new favorite treat."

"Ye're welcome. I'm glad ye like it," he said.

David escorted him to the exit.

"Be certain to bolt the door. I dinnae like that someone banged on it so soon after what happened yesterday."

"I agree. I will lock everything tight. Thanks for coming tonight. It was nice to see Shoshana smile. She hasn't had much of a reason to since coming to Edinburgh."

"I like her smile," he said before he could censor the words.

David grinned, and he couldn't help but think the man might be encouraging a relationship with his daughter.

THIRD NIGHT OF HANUKKAH

THE SUN HAD DISAPPEARED HOURS AGO, AND JAMES WAS JUST NOW walking toward the stable where his horse would be waiting. The evening was cold but still, and as he passed the Messingers' shop, he almost skipped a step as he took in the menorah lighting up the entrance.

The glow was like a beacon, and he wanted to turn in, knock on the door and drink in the sight of bonny brown eyes. But it wasn't just that. Shoshana loved who she was and where she'd come from. Her quiet confidence and sense of self drew him to her.

A desire to be near her invaded, but he pushed the longing away —it would pass. His thumbs grazed the inside of his hands, and he remembered the blisters he'd earned while trying to provide for his family. He was free and didn't want entanglements. Picking up his pace, he bolted for his horse and the silence of the home he had longed for since his parents' death.

~

Shoshana was startled awake by a banging at the shop's entrance. She bolted up, and as she made it to the kitchen, the sound of her father's footfalls on the steps reached her ears. Fear stabbed at her. It was late into the evening, and no one with good intent would be out on the city streets.

She glanced around for anything she could use as a weapon should someone breach the doors uninvited. Several months ago, a shopkeeper and his family a few streets over were attacked and found dead the next morning. She shuddered.

"Father," she called out as she moved down the stairs and noticed a small light flickering in the dark.

"There's no one there." He came to her side.

"Why is this happening?" It was too much of a coincidence.

"I'm not certain, but tomorrow, I'll speak with the magistrate and see if he'll put an extra patrol on the streets."

They returned to their beds, but she barely slept.

The next morning, as they opened the shop, her father received an urgent message from his supplier in Glasgow. A shipment had come in damaged, and his assistance was needed right away to sort out which merchandise he would accept. He would travel immediately, and she'd be spending the next few evenings alone.

Dread spiked in her veins. But she could do this. She and her grandmother had tended the shop in London together for years, and her father's apprentice would help during the day. She could handle a few nights here on her own.

FOURTH NIGHT OF HANUKKAH

THE APPRENTICE HAD LEFT, AND SHOSHANA WAS ABOUT TO CLOSE the store for the evening. It was raining again, but she was glad for it. The bad weather meant she would light her menorah inside again tonight and lock out anyone attempting to gain access to the shop. Perhaps the deluge would keep away anyone with ill intent as well.

A *swish* of air and *tinkle* of a small bell alerted her to another customer.

"Good evening." A smooth, familiar voice wrapped her in a comforting embrace.

She hadn't even glanced up, but she knew... James.

She fought back the excitement even as her heart thrummed in her chest. "Good evening." Why would he stop by? "Father is not here tonight. Are you looking for him?"

"Nae. He came to see me earlier in the day. He wanted me to check that all was well here tonight." Her father must have been more frightened by the recent intrusions than he'd let on.

"Well, I'm pleased to see you. Would you like to stay for a meal? I have plenty without my father here. I had not counted on his absence."

"I would be happy to join ye. I'm just going home to an empty house."

She'd not thought of it before. Despite doing business with her father, he was much younger. Closer in age to her, but she'd never thought he might have others waiting for him to come home. "Why? Are you not married?"

"I never wanted a wife." His eyes focused on her, then shifted away as he finished his statement. "Before."

He looked puzzled.

"Give me a moment to lock the doors and light the candles. Then we can head up."

"Aye. Can I help?"

"I have it, thanks."

James stood close by as she said her blessing and lit the wicks.

"'Tis a lovely prayer."

She dreamed of one day sharing these rituals with her own children as her grandmother had with her. It would be her way to honor her past and her people. And although this man beside her seemed to understand, he was not Jewish. Her stomach churned as she imagined her own children being forced to attend services of another religion as her family had been.

James was not an option for a husband.

"Thank you," she said and started up the steps.

"I hope you like soup," she said as she filled a bowl with the chicken and vegetables stewed in a broth. It was one of her favorites. With the rain today, she'd thought it would be comforting, and since there had been fewer customers, she'd also had an opportunity to bake bread. It would be a nice meal for them.

"It smells delicious."

"Would you like a glass of wine?"

"I would enjoy a glass. Thank ye."

She placed the drink in front of James, then slid in to take the seat opposite him.

"Tell me about yer move to Scotland. I ken David is happy to have ye here. He was always telling me stories of visiting ye in London."

"Edinburgh is quite different, but I like it here." She hadn't realized how true the statement was until now. She was afforded freedoms here that hadn't been possible in England.

"Do ye miss London?" He dipped his spoon into the soup.

"No. I miss the home of my youth though, before my uncle died and we went to care for his shop."

"This is delicious."

"Thank you."

He took another spoonful, then continued, "Where were ye before that?"

"Just outside of the city, but it was like a different world. There were birds singing in the mornings, peaceful evenings, and you could see all the stars."

"I can understand that." He gave her a warm smile, and she fancied there was a hint of something mischievous in it. She was flushed, perhaps from her wine, not the imagined interest she thought danced in his eyes.

"I'm sorry about yer grandmother. Ye were close." Now his gaze reflected her loss as if he understood.

"She was like my mother, since mine passed just after my birth. I think it's been hard on my father, not only that he lost her, but that he couldn't manage this place without help. I stayed with my grandmother and uncle, and he came to visit as frequently as possible."

"Yer father told me."

She was surprised her father had confided in James.

"Have you known him long?"

"For almost two years. He's a good man. I enjoy helping him with his accounts."

"And you have not been deterred by working for a Jewish man?" She bit the inside of her cheek, worried he'd be like most of the men in London, the ones who shunned others for beliefs that didn't match their own.

One of the neighborhood Englishmen had forced her family to attend church services once a month. It had been a law for as long as she could remember in England, a way to try to sway Jewish families to accept the Protestants' words as gospel and force the Jews to turn their back on their faith and traditions. It had made this move bearable, knowing she wouldn't be subjected to the same rules in Scotland.

"Nae. No' at all. I understand what it's like to no' have yer beliefs recognized. Mass was outlawed here for a long time, and we're still not allowed to celebrate some holidays."

"I didn't realize." But she did recall hearing of religious turmoil in Scotland over the years.

She also remembered that traditional tartan kilts had been outlawed at one point. Perhaps the people here were more understanding because of the trials they'd been through. The will forced upon them by the English was why she had only seen a few men in tartan. And when she did, it was typically for a special occasion.

"It's been going on for a long time. People should be able to practice their beliefs however they see fit."

She took a sip of wine and relaxed. There was something comforting about knowing he was so open to others despite their divergent views. But still, working with someone was different from raising a family. She was certain he would want his wife and children to hold his beliefs.

~

James leaned back in the chair as Shoshana unwrapped the remaining shortbread.

"I've been having one piece a night. Would you like one?"

"Aye. Thank ye." He took a section.

"Do you miss your family?" she asked.

"Aye. But my sisters are all married and have families of their own now." He glanced away and stared out the window, where a gentle rain still tapped on the pane. He mused if it were just a little bit colder, the droplets would be snow.

"What about your parents?"

He'd not talked about the past since coming to Edinburgh. But the intimate atmosphere in the small space made it seem like the right time to do so.

"They both died when I was young. Illnesses."

"Oh, I'm so sorry. I understand your loss. Did you go to live with family?" She placed her palm on his hand. The touch was light, comforting, but it made his whole body tingle.

"Nae. We didnae have any close by and we had a farm to run."

"Did you have an older sibling or anyone to help?" Her concern warmed him.

"I was the oldest and responsible for my sisters," he said as he flipped his hand to hold hers, wanting her to know he welcomed her caress. Her fingers curled into his. Contentment filled him.

"That must have been very hard on you."

"Aye. I managed, but it led me to appreciate the solitude I have now. I like having my home to myself." Her brown eyes were soft and possessed understanding but also a hint of sadness.

With his free hand, he ran his fingers along where he felt small calluses from his work at the market. The blisters from his days of tending the farm and raising three girls had healed. The rough skin reminded him; he was free of obligations now. No one's health and safety rested on his shoulders. When his last sister found a husband, he'd sworn he'd never be responsible for another. He was happy in his new life with no burdens.

So why could he not release his grip on Shoshana? And their meal was finished—why was he lingering?

One glance at the enthralling lass across from him answered his question. Shoshana was refreshing, unafraid to do whatever work must be done, open and honest with her conversations, and she had a generous heart. And he had a desire to kiss her.

She stood and began clearing the table.

"You have done well for your family and yourself. When did you come to Edinburgh?"

"My youngest sister and her husband still have the farm. I started by letting a table at the market and selling goods from home."

She filled their wine glasses, then eased back into her seat. He reached for her hand again. Somehow, he'd missed the few moments they'd not been connected.

"That was brave," she said.

He laughed, liking that she saw it that way, but he felt as if he'd run and hardly looked back. His thumb slid in circles on her soft skin.

"Once I was well-established, I started keeping accounts for some of the other merchants and word of my skill with numbers brought in more business. 'Tis how I met yer father."

"He respects you. It takes quite a bit to earn that from him." Her smile indicated she might see him in the same light. His chest swelled.

"I look up to him as well. He's worked hard to make this business thrive." *And to take care of his family.* James was thankful that her father had brought her here to live with him. He'd never taken the time to enjoy a lass's company before, and he was happy now to share the experience with Shoshana.

She tried to stifle a yawn. The time had grown late, the hours racing by as if they'd been mere minutes.

"I should let ye get some sleep." But he didn't want to let go of her hand.

"I will have to open the store on my own tomorrow." She nodded in agreement but made no move to stand.

"And I will need to be back at work as well."

"You can stay." Her gaze softened, and she looked unsure.

The blood in his veins heated.

"My father would let you use his bed," she said.

She was correct, after the strange occurrences the last few days, David would probably be more comfortable if he stayed to keep a watch on Shoshana. And suddenly, the thought of leaving her alone was unbearable.

He'd only intended to stop by to see to her safety tonight, to ensure she locked the shop up tightly, but he'd stayed for dinner and then enjoyed the conversation so much he'd remained much later than he should have. And now, he didn't want to leave. What if whoever had been harassing her and David returned tonight? And the thought of going out in the frigid rain to return to his cold home seemed daunting. His horse would most likely appreciate staying in the warm stable tonight as well.

"I'll stay." Her smile was all the reassurance he needed to know he'd made the right decision.

"Wonderful." She released his hand and stood.

He missed the connection, but she needed sleep. He doubted she'd gotten much with the fear of someone trying to break into the shop. As of yet, there had been no such incidents tonight. Hopefully whoever had been alarming them had moved on.

"Thank ye for the lovely meal and conversation."

"Let me know if you need anything tonight." A bonny blush stole across her cheeks.

Her gaze slid to his mouth, and her chest rose and fell, as if she thought he'd try to kiss her. His blood heated, but when he didn't move, she blinked and her eyes were again on his.

He wanted to taste her lips, to discover if they were as soft as they appeared, learn if she tasted of wine or honey. But he was only here to keep watch over her. She wasn't his, and giving in to the urge to touch her could destroy his carefully crafted world.

"A warm bed is enough. Thank ye."

Although his instincts fought him, he pivoted and strode toward David's room, afraid that if he stood there longer, he'd ask for her to wrap her arms around him.

As he slid under the covers, he imagined Shoshana snuggled beneath her own blankets. For the first time in years, he was under a roof with another person, and he was comforted by her nearness. She was safe.

He typically tossed and turned in his empty bed, but sleep claimed him almost immediately.

The next morning, he rose early and surprisingly refreshed. He pulled his boots on and righted the room. Shoshana had not yet returned to the kitchen, and he couldn't sneak away and bolt the door behind him. He would need to wake her.

He eased into her room and knelt by her bed. She looked peaceful and bonny. He was certain he could watch her sleep all day, and the urge to crawl into her bed and hold her in his embrace astonished him. Reaching out, he placed his palm on her shoulder.

She was warm, and the scent of honey reached his nostrils. He inhaled, then lightly shook her. "Shoshana." Her lids rose to reveal sleepy, seductive eyes. They focused on him, and she smiled, trusting. No one had ever looked at him in such a way.

He cleared his throat. "Good morning, lass."

"Did you sleep well?"

"Aye, I did."

"Thank you for staying."

He nodded.

"I need to go, but I didn't want to leave without ye up to bolt the door behind me."

She sat up and pushed back the covers. He stood, and as she rose to join him, he noticed her threadbare night rail. It looked comfortable and well-worn, but somehow, it was the loveliest sight he'd ever seen. Warm nights, coming home to cuddle under blankets, came to mind. He turned and walked from the room before he could let himself want something he'd never before desired.

She followed him to the kitchen, her bare feet poking out from beneath the white chemise. Her toes were small and clean, but they must be cold on the floor. Though the rain had stopped and the sky promised a bonny day, there was still a bite to the air.

"Do ye need me to get a fire started for ye?"

"I can do it. Thank you."

They headed downstairs and toward the door. He stopped, pivoted to thank her again, and she ran into his chest. His hands flew to her hips to steady her as her arms landed on his waist.

Their gazes met. Neither of them able to move, his eyes were locked on her. He didn't want to break the connection. The moment was perfect, as if his body had needed her touch to confirm last night really had existed.

When her lips parted, his heart stopped. Instinct swept through him, and he covered her mouth with his, needing her flavor. Her lips were soft and sweet as they moved on his. Deepening the embrace, he drew her into his body, the full length of her heating him and igniting desire in his core.

His tongue darted in to mingle with hers. He felt more than heard a sigh escape from her. This was perfection. His chest tightened as he reveled in the rightness of holding her in his arms. He didn't want to go anywhere, wanted to lose track of time and forever stay in this moment.

Hoofbeats, the crunch of wagon wheels on the pavement, and muffled shouts from the streets reached his ears. They were standing in front of the door. He couldn't let anyone see her like this, in his arms, in her faded gown. Reality set in. It was time to leave.

But he knew wherever he went and whatever the future brought, he would always remember this stolen morning.

FIFTH NIGHT OF HANUKKAH

SHOSHANA SAID A PRAYER AND LIT THE WICKS ON HER MENORAH before stepping back into the shop. It was cool this evening, but the sky had cleared and the air was still. She stood in the front, staring out the window as she had most of the day, hoping to catch a glimpse of James.

Would he stop by to check on her tonight?

Kissing him had made that gulf between them disappear, at least for a few moments. Yet she should remember they couldn't be. Their embrace had felt right, like they were meant to be together. But she would not give up her faith to the Puritans in England, and she wouldn't do it here for a man. No matter how her heart skipped a beat when he came to mind, they were too different. He was Catholic and he would eventually try to push his religion upon her, just as the Englishmen had. She had learned well...she couldn't trust them.

There was no reason for him to come back this evening. No one had tried to enter the shop last night, and there had been no odd noises. Perhaps the culprit had just been in his cups and had moved on. But she physically ached at the thought of not seeing James again.

Her fingers drifted to her lips for the hundredth time today. She wanted to kiss him again, feel the warmth of the muscles beneath his shirt. Would it be wrong to do it once more?

She turned to go upstairs, but a light rapping noise had her swinging around. James stood just on the other side of the glass panel. Her pulse quickened.

She opened the door, but he didn't step in. Perhaps he regretted the moment they'd shared. The thought etched a chasm in her chest.

"Good evening," he said.

"Hello, James." She had to stop this before she let herself get too involved. "I think it's safe now. I'll make certain to bolt the doors tight tonight. No need to worry."

"I was hoping ye would take a ride with me. 'Tis a bonny night, and I wanted to show ye something."

The excitement radiating from him sent a small thrill through her. Her pulse increased at the knowledge that he desired to spend more time with her. She should tell him to go—he'd hinted that he was happy alone. He said he had never wanted a wife, and she didn't want to raise children outside of her religion. A relationship between them could go no further than friendship, but she couldn't deny him or the eager glint in his warm eyes.

"I'd love to get out for a little while. Come in. I'll grab a jacket and the key." He stepped in and the smell of cedar, cinnamon, and warm nights strode in with him. A peace she'd missed during the day emerged and bathed her in contentment.

Once she'd locked the shop, they strolled down the street, and he took her hand in his. The touch was casual, but it sent a longing through her that was anything but innocent.

"Where are we going?"

"Here." He pulled her in through a door. Her side brushed against his, and a shiver ran through her.

"A stable?"

"This is only a stop."

A lad guided a horse toward them, and James helped her mount, then climbed up behind her. She leaned back into his chest as he pulled a warm plaid around both of them, and they trotted out into the street.

It was intimate to be cocooned in the blanket with him, even if his arms weren't wrapped directly around her as he guided the horse. She'd never felt so treasured.

As they headed out of the city, the crowded streets and lights disappearing behind them, she spoke. "Are you going to tell me where we are going?"

"There is something I think ye need to see, and tonight's the perfect night."

"I'm curious now." But she wasn't sure she wanted to arrive at their destination. The contentment enveloping her was magical.

~

James held his breath as his house came into view. The cottage was nestled on a large parcel of land, affording him plenty of open space. Here, he had the privacy he'd craved since he'd been thrust into adulthood, but he also had a place to escape the busy streets of Edinburgh. This had been his dream.

In the spring and summer, flowers and trees bloomed with life as birds sang sweetly, giving it an enchanted atmosphere. But now, in the heart of winter, with night upon them, it looked barren and abandoned.

His breath hitched as he waited for Shoshana's approval. For some reason, it was important to him that she like it.

"Is this yours?" A note of awe crept into her words, and he was able to breathe again.

"Aye."

"It's lovely," she said.

He had to admit it was a nice place and much larger than what one man would need, but when he'd purchased it, all he'd cared about was that he'd have all the space to himself.

"But that's not what I wanted to show ye. First, we'll eat. I'm certain I pulled ye away from yer evening meal."

He dismounted, then helped her down.

"Do ye mind holding this? 'Tis our dinner," he said as he handed her a satchel.

She took it, and he guided his horse into his small stable.

The dark winter night had already moved in, and the temperature dropped quickly. When they pushed in the door to his house, he stepped over the threshold and lit a candle. As the flame brightened the room, she smiled and pride washed over him. "I'll start a fire, then we can eat."

As he worked, Shoshana pulled items out of the bag and set them on the table. She stepped into the kitchen, then reappeared with trenchers and cups like she'd known exactly where everything should be. There was a comfort in the scene he'd not expected.

"This looks delicious."

"I ken 'tis simple, but the bread smelled wonderful and this cheese is one of my favorites." Many nights he walked by the baker's shop and purchased a roll, but never a loaf that would feed two. He'd also picked up wine and sweetmeats.

"It's fresh."

"I dinnae cook very often, but I thought ye deserved a night off." After years of feeling obligated to prepare food for his family, this easy meal was one of his favorites.

"It's lovely."

He poured them both a glass of wine as she sat at the table. They ate and talked about their days. The conversation was pleasant until Shoshana's gaze focused on something behind him. He knew the spot. It was the cross on the wall. He closed his eyes and took a deep breath as he hoped the sight didn't bother her.

He'd heard the tales of Puritans in the south pushing their views onto the Jewish population, just as they had to his ancestors over the years. He hoped she didn't think he would ever try to force his beliefs on her. But it was probably for the best that she be frightened off. He didn't need any responsibilities.

Perhaps it was time to do what he brought her here for and get her home. He was growing uncomfortable with how they'd relaxed into an ease that seemed natural. "Come. I didnae just bring ye here for a meal."

He guided her outside and to the clearing behind his cottage, then lay a blanket on the ground. Despite the rains of the previous two days, the earth had dried. "Sit," he instructed, and she did so without question. Rolling up another plaid, he placed it on one end of the blanket.

"Put yer head on it and look up."

She did.

It was a clear night, and after he'd eased down beside her, he could see her face. The amazement in her eyes pleased him. He'd thought she would like this, but he couldn't glance up to take in the expanse of stars with her because his regard was fixed on her. It was like the first time he'd seen her when he'd gone to visit David. It was so hard to glance at anything but her. He couldn't tear his attention away because he found he received more pleasure in viewing her enjoyment than he would the stars.

Finally, he stretched out beside her and placed his head next to hers, then pulled the last blanket over them. With her warmth and the additional blanket, the chill of the evening was kept at bay.

"Does it look like what you remember?"

"Even better."

Her hand clasped his, and she snuggled right up next to him. Shivers of awareness spread through his limbs. This was probably the closest to heaven he'd ever been, lying here with the bonny lass beside him. Sharing his world with her had seemed like the right thing to do, but after tonight, would he be able to stay in this world without remembering her every time he stepped outside?

A light streaked across the sky—a star telling him this was somehow where his trials had led him and this moment had been predestined.

"Did you see that?" The awe in her voice matched her intent gaze.

He was tempted to kiss her, but he knew if he did and she returned the embrace, he wouldn't want to stop. His plans were falling to pieces just as the universe was. Had bringing her been a mistake?

"Thank you," she whispered without tearing her eyes from the sight above them.

As the words washed over him, he knew he'd done the right thing.

"Ye deserve to see the beauty in the world. I'm glad ye like it."

"Do you do this often?"

"Nae." But he thought he would do it every chance he had if she were beside him. He still couldn't help but stare at her and wonder why she had chosen him to trust. She was perfection.

"You should."

"Ye can come visit anytime ye need a break from the city."

"Thank you." Her hand squeezed his, and she inched even closer to him.

He spent the next few moments fighting his body's reaction to her nearness. He was ready to tell her it was time he take her home when her eyelids shut and her breathing slowed. He'd thought her bonny before, but sleeping beneath the stars, she was ethereal. He soaked in the sight, knowing he couldn't do this again and walk away with his heart and his freedom.

Waking her from such a peaceful slumber seemed cruel, so he gently carried her inside to his bed, adding a blanket over her to keep her warm. He slid in under a separate blanket, purposely putting a barrier between them. He had thought about sleeping in the spare room, but he wasn't able to leave her in his bed without being near her.

Something in his chest fluttered at having her here, in his home. A strange comfort washed over him, joy and peace at her presence and knowing she was safe. He slid his arm over her torso and relaxed into her side, enjoying the scent of honey mingled with lavender soap.

The moment felt perfect, as if she was a piece of his world he'd been missing. Pushing the thought away, he inhaled her sweet scent and relaxed. He fell into a deep sleep and dreamed of endless days of hard labor on the farm and returning home to see small faces filled with hunger and dependent on him.

When he woke, Shoshana had disappeared. He walked out to

the main room as she placed a meal to break their fast on the table. It had been a long time since he'd even stopped to eat in the morning, but the moment felt real and right.

She glanced up to catch him watching her. Her cheeks reddened, and he had the urge to draw her near and kiss her. He swallowed. Despite reminding himself that he wanted to be alone, he didn't want to take her back to the city.

"Good morning." Her voice was soft and husky. It rolled through him like music.

"Did ye sleep well?"

"Aye. I did, but I fear I need to get back home. I have to open the shop."

She was right. He'd slept longer than intended, and his dream had reminded him this wasn't her home. He needed to get her back because he liked having her here more than he wanted to admit.

They ate quickly and rushed out to the stables.

When she turned for him to help her on the horse, her head tilted up and he couldn't resist. His arm coiled around her and drew her near. He took her mouth, and it was heaven. His tongue danced with hers as his entire body, flushed with need, came alive.

Everything about having her here had been perfect, but now he was glad he'd not tried to kiss her when they'd been in his bed. He was swept away, all control gone, and he realized he wanted her with a desire so fierce it shook his core. But he couldn't have her if he was to continue living the way he wished. The two of them were the stars they'd watched last night, on fire with life but never allowed to meet. Her arms tightened about his waist as she deepened the embrace.

He was lost.

The crow of a cock caused Shoshana to jerk back, then she laughed. "I haven't heard that sound in years."

"Did he startle ye?"

"Just for a moment." Her cheeks were rosy and lovely, and he wanted to pull her back in, but the bird's call came again, reminding him he needed to get her home, even as he thought that place should be here.

They rode back into the city, and he stabled his horse just as the sun was starting to rise.

He held her hand as they walked to her father's shop. When they reached the door, the sight of Shoshana's menorah stand knocked to the ground sent dread spiking into his chest. The next image stole his breath, and the world fell away as fear and anger assaulted him.

SIXTH NIGHT OF HANUKKAH

It had taken Shoshana all day, but in between helping her father's apprentice with customers, she managed to return the shop's storeroom to order. It was the room they used as an office and thankfully, her father kept his ledgers with him in his bag and the store's profits secured in a safe abovestairs. It was hidden well, and it appeared whoever had breached their building's security had not ascended the steps to enter their home.

Her thoughts returned to this morning and James. Everything had been perfect until they'd reached her door. She kept reliving the horror of discovering the damaged door and the ransacked office of the shop. She was grateful her grandmother's menorah was undamaged and somehow still full of oil.

Fear had stabbed into her chest as she examined the splintered wood of the door where the knob and lock had been attacked. James clasped her shoulders and swirled her behind him.

"Stay here," he ordered, but he was rushing in before she had a chance to reply or object to his dash into the building. The intruder could still be inside. She forgot how to breathe while he was gone, fear for his safety taking precedence over any harm that could have come to the shop.

It seemed like hours before he returned. When he did, he was shaking his head. "'Tis safe, but someone was here rummaging through the office." Dread and anger shone in his eyes.

He had stayed by her side until her father's apprentice arrived. Even then, James seemed reluctant to go, but she assured him she was all right and he needed to get to the market.

A man appeared later in the day, saying he'd been sent by James. He repaired the main door and added an additional lock to it as well as the back door. She hoped that would make her feel protected again, but the sense of violation wouldn't disappear. She wanted James to come back so he could hold her, tell her all would be well and that she was safe. They'd made no plans for tonight, and her father wouldn't be back for another day or two. The thought of spending a night alone in this sullied space terrified her.

As she closed the doors for the evening, she set the menorah and its stand back inside. The sun descended while she gathered the matches, then said her prayer and lit the wicks. The light was reassuring, and even though she was here by herself, she didn't feel as alone. She checked the locks again.

Settling into a chair, she watched the door as she remembered the kiss she and James had shared this morning and the events of the previous evening. He was everything she'd ever dreamed a man could be...considerate, attentive, and generous. If he were only Jewish.

But still, their embrace had reached into her bones and told her he was what she needed. Her life wouldn't be complete without him in it. As she touched her lips, her body sprang to life with a desire to be in his arms. To be loved by James.

Three steady knocks sounded, and she glanced up to see the man who hadn't left her thoughts all day. She flung open the door, then wrapped her arms around him in a fierce embrace. She hadn't realized she'd been cold since he'd left this morning. His warmth breathed reassurance into her.

"How are ye?" he asked as he held her enclosed in his strong arms, and she hoped he'd missed her too.

"Still a little shaken, but I've searched, and nothing is missing. I don't think whoever was here even went abovestairs. Perhaps they were scared off by something."

He leaned his forehead against hers as if he'd been worried. She breathed in the scent of fresh woods and cinnamon.

"The menorah looks lovely. I'm glad ye had yer faith to keep ye company until I could arrive. I would have been here sooner, but I couldn't get away."

It was the perfect thing to say. His words were an acknowledgment that her religion was something he respected and he cared that she'd had her beliefs to lean on. He had accepted her, but that was a far cry from wanting to be her husband or raise children the way she wished.

He released her, locked the door, then clasped her hand. She led him to the back room and showed him the progress she'd made on the papers, which had been strewn about upon their arrival this morning. Afterward, she made them a small meal, and they sat with glasses of wine as his hand held hers.

"And ye are sure there is nothing missing from up here?"

"Everything is in place, but I haven't been able to stop shaking all day."

He stood and pulled her up, then wrapped his arms around her. "I dinnae ken what would have happened had ye not been with me last night."

His embrace soothed her. "I agree, I was lucky to be at your house. Thank you for coming to check on me tonight." She glanced up to find his eyes on her, watching as if she were the most important person in the world. Her heart skipped a beat.

"There's nowhere else I want to be. I couldnae leave the market soon enough."

She rose on her toes to place a small kiss on his lips. Her gaze met his, and she saw her own need reflected in them. And she knew this was right, that there would never be another man who reached the place in her heart she'd hidden away.

She pulled back. She needed to know if there could be more between them. "If you were to ever take a wife, would she have to be the same religion as you?"

"Nae." He took a step back, and she thought for a moment he might run.

"Do you want children one day?"

"I never saw myself as a husband or with a family. I spent so long taking care of my sisters that I didn't want that responsibility."

She'd been correct...their differences were too great. Her chest ached, and the room tilted. As much as she wanted this man, they both had too much at stake.

"I think I will be all right now. Thanks for checking on me. I'll walk you out and lock up behind you." Her eyes stung, but she held her head high. If he couldn't accept her or having children with her, he wasn't the man she'd thought him to be.

～

Shoshana had misunderstood his denial. James had never wanted a wife. But he needed her more than he'd let himself admit these last few days. He'd been struggling with the promises he'd made himself and whether he should follow his heart. The heart that led him to Shoshana, whom he now knew was his only chance at happiness.

Somehow her safety and comfort had eclipsed his desire to never again be responsible for someone else. He'd just not admitted that to himself, at least not until she'd brought it up. He'd told himself she wouldn't want him anyway.

Her gaze dropped, and she spun for the stairs, but he caught her arm before she could retreat farther. His heart pounded so loudly that it vibrated in his ears. Now that he knew she wanted him as well, he would cling tightly to her and couldn't let her think for another minute that she was anything less than his world.

"Wait," he said.

She was worth it. *Hell*, if he were honest, she was the only person who mattered, and he now knew he wanted to provide and care for her. She had reached into his soul and latched on to what he'd lost when he'd been thrust into adulthood. Unlike before, he now had an option...he chose her.

And it had felt so right having her at his home last night. The thought of going back to the empty cottage without her left him barren and cold. Until now though, he'd not let himself fully contemplate marriage. He knew what a commitment family was because he'd raised three girls already. But he was ready for this. Whatever was growing between them would be on his own terms.

His hand caressed her cheek. "If I asked, would ye be willing to be my wife?" Doubt crept in that she might not want him.

"I would like that, but I cannot go into a marriage without discussing children. If we were blessed, would you be willing to raise them in my beliefs?"

He'd never thought to have a family of his own so the idea had never occurred to him, but she was right. They could have babes. Children needed guidance, and from what he'd witnessed from David and Shoshana, he trusted them. Everything he'd seen of the Jewish religion was beautiful. He wouldn't give up his own beliefs, but he could support hers.

"We could raise bairn in yer religion, but I'd like for them one day to know my beliefs. Then, when they are older, they can choose the best of everything."

She smiled, and her eyes shone like his declaration was what she'd needed to hear. "Kiss me," she said.

His spirits soared, his emotions floating like a cloud in a warm breeze on a sunny day. She wanted him too.

He dipped his lips to hers, and as his tongue entered her mouth and pleasure spiked in his blood, he was lost in a place where only he and she existed. A world he never wanted to leave and the closest thing he'd ever found to heaven on earth...

She sighed and flattened her body against his. He deepened their embrace and wrapped his arms around her, enjoying the feel of her curves beneath his fingertips.

He drew back. He had to know for certain before they couldn't undo what was happening between them. "Shoshana, will ye marry me?"

"Yes. Nothing would make me happier than to be your wife."

He kissed her again, and this time when he released her, she backed away and took his hand. "Stay with me tonight."

He'd not intended to leave her alone with the threat that whoever had been here might return, but he thought she wanted more. Her fingers trembled, and she swallowed as her gaze pleaded with him.

"I'm no' going anywhere."

"Please hold me. All I've wanted today is to be near you." She guided him to her room.

He took her in his arms and kissed her again, then let his lips trail across her cheek and to her neck, where he dotted gentle caresses with his mouth. Then he nibbled on the soft skin, and she gasped, arching into him and giving him better access.

He flushed as his whole body came alive. His hands rose to pull the pins from her hair, releasing her curls and their lavender scent. He inhaled deeply.

While her hands tightened on his sides, he pulled the gown from her shoulders and peeled it down the rest of her body. He wanted to know the glide of her flesh against his, so he drew his shirt over his head. Her fingers rose to explore his chest, and desire snared him.

She was his, and he would do anything for this woman. He studied her glowing complexion and curiosity. Shoshana was everything he'd never known he wanted, and he welcomed spending years providing for her and the family they would make together.

～

The brave, considerate, intelligent Highlander before her was going to be hers. Shoshana couldn't take her eyes from James. She'd wanted to learn more about him every time he'd visited her father, and now she knew he was the only man for her.

Taking her hand, he guided her to the bed. She lay down, and he climbed on beside her. The position and the cold air made her feel vulnerable, but only for a second before his lips returned to hers. Warm cinnamon and cedar enveloped her as she melted into the embrace.

His hand rested on her bare belly and skimmed up to clasp her breast. Sensations exploded in her core. She wanted more.

Her hand rose to his side and slid down his leg, taking in the smoothness of his heated skin. She explored until she noticed he'd stilled.

"Did I do something wrong?"

"Nae, lass. No' at all." Then his mouth was on her breast, and his hand slid down to the apex between her legs. Tingles erupted in places she'd never imaged could ache with such intensity as his finger slid across her nub. She moved into the touch.

James drew back to watch as he brushed back and forth. "Ye are so bonny, Shoshana. I promise to always take care of ye."

His dilated pupils studied her, and she saw the truth in his words. She felt safe and cherished.

He eased her legs apart and moved to rest between them. With the tip of his manhood poised at her opening, he massaged it up and down the entrance to her passage. Need enveloped her as pressure began building.

He slowly entered her. She tightened her grip on his side as a moment of pain wracked her. It faded, and then the completeness of him filling her brought her back into the moment. There was only James, only her, and this undeniable connection between them.

"Are ye all right?"

"Yes, I am." She lifted her hand to cup his cheek as their gazes remained locked.

He smiled, then started moving in and out, caressing her insides with his staff and rubbing against the sensitive part at her junction with the friction of his pelvis. The pressure intensified, and sweet tremors shook her core.

The world splintered around her as waves of pleasure invaded her senses. Then James was calling out, and his movements became erratic. He stilled, and with his raptured attention still on her, his breathing heavy, he said, "That was amazing."

And she agreed.

SEVENTH NIGHT OF HANUKKAH

S<small>HOSHANA HAD DINNER PREPARED EARLY AND LIT A LAMP UPSTAIRS.</small> The shop would be closed for Shabbat soon, and she wanted to have everything ready. James appeared just before sundown. After she said the Hanukkah prayer, he watched as she ignited the wicks of the menorah, then they locked the shop and headed upstairs to welcome Shabbat and enjoy the meal.

She handed him a cup of wine. "This is for the kiddush prayer I'm about to recite."

He nodded and she began. *"Blessed are You, the Lord our G-d, King of the universe, Creator of the fruit of the vine."*

She took a sip of the wine, and James followed suit.

"Now, we must wash our hands."

He smiled and followed her to the basin to cleanse away the dirt before they proceeded with the ritual. Afterward, she uncovered the braided challah bread she'd baked, then made a small cut in it. Holding up the loaf, she said another blessing. *"Blessed are you, Lord our G-d, King of the Universe, who brings forth bread from the earth."*

She placed it on the table and sprinkled it with salt before motioning for him to sit.

"That was lovely," he said as he eased into a chair.

"Thank you."

"I ken the shop will be closed tomorrow, but I will still need to work. Will that bother ye?" he asked.

His concern was genuine, and she could see that he truly did respect her choices. Her wariness of others with beliefs not matching her own faded, and she put her trust in him wholeheartedly.

"No. I am accustomed to others doing what they must." She sat across from him.

"I will always support yer beliefs and ken how important Shabbat is to ye."

"Thank you. I am happy to hear it. And I can do the same for you." She smiled.

"I ken yer father goes to a nearby service led by a rabbi. Will ye be going?" He tore off a piece of bread.

"Yes. It's a small group, but I will walk there."

"If I could be here I would escort ye."

She was pleased he knew of the service and was encouraging her to go. It showed he was a man of his word and would honor and respect her need to worship with others who shared her beliefs.

"Please be careful. We still dinnae ken who rifled through the shop."

"I promise to be watchful." She placed her hand in his. The touch was comforting and natural.

"I may no' be back before sunset. 'Twill be a busy day for me," he said.

"I understand." She was curious. "How much do you know of Judaism?"

"I ken more than ye would think. I've worked with yer father and a couple other Jewish traders for a few years now, and they have taught me a little. Some of the best people I ken."

"Then you know of our other holidays and traditions?" she asked.

"Aye. I think I ken most, but I also look forward to ye sharing with me what I dinnae ken."

They finished the meal, then spent the rest of the evening snuggled together discussing plans for the future. The next morning, James left her with a long kiss and a wish in her heart for the day to pass quickly so that she could see him again.

EIGHTH NIGHT OF HANUKKAH

AFTER SHABBAT HAD ENDED AND THE DARKNESS OF NIGHT HAD settled in, bathing the city in its coolness, Shoshana stepped outside and breathed in the fresh air. She glanced down the street toward the market, hoping to catch a glimpse of James striding her way, but he wasn't there. *Soon,* she thought.

As she turned to light the menorah, something heavy crashed into her back. A hand clutched her mouth and impeded her nostrils at the same time. She attempted to wrench free, but the hold was like a vise. She struggled to take in a breath. When she managed, the scent of heavy spirits and sweat assailed her. Her stomach lurched at the sour smell. The attacker pushed her toward the door.

"Get inside," a man's harsh voice ordered as ice filled her veins.

She tried to grasp the doorframe and obstruct their progress, but her hand slipped and the brute shoved her through. He pushed her to the ground, then turned and shut the door.

Glancing up, she recognized the man who had held a pistol on her a week ago. His hand went into his pocket, and he pulled out another one, aiming the weapon at her again.

"Get up."

She did as ordered and inched back to put some distance

between them. Too afraid to say anything, she contemplated running for the back exit, but she knew she couldn't beat the ball that would fire at her if the man pulled the trigger.

"Where is he?"

"Who?" Her voice shook.

"Dinnae play daft, lass. Yer father."

"He's not here." She regretted telling him because now he knew she was alone, but he would have figured it out anyway.

"Then where is he?"

"Away on business. He'll return tomorrow if you want to come back." The brute might not fall for it, but she had to try, anything to get him to leave.

"Then where's his books and the money?"

"There's nothing here." Perhaps if he thought it was all gone, he'd just give up. But the desperation in his shifty eyes warned her he might not leave a witness behind. She had to get out of the store.

"I can take you to him." She moved to the side as if she would walk around him toward the door.

"Halt. We're no' going anywhere lass. Give me the books."

"He keeps the ledgers with him."

The man growled, and in the scant light, she could make out his fist tightening on the base of the gun. He stood still for a moment, seeming to contemplate his next move. She edged farther away.

"The coin then."

She froze. If he got her upstairs, she didn't see a happy ending to this.

"Give me all the money, or I'll burn the whole place down with ye in it." He straightened the pistol so that it pointed at her chest. She had no choice. If she gave him what they had on hand, perhaps he would leave.

"It's upstairs." She nodded and backed up the steps, not taking her eyes from the beast who stumbled and cursed as they ascended. When they crested the top and the lantern light hit him, she saw his eyes were red, and he had rosy blotches on his face.

He was a large man, so there was no way to overpower him. But now, she thought she detected a weakness. "It's going to take me a minute to pull it out. My father has some rum. Would you like it while you wait?"

"Aye. Hand it over."

She retrieved a bottle and placed it on the table. He snatched it up and drank as if he'd not had a drink in days. The man eased into a chair, seeming to calm slightly.

"Well, go get the coin, lass," he bellowed then took another swig.

She rushed into her father's room to retrieve the money, but also to look for something she could use as a weapon. She had a feeling the spirits wouldn't appease the man for long.

∿

James expected to see Shoshana's menorah burning bright as he approached his destination. Maybe it wasn't outside tonight—there was a bit of a breeze. As he got closer, all he saw was darkness. He'd thought she would have lit it before he arrived, but perhaps she'd waited for him.

But as he drew near, something eerily disturbing about the darkness inside clutched at his heart. Holding his breath, he tried the door and discovered it was unlocked. Fear, more frigid than the Scottish night, wound its way through his blood.

From upstairs, an unfamiliar man's voice belted out garbled words he couldn't understand. Shoshana's reply reached his ears, and he knew she was safe for the moment. He sneaked to the bottom of the steps and inched up, letting his eyes adjust to the light coming from the top as he took in the silence.

"Hurry up, lass." The sound of a bottle hitting the table reached him, followed by a chair sliding across the floor. "Ye got any more of that stuff?"

The stairs opened into a short hall, and James twisted at the top to face the common room. A familiar form searched through cabinets. It was the man who'd run into the table at the market. The one he knew was unstable. Searching his memory, he came up with the name—Gordon MacAskill. He'd been intending to let his clients know the man was falling behind on payments to those who had lent him money.

Had David given MacAskill a loan? His heart thundered as he realized the friend who had been murdered last month had been a moneylender also.

Gordon pulled a bottle from the cabinet, sniffed it, then took a drink. "Where's that money? Ye better no' be lying to me."

A pistol lay on the table. *Hell*, the man had no intention of leaving a witness to his crimes. Gordon swiveled and started at the sight of him. They froze, then both dove for the weapon. The table tipped and crashed as its leg splintered. The gun flew across the room.

Gordon lunged for it, but James was able to grab his thigh and pull him back before he could reach it. The arse beat at his hand, then twisted and threw an awkward, unsteady punch. James dodged it, then sat up and threw his fist into the man's hip.

Kicking out at him, Gordon scored a hit on his shoulder. James's grip faltered, and the man scrambled for the weapon, but he was able to get in another strike to the man's side.

"My ribs," Gordon shouted as he hunched in on himself. "I yield."

James stood, and the arse rose to stand in front of him, clutching at his side.

Shoshana, who had been standing near her father's bedroom door, rushed over to check on James. "Are you hurt?" she asked.

Gordon lunged and pushed her into James, then pivoted and dove for the pistol. He rose and pointed it at them, then glared at her. "Give me the money, or he's dead."

She nodded and moved back toward David's chamber. Gordon's glower returned to him, a smug smile plastered on his face. From the corner of his eye, James saw Shoshana grab the empty bottle and throw it across the room.

As Gordon turned at the sound of the glass shattering, his arms dipped. The pistol aimed at the floor and his attention diverted, he didn't see Shoshana grab a pot from the fire. She flung what looked like boiling water onto the man's face as he swiveled back around.

He dropped the weapon as he attempted to tear his scalding clothes from his body.

James jumped, throwing a fist into the man's red face. Gordon stumbled back, and James attacked again. He struck one more time, and the dazed man fell to the floor, crying and writhing in pain.

James picked up the gun and aimed it at Gordon. And breathed. He could finally fill his lungs, knowing Shoshana was safe.

"Are you hurt?" she asked.

"Nae, I'm all right. Get some twine."

She nodded and ran from the room as he stood guard.

When she returned with the rope, he bound the arse's hands. "Why, Gordon?" he asked.

"Because I cannae repay my debts. If he's dead and there's no records, I dinnae owe him and he cannae go to the magistrate."

James's stomach churned at the implication. Gordon would have killed Shoshana and then come back for David.

He and Shoshana marched the arse to the magistrate's office, where they retold the story of what had happened. And James told them to look into Gordon's whereabouts on the night his other client and the man's family had been murdered. The authorities assured them that Gordon would never again see the light of day.

～

It was late into the evening when they returned to the shop, and Shoshana wanted nothing more than to climb the stairs and crawl into bed with James. She craved his strong arms around her.

Once they were inside and had bolted the door, James drew her close and held her. She breathed him in. Her hands still trembled. The fear at seeing that brute point a gun at him had terrified her, and now that she had him back here and unharmed, a tear trailed down her cheek.

"I thought he was going to kill you." Her breath hitched, and she pulled back to look into his eyes, to know that he was safe and real and not going anywhere.

"And I was afraid he would hurt ye." James's hand cupped her cheek. His touch was gentle and reassuring.

"I don't know what I would do without you now that I've found you."

"Well, ye dinnae have to find out because I'm no' going anywhere."

"I love you, James."

"And I love ye," he returned.

He kissed her, and her frayed nerves finally settled. It was a gentle, claiming kiss that told her she was his world. She was at peace and she couldn't wait for her father to return so that she could share the news that they would be wed as soon as possible. She had no doubt that he would be thrilled with the match.

When James drew back, she took his hand and started toward the steps.

"Wait." He stopped and spun her around to face him.

"What?"

"Ye are forgetting something."

She tried to remember, but honestly, all that mattered was that he was here with her.

"The menorah. I need to see all the wicks lit. I want to celebrate yer people's miracle and my own."

"And what miracle is that?" She smiled.

"Finding ye."

HARMONY LIGHTS

MINDY KLASKY

AUTHOR'S NOTE

Nestled in the fertile farmland of the Shenandoah Valley, the fictional small town of Harmony Springs has seen its share of miracles—returning veterans and spirited resistance to urban sprawl and heroic first responders. And what better time than winter, when lonely nights grow all too long, for a woman to face the demons of her past and discover her own personal miracle—true love? I hope you enjoy reading "Harmony Lights" as much as I enjoyed writing it.

FIRST NIGHT

IN RETROSPECT, IT WAS A GOOD THING ABBY COHEN WASN'T holding a skillet of boiling oil when she answered the front door.

In fact, when the doorbell rang, she was standing in the kitchen, sprinkling salt over the first batch of latkes. "Seth!" Abby called out to her good-for-nothing twin. "Could you grab that?"

But Seth was leading a take-no-prisoners game of dreidel in the sunroom, crowing with victory as he emptied the pot of gold-wrapped chocolate coins. He tuned out Abby as completely as he ignored the outraged wails from his trio of kids.

"That's not fair!" shouted Abby's youngest niece. "Daddy's taking all the gelt! Bubbe!"

Deborah laughed from her grand-maternal roost on the couch. Her right foot rested on the battered leather ottoman, toes peeking out from an overstuffed nest of gauze and elastic bandage. In Abby's expert opinion, her mother was still a week away from a hard cast. One month from a walking cast. Three from a full recovery. She'd mangled her ankle with one hell of a bad break.

Deborah shushed her granddaughter's pouting, pointing to the plastic top in the center of the floor. "That's the way the game is played. Now it's your turn to spin. Maybe *you'll* land on the *gimel* too."

As all the players ponied up to restock the pot, the doorbell rang again. Abby cast a weathered eye on her distracted family, adults and children alike, before she turned off the flame under her skillet of hot oil. The next batch of latkes would have to wait.

Her annoyance faded as she glanced into the parlor on her way to the door. The familiar brass menorah sat on a chipped white serving dish, secure in the middle of the card table Seth had carried up from the basement.

The blue candle in the first cup had already burned halfway down. The white shamash, the servant flame the kids had used to light the blue one, had burned even lower. Still, both candles flickered in the window, a beacon of welcome to the town of Harmony Springs.

Abby wiped her hands on her apron and opened the door.

And she barely managed to keep from slamming it closed again.

To be fair, Ethan Weiss looked as surprised as she was.

She hadn't seen him in twelve years. She'd never imagined his beard would grow in that full, with a lot more red than the brown curls atop his head. She'd never thought he would have six whole inches on her own five foot ten. And she'd definitely never dreamed that his shoulders would be so broad, or his waist so narrow. He looked like he spent his spare time swimming butterfly in the Olympics.

"Abby," he said.

His voice was the same—a calm, rich baritone. His eyes were the same, too—a brown so dark they looked black in the indirect light on the front porch. And his smile... His smile hadn't changed a bit. His lips curled in genuine glee, as if she were the only person in the world he'd ever hoped to see on the first night of Hannukah.

"What the hell, Ethan?"

He cleared his throat. "Your mother invited me over to light candles."

Abby glanced over her shoulder at the menorah in the parlor. "You're a little late for that."

"There was a tree across Highway 10, came down in the storm. I had to circle around to Hammond's Grove to get here."

She didn't care about traffic. She didn't care about weather. The only thing she cared about—the only thing she wanted in the entire world—was to get Ethan Weiss off her porch and out of her life, the way he'd been for the past twelve years.

"Abby?" Deborah's voice came from the sunroom. "Is the front door open? There's a draft back here."

Is the front door open? Ethan had just said Deborah invited him. Abby's mother knew damn well the front door was open.

And now, Abby couldn't send Ethan away, not without letting him into the house, into her *life*, at least for long enough to satisfy Deborah. Sighing with exasperation, Abby stepped back. Ethan ducked his head, something between a nod and a bow. She sucked in her breath as he passed by, determined to keep from touching him in the tight confines of the foyer.

She watched, furious, as Ethan strode down the hall to the sunroom. Of course he knew his way around the house. He'd practically grown up here.

"It's not Hanukkah without latkes!" he said as he passed through the kitchen. As Abby gaped, he plucked one of the crisp potato patties from its snow-white bed of paper towels. Without waiting for sour cream, even without waiting for applesauce, he pursed his lips —those lips!—and blew on the fried treat. Two bites, and it was gone.

And Abby was left screaming at herself not to think about Ethan Weiss's lips. Or any other part of his absolutely unwelcome anatomy.

"Ethan!" Deborah cried from the sunroom. "Come give me a kiss. You can see I'm in no shape to stand up and greet you like a civilized woman."

As Abby glared from the doorway, Ethan obeyed, brushing a kiss against her mother's cheek. Seth climbed to his feet, muttering something under his breath. Abby didn't catch the exact curse, but she understood the sentiment when her youngest niece shouted, "That's the *really* bad word, Daddy. *Two* quarters for the swear jar!"

Seth ignored his daughter. Instead, he whirled on Abby. "Is this your idea of a joke?"

Anger flared hotter than the oil she'd abandoned on the stovetop. Before she could invoke a few curse words of her own—swear jar be damned—Deborah spoke up. "This is *my* house. I ran into Ethan at services last week, and I invited him to join us for First Night."

"Mother—" Abby began.

Deborah interrupted her. "Seth, please get Ethan a beer. Abby? I think we're ready for latkes."

Apparently making the best of a bad situation, Ethan crossed to the kids and their abandoned game. "Hey!" he said, as if he'd just discovered the most exciting toy in the world. "Have you ever played Nuclear Dreidel?"

"What's that?" Abby's nephew asked, suspicion pinching the space between his eyebrows. He clearly considered Ethan a threat to steal his modest pile of chocolate gelt.

Ethan started to explain the rules, something involving double spins of the top and carefully hidden bets. The kids were immediately entranced. Seth muttered another fifty-cent word and stalked into the kitchen.

Abby crossed to the table beside her mother's throne. It only took a moment to get the child-proof cap off the bottle of pain pills. She shook out the evening dose and poured a glass of water from the carafe she'd placed on the table specifically for that purpose.

Once she was certain the kids—and Ethan—were fully occupied, she spoke to her mother in a harsh whisper. "What are you trying to do?"

Deborah's eyes opened wide with innocence. Or with something close enough that Abby couldn't claim otherwise. "Please, sweetheart. This rift between Seth and Ethan has gone on long enough."

"Between *Seth* and Ethan?" Abby almost choked on her effort to keep from shouting.

"Those boys were inseparable from their first day of kindergarten. It's high time they shook hands and made up.

Whatever they fought about, what was it? Twelve years ago? It can't mean anything this long after the fact."

"I wouldn't be so sure," Abby said darkly.

She knew *exactly* what they'd fought about. They'd fought about her.

Ethan Weiss had jilted her on prom night, senior year of high school. He'd left her standing in the very same parlor where the menorah burned. She'd worn a cobalt blue dress, with a tight bodice and a skirt short enough that she'd fought with her parents about it for weeks. She'd stood there waiting as the tall case clock in the foyer struck seven, then eight, then nine.

And the worst part had been, even as she'd fought to keep from sobbing, she'd known exactly why Ethan hadn't come. He'd stood her up because he'd already gotten what he'd wanted.

Sex.

In his high-school bedroom, on his high-school bed, both of them nervous and trembling and whispering even though his parents were out of town for the weekend.

She'd known she loved Ethan, and she'd thought he loved her back. He wouldn't walk out on her after weeks, months, years of screaming matches, the way her father had done to her mother, just the weekend before. Ethan would never pretend to be one thing—a loving, caring, family man—only to ditch her for a prettier girl, a better-paying job, and a more exciting home than Harmony Springs.

But the very next night Ethan had missed her prom. And the morning after, she'd left for DC, for a long-planned internship at Washington Hospital, a once-in-a-lifetime prospect that Deborah had pulled every string in the book for Abby to land.

Of course Abby had heard about what happened next. Seth had beaten up Ethan. Broken his nose to punish him for standing her up. Fourteen years of being best friends, gone with a surprisingly quick left hook.

Even then, she and Ethan might have gotten back together— after she'd had time to forget the mortification of being jilted, after his nose had healed. She'd known he was terrified that things had gotten so serious so quickly between them, especially after he'd dated half the girls in high school.

But he'd sent her an email the first night she was in DC. Not just a text, a full-blown email, from Ethan.Joel.Weiss@gmail.com. Like she was some college admissions board considering his application, not her social media friend, EDubTheFootballKing.

He'd called her names in that email. He'd blamed her for distracting him from his AP classes. He'd said she was the reason he wasn't going to Harvard in the fall. She was the biggest mistake of his life.

The specifics had been different from her father's angry screed, but the effect was the same. Ethan was abandoning her, rather than confronting his own weak nature.

It had been easy to block further emails from her phone. It had been a hell of a lot harder to block Ethan from her heart.

Abby had completed her convenient hospital internship. College. Med school. She'd settled into a lucrative concierge practice, providing elite medical care to a handful of overpaid lawyers in Washington DC. But in twelve long years, she'd never spent more than three consecutive nights in Harmony Springs.

Twelve years, a professional career, and half a dozen boyfriends, none serious enough to make her lose a minute of sleep. Ethan.Joel.Weiss may have ripped out her heart and stomped on the remains, but Abigail Cohen was doing just fine, thank you very much.

In fact, Abby wouldn't be here now, if her mother hadn't shattered her ankle by stepping wrong off a curb. Abby was her family's speaker-to-doctors, the one everybody called when they needed test results interpreted, when they had to understand what was going on with their health.

Seth, a foreman over at the Baked Rite cookie factory, wouldn't be much help in that department. And Deborah didn't want her son attending to her most personal needs. Besides, Seth had his hands full with the kids, since this was his year to have custody over winter break.

Of course Abby had come home. Family, education, and guilt—

the triple crown of Judaism. Those were the values Deborah had instilled in her from birth, literally driving the lesson home year after year, as she ferried Abby and Seth and Ethan to and from Winchester for Hebrew School.

"Aunt Abby?" She was pulled out of her reverie by Seth's oldest daughter.

"What is it, Sophie-cake?"

"Are you going to make the rest of the latkes?"

Abby caught her tongue between her teeth, reminding herself that past was past, and she was in absolute, perfect control of her present. If her mother wanted Seth and Ethan to make up, Abby would stay out of it. "Absolutely! It can't be Hanukkah without latkes, can it?"

The little girl giggled and turned back to the dreidel game. For just a heartbeat, Ethan's eyes met Abby's over the spray of golden coins. She hurried into the kitchen before either one of them needed to speak.

Along the way, she passed Seth, who was armed with a pair of IPAs in glistening brown bottles. She sighed and rolled her eyes toward the sunroom. "Have I ever told you that your mother drives me crazy?"

"Have *I* ever told *you* that *your* mother is an interfering old crone?"

She laughed because twins were twins, and she and Seth had always understood each other. Proof in point: He pointed back toward the kitchen with one of the beers. "I left one on the counter for you."

"You know, you're my favorite brother."

"Yeah, yeah," he said. "And your least favorite too."

She stuck out her tongue and returned to her work station. It took a while for the oil to heat up again. Before the final batch of latkes was done, she convinced herself she had a headache.

After putting the last potato pancake on a plate, she clutched her phone in the front pocket of her jeans. She should check email from the office. And she hadn't listened to voicemail since ten that morning. She should call Jess, too, make sure her neighbor had remembered to take in her mail.

That should keep her busy for a while. At least until the sunroom emptied out.

She glanced into the parlor as she headed upstairs. The candles had burned out in the menorah.

SECOND NIGHT

"Hey, Mom?" Abby asked, walking into the sunroom the following afternoon.

Deborah looked up from the couch where she'd taken up residence. It would be several weeks before she could handle the stairs to the master bedroom.

Abby asked, "Do you have a phone charger I can borrow?"

"What happened to yours?"

"I left it in the waiting room this morning." Abby tried to soften the annoyance in her tone. She'd been the idiot who'd left her phone cord in the doctor's office. Not her mother. "I called half an hour ago, but they couldn't find it."

Deborah shook her head. "Well, I'm afraid I can't help. You and your fancy Big City phone. My charger won't work on yours."

Abby smothered a tart reply. "I'll order a replacement online. Sometimes it's worth paying for overnight delivery."

"Tomorrow's Christmas," Deborah reminded her.

Abby rolled her eyes. Of course it was. She couldn't have lost her charger cord on an *ordinary* day in an *ordinary* town where she could go to an *ordinary* store and pick up a quick replacement.

Fighting the eternal frustration that was life in Harmony

Springs, Abby opened up a browser on her phone. A few taps, her thumb held over the sensor at the bottom of the screen, and a replacement cord was on its way. She'd just have to ration her use until Thursday.

Really ration her use.

Who was she kidding? She'd be out of juice by midnight.

"Are you going to light the candles, dear?"

Abby blinked.

"It's nearly sunset," Deborah added.

"Let me bring the menorah in here."

"No, sweetheart. Leave it in the window. I've always loved the idea of people walking by and seeing it."

Abby turned back to her mother. "Then let me help you get in there."

Deborah looked sad as she waved toward her well-wrapped foot. "It's hardly worth it," she said. "Go light them yourself, but say the blessing loud enough for me to hear."

Abby was torn. The child in her wanted her mother to participate in the holiday. But the doctor in her knew her patient would heal better if the ankle remained completely undisturbed at this delicate stage of healing. Finally, she said, "I'll be back in a minute."

Seth had left the candles and a book of matches on the mantel the night before. Opening the familiar blue-and-gold box, Abby smiled at the jumble of colors. As a child, she'd spent countless hours deciding which shade should be placed in the menorah on which nights… As an adult, she paid less attention to the array of colors. But she always chose a white candle for the shamash.

A green candle in the first cup, then. A yellow one in the second. Deborah struck the match and held it to the shamash, waiting for the wick to kindle. After the light flared high, she touched it to the other two.

"*Baruch atah adonai*," she recited, purposely pitching her voice loudly, so Deborah could hear. "*Eloheinu Melekh ha'olam, asher kid'shanu b'mitzvotav, v'tzivanu l'hadlik ner shel Hanukkah.*"

She watched the candles for a moment, letting her lips curl into a smile. The lights were cheerful, reflecting off the window in the darkened room and keeping her from seeing the winter night outside.

As a kid, she'd always wanted to watch the candles burn all the way down. Seth had been more interested in opening presents.

Well, she didn't have time to watch the candles tonight. She had to make dinner and give Deborah a sponge bath. Then she could check her email—

No. She'd hold off on that. She had to preserve her phone's limited power.

Before she could head back to the kitchen, the doorbell rang. She had a premonition before she opened the door.

Ethan.

"Let me guess," she said, before he could speak. "Mom invited you again."

"No." His hands were shoved deep in his pockets, which made his shoulders hunch. That was exactly the way he'd looked when he'd invited her to prom twelve years ago: *Hey. This prom thing. Wanna go?*

Tonight, though, he looked directly in her eyes. "We didn't get to talk last night."

"We don't have anything to say to each other." She started to close the door.

"Please," he said. He didn't move. He didn't block the door, didn't lay so much as a fingernail on her. But suddenly she *felt* that one word like a palm against her cheek.

He'd always had that effect on her. She'd always known exactly where he was, even when he was sitting in the back row of the classroom, banished to the hinterlands by alphabetic order as she was destined to stay up front. She'd felt his presence in gym class, as they'd competed on opposing volleyball teams and softball and more. She'd known when he was building Lego monsters with Seth in the sunroom, and later, when the boys had skateboarded around town, when he'd sneaked his first beer, and when he'd driven his father's car without permission.

She knew him. She'd always known him. That was why it had

hurt like ten thousand paper cuts when he'd left her standing in this room on prom night.

"I can't——" she said.

But he was fishing something out of his pocket. She recognized it immediately—a dreidel, carved out of olive wood. She'd given it to him for his bar mitzvah, because he was a December baby, and it had been beautiful, and a lot more interesting than a Kiddush cup.

"Please," he said again. "One game. Radical Dreidel."

She couldn't help herself. She laughed. "The kids took home all the gelt last night."

"We don't need gelt."

"Then how do we play?"

"Truth or dare," he said, and then he pointed at the four letters carved into the wooden top. "*Nun.* Ask me anything, and I'll tell you the truth. *Gimel.* Dare me to do anything. *Hey.* I'll ask you for the truth. *Shin.* I dare you."

Her belly flipped, low and slow. She didn't want to play games. She'd *never* wanted to play games. Not with Ethan. Not with her heart.

He grinned.

She knew that grin. It was the one he'd used when he'd urged her to enter the pie-eating contest for Harmony Days. It was the one that had driven half the girls in their high school class mad with crushes. It was the one that had given Ethan Weiss the indelible nickname Ethan Vice, because of all the rules he'd broken, all the reputations he'd made and ruined before the spring of their senior year.

"I have to…" She started the lie, unsure of how she would end it.

He put the dreidel on the surface of the card table and gave a single strong turn. Candlelight rippled over the spinning top—light wood, dark wood, light wood, dark. She caught her breath as it began to slow. She leaned forward, trying to predict which letter would surface. She started to cross her fingers, to make a wish, but she didn't have a clue which one she wanted to land.

"*Nun*," Ethan said when the dreidel finally stopped. "Truth. You ask me."

She already knew the answer to her question. She shouldn't have to say the words out loud. But Ethan was waiting for her, so she asked, "That night. Why didn't you come get me?"

He looked at her like she was nuts. "With Seth standing guard?"

"Not Sunday." She shook her head, impatient. The hurt was still as fresh as if it had happened yesterday. "Saturday night. Prom."

"I spent Saturday night at the hospital in Winchester. It took three hours to get a doctor to set my broken nose. And I waited till after midnight before they took an X-ray to see if Seth had broken my ribs."

Wait. That didn't make sense. Seth hadn't fought Ethan until *after* she'd been jilted. Until Sunday.

"You don't know," Ethan said, his voice flooding with realization.

"Know what?"

"Seth kicked my ass Saturday afternoon. The second he found out about…Friday night."

Friday night. When she and Ethan had made love.

Ethan went on, as if she'd actually said something out loud. "He came over to my house Saturday afternoon. Asked me if it was true. When I told him it was none of his business, he went nuts." Ethan rubbed his side with a rueful smile, as if his ribcage still ached.

She understood each individual word. But her entire universe was shifting on its axis. The foundation she'd thought was rock solid had suddenly turned to mush.

"Seth's always had a temper…" she finally said, reluctant to admit it. Seth had a temper like their father's.

"And I'd been an asshole to other girls," Ethan said, sounding every bit as unwilling as she was to face a filthy truth. "Seth knew that. I tried to tell him you and I were different. That I l…"

Abby cheeks flushed as Ethan trailed off. She was thirty years old and a successful doctor, but she was blushing like a teenager on her first date. She protected herself by sounding defiant. "Seth always let me believe he punched you *after* you stood me up."

Ethan shrugged. "I guess that made him more of a hero in his own mind."

"More of a jerkwad," Abby corrected. She wondered if that word would cost her a quarter, if Seth's kids had been around. "I guess that explains the email. You wanted to hurt me as much as Seth hurt you."

"Email?"

"The one you sent after prom." She wasn't about to quote his hateful words, even though she had them memorized, syllable by jagged syllable.

"You're the one who wrote to *me*," he said. "I was the reason you weren't going to Harvard in the fall. I was the biggest mistake of your life."

She knew the words before he said them. She knew the words because they were identical to the ones he'd written to her.

No.

Ethan hadn't sent the email.

Seth had.

"I'm going to murder him," Abby said.

"Not if I get to him first." But even in the first minute of discovering Seth's betrayal, Ethan didn't sound as angry as Abby felt.

"I can't believe he—"

"I can." Ethan's voice was strained. "He was crazy that whole semester. Things had gotten so bad with your mom and dad... Seth said they were fighting all the time. This house was like a battlefield."

"I lived here too. And I didn't go around making up emails—"

"You lived here." Ethan agreed. "But it wasn't the same. Your father did a number on Seth. Constantly told him he had to be the man of the house. Said he had to step up, to be responsible. Your dad knew he was leaving a long time before he actually walked out the door."

The more Ethan spoke, the more he seemed to believe his own words. He was already understanding Seth's actions. Already rewriting the past dozen years of lies and mistakes.

"But to make up emails from both of us…"

"He was a kid."

"We weren't babies! We were about to graduate high school!"

"He was scared," Ethan said gently. "And angry. Your father had left. You and I… He was afraid he'd lose both of us, to each other."

"So instead, he threw you under the bus!"

That brought Ethan up short. But after a moment, he shook his head. "He must have been terrified."

"How can you keep making excuses like that?"

"I'm trying to put things in context."

"What *context* is there for a guy to ruin his sister's life? His sister, and his best friend, both?"

But even as Abby contradicted Ethan, she thought about her own "context." She'd spent twelve years avoiding the wreckage her father had strewn when he'd abandoned the family. Twelve years being the Good Daughter, Good Sister, Good Aunt—but only long-distance. By Skype in a pinch. In person, only in the most dire of circumstances.

Seth had lashed out about their father in his way. She'd responded in her own.

And Ethan? Ethan was willing to stand here in her parlor. He was willing to figure out exactly what had gone wrong, and when, and how, and why. He was waiting for her to say something, to do something, to give him an idea of a direction for their next steps.

"I don't know what to say," she said truthfully. She didn't know what she wanted. She didn't know how to forget twelve years.

"Say we can light candles together tomorrow night."

"Light—?"

"I'll bring dinner."

She didn't trust the sudden breathlessness that made her dizzy. She retreated to familiar ground, offering up an excuse. "My mother—"

"I'll bring enough for three. Come on, Ab-Fab."

He hadn't called her that since they were ten years old. She teetered, unsure of what she should say.

And then he gave her another trademark grin. And her stomach

—no, something distinctly lower—gave another twisting, spinning drop.

"Okay," she said.

He pumped his fist like a kid who'd just mastered a skateboard kickflip on the public square. Before she could say anything else, he turned on his heel, let himself out the door, and swaggered down the walk to his car.

"Wait!" she called, just before he closed his door.

He paused, one hand on the roof of his dark sedan.

"Your dreidel!"

He laughed. "We'll play again tomorrow. Your spin."

Abby was still staring after his taillights when her mother called from the back of the house. "Abby?"

"Just a second!"

Dinner. Sponge bath. Email.

But first, she had business to attend to. Business that was well worth using a little of her phone's remaining power. She tapped Seth's number with a stiff finger.

It rang four times before it rolled over to his voicemail. "Hey, dogface," she said. "You've got a hell of a lot of explaining to do."

THIRD NIGHT

WEDNESDAY WAS A BAD PAIN DAY FOR DEBORAH.

It shouldn't have made any difference that it was Christmas. The Cohens didn't observe the holiday. But there was something about knowing that every business in Harmony Springs was shut down, that all the other families were gathered together, opening presents, sharing meals...

Abby made sure her patient was as comfortable as possible— pillows supporting Deborah's back, TV positioned at a convenient angle, a pitcher of ice water close at hand. As expected, the maximum dose of pain pills made Deborah sleepy—a mercy, under the circumstances. Abby set the baby monitor and headed upstairs to her childhood bedroom.

The space was still cluttered with the detritus of a teen-age girl's life. Spiral notebooks jammed the drawers of the student desk in the corner. Stuffed animals overflowed a basket in the corner. The closet leaked clothes that Abby couldn't imagine ever wearing again.

Armed with a dozen garbage bags, Abby went to work eliminating her past. The toys and ratty T-shirts were easy prey. Worn out tennis shoes, too. A strand of fairy lights that had forgotten how to twinkle was quickly tossed.

But those notebooks...

Abby started paging through her old journals. She'd bared her heart in each volume—entire conversations with classmates were dissected on the college-rule pages. The notebooks were filled with bad poetry, forced rhymes, and overflowing emotion that made her cringe now.

And there, in a journal from the spring of her senior year, like a prop from a bad movie about doomed teen love... Her careful handwriting, loops and swirls exactly as she'd been taught, before med school ruined her penmanship forever:

Mrs. Ethan Weiss.

Abby Weiss.

Abigail Cohen-Weiss.

Ethan and Abigail Cohen-Weiss.

She didn't remember scrawling the names. Even now, she blushed at the inanity. She started to rip the page out of the notebook, to crumple it and bury it in the trash. Before she could destroy her girlish daydreams, though, the doorbell rang.

Abby startled like a guilty thief. Looking up, she realized that the sky outside her bedroom window was nearly indigo.

"Abby?" Her mother's voice wavered through the baby monitor.

"It's okay, Mom," Abby called. "I'll get it. Ethan said he was coming by."

And there he was, waiting on the front porch, raising a heavy-duty paper bag like a trophy. "What's that?" she asked, trying not to smile like a fool.

"I said I'd bring dinner. If you'll invite me in."

"Come in!" She said the words too quickly. If only she could catch her breath... She shouldn't be so winded, just from running down the stairs. As she stepped aside to let him enter, she forced herself to act like a normal human being. "Where did you find a place that's open?"

"Hunan Palace," he said. "Around the corner from me in Marksburg. I wanted to make sure you had the traditional Christmas feast of our people."

She laughed and led the way into the kitchen. As Ethan set the large bag on the counter, Abby went into the sunroom.

"Hey, Mom," she said, automatically noting Deborah's high color. "How're you feeling?"

"I'll live," her mother grumbled. "But I won't be happy about it."

"Ethan brought dinner," Abby said, easing Deborah forward and fluffing the pillows into a more comfortable arrangement. "Chinese," she added.

Deborah shook her head. "I'm not hungry."

"Well, you have to eat something before you can take your meds."

Ethan chimed in from the doorway to the kitchen. "I brought wonton soup," he wheedled. "The Chinese version of Jewish penicillin."

"I guess I could have a little soup." Deborah relented.

Abby said, "Let me just set up a few trays in here—"

"Don't bother," Deborah interrupted. "You two can sit at the dining room table. No reason to crouch over a rickety TV tray with me." Before Abby could protest, her mother brandished the remote. "This is my last chance this year to watch *It's a Wonderful Life*."

Deborah's stubbornness seemed to banish the pain from her ankle. Secretly pleased that her mother had rallied, Abby gave in. "Let me put together a plate for you."

While Abby unpacked the white cardboard cartons, Ethan set up a single TV tray in the sunroom. He ferried in napkins and a fresh pitcher of ice water, chatting with Deborah in a voice too low for Abby to pick out individual words.

Hunan broccoli—Abby's favorite, a dish that usually required a special order because it wasn't on most menus. Mu shu chicken, complete with two extra pancakes and plum sauce. Ginger beef. Two containers of white rice and one of the chewy brown rice Abby loved. She piled a plate high for her mother and returned to the sunroom.

As Ethan helped Deborah maneuver into a more comfortable

position for eating, she pointed a chopstick at Abby. "Have you lit the candles yet?"

"Not yet. I was upstairs—"

"Do them now," Deborah said imperiously.

"But dinner—"

"Dinner can wait."

Abby muttered under her breath: "Says the woman with a plate full of food in front of her."

Ethan laughed as Deborah demanded, "What did you say?"

"Nothing," Abby said, marching into the parlor.

She shoved the box of candles into Ethan's hands as she fumbled for the matchbook. He was still chuckling as he filled the menorah's cups—blue and green and red, with a white shamash.

"I can't hear you!" called Deborah.

Abby gritted her teeth as she struck a match and held it to the white candle. "*Baruch*," she began in an over-loud voice, but she nearly swallowed the rest of the blessing when Ethan's hand covered hers.

She'd lit candles with people in the past. Deborah's hand had guided her when she was a child. She and Seth had performed the task together for countless Hanukkahs.

But she'd never felt an electric tingle like the one that suffused her hand now. After they said the last word together—*Hanukkah*—she was content to watch the candles in silence, with Ethan by her side.

Content, that was, until her stomach rumbled loudly. Embarrassed, she curled her fingers into fists, but Ethan only nudged her with his elbow. "I think that's the dinner bell."

She didn't realize he'd brought the dreidel into the dining room until she was settled at the table with her own plate of food. "Your turn," he said, pushing the top toward her.

Abby glanced over her shoulder at the sunroom. As if in response, Deborah cranked the TV up louder. George Bailey was saving his pharmacist from poisoning an unsuspecting resident of Bedford Falls.

Ethan's grin was a direct challenge that Abby couldn't let pass.

After setting her chopsticks across the edge of her plate, she reached over and spun the top.

Hey. Abby caught her tongue between her teeth. By Ethan's stupid rules, it was time for her to answer a question. Truthfully.

He looked from the dreidel to her, his face suddenly serious. She just had time to brace herself before he asked, "Are you happy?"

She opened her mouth. Closed it. Opened it again. Reached for her chopsticks. She thought about spinning the dreidel again, erasing the *hey*, but if she wasn't willing to accept Ethan's Truth, she was pretty sure she'd crumple at his Dare. And she didn't have the first idea what she'd ask him. Or command him to do.

Was she happy?

"I love my job," she finally said. "Or rather, I love being a *doctor*. The concierge thing... It pays well." When Ethan raised an eyebrow, she fumbled to explain. "My patients want me 24/7, but most of their needs are pretty boring." For the first time ever, she dared to put her most secret thoughts into words: "I want to see more patients. Help more people."

She waited, to see if that was enough of an answer. Nope. From the expectant look on Ethan's face, she still owed him more of a reply.

"I don't really have time for friends, or anything else outside the office. That 24/7 thing. And a lot of people from school are busy with babies or boyfriends or their own private lives."

She saw the spark of interest flare across Ethan's face, and she realized the answer she'd given without intending. She didn't have a baby. She didn't have a boyfriend. She didn't have a private life to speak of.

"The whole time I lived here, I couldn't wait to get to DC," she rushed on. "I was going to spend every free minute in the Smithsonian. I was going to get tickets for everything at the Kennedy Center. But I'm tired at night. And on the weekends..."

I'm lonely. She started to say it. Her mouth formed around the *I.* But Ethan had already parsed too much from her answer. She wasn't about to give him any more ammunition.

Ammunition? Were they fighting? It didn't seem so—not with

the serious look on Ethan's face, the sympathetic tilt of his eyebrows and the slight pout of his lips.

In a flash as hot as the Hannukah candles burning in the other room, she remembered the feeling of those lips against hers. Finding the soft spot behind her ear... Roaming down the arch of her throat...

"Yes!" she said, because she had to say something. "I'm happy!" But that was a lie, so she changed her answer. "I mean, no." And then she gave him the truth, because they were playing Truth or Dare. "I don't know."

He took pity on her and responded to the last thing she'd babbled about DC's shortcomings. "The theater department at Shenandoah puts on some great plays. Not Kennedy Center caliber, but really interesting productions. They just did *King Lear* with an all-female cast."

She nodded and asked him a question, something, anything, because she suddenly realized that she wanted to keep Ethan Weiss talking. And she wanted to keep him eating, so she passed him the container of ginger beef. And she wanted to keep him beside her, so she leaned forward, not shying away when her knee brushed his, under the table.

Just like that, they were talking, laughing, simply enjoying each other's company like the friends they'd been for all those years before they'd become lovers. They didn't notice when the candles burned down in the other room. They didn't realize their food had grown cold. They didn't even hear the TV in the sunroom, as a bell rang in Deborah's movie, loud and sharp and clear.

FOURTH NIGHT

ETHAN DIDN'T MAKE AN EXCUSE TO SHOW UP ON THURSDAY NIGHT.

Abby was checking the front porch, to see if her charger cord had somehow appeared in the twenty-seven minutes since she'd last peered out the front door. According to the email message displayed in living color on her phone screen, the cord had been left at 1:37 that afternoon—exactly when Abby and her mother had been sitting in the doctor's office, waiting for an update on Deborah's ankle.

The broken bones had been deemed three days shy of being re-set. Deborah had returned home, disappointed and exhausted. Abby had fed her a grilled-cheese sandwich and tucked her in for a long nap.

If Abby had been home in DC, she would have worried that someone had stolen the cord from her front porch. But this was Harmony Springs. No one took packages from anyone else's porch.

But some inattentive delivery person had left the charging cord at the wrong address. Someone in Harmony Springs was puzzling out a use for a brand-new cord for a phone they didn't own. And Abby was left offering grudging thanks for whatever miracle had left her with a sixty-three percent charge on her cell after four days.

In any case, she was closing the door in renewed disappointment when a now-familiar dark-blue sedan pulled up to the curb. Her first impulse was to smile and walk down the path, meeting Ethan half-way. Her second impulse was to slam the door and flee upstairs.

She froze. No door slamming. Deborah was still asleep.

"Is that a phone in your pocket?" Ethan asked. "Or are you just happy to see me?"

She rolled her eyes at the corny joke. "Come in," she said. "But we have to be quiet. Mom had a rough afternoon, and she's sleeping."

"What's wrong?" Ethan asked, immediately concerned.

Abby filled him in on the doctor's visit as she closed the front door. She glanced into the parlor. "I don't know if I should light candles now or wait for her to wake up."

"Your call," Ethan said. "I don't think you'll attract lightning bolts of divine retribution if you wait till after sunset."

"But Mom likes the neighbors to see them on their way home from work. Speaking of which, why aren't you at the office?"

"Winter break," Ethan said. "One of the best reasons to be a professor."

She huffed in disagreement. "Right. You spent five years at Cornell so you could have two weeks off in the middle of winter."

As soon as the words were out of her mouth, she cringed. She didn't want Ethan asking how she knew he'd gone to Cornell. She didn't want to admit she'd spent hours on her phone, filling in twelve years of gaps about him.

College at Williams. Grad school at Cornell. Full time appointment in the history department at Shenandoah College over in Marksburg. That was all easy enough to find at the *Harmony Springs Herald* website.

She'd had to dig deeper to learn that he'd lectured at a Historical Association conference in New York, and another event in Las Vegas. Both programs had included the same headshot, a professional photo that couldn't capture the glint in Ethan's eyes.

He'd looked happy, though, in a photo from the Shenandoah Shelter's annual Puppy Prom. He'd been buried under a litter of mutts, laughing as he was assaulted by tiny paws and noses and tongues.

And the *Herald* had a great picture of him coaching Little League. His hand looked heavy on his young catcher's shoulder as the kid looked up with hero-worshiping eyes.

And he'd made a huge hit at the local Rotary meeting, where he'd judged an essay contest with the theme *In My Youth I See*. The winning girl had written about the joys of growing up in Harmony Springs—the Save Our Stores campaign that had revived a dozen shops on Main Street, the Mayor for a Day fundraiser that had inspired hundreds of people to vote, the Christmas Fête that always brought everyone out in the middle of winter... Ethan had presented the essayist with a thousand-dollar check for college, and she'd pledged to use it at Shenandoah College.

While Abby had been reliving her research, Ethan had collected the box of candles from the mantel. She couldn't help but notice how long his fingers were as he filled the menorah's cups: Blue, gold, blue, gold.

She caught her breath as he reached into the box for the shamash. When he pulled out a white candle, it seemed like a sign.

Absurdly, her own fingers trembled as she took the box of matches he offered. Her first two strikes failed, and she thought about handing them back, but the flame caught on her third try. She let it kiss the shamash before she shook it out.

"*Baruch atah adonai*," she recited, letting Ethan's hand settle over hers as they lit the four colored candles from the white one. As it had the night before, his baritone matched hers, automatically pausing at the same places as they completed the ancient prayer.

She knew he kept his voice down because she'd told him Deborah was sleeping. But his reassuring rumble felt like he was settling a curtain around the two of them, sheltering them in a private corner where no one else could interfere.

One step. That was all she had to take, to press her back against his broad chest. He'd fold his arms around her. He'd touch his lips to her hair. The warmth of his body would melt something deep inside her, the frozen mass that had kept her strong enough to endure the past twelve years.

He stepped away.

She almost cried out at the loss, but he only walked to the fireplace. He picked up the dreidel from the mantel, where she'd placed it the night before. "My turn to spin?"

Her relief felt like a tangible thing, one of those weighted blankets that calmed nervous dogs in the middle of a thunderstorm. He wasn't leaving. Not yet. "Your turn," she agreed.

He placed the tip on the card table, far enough from the chipped plate that he wouldn't disturb the menorah. Suddenly, his grin seemed devilish in the firelight. He twisted his fingers, and they both watched the olive-wood top whirl in place.

"*Gimel*," she said, when it came to rest.

"Give me a dare."

She gasped an answer before she could chicken out. "Kiss me."

She may have answered with lightning speed, but Ethan responded slowly. He settled his palm against her cheek, making her heart jackrabbit even faster inside her chest. He must have felt her pulse spike. He had to feel the shock of blood warming her face. But he waited, holding himself steady and calm as she fought to keep her breath from hitching in her throat.

His gaze caught hers, his eyes made opaque by the menorah's light. She needed to do something, needed to move, needed to fight the fluttering thing trapped deep inside her, so she took a step closer, bridging the gap between them.

He took that as the permission she meant it to be.

His lips on hers were warm. They were firm. They felt familiar, like home, but they were different from anything she could remember about their child-like fumbling in the past.

She *knew* this kiss. She wanted it. And she wanted a hell of a lot more.

Knowing he would pull her close, she opened her mouth to his. She felt the promise of his tongue, secret and hot and exciting. She moaned a little, deep in her throat, an animal sound that made Ethan tighten his arms around her.

Her hands splayed across his back, clutching him, needing him. His fingers tangled in her hair, tilting her head to a better angle. His knee pressed between hers, melting her into his body.

He hadn't kissed her like that when they were in high school. No man had *ever* kissed her like that. Her lips were on fire. Her brain was ablaze. She wanted to stay here forever, exploring him, holding him, opening her body and mind and soul to his touch.

The front door crashed open.

"Holy shit!" Seth said.

Three things happened at precisely the same time.

All three of Seth's kids shouted "You owe a quarter!"

Abby leaped away from Ethan as if she'd been scalded by melted wax.

And Ethan stepped in front of her, shoulders squared, feet planted firmly on the parlor floor. His hands hung easy at his side, fingers curled, as he said, "Seth." His voice was husky.

Before anyone could respond, Deborah called from the sunroom. "Seth? Is that you?"

The kids screamed, "Bubbe!" and ran down the hall.

Abby finally asked, "What are *you* doing here?"

"I thought you and Mom would be at each other's throats by now. I figured I'd bring the kids over and we could order in pizza."

More like he figured he couldn't avoid her anger forever. And he'd brought the kids as protection.

"Great," Ethan said. "I'll take mushrooms and pepperoni."

"*You* aren't invited."

Abby grabbed Ethan's arm. "He *is* invited. *I* invite him."

Seth scowled. Before he could say something he couldn't take back, Abby said to Ethan, "Can you give us a minute?" When he hesitated, she added, "*Please.*"

Ethan clearly wasn't happy, but he headed back to the sunroom. "Hey, kids," Abby heard him say. "Did you light Hanukkah candles before you came over here?"

She didn't listen to the answer. Instead, she glared at her brother. "I don't need you to protect me."

"You don't know that guy," Seth said.

"I've known him since I was five years old."

"Not really, Abs. He's not the guy you thought he was."

"He's not the guy *you* thought he was. Come on, Seth. You haven't talked to him since you beat the crap out of him on Prom Night."

"He screwed—"

"I *chose* to be with him." Abby shook her head vigorously when Seth opened his mouth to protest. "No. I *chose* him. That was twelve years ago. Neither of us really knows *who* Ethan is now, tonight, here in Harmony Springs. You and your lying emails saw to that. But I'm willing to find out."

"Abby…"

She put her hand over his. "Seth. I know you thought you had to take care of me after Dad left. But you're not the boss of me. You never were."

"I'm your big brother," he said, unhappily.

"By all of fifteen minutes." She brushed a kiss against his cheek. "Thank you for being there. For watching out. But you were totally wrong to send those emails."

"I thought…"

"And you were worse for not bringing it up—ever—since I moved away."

"I wanted…"

She let him search for an explanation, knowing he'd never find the right words. And when he gave up with a sigh, she said, "I'm a grown-up now. I'm able to make my own decisions. I always have been."

She could see he wasn't happy. He wanted to argue with her. Wanted to tell her all the ways that she was wrong. Hell, he probably wanted to catch her in a headlock and rub a noogie into the crown of her skull.

But he sighed and shook his head. "Don't come running to me when this falls apart."

"I won't," she said. "I promise."

He started to say something else, but he caught the words at the back of his throat. "Fine," he finally said. "But there's no way in hell

I'm letting a pizza with *mushrooms* get past the front door of this house."

She laughed and led the way into the sunroom. When Ethan looked up with worried eyes, she crossed the room to sit beside him. All of the adults pretended not to notice when she wove her fingers between his.

"Okay," she said, taking out her phone before the truce could disintegrate. "Who wants what on their pizza?"

FIFTH NIGHT

FRIDAY NIGHT, SETH LOOKED WORRIED, PEERING AT THE LATE December sky as if the dark clouds were tarot cards. "It's going to snow, Abs. I don't think you should go."

"Nice try, Big Brother." She laughed as she settled her purse on her shoulder. "Admit it. You don't want to be responsible for Mom for an entire evening."

He didn't laugh at her joke. "I don't want you getting hurt."

She chose to ignore the true message behind his words. "We get snow in DC, too. I haven't forgotten how to drive in it."

"That's not what I meant."

"I know," she said. "Have fun. There's a new bag of gelt on the kitchen counter. Don't let the kids eat all of it."

She headed out the front door before Seth could come up with another argument. Settled in her Prius, her seatbelt safely secure, she looked back at Deborah's familiar house. The menorah was just visible inside the parlor, its candles not yet lit. She'd set everything up for Seth and the kids. The white shamash stood ready to do its job.

Sudden butterflies assaulted her stomach as she remembered the feel of Ethan's hand atop hers when they'd lit the candles the night before.

She could do this, she remonstrated with her herself. She was a grown-up.

With determination, she set her phone in the nearest cup-holder. She'd already keyed in her destination. All she needed to do was tap the green rectangle: Go.

Maybe Seth was right. Mountain snow was different from the storms that slipped in and out of DC. And what if Deborah needed her? Even if Seth was able to provide basic care, he'd be distracted with the kids.

She bit her lip. She was just looking for reasons to delay. Well, twelve years was long enough. She turned her key in the ignition. Waited a moment. Turned the key to *Off*.

She hadn't even called Ethan, hadn't told him she was coming to Marksburg. This trip was some sort of test. Of Seth. Of herself. Of Ethan… She didn't want to put that into words.

What if her phone didn't maintain connectivity as she drove over the ridge to Marksburg? The charger cord she'd ordered had finally arrived, but the damned thing hadn't worked. The white plastic casing was frayed, stained brown where overheated wires had rubbed against the surface. The vendor had tried to pawn off a used cord. She'd demanded a replacement, sent overnight. But for now, her phone still had fifty-one percent of its battery power left.

Enough. She was obsessing about storms and her mother's ankle and her phone because she was flat-out scared. *Chicken! Chicken!* She could hear Seth and Ethan clucking at her when she was six years old, when she'd been terrified to enter the ramshackle barn at Old Man Marshall's house.

She'd found her courage then. She'd damn well use it now.

She started the car again, put it in gear, and tapped the screen of her phone. She was on her way to Marksburg.

Her cell held out, guiding her without a hiccup. One quick stop, at a Walgreen's on the edge of the Shenandoah College campus. Then over to a small brick house, where a parking space was conveniently available, right in front. Ethan's car sat in the driveway, signaling that he was home.

Everything was right. Everything was exactly the way it was meant to be. But she was still as nervous as a hospital resident, making rounds for the very first time. The first flakes of snow fell as she rang the doorbell.

Almost a minute later, Ethan opened the door, wearing only a pair of sweatpants. His wet hair stood up in little spikes. She could smell shampoo and soap—good, clean smells that made her mouth water.

"Abby!" he said, surprise sharpening his tone.

"Ethan," she said levelly, pretending she hadn't been about to run away.

"Come in." He stepped back so she could enter his home. "I just got back from the gym. I was in the shower."

She took the dreidel out of her pocket, surprised by how warm the wood felt beneath her fingers. She asked her question before she could make up an excuse to flee. "Want to play a game?"

He laughed. "You came all the way over here to spin a dreidel?"

No. She'd come all the way over here to prove that she could finish what they'd started the night before. And Seth wasn't here to interrupt. Seth wasn't here, and the kids weren't here, and Deborah wasn't here. No excuses.

But Abby was afraid she wouldn't have the nerve to spin the wooden top, to play the game until it fell on the *shin*, until she could demand that Ethan meet her Dare.

So she threw caution to the winds and said, "I came all the way over here for this."

She felt his surprise as she moved forward for a kiss. For just an instant, his lips were hard. But then his arms wrapped around her, and he pulled her close, and his mouth opened to hers, and they were eighteen years old again, or maybe they were thirty.

His lips moved down her throat. He found the sensitive place where her pulse beat hard, just beneath her jaw. She moaned as he nuzzled her, pulling away by reflex before her fingers found his hips, and she clutched him close.

Then, everything grew easy.

It was no problem to slip her fingers beneath the waistband of those sweatpants. Simple to discover that he hadn't pulled on any other clothes when he'd hurried to answer the door.

His breath stuttered in his throat as her fingers closed around his velvet hardness. When they'd been seniors in high school, she hadn't understood the power she commanded when her fingers wrapped around him. Now, she knew exactly what she was doing as she tightened her grip, as she felt him leap in eager response.

"Abby," he breathed into her hair, just before his own hands began to work their magic. His palms were warm as they slipped beneath her sweater, as they eased up her back. She had to release him as she raised her hands over her head, but she heard his appreciative chuckle as she wriggled free of her cashmere sleeves.

She shivered as her skin was exposed, but he folded her into his heat. His chest was fire, the soft curls of his dark hair sparking against her smooth flesh. His hands molded the curve of her spine, pulling her closer. She arched her back, pressing her belly against his, reveling in the support of his broad fingers, spread wide to keep her safe.

He lowered his head to kiss the lacy line of her bra. She moaned something that might have been his name, but she forgot how to string together syllables as his lips moved lower.

Her nipples strained as he teased her through soft silk, first suckling one and then the other. She needed to feel more of him, to bring him close, so she slipped her hands beneath his sweatpants once again. Her fingers spread across the firm muscles of his ass, digging in with a silent command.

His laugh was smothered against her flesh, but he obediently worked the clasp of her bra. She gasped at the sudden feeling of freedom, a soft sound that grew sharp as his teeth grazed the tip of her right breast. She rewarded him by once again closing her grip around the steel that pressed hard against her thigh.

"Oh, God," he murmured, his lips moving back to the knot of nerves behind her ear, the same sweet spot he'd found the night before. He slipped her bra from her shoulders as a shock of pleasure rippled through her, leaving her knees weak and trembling. She tightened her grip on him to keep from swaying.

She couldn't say if he moved toward the bedroom first or if she did. All she knew was that she was lying on his bed, comforter flung back, blanket cast away, flat sheet thrown to the foot of the bed.

She reached for the cord that tied his sweatpants, but he eased her hands back to her sides. His own fingers were steady and decisive, slipping off her shoes and socks, letting them fall beside the bed. He worked the zipper on her jeans, sliding the soft denim over her thighs, her calves, her feet, taking her lace panties in the same sure movement.

She lay before him, naked, exposed. With another man, she would have covered her breasts. With another man, she would have settled a coy hand across the neatly trimmed V at the top of her thighs. With another man, she would have looked away, blushing.

But this was Ethan. Her first. The man she'd dreamed of for over a decade, wondering what magic they could weave as knowing adults, confident of their desire, certain of their skills.

This time, she didn't let him push her hands away. Instead, she untied the loose knot at his waist. She slipped the waistband over the jut of his hip bones. She peeled away the grey fleece, adding it to the tangle of her clothes on the bedroom floor. She pulled him down, needing the weight of his chest, longing for the tangle of his legs between hers.

The scruff of his five-o'clock shadow against her lips ignited a white hot flame deep inside her body. She writhed as he kindled another fire in the hollow of her throat, against her right breast, then her left, then in the hard, hot button at the top of her cleft.

He worshiped her. He served her. He left her whimpering and mewing, panting like a mad thing. Until that evening, she hadn't realized how much she'd needed him, how hard she'd longed for him. She hadn't known how desperate she was for his touch.

Her fingers raked through his hair, pulling him back so his chin rested against her belly. "I want you," she said, as frankly as she knew how to speak. "Now."

To emphasize her desire, she fought to sit up. Her head spun a little, as if she'd drunk an entire bottle of rich red wine. She reached down for her jeans, though, for the trio of foil-wrapped condoms she'd slipped into her pocket after her stop at the drug store.

The packets were as bright as Hannukah gelt. Ethan laughed as her trembling fingers fumbled the unwrapping of the first. She silenced him soon enough, though, rolling the condom onto his ready length.

His gaze snared hers as she finished the task. One of his broad hands spread across her hip, his fingers branding her, claiming her. She felt the energy inside him, the molten power scarcely held in check.

She shifted her weight, pulling him on top of her. She gasped as he filled her, as his belly came to rest against hers. And then he was moving; they were moving together, and the spark caught and the flame grew and the fire enveloped every last nerve in her body.

SIXTH NIGHT

Abby woke before dawn. For a moment, she lay in Ethan's large bed, listening to him breathe. Before they'd collapsed onto the pillows, exhausted by a long night of lovemaking, they'd pulled the sheets and blanket up from the foot of the bed. Sometime during the night, Ethan had added the comforter as well.

Lying still, feeling the heat from his body radiate against her side, Abby wondered why she'd waited so long to make her peace with him. Sure, he'd embarrassed her by standing her up—and she'd been devastated by the emails she'd thought he'd sent.

But there'd been more to it than that.

Ethan had been the heart of her childhood. He'd been the safety and stability of Harmony Springs, the essence of *home*.

But her father had toppled that so-called safety, that imagined stability, the day he'd abandoned her family. Abby had consciously refused to let herself to be vulnerable with any man ever again. Even with—*especially* with—Ethan, whose physical and emotional love had been so tangled with her own father's desertion.

Okay. Great. She'd proved something to herself last night. She'd told Ethan what she wanted, and he'd obliged, and they'd had an amazing time in bed.

It was time for her to get back to the real world. She had to drive back to Harmony Springs. She had to give Deborah her morning meds. She had to be calm and controlled, logical as ever, Dr. Abigail Cohen.

The alternative was being the wordless, needy creature who had writhed beneath Ethan's touch, eager to get more. Eager to give more.

The alternative was terrifying.

Trying not to wake Ethan, Abby slipped out of bed, collecting her strewn clothing on her way to the living room. Looking out the bay window, she was shocked to realize how much snow had accumulated—at least five or six inches. The weather report hadn't forecast that much.

She made short work of getting dressed, pulling on her abandoned sweater against the early-morning chill. The denim of her jeans was freezing against her legs.

Swallowing a few choice curses at the cold, Abby pulled her phone from her pocket. The screen sprang to life at her touch. She scarcely had a second to register that it still had power before she saw a cascade of texts—seven in all.

Message 1, from Seth:

Abs — Give me a call.

She could picture Seth's exasperated face as he typed his command. He'd probably come up with yet another reason she shouldn't be with Ethan. Or maybe he just wanted some reassurance that she wouldn't walk out on him the way their father had.

She scrolled down to the second message:

A — Pick up your phone.

She glanced at the red badge telling her she had half a dozen voice mails. Rather than waste time listening, she scrolled down to Seth's next message:

Mom fell. Heading to hospital now.

Abby's heart clutched tight in her chest. There wasn't a hospital in Harmony Springs. Seth would have taken Deborah to Winchester. Had he thought to call an ambulance, or had he tried to drive Mom himself? What had he done with the kids?

It took her less than a minute to skim the rest of the messages. They'd sat in Emergency for almost three hours—heart attacks and God knows what else had taken precedence. Another two hours waiting for X-ray. Confirmation that Deborah had re-injured the ankle. Emergency surgery at five in the morning.

Abby didn't remember making a noise, but she must have, because Ethan was standing in the doorway of his bedroom, gloriously, indifferently naked. "Abs?" he asked.

She looked up from the phone, feeling faint. "It's Mom," she said. "She fell last night."

Speaking the words released something inside her. She was finally able to toss her phone into her purse, the way she should have done the instant she read Seth's first message. She shoved her feet into her shoes and scrambled for her coat.

"Wait," Ethan said. "Let me get dressed."

But she didn't have time to wait. She'd waited too long already. She'd spent an entire night making love when she should have been home with the family that needed her. She was as bad as her father had been. Worse, because the entire reason she'd come back to Harmony Springs was to help her mother.

She yanked open the front door and stumbled down the walk to her car. The snow crunched under her shoes, each sharp, clear bite driving a wedge of urgency deeper into her skull.

She didn't bother with the brush and scraper inside the car. Instead, she dragged her arm across her windshield, ignoring the cold burn as snow burrowed up her sleeve. Another swipe, a third, and the driver's side was almost clear.

She yanked open her door and pressed the keyless ignition. The instant the engine roared to life, she threw the front and rear defrost on high. By the time she'd emerged to attack the back window with a quickly scavenged scraper, Ethan was stumbling to the car, still pulling on his parka.

"Abby," he said. "What's going on? Where's your mother now?"

"In Winchester. At the hospital," Abby said. Her voice was too high. Her breath was coming in short, sharp pants, and the clinical voice at the back of her mind warned her she was going to hyperventilate.

"Is Seth with her?"

"Of *course* Seth is with her. What sort of monster do you think he is?" She hiccuped on the last word, and she realized she was crying.

No one had called Seth a monster. But *she* was the monster. She'd been screwing her high school boyfriend, when she was supposed to be taking care of her mother.

Her snow brush caught on the windshield wiper at the base of the window. She twisted the plastic handle, trying to wrench it free but it only broke in her hand.

Ethan said, "Let me help."

"You've done enough!" she shouted, because it didn't do any good to holler at the shattered plastic, because she couldn't change her mind about leaving her mother the night before, because she couldn't turn back time to keep Deborah from breaking her ankle in the first place.

"Abby," Ethan said, his voice calm and reassuring.

But she didn't have time to be calm. She had no right to be reassured. She'd failed as a daughter, failed as a sister, failed as a doctor. She didn't deserve the look of quiet compassion on Ethan's face.

"I never should have come here," she said.

There was a moment—when his mouth opened with shock— that she could have taken it back. She could have taken a breath, held it, and counted to ten. She could have explained that she was angry with herself, not with him.

But she didn't have time for that. She didn't have time for anything. So to make sure he didn't say anything else, that he didn't try to keep her from leaving, she gritted out her greatest fear. "Seth was wrong when he sent those emails twelve years ago. *Last* night was the worst mistake of my life."

She threw herself into the car before she could see how Ethan took the blow. Her initial impulse was to gun the Prius down the snow-choked road, but she remembered just in time that she had to baby the accelerator, press it slow and steady.

The car fishtailed out of her parking spot, but she made it to the corner. She ignored the stop sign, making a wide turn onto the cross street. She fed the car more gas as she headed toward campus. She only slipped a little as she made the next turn, and then she was on a road that had been plowed. With the cleared pavement ahead, she quickly left behind Ethan Weiss and the biggest lie she'd ever told.

SEVENTH NIGHT

BY THE TIME ABBY ARRIVED AT THE HOSPITAL, HER HANDS WERE cramped around the steering wheel. Her neck ached from her unnatural stretch as she peered ahead at the icy road. There were no interstates joining towns in the Shenandoah Valley; she'd been forced to drive along country roads.

With every mile she put between herself and Ethan, she replayed recriminations in her skull.

She shouldn't have left her mother in the first place.

Having left, she shouldn't have ignored message after message on her phone.

Having ignored messages on her phone, she shouldn't have spent the entire night with Ethan.

Having spent the entire night with Ethan, she shouldn't have left him standing in the snow, confusion warring with frustration on his face as she pulled away like the proverbial bat out of hell.

She shouldn't have left her mother in the first place.

At least she had no trouble finding a parking place at the hospital. And she easily followed the volunteer's directions to the second floor. And the only people in the waiting room at the end of the hall were her two nieces and nephew, staring like zombies at cartoons on the silent TV and eating mini donuts that looked like they'd come out of a vending machine.

"Hey kiddos!" she said, with fake cheer that wouldn't have fooled a newborn. "Where's Dad?"

"So the prodigal daughter returns." Seth's voice sounded as exhausted as she felt. She took her time turning around to face him.

"How bad is it?"

He jutted his chin toward the kids and said, "She's fine."

Fighting a tidal wave of exasperation, Abby grabbed his arm and pulled him halfway down the hall. She kept her voice low as she said, "Okay. Tell me. How's Mom?"

"What do you care?"

"Seth—"

"I didn't know what to do, Abs. The kids were screaming. Mom couldn't even *talk*, she was in so much pain."

She heard the remnants of panic in his voice. Her belly twisted with remorse as she said, "I'm sorry, Seth. I should have been there."

"Yeah," he said, his voice breaking across the single syllable. She couldn't remember the last time she'd seen Seth cry, but he dashed a hand across his eyes as he said, "You should've."

His agreement made everything worse. She wanted him to yell at her. To tell her to get the hell back to DC. To tell her they didn't need her here, at the hospital, and they definitely didn't need her in Harmony Springs.

Call it Jewish guilt, mastered decades ago at Hebrew School. But she deserved it. She'd known her mother was fragile. She'd known Seth had the kids. She'd left them because she wanted a little *nookie*. She was disgusting. She didn't deserve to call herself a doctor.

Suddenly exhausted, she asked, "How long are they keeping her here?"

"At least until tomorrow."

She nodded and offered the only apology she could think of. "Go home. Take the kids. I'll stay."

He wanted to fight. She could see that. But he wanted to get out of the hospital more. Without saying another word, he turned back to the waiting room.

Abby sighed and found her way to her mother's room. She braced herself before she entered, putting on another fake smile. She needn't have bothered. Her mother was out cold, her foot elevated in her hospital bed.

Abby gasped when she saw the metal cage around her mother's ankle. She should have expected the external fixation device. She understood the orthopedic need, but she couldn't help but think that the metal contraption looked like a torture device.

Glancing at the computer monitors, Abby quickly reviewed her mother's status. Her temperature was slightly elevated. Her systolic BP was high. Her heart rate, though, was steady, spinning out jagged peak after jagged peak on the monitor's endless loop.

Abby studied the white board at the foot of the bed. Deborah was on heavy-duty pain meds, along with a broad spectrum antibiotic. No wonder she was sleeping.

Abby smoothed her mother's hair off her forehead. She moved Deborah's hands into a position that looked more comfortable. She straightened the white cotton blanket across her mother's chest, folding down the edge.

After that, there was nothing to do but wait. She pulled the plastic chair to the side of the bed, so she'd be in her mother's field of vision when Deborah opened her eyes. Her thighs twinged as she sat, the soft ache reminding her of everything she'd done the night before.

With Ethan. When she should have been with Deborah.

Setting her teeth against the increasingly familiar wave of guilt, she took out her phone. Ethan had called, but she didn't want to listen to his message. What could she possibly say to him?

She'd seen his pain. She'd understood it. But still, she'd driven off, run away, the same way she'd run in high school, in college, in med school. She'd been running her entire life. That's who she was. That's what she did.

At least she took some responsibility as a doctor. She was more faithful to her job than she was to the people in her life.

Determined to ignore the voicemail from Ethan, she opened up her office email. There was the usual reminder to get billing paperwork in by month-end. An announcement that someone had left an umbrella at the holiday party the week before. A handful of questions about staffing, about vacations.

But not a single message from a patient. The clients who paid for her services wouldn't wait for her to finish frittering away a so-called vacation. Their needs would be met by other doctors long before Abby returned to the office. She was a cog in a machine. A machine that spit out money, certainly, but a cold, emotionless machine nonetheless.

She deleted every last email. She got rid of Seth's messages, and his phone calls too. Her finger hovered over Ethan's voicemail, but she still couldn't bear to listen to his voice.

She *knew* how it felt to be walked out on, but when push came to shove, she hadn't hesitated to inflict that sort of pain on someone else. She was as bad as her father. As bad as she'd always believed Ethan to be, after prom.

She couldn't think any more. Couldn't *feel* any more.

Instead, she pulled up a mindless game on her phone and started sliding colored blocks into neat rows, line after line of perfect, emotionless shapes that disappeared into the ether. According to the battery gauge on the screen, she had thirty-two percent of her power left. She could splurge on a little distraction. At least for a while.

EIGHTH NIGHT

MONDAY MORNING, THE DOCTORS ANNOUNCED THAT DEBORAH could go home. But it didn't take a medical degree to see that Abby couldn't drive her back to Harmony Springs. The passenger seat in the Prius could only push back so far. There wasn't enough room for the fixation device.

Reluctantly, Abby called Seth from the waiting room.

"I'd do this alone, if I could," she said.

"I can be there by noon." At least he sounded matter-of-fact. One thing about Seth—he'd never kicked her when she was down. Even when he was the one who'd toppled her in the first place.

"I'll head home now," she said. "Get things set up. Do some laundry. Make some dinner."

"Fine," Seth said.

"Fine," she responded, even though nothing was fine. Nothing would ever be fine again.

Abby returned to her mother's room and laid out the battle plan. Deborah's color was much improved, even though she looked exhausted. Hospitals were a crappy place for anyone trying to sleep.

"Thank you," Deborah said.

"For what?"

"For being here. For staying with me."

"I never should have let things get to this point. If I'd been home on Friday night..."

"If you'd been home on Friday night, I still would have tried to light the candles. You know how much I love Shabbat during Hanukkah."

Abby's smile was faint. She'd known that when she was a child. She'd forgotten it as an adult.

Deborah insisted: "Sometimes bad things happen. I moved faster than I should have, and I fell. You had no ability to keep that from happening. Don't take on more of a burden than you can carry."

Abby shook her head. She wasn't convinced. But she wasn't going to stand there arguing with a hospital patient. "I'm going home, to get things ready. Seth should be here in an hour or two. Call if you need anything?"

"Don't worry about me."

Fat chance. But it was nice of Deborah to say so. Abby headed out to her car.

The roads were substantially more clear than they'd been on her break-neck trip to the hospital. The sun was out too—almost blinding on the clean white blanket of snow.

Arriving at the house, she was surprised to see that the driveway had been shoveled. The sidewalk, too, and the flagstone path to the front door. Someone had carefully removed the snow, spreading salt evenly to keep slick patches from re-freezing.

Well, that was Harmony Springs. Some neighbor must have stepped up to the task. One of the advantages of life in a small town.

Slipping her key home, Abby was surprised to find the door unlocked. Seth must have left things open in the chaos of getting Deborah loaded into the ambulance, of getting his kids into his own car. Chalk up another advantage of Harmony Springs—no one had ransacked the unattended house.

But someone *had* come in to cook.

Abby recognized the aroma of chicken soup immediately—so

rich and hearty her mouth started to water. She couldn't remember the last real meal she'd eaten, but she could recite the contents of the hospital vending machine, row by sugar-laden row.

She wondered if she and Seth had gotten their wires crossed, and he'd come here instead of going to the hospital. But she was pretty sure the only chicken soup Seth knew how to make came out of a red-and-white can.

She glanced into the parlor, just to make sure her snow-clearing, soup-cooking benefactor wasn't sitting in one of the overstuffed chairs.

The chairs were empty.

But the menorah was full.

Eight candles stood at attention—red and blue and green and yellow. A single white candle was ready to serve as the shamash.

"Hello?" Abby called out, buffering her confusion with a smile. Someone *understood* how the candles should be placed.

"Back here!" came a reply from the kitchen. A baritone reply. A voice she'd never thought she'd hear again.

"Ethan?" she asked, pulling up short in the doorway to the kitchen.

He turned around from the refrigerator, where he was placing a huge bowl of green salad on one of the shelves. A loaf of crusty bread sat on the counter, along with a clamshell of red grapes.

"What are you doing here?" she asked, her voice little more than a squeak.

"Seth said he'd be getting your mother home sometime this afternoon. I figured she needed a little more nourishment than leftover Hanukkah gelt."

"*Seth* said," she repeated, like this was her first day speaking English. "When did you talk to Seth?"

"Most recently, about two hours ago."

"But I thought you two… I thought he wasn't…"

"Talking to me? He probably wouldn't have answered his phone Saturday morning, if he'd recognized my number. But he didn't hang up. He must have heard the panic in my voice."

"Saturday morning…" She felt like she was moving too slowly. Like she'd lost all ability to understand the world around her.

"I called him after you left," Ethan said, and his voice was impossibly gentle. "I was worried about you. Terrified, actually. The roads were in horrible shape."

So he'd called Seth. The guy who'd beaten him up for caring about her. The guy who'd lied to protect her. The guy who'd practically clocked him for ordering a pizza with mushrooms not four nights ago.

Ethan had called. And Seth had answered.

"Sit," Ethan said, turning the word into an invitation, instead of a command. She realized he'd cut a thick slice of bread for her and slathered it with butter.

Too many words were running through her head. Too many emotions. So she did the simplest thing she could think of.

She sat.

She sat, and she took a huge bite of bread, and she chewed until she could swallow. Only then did she ask, "Seth let you in?"

"He didn't have to. I sneaked in and out of this house enough times as a kid. But that basement window's a much tighter fit these days." He offered a rueful smile as he shrugged his broad shoulders. She had to laugh.

Before she could think of the right thing to say, the tea kettle whistled at the back of the stove. She hadn't seen Ethan fill it.

She hadn't seen a lot of things.

But now, she watched as he opened the pantry door. He reached unerringly for the shelf where Deborah had always kept the tea. His fingers flipped through the offerings quickly, until he came up with a bright blue bag, the Lady Grey that Abby loved.

Just as easily, Ethan found a mug in the cabinet beside the sink. He poured the boiling water carefully, stopping well short of the rim. He returned to the fridge for a carton of 2% milk, adding just enough to create the perfect tawny shade.

He remembered. He remembered everything about how she took her tea.

And just like that, an ancient rusty spring disintegrated inside her chest.

She hadn't lived in Harmony Springs for a dozen years, but a perfect niche waited for her here.

She no longer felt the compulsion, the all-consuming need to be on the move, to get out of town, to leave behind family and friends. She no longer felt the urge to flee Harmony Springs and all that it meant, all that it could be. She didn't have to make her father's mistakes. She didn't have to destroy her life and everyone else's.

And with a clarity born of tea and belonging, she realized she didn't need to go back to DC either. Someone else could step into her concierge practice, her high-end medical babysitting.

Because she was in her mother's kitchen, because Ethan had made it safe, she dared to say the words out loud. "I'm staying in Harmony Springs."

He didn't laugh. He didn't point out the craziness of her split-second decision. He didn't tell her she couldn't make a change that big without thinking it through, without drawing up a plan and a fallback and a reliable third course of action.

"I'm glad to hear that," he said.

"I don't know what I'm going to do." She heard the awe in her voice, the sudden confusion as she realized exactly what she was saying. "I'll need to find a place to live. A place to *work*. I need to figure out everything."

"We can figure it out together."

She folded her fingers around the mug of tea, suddenly too shy to meet his gaze. But he deserved her words, so she said, "Aren't you angry with me?"

He did her the favor of not faking confusion. "You were scared."

"I shouldn't have been. I knew Mom was in the hospital. They were caring for her better than I could."

"Your mother's health wasn't the only thing that scared you."

How did he do that? How did he know exactly what was in the darkest corners of her mind? Exactly what was in her heart?

"Ethan—"

She started the sentence because she had to say something. He was standing there, right in front of her. He was waiting. He could read her mind because he'd known her since she was five years old, since he and Seth had first rolled around in the sandbox and called each other best friends.

And *she* knew *him*. She loved him. Distinctly *not* in a brotherly way.

Because of that, she had to say, "I'm sorry." She was sorry for leaving him standing in the snow. She was sorry for not reaching out to him in high school, the morning after prom. She was sorry for losing a dozen years they could have spent together. "I am so, so sorry."

He moved close enough to tuck a stray lock of hair behind her ear, and his palm settled against the side of her face. "Are you going to run out of here if I tell you I love you?"

She heard the Dare in his question. Heard the Truth as well. She swallowed hard but didn't pull away. "Will you tell me you love me if I stay?"

Stepping into the circle of his arms felt like coming home. She heard his heart beating through his shirt. She felt his fingers spread across the back of her head. She held him, clutched him, realizing just how much she needed him where he'd always been—at the center of her life.

She turned her face up for his kiss, but before he could oblige, her phone rang. With a rueful laugh, she dug it out of her pocket.

"Seth," she said, answering the call.

"We're on our way home," her brother said. "Should be there in an hour."

"Great," she replied. "Ethan and I will be here."

The call had taken the sheen off the perfect magic of their embrace. Ethan shifted a grocery bag on the counter, digging down to a padded manila envelope. "This was leaning against the door when I got here. It's marked *Urgent*."

Studying the shipping label, she slipped her finger under the glued flap. She laughed as a coiled white cord fell into her hand. "It's the charger. For my phone."

"Didn't you order that last week?"

"Eight days ago." She set her phone on the counter. "It held a charge all that time. It's a Hanukkah miracle."

Ethan laughed and nodded toward the parlor. "There are extra candles in there. We missed the last three nights."

We.

She shrugged. "At least we'll light them tonight. With everyone here."

"How long did Seth say they'd be?"

"About an hour."

A broad grin spread across his face. "Any idea what we can do for an hour?"

"One or two things come to mind." She found herself answering his smile.

"Only one or two?"

"For now," she said, speaking quickly before his clever fingers distracted her. "We can make a longer list for later."

"For tonight?" Ethan murmured.

"And tomorrow night. And the next one, and the…"

He didn't give her a chance to finish counting.

CAN'T HELP FALLING

ROSE GREY

AUTHOR'S NOTE

WHEN THE OLD MINISTER ACROSS THE HALL DIES, LEAVING BEHIND AN apartment crammed with hoarded trash, Gail offers to help out. But his nephew, James, is suspicious of her motives. Especially when he discovers a tarnished menorah in the mess and Gail claims it as a family heirloom.

"SHOOT, SHOOT, SHOOT!"

Gail lowered her bags of groceries to the asphalt. One bag tipped and a jar of salsa rolled out while she rummaged in her purse for the buzzing phone. Debbie. Great. She briefly considered letting her stepdaughter go to voicemail and then pretending she had never received the message.

"Hey, honey. What's up?"

"I'm coming to visit for Christmas."

"Well. That would be—" Gail winced at the lack of enthusiasm in her tone, but it didn't matter. Debbie wasn't listening anyway.

"I'll be at the airport at 11:00 a.m. on Christmas Eve so you can pick me up at Gate C."

"Maybe you could—" But Debbie had hung up.

Gail gazed at the phone until she realized the salsa was now under her car. She wasn't sure why she had bought it. Larry was the one who had liked salsa. She fished the jar out from behind the tire and tucked it back into the bag. Maybe she would donate it to the rehab center.

Or on second thought, maybe not. She replayed the conversation with the director of volunteers at Mill Harbor

Rehabilitation Center. The woman had given her the furrowed-brow look, the one she used to convey deep sincerity and compassion.

"We *so* appreciate the help you've given us since Larry passed. But since our first book lady is back from her sick leave, she wants her old job again."

It wasn't fair. Gail had put off her vacation from the insurance company where she worked as a secretary for as long as she could. But her boss had insisted.

"Spend some time with friends," he had urged her. "You work hard—you deserve a break. Besides, it's Christmas."

She hadn't been able to bear the ignominy of admitting she didn't have any friends outside of work. And she wasn't about to bring up the Jewish thing. So she had planned to fill the next two weeks with volunteer work at the rehab center where Larry had spent his last days. And now she was faced with two weeks at home with nothing to do and no one to do it with. Even that might have been preferable to hosting Larry's daughter for an indeterminate period of time.

She snatched the bags up and headed toward her condo, wishing she was wearing something fiercer than sneakers. Stilettos maybe. Or steel-toed boots. She stifled a sudden smile at the image. Residents of Marion Gables Retirement Community in Phoenix didn't wear steel-toed boots. They tended toward the fashionable and unfriendly. She caught a glimpse of herself in the mirrored panels of the elevator and winced. Her linen slacks had been scuffed when she knelt on the asphalt. Larry would have had a fit.

Gail headed down the hall toward her condo, but as she turned the corner she saw Harold's door was ajar. Harold Williams must have been in his nineties. She saw him in the mornings when he reached out to his welcome mat to pick up his newspaper. She would smile and say "Hello," and he would glare at her before closing his door with a firm *snick*.

She got why he might be self-protective. Being Jewish was complicated, but at least people couldn't tell your religion just by looking at you. She guessed it would be even harder to be one of the few African Americans in Marion Gables. Still, his suspicious frown had always stung a little.

Now she wondered if she should have been more aggressive about reaching out. An old man living alone—what if he had been robbed? Or fallen ill? She would just peek, she told herself. If it looked like everything was all right, she would sneak back home and mind her own business. She pushed the door a little further open and clapped her hands over her mouth to stifle a gasp. Her feet rested on the floor where the door had cleared a path, but as far as she could see, that was the only spot of clear floor space in the room. Gail wrinkled her nose and tried not to notice the smell.

No one could live like this and be all right. She took a step forward, trying to ignore whatever squished beneath her sneaker. It was hard to imagine the prim disdainful man living in such squalor —mounds of clothing, newspapers, empty soda bottles, and boxes overflowing with a hodgepodge of items. And the smell was an assault, a dense pungent mingling of rotten food, unwashed clothing, and mildew.

At least his mattress was empty. She heaved a sigh of relief and felt silly for having pulled out her cell phone to dial 911. In the five years since she and Larry moved in, she had only seen Harold leave his apartment twice. She had just assumed he ordered his groceries delivered through the concierge. But he must have gone out. She should leave before he came back.

She turned to do so but stopped as she glimpsed the bathroom door. She didn't want to open it. She turned the doorknob and pushed gently until whatever was on the other side gave way. Worse. Much worse. Because Harold was curled on the filthy floor, blinking slowly as he looked up at her, his face a mask of fear and confusion.

～

James Jackson thought he had been lucky to arrive before the hospital cafeteria grill closed for the night. Although now, given the quality of the burger, he wasn't sure whether it counted as good luck. He glanced around the deserted room. The sparse Christmas decorations on the walls didn't manage to cheer the place. But maybe nothing could.

One more day, two at the most, and James could get back to his office in Baltimore. Since the divorce, his house was just a place to sleep poorly. It was his office, with its comforting smell of files, printer ink, and day-old coffee that was home. He missed it already. But once he had dealt with Harold, he could leave the past behind for good.

A lone taxicab idled in the curved driveway in front of the hospital lobby and on impulse James closed the ride share app and waved to the driver. Couldn't be easy being a cabbie these days.

"Long day, sir?" The driver glanced at James in the rear-view mirror with a sympathetic look.

"You could say that."

James repeated the address from memory and then stared at his phone as though fascinated with the opening screen. He didn't want to talk about Harold. Not about how much he despised his uncle nor about the weird momentary surge of sorrow he had felt when he saw the shrunken old man huddled amid the oddly silent machines. He had missed Harold's passing by half an hour.

Twenty minutes later he handed the driver a generous tip and watched the red taillights disappear into the distance before turning to look at the main building of Marion Gables Retirement Community. It was strange standing outside, with only a suit jacket for warmth in December. He thought longingly of the snow that was predicted to fall in Baltimore while he was away. People in Arizona didn't know what they were missing.

The complex looked attractive enough. He hadn't ever visited his uncle's home, but he remembered the picture on the website from researching living options for Harold. It was affordable and far from Baltimore. That was all that had mattered. He reminded himself of that every time he sent the mortgage check.

He pulled his shoulders back and strode into the lobby. The night concierge expressed unnecessary sympathies and offered to escort him to Harold's condo. It took effort to be gracious in his refusal, but five minutes later James stepped into the elevator, blessedly alone.

Unit 611. He slid the key into the lock and turned the knob before he heard someone clear her throat behind him. He meant to ignore whoever the busybody was, but he had to fiddle with the key to get it out of the lock, which unfortunately gave her just enough time to speak.

"Are you related to Mr. Williams?"

He tried to stifle his annoyance as he turned, but suspected he only half succeeded. She was middle-aged, a head shorter than his six feet, and she stared up at him, the round lenses of her glasses accentuating the owlish quality of her gaze. Her eyes were the most extraordinary shade of nutmeg, shot through with gold. Her lips were full and a little puffy as though she had been nibbling them. As quickly as he registered her lush figure, he dismissed it. Wrong time, wrong place, even if his body disagreed. Besides she wore a wedding ring.

"I'm his nephew, James Jackson."

"I'm Gail Costanza." She gestured unnecessarily at the door behind her. "Is Mr. Wilson okay?"

"He's dead."

"Oh, no!" She looked distressed, which meant she couldn't actually have known Harold. "He was breathing when the EMTs came. So I hoped—"

"I appreciate your concern."

He used the firm grateful tone he always used to end business conversations that threatened to go on too long. She kept talking anyway.

"I'm glad the hospital managed to locate a relative. Did you come from far away?"

"Baltimore."

"My goodness, you must be exhausted. Where are you staying?"

"Here." He turned back to the door, determined to close it between himself and the pesky woman.

"Oh, no! You can't."

Despite himself, he turned instinctively toward her gasp of distress.

"You can't stay in there," she insisted.

Something cold grew in his chest.

"I assure you, Ma'am. I can."

"But there isn't—you don't understand."

He certainly did understand. An old black man across the hall was one thing. You could look at him as local color. But a healthy middle-aged black man was a little too rich for this white matron's taste. The icy spot inside his rib cage broadened a little.

"Thanks for your opinion, Ma'am. Good night."

Irritated that he had let her get to him, he shoved the recalcitrant door open and fumbled for the light switch. The smell hit him just as the light flicked on. He inhaled in surprise and was sorry he had, but he couldn't contain a gasp at the state of the room.

"Holy God!"

He was so occupied fighting his gag reflex, it took a moment before he registered her warm hand on his arm. Bewildered, he let her tug him back into the corridor. She pulled the door shut on the horror that was Harold's condo and shepherded him across the hall into her own living room.

She didn't ask any more questions, just left him standing in the foyer and walked toward the kitchen. He shook his head. He could have been anyone, a grifter, a con man. She was either supremely careless or supremely cocky, because whoever had chosen the decor in Unit 613 had money. The vase on the sideboard was a Baccarat and the painting over it was a large aggressive piece of work. A Schnabel, maybe.

He winced as he pulled his phone from his jacket pocket. The stench clung to his clothes. Methodically, he dialed one hotel after another. Six "we're booked up" conversations later he looked up and met his hostess' eyes. It was nearly midnight. He realized belatedly he had been talking in a normal tone of voice.

"I apologize for the inconvenience. I don't want to wake up your husband."

"You'd have to talk a lot louder than that. Larry's been gone a couple years now."

"I'm sorry."

"It's okay. I mean it wasn't okay at the time, but—you should eat." She gestured toward the table.

When he was able to focus again, he took a sip of the truly excellent coffee and watched her over the edge of the cup. It was embarrassing how ravenous he had felt at the sight of the crackers, cheese, and fruit she had arranged on a pretty tray. At least he hadn't licked his plate.

"Did you find a hotel?" she asked.

"Not yet. Apparently Uncle Harold should have had the courtesy to collapse after—" he looked around the room for a Christmas decoration to gesture at, but found none, "—the holidays."

She nodded. "That must make it harder for you, having a sick relative so near Christmas."

She was wrong. This time of year had always been painful. When his mother was alive, James had visited her regularly, but he always found excuses to avoid holiday meals with the extended family. Particularly Christmas. The image of his uncle flashed unbidden, unwelcome. Harold had always dressed impeccably, pressed suit set off by a silk tie, shoes shined. But then a minister had to look good on the outside.

James forced himself back on track. The food would give him energy for a little while, but jet lag was going to kick in soon and he would need a bed. Surely *one* of the cruddy motels he had driven by near the airport would have a room. No matter how dingy it was, it couldn't possibly be as bad as Harold's bedroom.

"I'll make a few more calls and then I'll get out of your hair," he said. "And thanks for the food. I didn't realize I was so hungry."

She smiled. "I'm glad I went shopping this afternoon. Otherwise it would have been anchovies and frozen mango. You could stay here."

He stared. She stopped abruptly as if she hadn't planned to say the last four words. She probably wished she could take them back, but hell if he would give her the chance. The couch would be short for his six-foot frame, but exhaustion was hitting him hard now and he knew the moment he lay down, he would be out for the count.

"Thanks," he said. "All I need is a spare blanket if you have one. I'll be out of your hair in the morning."

"You could—I have a bed."

He dragged his eyes open and stared at her incredulously. "Lady, I don't know how you do things in Arizona, but back in Baltimore we like to get to know each other first."

"Oh, no. That is, I'm sure you would be wonderful. But I—" She blushed furiously and gestured behind him toward the other end of the living room. "I have a spare bedroom."

Later, it occurred to him as he slid between the blessedly clean smelling cotton sheets that he would have to find other arrangements quickly. Gail seemed like a nice woman, but nothing in life came free. And he couldn't afford a woman in his life.

～

Gail woke with a start, thinking she had missed her alarm. But then she remembered it was Saturday and wondered whether she had left the television on. Her eyes shot open. James. Last night as she handed him a bath towel, he had apologized for misinterpreting her invitation. That conversation had been almost as embarrassing as his original error. Her face grew hot at the memory.

She showered quickly but hesitated at her closet. She didn't have much in the way of leisure wear, but she was on vacation. Technically. She reached for the lone pair of jeans she had bought in a moment of rebellion and then never worn. Rejecting the row of staid blouses she kept arranged by color, she reached deep into the bottom drawer of her bureau and pulled out a well worn t-shirt from her cache. Barefoot, she padded into the living room.

James' broad back was to her, his cell phone to his ear. Great. *He* had dressed as if he was headed to a business meeting. He filled out his clothes as though he had been sculpted when God was having a particularly good day. His skin was rich and dark. His hair was cut short, so she could see the shape of his head from the back. It gave him an endearing little-boy look. Especially since he was scowling a bit as he turned to her. If it weren't for his personality, she would have been smitten.

"Eavesdropping?"

Jerk. If he hadn't found a hotel by this afternoon, she would start making calls herself. There had to be *something* available. She opened her mouth to tell him so, but he held a hand up.

"I'm sorry." He dry washed his face. "I figured I'd only have to close my antiques business for a few days, but now—this is a mess. Literally and figuratively."

"Was that your wife on the phone?"

"Secretary. I'm divorced."

"I'm widowed, but you already knew that." She turned the ring on her finger. "Any kids?"

"No."

"I have a step-daughter, Debbie. She's twenty-three."

She rummaged in the refrigerator for omelet ingredients and was suddenly and acutely aware of how silly she must look with her rump sticking out. And at the same time the very thought made her feel pathetic. She rolled her eyes and reached for a jar of sun-dried tomatoes. A man like James could have any woman he wanted. It was signally unfair. He couldn't be much older than her sixty-two years but he looked terrific. She tossed a packet of goat cheese onto the counter with a vengeful thump.

"If you don't want to cook, just say so." He sounded annoyed. She looked up, startled.

"Sorry," she said automatically and then mentally rescinded the apology. "Are you always this grouchy?"

He looked taken aback. Then he grinned and for a moment she couldn't breathe. "Most of the time," he said. "Eager to get rid of me already?"

"Not at all. But this time of year it may be hard to find a cleaning company with openings in its schedule. If you're planning to stay until you succeed at making arrangements, you may be in town a while."

When their plates were empty and they were sipping their coffee, she said, "I know a good funeral home."

"There's a conversation starter you don't hear every day."

She flushed and reached across the table to pick up his empty plate. But he rose and deftly stacked the dishes, silverware and cups.

"You cooked. I'll wash. And I'd appreciate that funeral home information. The hospital wants to do an autopsy on Harold, just to be sure what he died of. So I have a couple of days to make arrangements, but obviously the sooner I do, the better."

She stared at his back as he headed toward the sink. He sounded peculiarly companionable. He had hung his blazer on the back of his chair and she swallowed as he rolled up his shirt sleeves. She reached for a dish towel and intercepted a dripping plate on its way from the sink.

"Maybe I could help you—"

"The whole point of a dish rack is to save on hand drying." He shot her a disapproving look.

"—with your uncle's condo. I mean, if you want me to."

He turned off the water and stared at her.

"Uncle Harold's condominium is an environmental hazard. I'll be lucky if it doesn't get cited by the Board of Health. Plus, you'd need an army to clear that mess out."

"I don't think so," she said. "His living space is half the size of mine. The units on your uncle's side only have one bedroom. The living room is small too. Still, we would need a lot of garbage bags. And we'll have to find a way to open the windows while we're working."

"You're serious."

She nodded, hoping he'd agree. Not so much because she wanted more time with him. Although, strangely, she did. But because even the idea of such a ridiculous project was like a glowing beacon compared to the two-week tunnel of darkness that was vacation. She watched her hand rub the towel in circles on the dry plate, willing him to agree.

"I guess we could try it," he said. "But if you come down with the plague, don't blame me." Doubt laced his tone, but he hadn't said no. She felt like dancing.

~

James' heart sank. Her face had lit up as if he had offered her a free trip to Paris. No one could look forward to cleaning that much. Which meant she had another agenda. It could be she was just a busybody. Or she wanted the opportunity to sift through Harold's goods for valuables. She had plenty of those at home, but some people, like his ex-wife Denise, were never satisfied with what they had. Even if it was a man's heart.

He sighed. Maybe he was looking a gift horse in the mouth. Gail was right. The chances of finding a cleaning company willing to devote an entire week to digging out Harold's dump during the Christmas season were slim. And waiting until after the New Year wasn't a good solution. The sooner he found a tenant for the condo, the easier it would be to pay Harold's medical and funeral expenses. It was the wrong time of year to list it for sale, but a short term rental until the spring market opened up would work.

But the real problem was Gail herself. Ever since Denise, James had steered clear of women. For the most part, that hadn't been a hardship. He simply hadn't found himself attracted. He had guessed it was a matter of maturity, which was a nice way of saying at sixty-five he was getting old. It didn't help to know Denise had been stepping out with a younger man.

Which made the way he was feeling about Gail not only surprising but unwelcome. The way her curly hair refused to stay put, her capable-looking hands, that lush body… He could feel his skin tingle as he remembered the way she stretched to reach for the cream pitcher on a high shelf. But he wasn't going to act on it. That ship had sailed the day Denise walked away. Keeping his distance from Gail would be a good idea. Just as soon as he could find a hotel room.

He took a last deep breath of fresh air as they opened Harold's door, snagged a roll of trash bags, and headed toward the bedroom.

There wasn't enough empty floor space for him to work in the same room as Gail—a fact for which he was grateful.

He had assumed the odor wouldn't come as a surprise since he had smelled it yesterday and was expecting it. He was wrong. He edged between the stacks of assorted goods, wondering where to start. There must have been furniture here originally, a bed, a bureau, and a night table. But whatever furnishings Harold had moved in with were covered over, like long-fallen oaks smothered in choking ivy.

By lunchtime, James had settled into a rhythm—one bag for donations to Goodwill, one for trash and one for keeping. The bag of keepsakes was nearly empty. So far it had one framed portrait of James' mother. The glass in the frame was long gone. Every now and then, Gail would pop her head into the room and silently remove filled bags. James had accumulated half a bag of items he thought qualified for Goodwill donations when he came across a hard object wrapped in a bundle of musty old newspapers.

Tugging at the masking tape, he managed to free a dull black hunk of metal. It was a candelabrum, but a strange one. Lions supported the wide central column, and as James ran his fingertip along the flowers etched into the tarnished surface, he felt two tiny knobs. The room was dim and the twenty-five-watt bulb overhead wasn't strong enough let him assess it properly. He stepped into the living room to take advantage of the natural light there.

∼

Gail looked up from the armload of clothing she was stuffing into a trash bag but her smile faded as she stared at the menorah. It couldn't be. And then, a far worse, colder thought came. Because how could Tante Leah's Hanukkah menorah have turned up here?

"Where did you find that?"

Her throat was so tight she barely made it through the question without coughing. She glanced around and reached for a newly freed dining chair. It wasn't so much that she needed to sit down, although she was suddenly feeling short of breath. But she needed to hold onto something solid. Because nothing made sense.

"In the bedroom." He gave her a quizzical look. "Do you recognize it?"

She sank into the chair. Tante Leah, blue checked apron, the little box of colored candles, and Tante Leah's hand on hers as six-year-old Gail touched the flame to one wick and then the next.

"Are you okay?" He knelt before her now, his find seemingly forgotten as he peered at her. "You look like you saw a ghost."

Wordless, she reached toward the menorah and pulled it to her lap, patting her fingertips over the surface as though to assure it and herself that it was unhurt. When she could speak again, she struggled for the words.

"This shouldn't be here."

"No kidding." James stood up but made no effort to take it from her. "Maybe Harold picked it up from the trash."

She frowned. "It couldn't have been in the trash. Or if it was, I didn't put it there. And I have no idea how it could have ended up in Harold's place. After we settled into the condo, I looked for it. I thought I had misplaced it in the move somehow. At least, that's what Larry said."

James' skeptical expression was understandable, she guessed. What she was saying must sound ridiculous. Things didn't just disappear.

"What is it for?" He asked.

"It's a Hanukkah menorah. It's kind of a childhood memory."

"You're Jewish?"

She shrugged and dragged her gaze away from the candelabrum to his face. To her surprise, he looked intrigued.

"I'm off the—," She paused and tried again. "I used to be observant. Very observant. I grew up that way."

"I understand about observance." He nodded. "When I was a boy, we attended church every Sunday, rain or shine. My mother insisted on it and for the most part I didn't mind. Our entire social circle was there. All my friends. All her friends. And Uncle Harold was the big shot—Pastor Williams. Mom was so proud of him."

"And you?" She held her breath. The bridge they were building seemed so frail, as though the least disturbance could send it tumbling.

"I was too, until he accused me of stealing the church silver."

"Oh, no!"

"To be fair, I was a wild kid. My Dad died when I was seven and Harold tried to be that father figure I needed. But compared to my Dad, Harold was stuffy and full of himself and a terrible listener. Mom was too busy holding down two jobs to keep me in line. And when I was eight, I got caught shoplifting. A butterscotch candy cane. I still hate butterscotch."

Looking troubled, Gail shook her head. "But stealing when you're eight doesn't show a fatal character flaw. You were just a little boy in pain."

"Yeah, well. Uncle Harold couldn't get over it. You would have thought I had stolen bread from the mouths of orphans." He paused and cleared his throat before continuing. "That's why when I was nineteen, and the church silver went missing, Harold was pretty sure it was me. Didn't matter what I said. My mother believed in me, but once Harold had his say, no one else in the congregation did. So, if you wondered why I seem so unaffected by the loss of my uncle, now you know."

"That's a terrible story."

"Everybody's got at least one terrible story." He shrugged. "What about you, Gail? What's your tragic tale?"

She clutched the menorah a little tighter. "It's not a very interesting one."

He grinned. "My other option is shoveling out Harold's underwear drawer. Any excuse to take a break sounds great about now."

"My parents raised me religious, but it was all ritual and no depth. So when I went to college, I drifted away from Judaism. Like you, I lost my community. But this had meaning." She patted the menorah. "It was a wedding gift to my great grandmother. It travelled to this country in her suitcase when she arrived at Ellis Island. But mostly I loved this menorah because it belonged to my

Aunt Leah. And when I visited Tante Leah, the rituals all seemed to have a purpose."

She looked at him to make sure he understood.

"And the purpose of this?" He gestured.

"To bring light. Well, obviously. But not just physical light. A sort of light of the spirit."

"So how did it end up in my Uncle Harold's bedroom? I mean, no disrespect, but a mess like this is not where you expect to find a lightness of spirit. I can't imagine how he would have come across it. Did you ever invite him to visit you?"

"No, and I don't think he would have accepted an invitation," she said. "He didn't seem to approve of me."

James chuckled but his eyes were somber. "How can you be sure this is the same exact menorah you remember?"

"I'm not sure how it ended up here," she said. "But I am positive it's my menorah. See these doorknobs?" She pointed to the little protrusions. "I can tell you what's inside these doors."

~

Before responding, James flipped the candelabra over and checked for a maker's mark. Silver. If she was wrong, he could probably get a couple thousand for it to defray some of Harold's funeral costs. Unless Harold had stolen it.

"Okay. Tell me. Before I open them, what's behind doors number one and two?"

"A little dreidel, that's a four sided spinning top, with a nick at the tip of the handle. And an engraving of the ten commandments with just the first couple words for each commandment in Hebrew."

He blinked. She was taking a risk by being so specific. On the other hand, if she was right, it belonged to her. In that case, he wanted to know how Harold had gotten hold of it. Too bad Harold wasn't in position to explain. James would have enjoyed that conversation. He set the menorah on a newly cleared table edge and tugged gently at the tiny knobs.

He couldn't contain his intake of breath when the doors gave. A tiny blackened top tumbled out onto his palm. The inside wall of the compartment was as tarnished as the outside, but even so he could pick out what looked like a miniature bas relief pair of tablets. He shook his head in wonder.

"Looks like it's yours."

"See the nick on the top of the dreidel?" She cupped the top in her hand and pointed to the tiny deformity. "That's because I dropped it onto the stucco floor of Tante Leah's balcony once."

"She let you play with a solid silver antique. On a balcony."

"It was meant to be played with," Gail said. "It's a top."

"I'm not criticizing." And he wasn't, exactly. But Gail's whole manner had changed at the sight of the menorah, as though it brought out a different side of her, a side she had missed. If it was possible to be envious of a tarnished bit of silver, he was. Which was downright pathetic.

"Want to break for lunch?" he asked. "Pick your favorite place. My treat."

The fresh air on the walk to the café was a gift. James felt as if he was breathing more oxygen than usual. Or maybe that was Gail. She bobbed along at his side, nearly skipping in her enthusiasm. The tables inside were occupied, but there was seating on the patio in the deep shade of a large awning.

"I love eating outside," she said once they had placed their orders. "But I hardly ever do so. Isn't it strange how often we deprive ourselves of harmless pleasures?"

He nodded, but didn't explore the topic. There was a companionable quality to being with Gail he didn't care to delve into, but he had wanted to catch her hand in his as they walked, to lace his fingers between hers. And now he wanted to reach across the table and tuck a wayward curl behind her ear, and that was even more of a problem. He reached for his napkin instead, spread it on his lap, and settled on a safe topic.

"How do you think Harold got hold of your family heirloom?"

She shot him a long look. "I'm not sure I want to know."

"Best guess. Do you think he stole it?"

"I don't see how he could have."

A shadow flickered in her eyes. But then she tightened her jaw and the shadow was gone before he could be sure he had seen it. She picked up her glass but set it down again without drinking.

"Larry," she said. "You can't change people in my experience, but Larry thought you could. Mold them. Make them suit your needs. He should have figured out he wouldn't be able to change me before he married me, but by the time he did, we were a few years in and he was getting sick. We moved here around then. This condo and almost everything in it was his lifelong dream. He knew exactly how he wanted every furnishing placed, down to the last vase. And I was part of the furnishing, in a way. So any part of me that didn't fit with the image had to go." She gestured toward her jeans and t-shirt. "Larry was still mobile when we moved here. And he always insisted on being the one to bring out the trash. I think he decided my Tante Leah's menorah didn't fit the decor, even though I generally kept it out of sight."

"But you used it for Hanukkah, right?"

"No. I—well, once. The first year we were married. But later, not so much. It's a communal activity, lighting candles, playing games, singing the songs. And Larry didn't want any part of it. Larry wanted me to fit into his world. So it was easier to give in than to take a stand about something that didn't matter."

But clearly, her religion had mattered to Gail. James relaxed his hand, which had unaccountably tightened into a fist. He was glad he would never have the opportunity to meet Larry. The guy sounded like an idiot.

∽

Gail watched James across the table as he scrolled through whatever was on his phone. Business email, maybe. She felt a twinge at the thought of him leaving. He would fly back to Baltimore as soon as his obligations in Arizona were met. And even with their short acquaintance, she would miss him. He stared at the screen for a moment and then tucked the device away in his pocket.

"Hanukkah starts tonight," he said abruptly. "Are you going to light the candles this year?"

There was a sudden lump in her throat so she put her sandwich down on her plate.

"I hadn't thought about it. I don't suppose your uncle also has silver polish and Hanukkah candles in his bedroom?" She tried to keep her tone light but it came out forlorn.

"I don't know about candles, but the supermarket across the street probably carries silver polish." He sounded so reasonable, she couldn't figure out why her eyes were moist. Larry had always said she was too emotional. She pushed her plate aside, her appetite dwindling.

"You should finish your lunch," James commented.

"I'm not as hungry as I thought, but that's okay. I could stand to lose a few pounds," she said.

"I don't think so." He seemed oblivious to her disbelieving stare as he took another bite. "This is an excellent pickle. What's Hanukkah about, anyway?"

She sat back and shook her head. "The short version is that a band of Jews recaptured the Holy Temple from the Syrian-Greeks sometime around 167 BC. But when they cleaned the Temple up, they only found enough remaining pure oil to light the big menorah for one day. The process of producing more pure olive oil would have taken eight days. But a miracle happened. The little bit of oil they found lasted all eight days."

He nodded. "That's why Hanukkah is eight days long?"

"Right," she said. "You light one additional candle each night."

"But the menorah we found has nine candle holders."

"That's a little confusing," she admitted. "The extra candle that isn't on the same level as the others is called a *shamash*. You use it to light the other candles."

He frowned. "So the *shamash* is kind of like a servant."

She shook her head. "Nope. The *shamash* is critical. Hanukkah candles are purely for enjoyment. You can't use them to work by. You can't even use them to light each other. Only the *shamash* can light Hanukkah candles."

He sat silently for a moment, looking at her. Then he shook his head and rose to pay the bill. She stood to follow him but stopped in her tracks. He wasn't a friend. He was just being polite, she reminded herself. And practical, since she was helping him out. The cashier smiled up at him and said something Gail was too far away to hear. Flirting, probably. James turned to look at Gail and beckoned impatiently.

"You made a conquest." She glanced at him as they stepped onto the sidewalk. He gave her a withering look and strode ahead, slowing only to hold the door for her as they headed into the supermarket. The store had a special display up front which included Hanukkah candles, chocolate coins, Passover matzoh, jars of borscht, and a platter of triangular hamantaschen cookies. She felt a little sorry for the confused store manager, at sea in the complexity that was the Jewish year, but it made her smile too. Shaking her head, she plucked a box of matzoh from James' hand and led him toward the silver polish. On a whim, she also added potatoes, onions, sour cream, and apples to her basket.

By unspoken agreement, they bypassed Harold's door and headed straight to Gail's. It was just as well, she thought. Latkes, potato pancakes, took a long time to fry even if she was preparing them for only two. She flicked on the radio and tuned it to her favorite oldies station, swaying to the music as she dug out her stained recipe card. She glanced toward the dining room table. James frowned in concentration as he smoothed the silver paste onto the menorah.

"How's it coming?"

His hand stopped and he looked up at her. "I work better when I'm not rushed."

She fiddled with the food processor to hide her flushed face. It was embarrassing enough to be developing a crush on a house guest, but to misinterpret his words to mean something he couldn't possibly have intended was out of line. She turned on the cold water to wash the potatoes and surreptitiously splashed some on her face and neck. Darn hot flashes.

She had just taken a saucepan of simmering applesauce off the stove to cool when she sensed him behind her. She turned and her vision blurred with tears. The menorah shone gently, almost glowing in his capable hands.

"Thank you," she whispered. And without pausing to think, she threw her arms around him.

He stiffened and she knew she had made a terrible mistake. She stepped back, prepared to stammer out an apology. He shook his head and her heart sank as he placed the menorah on the counter. He would walk out now, she thought dully, and he would be right to. Or, worse, he would stay and pretend she had done nothing wrong and it would be awkward and awful. She looked at the floor, searching for something to say to make it right.

The last chords of the Monkees singing about a Pleasant Valley Sunday faded away on the radio and were replaced by a deliberately paced piano introduction. His shoes still hadn't moved. She looked up at him, miserable. But he reached for her, drawing her into his arms. His forehead pressed against hers, his eyes serious as he swayed gently to the rhythm. It was Elvis singing *Can't Help Falling In Love With You*. But it was James too, his voice unexpectedly soothing, rumbling in his chest as she pressed her ear against his shirt.

His hand rested warm against the small of her back. And slowly, slowly they came to a halt as the song finished, his lips so close to hers she could almost taste his breath. He was waiting for something —permission, maybe. So she edged upwards and brushed her own lips against his. She expected nice, even sweet. She hadn't anticipated a surge of current, as though she had accidentally managed to connect the only two functional wires in a tangled mess of cords. He pulled back a moment and studied her face carefully.

"More?" He sounded hoarse.

"More." Definitely more. It was possible this would give her a heart attack but it would be worth it. She took his hand and led him toward her bedroom before she could change her mind. Before he could change his too.

～

"That was—" She searched for the right term.

"Spectacular? Phenomenal? Best you ever had?"

His tone was light but there was an undercurrent of seriousness there. She knew she should say something. She wasn't inexperienced, but the best she had ever had wasn't setting the bar very high. In any case, making love with James was more like stepping into a different dimension. It was impossible to compare an apple to an hour. Both were good, but there was no scale with the capacity to measure the difference.

He lay on his side next to her, gently tracing the line of her clavicle with one finger and occasionally dipping to give her a leisurely kiss. And she felt indolent. And somehow at the same time entitled to that laziness. It was a strange sensation.

"I'm still trying to figure out the appropriate terminology," she said. "But I don't think I've ever been so relaxed in my life. I'm not sure you are good for my self-discipline, James Jackson."

He flopped onto his back dramatically.

"But everyone told me this new method was the best way to build character," he groaned. "Now we'll have to go back to the old-fashioned way of doing it."

She turned toward him and placed a hand on his belly, enjoying the way his gaze sharpened at her touch. She felt oddly powerful knowing she had that effect on him. And at the same time, it humbled her.

"Which way is that?"

He looked at her darkly. "It involves whipped cream."

She grinned. "Now I'm wishing I'd thought ahead at the supermarket. But sour cream's all I've got and that's for the latkes. I'm surprisingly hungry. You?"

"Starving."

He sat up and reached for his trousers. She stopped to appreciate exactly how handsome he was—his smooth muscled back and the indented line along his spine. A little shiver went through her. He was a beautiful man.

There was a new awareness in her as she placed latkes on his plate and lifted up her own for him to ladle out the applesauce. His hand brushed hers as they reached for the sour cream at the same time. She watched his teeth bite into the crispy crust of the pancake —the way the tip of his tongue licked a smidgen of sour cream from his upper lip. And she wanted him all over again.

It was greedy to want more than your portion. Or maybe that was coveting. She had never been too clear on the difference. She couldn't have James forever, even if he was willing. But she could have him for now. And that would have to do.

∾

James watched as Gail lit a match and slid the base of the slim green candle through the flame, softening the wax just enough so it would stick upright in its holder. Then she plucked a blue candle from the box and set it next to the matchbox on the counter.

He edged closer, curious. "So what happens now?"

She hesitated. "Ideally you set the menorah near a window so people can see the lights when they pass by."

"How about that one?" He gestured toward the wide windowsill of her picture window overlooking the front of the building.

"I don't know." She looked uneasy.

"Are you worried about damaging the sill?"

"No, no. It's just that no one here knows I'm Jewish. So far. Larry asked me to keep it to myself and I did. We have this concept in Judaism called *Shalom Bayit*, peace in the house. It basically means that you value harmony in the home above your own wishes. So I honored his request. Not even my step-daughter knows."

"No disrespect, but why would anyone care?"

He must have looked as mystified as he felt. If anything, she seemed more uncomfortable now. She threw up her hands and headed toward the couch where she sank into the cushions with a sigh.

"Nobody should care. Ideally. But inevitably, some people do. The same sorts of people, probably who would care about what color skin you have. Or the fact that you and I are, well..." She blushed but pushed on. "It was easier for Tante Leah. She lived in a

Jewish neighborhood in New Jersey where everyone put their menorahs in the window on Hanukkah. Even so, one year some teens ran through the neighborhood throwing bricks. My aunt's window wasn't broken, but her neighbor's was."

"We're on the sixth floor," he said. "The complex has a wall around it. And a security guard. I think you're safe."

He sat beside her and wrapped an arm around her shoulders. She smelled good, latkes and applesauce and that particular vanilla scent he thought might be a natural part of her skin.

"Maybe," she frowned. "I probably only have to worry about anti-Semites who are residents, have access to bricks, and have fabulous throwing arms. How many of those can there possibly be?"

He couldn't help smiling at her logic. "Do you worry about this type of thing a lot?"

"Not a lot. But some. Probably not as much as you worry about racist behavior. I can't imagine what it's like to be a black man in America. Scary, I would think. Not to mention infuriating. I'm furious just thinking about what it must have been like for you as a teenage boy. And how it feels now for you to walk down the street."

He glanced at her, amused. Her curly hair was standing out more than usual, as though she was channeling an electric current. And her eyes flashed. She looked like an angry owlet.

"You have to pick your battles, obviously." He kept his tone gentle. "But I'm not willing to allow prejudice to run my life. My mother used to say, 'If I stop sitting in the front of the bus, they've won.' If you light your menorah with the shades down, they also win."

She nodded. "Your mother was a wise woman."

His eyes stung. He wasn't sure how his mother would have felt about what he was doing right now. Worried, probably. Not that he would do something wrong. She had believed in him when no one else had. But that he would be hurt in the end.

He watched Gail place a square of aluminum foil on the window sill and then the menorah on top of that. She turned toward him and he shook his head. This was not his story, his tradition, his life. It was hers. And he could never truly be a part of it. Pretending otherwise would be foolish.

"What's the matter?" She raised one brow. "Afraid of a little brick?"

He snorted but got to his feet. Standing at her side, he watched her touch the lit wick of the *shamash* to the green candle. For a moment it looked as if the flame would die, but after a brief heart-stopping moment of guttering, the wick caught and burned steadily.

"*Baruch atah...*" Her voice wavered and she stopped. He ducked his head to see her face. Her cheeks were wet. He wrapped his arm around her shoulders to pull her into a hug, but she shook her head fiercely and stood her ground. Breathing deeply, she tried again and this time the melody rang out, sweet and true. He couldn't understand the words, but the message was clear.

～

They settled into a routine. Mornings they cleaned. When they couldn't bear the mess anymore, they broke for lunch. Afternoons were filled with trips to drop off trash in the dumpster, donations to Goodwill, and to pick up more trash bags. After the first day, they switched to industrial strength bags and began using gloves as well. And once they had cleaned out enough foot room, they worked together.

There was an intimacy to their rhythm, to the way she ducked under his arm to snag another trash bag. The way she shoved her hip against his companionably when he was in her way. Her snort of disbelief at yet another set of headphones. So far, they had found twenty-seven of them in varying states of disrepair.

Gail was good company and that was disturbing. Because he might love her a little, but he couldn't afford to like her. He had loved Denise once, passionately. But he wasn't sure now if either of them had liked the other. In retrospect, that might have made their breakup easier. And more understandable.

But if the love of his youth had been an urgent flash of flame, this thing with Gail was a slow-building fire that grew from embers.

It was built on a foundation of warmth. Losing that sort of fire could break a man.

Worse, Gail was becoming attached to him. That was in nobody's best interest. So he kept things as light as he could.

But nights were a different matter. The intensity of what was happening between him and Gail was a lot easier to ignore in daylight. It wasn't the sex that was the defining measure, although that was well beyond good. It was more about Gail's contented sigh as she settled next to him on the couch in the evening. The warmth of her against his back as he was slipping into sleep. She snored a little at night, not enough to keep him awake, but enough to remind him she was there.

He felt safe with Gail and it had been a long time since he had felt that way. Probably since he was seven, he guessed. But this was exactly why he had to nip his attachment in the bud. It would be a dangerous mistake to pretend he could be with a woman like Gail.

He stopped mid-motion to watch as she assessed a rumpled Hawaiian print shirt, her nose wrinkled. She held it briefly over the Goodwill bag, then she shrugged and stuffed it in the trash bag. And that, in a nutshell, was why this could never work. Because Uncle Harold had understood that even an ugly shirt was still a shirt. Because sometimes you didn't even have a shirt. James had lived with that knowledge his whole life. The taint of poverty never left a person. And he didn't want that rubbing off on Gail.

Gail would never understand where he had come from. She couldn't. Because all the explaining in the world couldn't give her the sounds and the smells of growing up in the worst neighborhood of Baltimore. He remembered standing in the middle of an intersection early one Sunday morning, when the addicts were still sleeping. No matter which way he looked, row houses stretched into the distance, tiny unreachable toys as they touched the horizon. It had been impossible for him to conceive of the sort of world Gail lived in, never mind imagine himself a part of it.

Then there was the color thing of course. Some women were specifically attracted to "exotic" men. Kenny, a cashier on the graveyard shift at Wendy's when James was working his way through

college, called them *Gourmandes*. James had found these women
tended to tire of the latest trendy flavor quickly. But Gail hadn't
struck him that way. For one thing, she didn't have a *Gourmande's*
signature predatory air.

The difference in religion wasn't an issue per se. But he didn't
like how he felt when Gail held his hand and sang the blessings. The
memory of Uncle Harold's chilly precision as he denounced the
wages of sin was a world away from laughing over a silly game with
a top and eating donuts by candlelight. A part of James stung at
how unfair it was that Gail was able to surround herself with rituals
of such warmth and comfort. There was a strength to the slim
candles with their delicate wicks, a kind of life despite their delicacy.
More, there was a resilience to the story of Hanukkah that appealed
to him. Still, it would be foolish to confuse his envy of Gail's
religious practice with interest in a love relationship.

~

Gail glanced uneasily at the five little flames sputtering out against
the backdrop of night in her window. Something was nagging at
her, something she should be remembering. She shrugged and tried
to let it go.

Tomorrow was Friday. Maybe she would make challah. She
hadn't taken the time to bake the sweet braided bread in years.
James would like it. She glanced toward the dining room and
smiled. He was completely focused on paperwork, a tiny crease
between his eyebrows as he compared whatever was on his laptop
with the figures on the stack of papers next to it.

She loved watching him concentrate. It reminded her of the way
he made love. Utter focus. There was something addictive about
being the object of such concentrated energy. Maybe a little
dangerous too. Because being with James made her feel as though
nothing else mattered. It was a seductive sensation, like lolling in a
hammock on a lazy day in summer with no greater requirement
than reaching out for an icy glass of lemonade.

She walked to his chair and rested her hands on his shoulders, reveling in his moan of appreciation as she kneaded the tight muscles. She breathed in his scent. He smelled like home. For no reason she could pinpoint, she felt a sense of urgency as she tugged him toward the bedroom.

But once there, James refused to hurry. He took off his shoes and waited as she removed hers. Then socks. Then belt. The slow pace gave each movement a weight of intent. They had both removed their shirts when she heard the front door click open. She snatched her T-shirt from the bed and jammed it on. James looked a question and she shook her head. Toes curling on the carpet, she crept toward the living room and peeped around the door frame.

A bulging suitcase slouched on the floor in the foyer. There was a trail of clothing, a jacket, a sweater, and a hat leading into the living room. She could just see the top of a young woman's head over the back of the couch, straight blonde hair, with an obligatory purple streak.

"Debbie?" Gail's voice sounded squeaky. "I for—wait, today is Thursday. Christmas eve isn't until—"

Debbie didn't bother to get up, but one foot clad in a grimy flip-flop wriggled slightly as it poked off its perch on the armrest of the couch.

"Change in plans."

Gail shook her head. There was something about knowing James was in the bedroom behind her that changed things. She strode into the living room and turned to face her step-daughter, hands on her hips.

"You should have told me you were arriving today."

"Why?"

"I have a guest."

"Right." Debbie snapped her gum and tapped at her cell phone without looking up. "Funny. Ha, ha."

Gail's lips tightened. Fighting rudeness with more rudeness wasn't effective. Didn't change her desire to bat the girl over the head with one of the sofa pillows.

"Hello." James was fully dressed, which would have been

disappointing if Gail hadn't also been relieved. Scrambling to her feet, Debbie stared, her mouth an O of surprise.

"James, this is my step-daughter, Debbie Costanza. Debbie, this is my guest, James Jackson."

"But *I* need the guest room."

"No problem." James said.

Gail watched Debbie's expression morph from surprise to embarrassment to anger. The same way she had looked at Gail when Larry first informed sixteen-year-old Debbie he was marrying again. And no amount of friendly overtures, family meals, or thoughtfully chosen gifts had helped.

Gail had worked hard to build trust with Debbie since then and she had thought they had reached a sort of détente. Not friends exactly. But not enemies either. Now, given Debbie's spiteful expression, she wondered if she had been kidding herself. "Is he rich? I mean that's what you tend to look for in a guy, right?"

James eyed Debbie as if she were a peculiar and slightly disgusting insect and then turned his gaze toward Gail. But Gail couldn't meet his eyes. And then, when she finally did look up, James' expression was polite but distant.

"I'll be heading out shortly, Gail," he said finally. "Thanks for all your help."

Debbie snorted. Gail opened her mouth to protest and then shut it again. Debbie was right. Not about the money, of course. That was just ridiculous. But she was right that Gail wasn't exactly romantic heroine material. She remembered watching a pair of mallard ducks, the female a pale version of the vibrant male. She had felt that way with Larry. And now she was even older. More foolish too.

~

James shook his head as he watched Gail head toward the kitchen. It would have been easy to leave now. On the other hand, Gail had been good to him and he couldn't see abandoning her to deal with

Debbie alone. He'd stay through dinner and then he'd come up with an excuse.

Debbie had settled back onto the couch with her phone, presumably communicating with other like-minded harpies, so he followed Gail into the kitchen. There was a circular mirror on the wall over the sink, framed in cheerful plastic orange petals like a flower. His mother would have liked it, but given the carefully curated decor, it looked as out of place as the menorah did. He wondered who had chosen it. And who had chosen to place it there. Gail leaned against the edge of the sink, her eyes fixed on her reflection.

"I got a text from one of the hotels I contacted the night I arrived," he lied. "They had a cancellation."

"That's great!" Her tone was chipper as she turned to pull a lasagna from the oven, but her shoulders had slumped.

"I want you to know how much I appreciate your hospitality." He winced the moment it was out of his mouth. He would have done anything to pull the words back.

"It's no trouble at all. I hope Debbie didn't make you feel unwelcome." Her tone was even, but her cheeks were as red as if they had been slapped.

"Not at all."

She smiled politely, but there was hurt there too, in her eyes, at the corners of her mouth. He could feel the wall of pleasantries growing between them—a kind of mesh made of words. It looked porous. Anyone aside from the two of them wouldn't have even known it was there.

Dinner would have been awkward anyway, but Debbie made it downright unpleasant. She refused garlic bread with a frown and wondered aloud how many carbohydrates were in a piece of lasagna. She asked for a mint leaf in her water glass and when Gail told her there was no mint in the house, she groaned theatrically.

"You're so lazy. Why don't you just grow some? It's super easy. My mother does it."

He could see Gail tighten her lips and wondered why she was resisting the obvious retort. Because if anyone needed a swift virtual kick in the behind, it was Debbie. Instead, Gail served berries with whipped cream, which Debbie picked around fastidiously, huffing with indignation.

Later, he washed dishes while Gail dried. The kitchen felt like a refuge compared to the one-sided war zone that was now the living room. Leaving would be the right thing to do, at least for him. But Gail seemed in no hurry to show him out. Instead she put on a pot of coffee.

"Why do you let her talk to you that way?" He kept his voice low as he watched her fiddle with the sugar bowl.

She shrugged. "It's complicated."

He followed Gail into the dining room, carrying the mugs and a plate of cookies while she brought the coffee pot to the table. To his surprise, Debbie ambled over to join them, pouring herself half a cup of coffee and crumbling a cookie into her napkin.

"How's school going?" Gail asked.

Debbie shrugged.

"Debbie is studying economics at Colfax University. We're all very proud of her."

"Economics a good field." James kept his tone non-committal.

"It's BS. I hate it," Debbie muttered.

"Then why study it?" he said.

"Because—aaargh!" She pushed the napkin away from her and stomped back to the couch.

He shot a startled look at Gail. She leaned forward as though to explain and then beckoned to him to follow her into the kitchen.

"She has to study economics." Gail glanced over her shoulder and kept her tone low. "Larry's estate only pays her tuition if she does."

Rich people problems. James had worked his way through state college and it had taken him an extra year to do it. He had barely finished paying off the loans when his mother had first asked for help with Harold's rent. A degree in economics would have been helpful.

∾

Gail checked the peephole to the hallway for what felt like the twentieth time. Harold's door was ajar. Mumbling something over her shoulder about checking the mail, she slipped out the door and followed the rustling sound into Harold's condo.

There wasn't much left to do now. The items of furniture too large to be easily disposed of were scheduled to be picked up by the Goodwill truck after Christmas. Now it was just a matter of cleaning and, after the furniture was gone, painting. James, looking unusually rumpled, stopped sweeping and looked up, his expression courteous. Guarded.

"How was the hotel?"

He paused, as though considering the implications of his response.

"Fine."

"I wish—" She stopped. "I didn't expect Debbie until today. Although, to be honest, I'm embarrassed to say I forgot she was coming at all. Usually she comes to visit for spring break, but she hasn't come home for Christmas in years."

"No need to apologize." His air of distant courtesy kindled a kind of visceral irritation in her. It was as though he was slowly erasing everything that had grown between them. The heat, the laughter, the maybe-even-love…

"I wasn't apologizing," she snapped. "Where's the vacuum cleaner?"

He frowned. "What's the matter?"

"Nothing." She said it a little louder than she intended and stomped toward the bedroom. She had left the aged vacuum cleaner in the linen closet for just this purpose.

"Don't." James spoke sharply but he was too late. His suitcase lay open on the bedroom floor. The surface of the stained mattress was wrapped with what looked like a new shower curtain. A quilt she didn't recognize was folded neatly at its foot. She felt the blood drain from her face.

"There was no hotel. You lied," she whispered.

He stiffened. "It wasn't a lie. Exactly."

"Then what *exactly* was it?"

"You have a houseguest. I didn't want to be in the way."

"You didn't want to be seen with me," she corrected. "It was all very well to sleep with me when no one knew about it. I was convenient."

"Not true," he thundered.

"Right," she countered. "How do you think it makes me feel to know you prefer this," she gestured at the sad mattress, "to me?"

"I don't!" He looked shocked at the idea.

For a moment, she wondered if she was wrong. But then she caught a glimpse of her reflection in the full-length mirror mounted on the bathroom door. "Such a pretty woman," he had whispered in the dark. "You are beautiful." And in the moment, she had wanted to believe him. But it was day now, and she knew he had lied about that too.

~

Gail was crazy. There could be no other explanation. James stared at the door she had just marched out of. Maybe it was her stepdaughter. One evening had been enough for him, but Gail had seven years in. He guessed that could drive anyone nuts. Or maybe, she had finally come to her senses about a relationship with a man she barely knew. In that case, it was about time he did too.

He pulled out the ancient vacuum cleaner and shook his head. He hadn't wanted to keep it, but she had insisted. Something rattled in the base as he unwrapped the cord. He turned the vacuum over and shook it until a large button fell out. He cradled it in his palm and studied it.

There would have been no point to a wool overcoat in Arizona, but this button, brown with a streak of gold, looked like a remnant of the tan Chesterfield Harold had worn so proudly in Baltimore. The coat had epitomized the prosperity and elegance Harold had aspired to. James looked around for his trash bag and realized he had already knotted it shut. So he slipped the button into his pocket. It could serve as a reminder of the dangers of prioritizing social status. Although if anyone was guilty of that, it was Gail.

James shook his head and pressed the power button on the vacuum. Nothing happened. He felt like kicking it. With a grunt of irritation, he picked the vacuum cleaner up and carried it to the trash collection room. There was no point in holding on to something that didn't work. He had told Gail that but she hadn't listened. And now there was no point in telling her anything. Because, like Denise, like Uncle Harold, she had seen what James was and didn't like what she saw.

If he couldn't vacuum, at least he could scrub the kitchen floor. He had just filled the bucket when the call came. Harold's autopsy was complete and the coroner's office had sent the body, per James' instruction, to Blessed Rest Crematory in Scottsdale.

He felt a brief pang of sorrow and quelled it. Harold didn't deserve his pity. James had grown up in the same circumstances Harold had. Maybe worse, since Harold had a father to guide him. And all James had was a vindictive malicious uncle. Still, there was something pathetic about what Harold had become.

Closing his eyes, he saw the image of his mother as she had looked the last day he saw her, fighting for breath in her hospital bed. She had squeezed his hand with surprising strength. "Take care of my brother," she whispered, her voice hoarse from coughing. "He doesn't deserve you, but take care of him anyway. Because you are the better man. And because you love me."

Looking around the sad collection of goods remaining, he wasn't sure just paying Harold's bills had met his mother's standards. His hand hurt. He looked down and saw he was clenching the metal bucket handle, the hard wire jammed into the flesh of his palm. For the first time in years, he felt like crying, and he was pretty sure it wasn't because of Uncle Harold.

He knelt on the floor, dunked the scrub brush into the soapsuds and swore as he pushed the bristles against the sticky tiles. He didn't want to feel sad about Harold—Harold didn't deserve his sorrow. But the plain fact was, he did feel sad. Not because Harold had died, but because he had died alone and unloved. James wiped the square of floor he had scrubbed and watched the water in the bucket darken before he started on the next patch of sticky, greasy tile.

Tomorrow he would call Blessed Rest and complete his obligations. Then, he decided, he would buy a plane ticket back to Baltimore. En route to the airport, he would call a rental agent to find a tenant for the condominium. The rental agent could make arrangements to have the unit cleaned, freshened and painted. Abruptly, he got to his feet. There was no need for him to do any more work here. Ever.

He felt a pang at the image of Gail grinning up at him as they dredged out the mess that had been Harold's crowded living space. At the scent memory of her when she cupped his face and brought it to hers for a kiss. The taste of her shoulder after a day of hard work, sweat-salted with a tinge of vanilla. He had thought there was a chance for love there. But he had been wrong.

He looked around the condo. It was a perfectly fine space, he reminded himself. But he couldn't help feeling it was empty without Gail working beside him. Desolate, actually. Maybe that was why Harold had kept trying to fill it.

～

Gail glared at the kitchen sink. For a person who counted calories incessantly, Debbie still managed to produce an astounding amount of dirty dishware. Sighing, Gail rolled up her sleeves and got to work.

She had been right to call it off with James, she reminded herself wretchedly. She was sure once she accepted that fact she would get back to her usual self. A dish slipped from her hand on the way to the drying rack and hit the floor, shattering into a dozen shards.

She just made it to her bedroom in time. Closing the door with a gentle click, she leaned against it and gave way to a flood of tears. It wasn't just losing James that hurt so badly, although that was truly painful. It was the idea of going back to the Gail of before James. It would be like returning forever to a cave after having experienced sunshine for the first time. She sobbed now, gulping and gasping for air. Blindly, she staggered toward the tissue box on her night table and collapsed onto the edge of the bed.

"Gail? Where are you?" There was an impatient rustling sound just outside the bedroom door.

Gail wiped her face with a wad of tissues and tried to breathe deeply and evenly. Maybe Debbie would think she was napping. But then Gail hiccuped. Loudly.

"Gail, are you okay?" Without waiting for an invitation, Debbie poked her head into the room and froze. "I'm sorry about the dishes, all right?" She gestured impatiently. "You could have just told me you were mad instead of breaking them."

Gail laughed now, but it was a paroxysm. Not sprung from joy but born of a weird amalgam of humor and pain. It hurt. She didn't think she could bear any sarcasm just now and took a breath to tell Debbie so. But to her surprise, Debbie sank down next to her and held her close, rocking gently.

"So where's your boyfriend?"

Gail blinked and stared at her. But Debbie looked bored as always. Maybe a little irritable.

"He's not my boyfriend." Gail swallowed the sob that threatened to erupt.

"Yeah, right." Debbie shot her a skeptical look. "I guess you're all worked up about that plate you broke."

She rose and wandered around the room idly, stopping to run an index finger over the ceramic bowl on Gail's bureau, the carved back of her hairbrush. Then she turned to lean her backside against the bureau, her arms folded across her chest, her expression curiously vulnerable.

"Why are you so nice to me?" she asked.

Gail blinked. "Why not?"

"I was always obnoxious to you," Debbie said. "I never understood why you put up with it."

Gail dismissed her instinctive response and thought a moment. "I think because you needed someone to love you. And I was it."

Debbie snorted. "You make it sound like a chore."

"It is, sometimes," Gail said, shrugging.

Debbie nodded. "You haven't put up the tree."

Gail took a deep breath. "Your father was Christian. I'm Jewish. But if you want to put the tree up, you can. It's still in our storage unit in the basement. Just as long as you're in charge of taking it down again afterwards. I've always hated tinsel."

She waited for the inevitable protest. But Debbie looked at her and nodded.

"Okay."

There was a hint of respect in her tone. Debbie studied Gail for a minute more and took a deep breath.

"I'm quitting school."

Gail stared at her. "Why?"

"Because I hate Economics. And because I want to study French Literature."

"So switch majors."

"I can't. Remember the stupid will?" Debbie's tone was strangled now.

"Of course you can," Gail stood. There was anger in her now, not the managed flame that could form a weapon. This was wild fury, an uncontrolled burn. Gail clenched her fists and concentrated on not growling. "Call the financial aid office and take out a student loan. I'll contribute as much as I can afford. Your father doesn't get to direct your life after he's dead. Not unless you let him."

"Bull," Debbie spat. "This place looks exactly the way it did when Daddy died. You haven't changed anything except that mirror over the kitchen sink. It's like a frikkin' museum dedicated to the memory of a control freak."

Gail felt the blood drain from her face and she sank back to edge of the bed.

"You're right," she whispered. The words scraped her throat. "I'm no better."

"Right? What was your first clue, Sherlock? His pants still hanging in your closet?" Debbie's eyes flashed. "You want me call the financial aid office? I'll do it if you walk across the hall and tell your boyfriend you love him. Double dare you."

Debbie was glaring at her now. That implicit challenge that said *I won't allow you to love me*. But it was too late. She did love Debbie. And she did love James—not that it mattered. Gail's shoes scuffed against the carpet as she trudged across the living room. It occurred to her that if she tripped and fell, she might have an excuse not to speak to James at all. But that would also give Debbie an excuse not to make the call. So she picked up her feet and kept walking.

Gail's hand trembled as she clenched her front door knob and stared through the peephole. Harold's door was shut, so maybe James had left town. In any case, he wouldn't want to see her again. She winced at the memory. She had yelled at him. Stomped out. But when she looked over her shoulder to plead for mercy, she saw Debbie's finger trembling too, poised over her cell phone. For all her bravado, Debbie looked about as scared as Gail felt.

Gail looked down at her hand, clasping the doorknob. If she was going to hold up her end of the agreement, she couldn't do it in half measures. Slowly, she twisted her engagement ring over her knuckle. The wedding ring was a bit tighter. But just as she thought she might have to soap her finger, the ring slipped off. Her finger, with its indentation, looked strangely empty without them. She slid both rings into her pocket, and turned the doorknob.

She left the door open as she crossed the hall and knocked. She wanted Debbie to see her try. But then she heard the echo of footsteps within and her breath caught in her throat. The door swung open and she took a step back. For a split second, before James' screen of civility descended, she saw a kind of wild grief in his eyes.

Without thinking, she stepped forward and wrapped her arms around him. He froze and then she felt his chest heave as though he had been holding his breath until that moment. Then his arms were tight around her, his face buried in her hair as great wrenching sobs gutted him. Alarmed, she guided him to a chair, rubbing his back in an attempt to comfort him. Slowly he calmed. His face was buried in his hands but he was breathing more normally now.

"What happened?" An array of possibilities flitted through her mind. None of them good.

"I don't know," he admitted finally. "The funeral home called and ever since then, I've been a mess. I can't understand it. I hated the guy. It's not as though I loved him and have to go to his funeral."

"Maybe you aren't grieving for him so much as for the loss of opportunity," she said. "Now he is dead, and all the things that were wrong in your relationship can never be fixed. But I think you need to attend a funeral, or at least be there at the end. It will help you let go of some of that pain," she said. "And I'm going with you."

He rubbed his eyes and as he reached for the tissues she offered him, she straightened, standing tall. This was something she could do for him, a way to compensate for any part of his pain she had caused. It wasn't an outright declaration of love, but it would do. For now.

～

James scowled. "You don't have to wear black."

"It's a funeral. Kind of." Gail kept her tone reasonable.

James had been increasingly difficult all morning. First, he stubbed his toe on the shoes Debbie had left under the coffee table. Then he had chipped a teacup. Gail hadn't cared, but he had been upset. And now he was mumbling to himself as he ironed invisible wrinkles from his dress shirt. He looked like a thundercloud.

She didn't mind it. There was no malice to James, so in that way he was quite different than Larry. She had been married to Larry for seven years and she had known James less than two weeks. But in some ways she felt more comfortable with James than she ever had with Larry. And that felt like the ultimate betrayal. Of Larry. Of herself. Of the kind of woman she had believed she was. The sort of woman who lived with her mistakes and tried to make the best of them. A woman who stood up for a child who was hard to love. Or even one who just didn't fit in. The way Tante Leah had done for her.

Gail wasn't intentionally quiet as James drove toward the funeral home, but her sudden sense of disloyalty made it hard to talk of inconsequential things. And anyway, they were going to a funeral.

Sort of. Apparently, it was more of a signing a waiver type of thing. The in-house chaplain was out of town for the holidays.

Just as well, since she and James would be the only ones present. As far as she knew Harold had no friends in the complex and no family but James. Her heart hurt at the thought. Harold had to have been terribly lonely. Loneliness could make a person do foolish things, maybe even terrible things. To oneself. To others.

She glanced at James' profile as he pulled into the parking spot in the nearly empty parking lot. He kept his grip on the steering wheel even as the engine cooled. The funeral home was drab, a cement block structure painted pale apricot. A few discouraged yew bushes lined the edges of the driveway as it curved under the obligatory portico.

"It's not your fault," she said suddenly.

He shot her a suspicious look.

"What's not?"

"That he lived and died alone. His choice. Not yours. Because I'm guessing if he had wanted a relationship with you, he could have had one. Right? I mean, if he'd apologized."

James swallowed and turned away to look out his window.

"I've been having this conversation with myself too." She forged on against the weight of his silence. "About what my responsibility was to Larry when he was alive. And what that responsibility is now."

"And?" He turned to face her, the force of his gaze almost physical.

She hesitated, tentative now. "I was single a long time before Larry came along. And when I met him, he didn't so much woo me as wear me down. He seemed so sure of everything, that it seemed easier to just give in to him. I did push back occasionally. My mother's mirror is over the kitchen sink. Although if Larry had lived longer, the mirror might have gone the same way as the menorah. But mostly, I just went along with whatever he wanted. I'm not proud of it.

"I wasn't happy and I don't think he was either. Maybe I should have left him, but there was Debbie to consider. You think she's bad now? You never met a more prickly teen. And she had reason. Her mother wafted from fad to fad. She may grow mint now, but it was marijuana a couple years ago, when it was illegal. And then she moved into a yurt with outdoor plumbing for a while. Larry was on the other end of the spectrum. He had crazy expectations for his daughter. No. If Debbie was ever going to have a taste of normalcy, I was it.

"So I stayed. And I think I made the right decision then. But I'd like to have the chance to make a better decision now. Because I love you, James Jackson."

He stared at her for a moment before replying.

"Is this your way to make me feel better?"

"Is it working?" She smiled.

"Maybe a little." His lips twitched. "I thought you were mad at me."

"I was. Temporarily. That's the new Gail. No holds barred. I might need a little fine tuning," she admitted. "Are you angry with me?"

He reached for her hand and slowly ran his index finger along the creases of her palm before touching his lips to them.

"No," he said. "For a moment there, you had me worried I had fallen in love with a crazy woman. And what worried me most was I didn't care. I figure, worse comes to worst, we can be crazy together."

∾

It was the eighth night. The last. And always a little bittersweet. Gail glanced at the tray of latkes in the oven and turned down the heat on the applesauce. Debbie had insisted on buying another box of candles since she said the last nine candles in the original box were too boring. Now she sat at the dining-room table silently debating candle-color schemes before arranging them in the menorah.

"I heard back from the financial aid office," she said.

Gail put down her spatula. "And?"

"Like you said, they'll give me loans. Plus, it turns out there's a fund for students changing majors from Business to Humanities. Something about encouraging the arts. They said Economics is close enough and they'll make an exception in my case. I'll probably have to do an extra semester or two—"

Gail whooped and strode across the room to hug her step-daughter. Debbie stiffened at the embrace but didn't wriggle away. Progress. Gail stepped back and patted Debbie's shoulder.

"I'm proud of you," she said.

Debbie stared at the corner of the ceiling, arms folded over her chest. But her cheeks were unusually rosy and Gail knew she was pleased with the praise.

"James must be running late. But he'll be excited to hear the good news too," she said.

Debbie nodded. "He's going to freak."

Debbie had come to the conclusion that James was not a dork. This was tantamount to a scream of approval. Of course some of that had to do with James' offer to buy a new mattress and to let Debbie use Harold's condo for the remainder of her stay. Debbie had accepted with an air of reluctance, but she was clearly relieved to avoid having to witness James and Gail holding hands. Or worse.

Since James first told Gail he loved her, he had made a point of repeating it. Not as though the words were an obligation but with an air of wonder and almost disbelief. As though the emotion itself was a miracle. And maybe for him, it was.

He had gone to the library to research the logistics of moving his business to Arizona. But Gail thought she might take a trip with him to Baltimore before he went any further than research. Arizona had been Larry's dream, not hers. It would be good to chase a dream of her own.

She was just beginning to worry when she heard the doorknob rattle. As far as she knew there was no construction in the hallway, yet James' shoulders and hair were covered with a fine white powder. And his face was alight with pleasure.

"Come quick." He beckoned. "You have to see."

She glanced at Debbie who looked equally mystified. But they followed him into the elevator and through the silent lobby out the front door and into the parking lot. Snow. She reached for James with one hand and for Debbie with the other and looked up into the sky where snowflakes had temporarily displaced the stars.

Gail had forgotten the hush of snow, the grandeur of millions of flakes swirling downward from a silent sky. Only now did she realize how much she had missed it. Not the shoveling and the slush, but the bite of it, the way the flakes caught the light of the street lamp and sparkled for a split second as they fell.

It wouldn't last. She guessed it would melt by morning. But for now, it was a rare thing of incomparable beauty. A miracle.

Later that night, when Debbie left to attend a free lecture about Sartre, Gail sank onto the couch with James to watch the candles burn low. One by one, the flames winked out until the only one left burning was the *shamash*. The bringer of light. The snowflakes fluttering against the window had morphed into raindrops.

"Debbie's happy," Gail said. "Or at least as happy as I've ever seen her."

"And you?" James smiled, but his eyes were intent on hers.

"More than happy," she said. "Joyful. In my heart. I love you, James."

"Good," he said. "Because you kindled joy in me too, the first time I saw you smile, Gail. I love you. As you are. As you will become. Always."

The *shamash* was a puddle of wax and wick now. Silently, she cheered the guttering flame on. But finally it gave in to the inevitable and vanished with a *sizzle* and a wisp of smoke. She looked down at her hand, fingers laced with James'. They would celebrate again next year and the year after that. They would light more candles. There would be singing and fighting and laughter and loving. And their individual flames would join together to make a far greater light than either one of them could have created alone.

FRISKY CONNECTIONS

MICHELLE MARS

AUTHOR'S NOTE

BEING AN AVID ROMANCE READER, I'VE OFTEN WISHED MORE represented me, someone Jewish. When I saw a posting for a Hanukkah anthology, I had to jump at the opportunity to write my own. It just so happened, that I had a series planned for release in 2020 which was perfect for such a story. Enter "Frisky Connections" into The Frisky Bean universe. Nothing says holidays quite like food and family, and for Shira and Aaron, both play a part in giving them the life-long connection they seek. Hope you enjoy the blind date, the holiday magic, and the Lace-Me-Up Latkes.

CHAPTER 1

"Really. It's fine, honey. You couldn't have predicted a bird-bombing as soon as you stepped out of the house. I'd turn right around and need a shower too." Shira Abramson spoke into her phone, tempering her disappointment and comforting her friend, Keren Sabinski, once again.

As her friend apologized for the hundredth time, she returned, "I *know* you'd come if you could. We both knew this was going to have to be a quick get together as it was."

Keren finally said, "I know. I know. It's just that I was so fucking excited to see you. It's been too long. I feel sooo bad. And instead of girl chat, I get to remove bird shit from my hair. Ew."

"I think I come out just fine compared to you, so don't worry even for a second. I'll just grab a quick coffee and get some work done. No biggie."

"Actually, if you still plan to grab a coffee, might I suggest you try out my company's new app?"

"Which app?"

"Immedia-Date."

"The dating app you described to me last month?"

"Yep. The very one. It came out this week and we've already

had a ton of people sign up. Give it a try. Maybe you'll meet Mr. Right today, and shitting birds will have a silver lining. It would be good for your blog *and* you can provide me with feedback."

"You're such a yenta."

"I'll wear that matchmaking badge with pride, thank you very much. Yenta heart. Business brain. Now give it a go, and I'm going to wash my hair a million times over and then head to my meeting."

"Fine. If I end up dead in a ditch somewhere, I'll know who to blame." Shira grumbled.

"Enjoy. Avoid the ditch. Text your bitch. That sounded a lot better in my head than out loud. You know what I mean, though. Text me when you're done. Bye."

With that, the line went dead.

What had she just agreed to? Shira opened up the app store and searched for Immedia-Date. She located it and had it downloaded quickly. She was impressed right away with the ease of setting it up. The streamlined process was a snap. Answer a few simple questions and it created a basic profile with what you were looking for. Tall, dark, Jewish a bonus, and handsome a desire. The app prompted that all she needed to do now, was turn her profile to 'currently available' and it would search her vicinity for any available matches interested in a short pop-up date. So she did just that. Easy peasy.

Her phone dinged almost right away, making her jump. Someone was available and interested in meeting up with her. *Well, that was fast.*

She opened the app back up, clicked on the profile of the interested party, and had to blink a few times. This had to be a scam. No one joined a dating app and got one of the hottest guys she'd ever seen in the first couple of minutes. She bet it was someone catfishing with a fake picture, but that could be resolved quickly when they met, so she clicked "Interested." The app then took a minute to search the area between them for a highly rated coffee shop or café within a short distance.

Her phone dinged again with the address to the shop. Shira figured she would at least discover a new place to get her caffeine fix out of this ill-advised adventure into modern dating. Coffee was life, after all. She pulled out of the parking lot where she had meant to meet Keren and headed to her Immedia-Date with some trepidation laced with excitement.

She arrived a few minutes later at her destination and was intrigued by the place right away. She checked out the map on the app and her date was still a few minutes away, so she decided to investigate the place on her own. The front window boasted a sign that read:

> *Welcome to The Frisky Bean*
> *Coffee to Wake You Up*
> *Pastries to Turn You On*

Shira was now more than intrigued. What kind of crazy coffee place was this? And was it really appropriate for a first date? She shrugged and stepped inside. Right away, she realized she didn't care. The scents in this café made her mouth water, and she nearly moaned out loud in pleasure. Well, damn. New favorite café indeed.

"Hi there! Welcome to The Frisky Bean. Have you been here before? Probably not, since I'd remember if you had and of course we've only been open for eight months, so quite new. What can I get for you?"

That was all said with such speed and exuberance, Shira nearly flinched. She had to wonder if this could still be her favorite new place with the overly cheery person working behind the counter. Was there a way to maybe avoid her? Order ahead? Her consternation with being overwhelmed with perkiness must have shown on her face because the woman with the stunning, messy, curly red hair grimaced and said with less exuberance, "Too much, huh?" Her voice dropped to nearly a whisper. "Sorry. You're obviously one of the people who needs some coffee defenses before I approach you. Let's try that again." And with a dramatically less excited, almost comically even tone she said, "Is there something I can help you with?"

Comical it might be, but it worked. Shira was now ready to answer. "Sorry. Coffee first may as well be my motto, but so should,

'Oscar the Grouch was misunderstood.'" She winked, hoping to diffuse the tension she'd accidentally created. It seemed to have worked, as the woman behind the counter visibly relaxed. So she continued: "I'm meeting someone here. They should be arriving any minute. Do you have a menu I can look at until then?"

"Sure." The woman handed her a card and then continued, still in a friendly but calm tone, "My name is Summer. Let me know when you're ready to order."

"Thanks."

"No problem. Take your time."

As she perused the menu, Shira's eyes opened wide and she felt a blush creeping up her cheeks. That slogan on the window wasn't kidding around. A bell sounded behind her, but she was so engrossed in the menu items, she forgot to keep a lookout for her date. She was oblivious until she heard a deep, sexy male voice coming from right next to her. "See something you like?" In fact, it came from too close. She reacted before she could think better of it, leaving her full of regrets the moment after.

CHAPTER 2

Aaron Sanders couldn't believe his luck. He'd just decided to test his company's new app when his phone let him know someone was in his vicinity. And boy was she beautiful. Or maybe more: striking. In her picture, she had long blackish-brown curly hair and almond-shaped, dark brown eyes. Intense eyes. The image looked kind of like a professional headshot, and he wondered what she did for a living. Of course, there was always the possibility that she used a fake photo or that no one would come. He had to try, though. That was the point of his app.

If a person didn't show up, wasn't who they seemed, or there was no chemistry, you were only committing a short amount of time to each date. Just enough to grab a cup of coffee and then you could get back to your life. No exchange of phone numbers or addresses or emails. No commitment at all. And, if no one showed up, at least maybe you'd discovered a cool new spot, so not a total loss.

When he'd walked up to The Frisky Bean, he had to admit to being a little concerned it had been included on the app because people might get weirded out at having a first date at such a provocative location. That was true only until he'd made his way inside. The place smelled incredible and had a very welcoming air about it. He noticed the gorgeous redhead standing behind the counter first and waved a hand at her in greeting, hoping to silence whatever she had been about to say. It worked, which was a good thing, because his eyes locked on the same hair he'd seen in the picture. The tresses crowned a soft, full-figured body with a deliciously rounded bottom. He liked an ass he could sink his teeth into. He was such an ass man.

At that moment, his date seemed preoccupied. She hadn't even turned toward him when he'd entered. While that stung his ego a bit, he was curious about what held her so completely enthralled.

He scanned the food items listed from over her shoulder and had to bite his tongue to keep from laughing. Instead he looked at her and saw the blush that colored her cheeks. Lovely. Her face was just as arresting in person. He really had hit the jackpot. His app was the best thing ever made. Clearly. Trying not to startle her, in his most soothing tone he leaned in and inquired, "See something you like?"

Not soothing enough apparently, because she startled anyway and slammed both of her palms into his chest. Hard. Since her reaction had caught him completely off guard, he toppled. It was almost worth the bruise to his butt and ego to see those amazingly expressive eyes grow round with the comical realization of what she'd just done. Somewhere in the background, his brain registered the exclamation of shock from the woman behind the counter, but he only had eyes for the woman in front of him, who reached to help him up.

"I'm so sorry! I can't believe I did that. But... You know... You really shouldn't stand so close to a woman when she isn't expecting it. You might find yourself facing a self-defense trainer who reacts decisively to such things."

"Yes. I think that lesson was just thrust into me. What a good instructor you are."

She snickered as he took her proffered hand and made his way to standing.

He continued, "Shall we try this again?"

"Yes. I suppose that would make more sense than slinking off and claiming an emergency embarrass-ectomy."

"I know which I prefer." He enjoyed the warmth that crept into her eyes as he smiled at her. "Hi. I'm Aaron and I would very much enjoy getting you whatever you want off of that highly inappropriate and yet enticing menu."

"I'm Shira, and I would very much like a, um, Moaning Mocha." He appreciated the way her voice grew huskier and she looked at him directly, as she told him what she wanted. *Hot.*

He turned to the woman at the counter who was beaming at them. She seemed like the kind of person who was awfully chipper. Maybe she dipped into the coffee a little too much. She woke from her contemplation, straightening and talking with her hands as she said, "What can I get—ow!" One of her hands collided with the cash register next to her. She grimaced and scowled at the register but then continued, "—you?"

He looked over at Shira and saw her biting her slightly quivering lip. It was obvious she was trying not to laugh at the antics of the barista. He picked up a menu from the counter and said, "One Moaning Mocha, one Escapist Espresso, and, do you have any recommendations for a baked good to go with our drinks? What's good here?"

The cashier's face perked up. "Obviously, since I'm a co-owner, I have to say everything here is delicious, but our best seller is the Bondage Banana Bread also called the 3B. We also make killer scones. Right now we have the Rock-Your-Socks Blueberry Scones straight from the oven." She began pointing inside the display case and said, "We also have a couple of seasonal items right now, with the holidays around the corner. The Well-Hung Gingerbread Man, Peppermint Bark and Bite, Yule Cream My Log, Candy My Yam Muffin, Lace-Me-Up Latkes, and finally, Stripped Down Sufganiyot."

That was a lot of information. Shira must have thought so too, because when he looked over at her, her eyes seemed a little glazed over. She blinked a couple of times and looked back at him. She opened her mouth to say something but closed it again.

From behind the counter he heard, "Oh no. I did it again. Sorry. How about I work on your drink orders and let you get back to me."

"Sounds like a good idea. Thanks," he responded.

Shira suddenly smiled, and it was breathtaking. Her whole face lit up with just the small twist of her lips. She mock-whispered to him, "I think Summer is going to kick me out for my lack of perk soon."

Before he could ask who Summer was, the woman behind the counter yelled over the top of the steaming sound, "Never, my new grumpy friend."

They all began to crack up but he was completely transfixed by Shira's gregarious laugh. He guessed that she was reserved until, well, she wasn't. What else wasn't she reserved about? He found he wanted to know.

When she finally sobered, she said, "I'd like to try the two Hanukkah-themed items and I'm willing to share. How about you? Interested?"

Oh. He was interested. Very, very interested. Instead of responding, he turned back to Summer and said, "One of the latkes, one of the *sufganiyot*, and one of the gingerbread men please."

"You like them well-endowed, too? Nice," his date commented.

"I just thought you could take it with you to remember me by."

It took only a heartbeat for her to understand his meaning and she laughed again, and it was everything he hoped to achieve with that order. Music. Just lovely. His app was the absolute best for this encounter alone. A few minutes together and he was entranced.

CHAPTER 3

Once Shira was able to catch her breath again, she said, "Well… that *is* a great alternative to the traditional dick pic." And then her amusement overcame her. Again. She had been ready for the worst but totally unprepared for the reality that was her blind date. Aaron was just as gorgeous in-person as his picture made him out to be. While that was a pleasant surprise, she was completely floored by his ability to make her laugh and his seemingly laid-back personality.

She still couldn't believe she'd knocked him down, but the ease with which he handled it was impressive. Also, considering the food they were ordering, his joke had been subtle, instead of getting downright dirty or leering like a teenager—also big bonus points. She was actually looking forward to sitting with him and getting to know him for the short time they had.

Aaron paid for their food after she tried to cover her half with no success. Ultimately, they agreed she could grab the next coffee. And already talking about a next time worked just fine for her. They grabbed their drinks and headed to one of the two-person tables in the lovely café. The walls were a warm mustard yellow with risqué black and white photos for sale throughout. It was a perfect balance between inviting and sensual. Like a warm comforting hug from your lover that develops into an unexpected boner. Bonus!

What she found surprising was that she was suddenly tongue-tied. It had been a while since she'd gone on a blind date, and she wasn't sure what to talk about first. The ease with which they'd bantered just a minute ago gave way to normal first date insecurity. Luckily, Aaron didn't seem to suffer from the same problem.

"So. You're a self-defense instructor? Is that your day job?"

In the background she heard Summer putting together the rest of their order as she considered her answer.

"I am, but no, it's not my day job. I'm a blogger and freelance writer. So, Immedia-Date has found me a new place to work."

"Nice. What do you blog or write about?"

This is when things usually became awkward, because most guys would back off quick when they heard what she wrote about. Because she really liked Aaron, she decided to hedge. If things moved to a second date, she could always go into more detail then. "I blog about things in daily life, as well as offer reviews to my readers."

For a moment she wondered if he could tell she wasn't being completely forthcoming as he studied her instead of replying. Then it seemed he accepted her answer because his face relaxed, and he did respond. "You must be very good if that's your day job. It's quite a saturated market."

"I am." She wasn't being boastful. She was considered one of the best in her corner of the blogosphere, and she had the traffic and advertising dollars to prove it.

"Confident."

"You bet. And you? What do you do?"

He seemed to pause again before he continued with, "I'm part of a startup that creates apps."

"And you're not located in Silicon Valley?"

"Why be in Silicon Valley when you can be in Silicon Beach?"

"Good point. Venice Beach has definitely changed a whole lot in recent years. Does that mean you're a surfer as well?"

"Oh. Absolutely."

"Sounds like we each have our side gigs."

"What's life without a little bit of this and a little bit of that?"

"Indeed." That came from Summer who walked up with several plates she placed between them. "I threw in our popular 3B for you to try for your first visit. Hopefully, we get to see you both in here from now on." She smiled at them and wandered off.

"Wow. It's not just the names." Shira studied each item before them.

"Do those latkes actually have a corset lacing design?" Aaron's voice was filled with awe.

"I think so. And wow, the bread really is tied up with that banana."

"And damn, *sufganiyot* holes to dip in six different toppings. Genius."

That was when they both looked at the gingerbread man, looked at each other, and began to laugh all over again, because really, it was all too much fun. Shira had experienced more pure enjoyment on this date in the first fifteen minutes than she had in the whole of some of her relationships. And wasn't that a sad state of affairs?

They spent the next thirty minutes indulging in the decadent, delicious, and downright divine drink, food and conversation. It was Aaron who finally said, "I need to get back to work, but I want to see you again if you're interested."

Shira had to bite her lip to keep from shouting "Yes!" She took a breath and then with a more even voice replied, "I'd like that too." Now she had to wonder, since she knew how these things often went, what route he would take. Exchange numbers and then keep her waiting for a few days before he reached out? Ask her for a date someday in the obscure future? Finish with, "I'll be in touch?" She'd heard it all before. And maybe that made her just a bit too jaded, because that wasn't what he said at all.

"How about tonight? What are you doing later?"

It took her a beat to recover from her shock to answer, "I don't have any plans. I'd love to get together tonight."

The warmest smile spread across his handsome face. She'd gotten caught on just staring at that face during their brief time together. Chiseled chin covered with a seemingly permanent five o-clock shadow… His dark brown hair trimmed short in a classic style… And his eyes a stunning hazel… Now those eyes were shining with such warmth, along with his smile, and she sent a prayer up to whoever would listen that this was for real. He seemed like an answer to an unacknowledged wish from deep inside her fantasies.

She opened her phone and saw the app staring back at her. So she made a mental note to thank Keren's company with a review for coming up with Immedia-Date and her friend for asking her to test it. She clicked away from the app and into her contacts. Then she handed her phone to Aaron.

"Go ahead and put your information in here and I'll call you so you have mine."

She continued to let her eyes and soul feast as he did just that. After he called himself, he handed her the phone, and entered her information into his contacts. Then he fiddled some more with it, and her phone vibrated.

She looked at the screen and she'd received a text from him. She smiled goofily and opened the message. It read:

How does dinner sound? I can be ready at six. How about you? And where should I pick you up? Or would you be happier meeting at the restaurant?

She thought about answering him directly, but it was too enticingly fun to play along. So she wrote back:

It's not a good sign if we are already both on our phones when we're together. Jumped straight from first date to married couple of thirty years. Sad. Sad. Sad. Wink emoji. I would prefer to meet at the restaurant for now. Just text me where and when, and I'll be there.

Their eyes caught and held after he read and replied to the message. Before she could see what he'd texted, he got up, leaned down, and pressed his rough, stubbled cheek to hers, causing all sorts of lusty sensations to course through her system as he whispered, "It's a date."

She was still sitting there, her body tingling, as Summer and a man she hadn't seen before sat down across from her. Where had the extra chair come from? She looked up at the other woman and expelled the breath she hadn't realized she was holding.

Summer leaned in and spoke in a loud whisper. "Well, that was something. Was it as good as it looked from over there?"

"Oh, yeah. I'd have to go with, better." She tentatively smiled at them both.

The new guy was a gorgeous dark-brown-skinned man with laughing eyes who was busy fanning himself. He said, "If it was any better, we would need to spray you down with ice water. In fact, I may need to be sprayed down with ice water just watching you two. I'm Kevin, by the way. Co-owner and baker extraordinaire."

"Nice to meet you. And how does one go about eating what you make and looking like you do?"

He winked at her and answered, even as Summer snorted. "Trade secret, honey."

Summer snorted again and said, "You're so full of shit. Simple answer. Be too busy to actually indulge in eating much of what you make. Plus enjoy being a gym rat." She nudged him and he winked back at her. Then Summer turned to Shira, "Looked like you scheduled a second date?"

"Yep. Tonight."

"Awesome! You'll have to come back and tell us how it went. I think you're our first First Date. I feel really invested now. Like our very own live and in-person Blind Dates show."

"You do realize I'm not actually a reality TV show? Right? Buuut, if you want to know more about my dating life, follow my blog." Shira pulled out one of her cards and handed it to Summer, who read it out loud to Kevin.

"Rae Ramson. Bold Bitch Guide for Dating and Defense. Rae Ramson?" Summer looked up and tilted her head enquiringly.

"Altered version of my name. Pseudonym. I like having some anonymity."

"Of course. Consider me your newest follower."

"You know this bold bitch will be reading," Kevin confirmed, and then he grimaced. "Assuming I have any time, that is. I may have to get the CliffsNotes from this one." He indicated Summer. "Planning, perfecting, and implementing all of our baked con-perfect-ions does not allow for much downtime."

A few minutes later and with a bagged well-hung gingerbread man in hand—to remember Aaron by, as if she could forget—Shira left her two new friends. She pulled out her phone as she approached her car to text Keren and was reminded that she still hadn't read the last thing Aaron had texted her before he left.

Maybe we'll get to see about that thirty year couple situation one day. It's been a true pleasure meeting you and I can't wait to see you tonight.

Warmth saturated every cell in her body, and she stood rooted as she reread the message four more times. Okay. Five. She finally entered her car and proceeded to text Keren.

Your app rocks! I met the greatest guy. I'll talk to you later, after he and I have our second date tonight. Wink emoji.

Nice! So happy it went well. Can't wait to hear more. Entering my meeting now. Give me the goods later.

Shira couldn't help but hope that there would be a lot of goods to share.

~

Aaron waited anxiously for Shira to arrive. He'd chosen a delicious, casual Thai place he liked to frequent, not too far from The Frisky Bean. Since he had no idea where Shira lived, he figured he'd take a chance she wouldn't have to travel too far if he stayed in the same basic area. Her last text said she was on her way. Since he'd left first that morning, he had no idea what kind of car he should watch for.

He couldn't remember ever feeling as nervous about a date as he was for this one. Something about Shira told him that this was going to be life-altering. He would have said it was ridiculous to feel like that after knowing someone for only an hour. Yet, he was sure deep down that his life was about to head in a new direction.

He saw lights pulling into the parking lot, then shut down as a car parked. Was it her? His hands got a little clammy and he was forced to roll his eyes at himself. *You're a fucking CEO, dammit. Clammy hands? Really?* He quickly dried them on his pants as a vision walked toward him.

Shira had changed from earlier in the day and was now wearing a pair of skinny jeans that had to have been painted on her and heeled, calf-climbing boots. He couldn't tell what she sported on top because she wore a black, form-fitting jacket. Her hair was still down, though, and her curls bounced with every step. The lights along the parking lot illuminated her face and even from a bit of a distance, he could see she wore red lipstick. He was screwed.

He calmed his racing heart and covertly adjusted his pants. He was ready when she opened the glass door and came in with her sexy red smile. "Hi. I hope this place is to your liking. You look beautiful." The last he said as he leaned down and allowed himself a press of their cheeks and air kisses in welcome. She probably didn't realize just how much he loved the smell of her. In fact, he couldn't get her sweet scent out of his mind the whole time he'd been in his meeting, earlier. And now he used their welcoming moments to inhale her once again.

"Hi. I love this place, actually. I don't live too far from here."

"Wow. Me either. Wouldn't it be funny if we were neighbors?"

"Funny or creepy? I guess depending on how tonight goes, we shall see which it is." She winked.

When the host indicated, he ushered her into a booth and they both placed their orders. When green tea arrived, he lifted his glass. "I have a good feeling about tonight. So perhaps we can toast to new possibilities?"

She raised her glass as well and said, "To new possibilities, surprising compatibilities, and hopeful opportunities."

"Well said. *L'chaim*." He reached out his cup and she clinked hers to his.

"*L'chaim*."

Had they just sealed some sort of deal? Some sort of fate? It felt like they had, and he was—surprisingly—totally okay with that. His only unease was knowing he hadn't been completely forthcoming about what he did. There would be time for that, though. Right?

No matter how sure he felt, he needed to see that he wasn't just infatuated. That there was substance to his sudden feelings. Maybe on their next date, if there was one, would be the right time to share that information. Not tonight. Tonight was for getting to know each other.

CHAPTER 4

Shira: *How is it possible that the best date I've ever been on ends with just a kiss. I mean. It was a helluva kiss, but still. Have I lost my touch that much? <sigh> I did have the best night ever. Conversation along with flirtation flowed so easily with him. We decided to focus on who we are instead of work, which was great for me, since I still haven't told him what I blog about, maybe next time, and he was just as amazing as at the coffee shop. There is too much more to share in text. But why just a kiss?!?! Cry emoji.*

Keren: *Sounds both fantastic and frustrating. You poor, poor thing. A guy who shows you an amazing time and respects you. My heart bleeds.*

Shira: *Your sarcasm is unwelcome and noted, young lady. I may just not tell you at all. You'll have to just read about my dating life on my blog like everyone else.*

Two weeks later:

Keren: *You're really going to make me keep reading about your new guy on your blog? Seven dates in two weeks?!? This sounds like it's really getting serious. I can't talk until this weekend, but you better be on my phone this Saturday. You hear me?*

Shira: *I hear you. Honestly, I would have called, but between your schedule, my schedule, and the dates, I haven't had time for a call. Seven dates. Seven dates and no sex. The best dates ever and no sex. I'll need to have that conversation on Saturday if for no other reason than for you to confirm that I'm not imagining the attraction between him and me because I am so ready and he keeps giving me devastating kisses that lead absolutely nowhere. Can't he respect me in the morning instead?*

Friday Night:

Shira was losing her ever-loving mind. Okay. Most people might hold off on sex for longer than two weeks, but those people hadn't had seven of the most wonderful, romantic, funny, and sexy dates that had ever been dated. Not to mention, there was nothing wrong with getting intimate quick if both parties were onboard. It just gave that much more data to decide if they were compatible, really. And so far, she and Aaron were about as compatible as two people could be, so why? Why wouldn't he sleep with her?

They'd even already made plans to celebrate Hanukkah with each of their families in three weeks. In fact, they'd already placed an order for sexy, fun food from The Frisky Bean to bring along to both parties. With everything being so good, why weren't they sleeping together? Or even getting to second base? Was she that unattractive to him? Maybe he liked everything else about her but didn't like her like that? A convenient Jewish girlfriend for the holidays? It didn't feel that way.

Then why?

Well, tonight, she was going to make a bold move and see where that got her. Forget waiting around for him to do it or getting shut down when she tried to gently press. She would make her play, and if he still wasn't interested, then they would need to have a little talk.

Everything else was going so well. She hadn't felt this connected to another person before. Well, except for the fact that she still hadn't gotten around to telling him about the specifics of her blog…

But they always found so many more interesting things to talk about. And maybe she was being a bit of a chicken shit. Probably, but she would tell him soon.

She was more concerned at the moment with whether he was attracted to her. The press of his hard cock through his pants always said yes, but his brushing her off after melting her panties with kisses at the end of each date said maybe not.

She was so confused but things would change tonight. She checked her purse and yes, the condoms she'd bought for their second date were still there. She looked around her place and yep, everything was relatively tidy, and her bed was ready for mayhem of the best kind. Tonight, she was going to be the bold bitch she billed herself as being. Sex or a deep conversation about it. One way or another she would understand what was holding them back. The eighth date would be the charm.

～

Aaron couldn't believe how great things were going with Shira. His balls couldn't believe what an idiot he was.

How hadn't they slept together yet? He knew why, though, even if his balls weren't too keen on the events, or lack thereof. He had never liked another woman more, and yet he hadn't come clean about owning the company that made Immedia-Date. At first he didn't tell her because he thought it might be weird for him to be using his own app. But after how great things were going, it felt creepy he hadn't told her to begin with. The longer he went without saying something, of course, the weirder and creepier it got. Why hadn't he just told her when they met?

He knew, though. It wasn't just that he was using his own app. Women always treated him differently once they found out he was the CEO of a successful startup. Especially one that made dating apps. Immedia-Date was just the latest in a string of apps he had developed to help people get together in the modern age. He didn't want Shira to like him for being a CEO or dislike him for his dating apps. Sometimes, people who had a bad date that originated on one of his apps blamed the app. Matching algorithms could only do so much, and there were no miracles.

Well, at least, that was true most of the time. But Aaron had begun to believe he had exactly that kind of miracle. Shira was everything he had ever looked for in a potential partner. He assumed from their kisses that she might also be everything he was looking for in a lover. Of course, since he was uncomfortable sleeping with her without telling her the truth, and he kept avoiding the truth because of how wonderful a time they were having…

Well, shit. He was being ridiculous. Time to get off this rollercoaster and just confess. Tonight. He'd see just how far she wanted to go, if at all, once he told her the truth.

It was almost time to pick up Shira. By date two, she had given him her address, which—as she'd said—wasn't far from where they originally met. It wasn't far from where he lived, either, though thinking about that made him cringe. He'd been hedging about his home because if she saw his place, it would be clear he wasn't completely forthcoming about his position in the company. If she came in, she'd see things with his company logo.

He'd been brought up better than this. Shame flushed through him.

Tonight he would clear everything up and hope he didn't lose her in the process.

CHAPTER 5

Shira's heart thudded loudly in her ears when the knock sounded at her door. Why was she so fucking nervous? *Pull yourself together. You don't even plan on jumping him until later. For now, this is just like any other date.* Her pep talk did nothing for her. Her fingertips were all tingles as she opened the door. He was so beautiful. She wanted to pull him by the neck of his shirt into her house right now and play naked tackle football. Clearly her libido was out of control.

She tried for nonchalant humor when she spoke, but failed miserably. Her voice came out much deeper and huskier than intended. Her "Hi stranger," took on a very seductive, role-play-like nature, instead of the joke she'd intended. His intense perusal of her body as he didn't answer made it clear he had heard it as well.

Don't panic!

His gaze felt like a caress running from her strappy sandals, up her mid-thigh-length form-fitting dress, all the way to her heaving (*Was she heaving? Oh God! She was heaving.*) breasts. She was going to hyperventilate if something didn't happen, and soon. Well, fuck this.

She reached out, grabbed his shirt collar and did what she'd wanted when she first saw him. He was inside, door closed, and playing tongue tango with her in an instant. And he was definitely participating. *Yes!*

Maybe they weren't going out tonight after all. Now was as good a time as any. Carpe diem and all that jazz. Their kisses during their past dates had been hot. But not just hot. More like H-A-W-T *hawt.* This kiss? This kiss put all those kisses in the kiddie pool. This kiss was scorched earth. He absolutely devasted her when he began to devour her lips with his.

He was firm and demanding and she yielded everything to him. At least at first. But she was not just a giver, she was also a taker and so when her senses came back online a few minutes later, she began to press her own kisses back at him, nipping and sucking on his bottom lip like she wanted to do to other parts of his anatomy. He groaned as she did, with clear invitation for more.

At that point, Shira was ready for anything. Wall? Couch? Bed? Clothes on? Clothes off? She really didn't care. She just wanted to feel every inch of the hard length poking her through their clothes pumping hard inside of her. She would beg if he needed her to. Did he enjoy begging? She could do some damn fine sexual begging. Of course, she could also make him beg, but that might have to wait for another time. She was too far gone in lust to play at that game tonight. She was ready dammit. Anything!

Except him backing away.

She practically fell to the floor, because her knees went weak. She braced herself with a hand against the wall and thought maybe he'd backed up to position them somewhere else, or to look for a condom, or something else along those lines. One look at his face, and it was clear that wasn't it at all.

What had she done wrong? Had she moved too fast? Well fuck him, if that was it. She was a modern woman. If she wanted sex, she wasn't going to be shamed by anyone for being clear about what she wanted.

She didn't see condemnation in his eyes, though. Before she spoke and made things worse by jumping to conclusions, she observed him and waited for him to say something, because what she did see there was trepidation. Was he breaking up with her? That couldn't be it after that kiss, could it?

She needed to take control of her damn imagination. She decided to help him spit it out with a question, instead of any accusations or suspicions. "What's wrong?"

He finally looked up, met her eyes, and said, "I have something I need us to talk about before we take this—" he waved between them, clearly indicating their bodies "—further."

"Sounds rather ominous. Should I sit down or are you planning on leaving soon?"

"I'm sorry. I don't mean to make it sound bad. I hope you don't think it is, and I don't plan on leaving. Unless I'm asked to."

"Okay. Then let's sit down."

She turned from the door and within a few steps, she was sitting on her couch. He followed and sat next to her, turned toward her, and grabbed her hands in his. Sheesh. Didn't he know this position never meant anything good was coming? All the movies and TV shows taught you that. Nervousness permeated her being and infiltrated the air around her. The room felt even smaller than usual, and it was hard to breathe.

"Just tell me, because it can't be worse than the anticipation you're creating."

"I know you're right. I just feel kind of stupid about it all. Okay. Here's the deal. I haven't been completely up front with you about what I do. And I didn't want to sleep with you until there was nothing but honesty between us."

Well, shit. Apparently, he was a more upstanding guy than she was a girl because she hadn't been upfront about what she did either, and she had no qualms about wanting to sleep with him. She flushed with embarrassment and that seemed to confuse him so she rushed to admit her own shame. "Um, funny you should mention that. I haven't been totally upfront with you either."

∽

Aaron wasn't sure what reaction he had expected. After that

entryway mauling from them both, he'd known it was now or never, and he really didn't want to ruin everything by going in with a lie. What he definitely had not been expecting was that she had a confession to make as well. The absurdity of it all hit him and there was no preventing the laughter that broke out.

Of course, expressing amusement in the face of someone's confession was usually not the right thing to do, but this was why he felt—even after such a short time—that they were meant for each other. Across from him, Shira was loudly entertained. Lovely. All the horrible tension that had built up around them in the wake of their make-out session diffused almost completely.

In the aftermath, Shira wiped away tears from laughing so hard, and he was relaxed and ready to talk. "What a pair we make."

"Yes. Apparently. Who goes first?"

"I will. Since I started it." He snorted. "Quite literally. You see, I own the company that created Immedia-Date."

Her eyes got big and her hands tensed in his. "You what? Could you repeat that?"

He thought he'd been done being nervous until she reacted with total shock at his pronouncement. *Fuck.* "I'm the CEO of the company that made the dating app we used to meet each other."

"Huh. That's what I thought you said."

She looked pensive and didn't speak for a while, and his anxiety started to rise with each passing heartbeat. He really had fucked this up. He was about to say, "I can explain," which, of course, he couldn't, not really, but it was the kind of thing you always said when trying to salvage a relationship. Before he could stick his foot in his mouth, though, she began to talk.

"Do you know Keren Sabinski?"

"Um. Yes. Why?" Not what he expected.

"She's the reason we're here today. She's one of my best friends and she asked me to test her company's, well, *your* company's latest app for her when she had to bail on a get-together." She paused, staring off into the distance. Then…she giggled.

He hoped that her amusement was a good sign, but he wasn't ready to drop his wariness just yet. It would be best to get some direction from her about the turn in their conversation. He asked, "And that's funny?"

"It is when you realize that the only reason you and I met was because some birds shit-bombed Keren."

He had to laugh too. He remembered walking into the meeting that first day he'd met Shira and seeing a disorganized Keren with wet hair, which wasn't what he was used to from her. "I wondered about that, at the meeting that day. Her wet hair and all."

"Yes. I'm sure, knowing her, she washed her hair at least ten times."

His heart stopped racing and his fingers, which he hadn't realized had started gripping her hands too tight, relaxed. One of the reasons he'd fallen so hard for this woman was because she had a quick mind and a relaxed nature. Whenever they stumbled onto topics they couldn't agree on, it was very easy to debate with each other but ultimately, to walk away comfortable with not agreeing. Of course, they agreed on the important things, but knowing how to argue with someone—he'd learned from his parents—was one of the tricks that led to a long, happy relationship. If this was any indication, they argued well. Still, he hedged. "We okay?"

Her eyes startled to his, and her brows were drawn. "Of course. Why would I care if you're the CEO of that company or any other? I assume you didn't tell me because it would have been awkward, which is a great segue into my confession."

"Oh? Are you the CEO of a company too?" When she smiled, he took it as a reward for trying to lighten the mood. That smile was what he wanted to see each morning and night and many times in-between. He knew things were moving fast, but he was pretty sure he was in love with her. Saying that would *definitely* be moving too fast, so he kept it to himself.

"I *am* a blogger. I write about dating and self-defense. Most guys freak out when they hear that I share information about my dating life, so I tend to keep that to myself."

He had hoped to take her news as easily as she had his, but he had to admit that he was taken aback. "Have you written about us?" Clearly his anger showed on his face, or in his tone, or both because she looked hurt and yanked her hands from his as she stood up and faced him. She was closing down. All her innate openness and humor from a moment before? Gone. He hated it, but he also hated thinking about his life being used as fodder for gossip. "Without asking me first?"

"And this is why I don't tell anyone. Yes, I have. If you understood me at all, you wouldn't be so upset. You would trust me not to do something to hurt you. But, maybe you don't. So... If you need to leave, then go."

CHAPTER 6

SHIRA BEGAN TO PACE. SHE COULDN'T BELIEVE IT WAS HAPPENING again, with Aaron. She had been so sure of him, of them, just a short while ago. Hell, she hadn't even cared and even *understood* why he hadn't told her about his true occupation. But now he couldn't do the same for her? He was going to react like every other guy?

They never bothered to check what she wrote, they just got upset that she wrote about them at all. The least someone could afford her was the courtesy of getting mad about something she actually did. Not some imagined offense. Fuck it. If he wanted to leave, fine.

She crossed her arms over her chest and faced him. She knew it was a defensive pose, but she was feeling damn defensive. He wasn't looking at her, though. He was looking down at his hands, which were still in the position she had left them when she pulled away. It made it look like he'd been holding something precious that had slipped through his fingers.

She was right here. He didn't have to let her go.

He finally looked up and spoke, his expression closed off. "I don't want to leave. Will you tell me your blog name so I can read it for myself?"

Holy shit. He actually *did* want to do his research. She fought to keep her hope tempered, because there was every likelihood that this still ended badly for her. "Yes. It's called Bold Bitch Guide for Dating and Defense."

He quirked an eyebrow at the name and smirked even as he entered it on his phone. "I thought it was a bad thing to call a woman a bitch."

"Guys should never use it, but women have reclaimed the word and affectionately use it with each other."

"Noted."

As she watched him search for her site, she began pacing again. What else was she going to do? Oh wait. That's right. Wine. She was going to do wine.

She went into the kitchen and grabbed a couple of glasses. She poured a helping of her latest Wine-of-the-Month bottle of pinot noir into each, and came back, putting one on the coffee table near Aaron and nursing her own as she continued pacing. How long could it take to read about seven dates? Well, eight, if you counted The Frisky Bean. So perhaps this was their ninth date?

For some reason an image of a fully lit hanukkiah flashed through her mind. It was warm and full of light. An indication of miracles. She wasn't sure why that popped into her head, but she did know she was hoping for a miracle. She didn't want things to end for them. She also loved what she did and would not apologize for it.

She paused to take a sip of wine and stared out one of her windows into the night. He must have moved quite silently, because even as she realized she was staring at his reflection behind hers, she felt his arms close around her, his chin resting gently over her shoulder, bringing him cheek to cheek with her. She held her breath, air a commodity she wasn't trading in at the moment.

"You are an amazing writer. I admit, I had a lot of concerns when I began to read, but, I have to say, I fell for you, for us, all over again reading your words." She felt more than saw his smirk, with the bunching of his cheek next to hers. "And you gave our app quite the review. We wondered why there was an uptick in sales at the end of last week. Thank you."

She relaxed into his body, and the cold that only the wine had kept at bay was banished in the heat radiating off of him, body and spirit. "You're welcome. Are...Are we good?"

"Honey, we are more than good. We are great."

She closed her eyes with relief and took a deep breath, taking in the scent of him all around her. She reached her hand out, placing her glass on the nearby bookshelf before spinning in his arms to face him. She fought the tears that threatened to overflow. So much emotion and tension and anxiety and relief left her feeling a bit unbalanced. She'd started the night wanting to have sex with her hot boyfriend. Casual fun.

Now, after all they revealed and accepted about each other and the emotional connection they formed, she wanted to create an intimate physical bond. All her defenses were down and her soul called out to his.

His responded.

She felt the link in her very bones.

Their mouths met in the middle of the sweetest kiss they had ever shared. Unlike the blazes and bonfires of before, this was a slow burn, like a match prepared to set a candle ablaze. The kiss deepened and morphed by slow, deliberate degrees. Shira was a total goner. She knew it. And while she wasn't ready to say it, she was oh so ready to show it.

To feel it.

To feel him.

To feel them.

Aaron swooped her up into his arms and started toward the back of her place, where he must have assumed her bedroom was. He was right, of course, because there really was nowhere else to go, but she said, "Wait!"

Concern flashed through his eyes, "If you aren't ready for this—"

"No! I am!" She may have said that a little too enthusiastically, but whatever. She was. "I just need to grab the condoms from my purse."

A sexy grin came over his face, and he said, "Why don't we start with the two I stuffed into my wallet since that's already on me?"

She couldn't help but smile back. "Two sounds like a good beginning."

"How many times do you plan to take advantage of me exactly?"

She cupped his cheek with one hand and wrapped the other around the back of his neck, leaning up to whisper in his ear, "As many as I can."

He gave a mock-suffering sigh, but she felt a shiver as it ran down his spine, as he crossed the threshold into her bedroom.

"Be gentle with me," he joked.

"We'll see."

"Evil vixen. I bet you even ate poor, well-hung Aaron's pecker off. Didn't you?"

She gasped and then laughed even as he dumped her—not placed, but *dumped* her—on her bed. "Of course I did!"

Aaron ran a hand down the length of her leg, from the hem of her dress to her foot, causing every nerve to come to attention. He lifted her foot to his lips and placed a soft kiss on the inside of her ankle. Then, he slowly removed that strappy sandal and dropped it to the floor. He continued nuzzling the inside of that leg a little while longer, but eventually lifted the other leg to do the same.

She was left to watch him and feel him and moan. Every scrape of his chin against the sensitive skin of her inner calf made her breath hitch. She was so focused on the sensations he was evoking, she hadn't even realized she'd left her first foot on top of his shoulder. She wasn't aware until he had both of her legs propped up and began to lean forward, pushing her knees up toward her chest. What was he doing? He wasn't going to... oh...he was.

Aaron skimmed his face along the inside of her knees, against her thighs, inching her knees ever closer to her chest. He opened her in such a way that the hem of her skirt posed no protection from his eyes on her black, lace-clad pussy. Wet lace-clad pussy. And getting wetter by the eyeful.

As his face got within an inch of said soaked lace, he inhaled. "I can tell how turned on you are by this musk alone. So fucking hot." He pushed his face into the lace, kissing her through it.

"Aaron." His name came out a plea because she needed him to touch her. She reached her hand down and ran her fingers into his hair, delighting in the silky softness of it. "Please lick me. I want your mouth on me."

"Your wish is…something I'll be doing soon."

"What happened to 'my command?'" She gasped as he rubbed his nose along her clit, through the lace, which gave the caress a slight rough, scraping sensation.

"Right now, I command."

Fuck yeah. Her heart rate sped up even more.

She moaned at the cold rush of air as he finally moved her underwear to the side and blew. She barely had time to register her sudden transition from warm to cold before she moved on to hot because his lips and tongue began caressing and sucking her pussy lips and clit. She arched up on a moan of pure pleasure as he settled in and began to feast.

This was not going to take long. She wasn't usually this quick to orgasm, but with how hot he had made her every night they'd gone out, she'd been edging for two weeks, refusing to take care of it by herself.

She usually did. That's why Magic Wands were invented after all. But something had made her want to wait. Something instinctual told her that since he generated the lust, he should be the one to address it. On top of that, she knew it would be that much better if she waited. And damn, it was.

Before long, her insides coiling tighter and tighter, she was prepared to explode in spasms. When she got oh-so-close, he placed two fingers inside her opening with a gentle but firm thrust. Then he curled them, hitting her G-spot even as he sucked her clitoris. The pleasure arched her straight off the bed, gasping, "Aaron!" as she shook and came.

⁓

Aaron loved her responsiveness and her taste. Shira was simply exquisite. He gave her a moment to relax as he leaned back and began to yank his clothes off. He was ready for some skin-to-skin contact. He made sure to place the condoms on the nightstand before throwing his pants into the pile of clothes he'd made.

He felt—before he saw—her eyes on him. It felt like an actual caress running down his abdomen and straight to his engorged and bouncing cock. His cock that was so ready... Even now the tip was wet with precum. He was about to sit Shira up so he could pull her dress from her, when she flipped to her stomach, facing him, and took hold of his penis at the root. All he could do was helplessly groan as he watched her tongue dart to lick that precum from him. He was about to tell her to save the oral for another time, but he was too late.

Her mouth engulfed the head of his cock in warm heat, and it was all he could do not to thrust farther in. The pleasure her mouth gave him was intense, especially with her taste still tripping along his tongue.

But he was not going to come in her mouth. Not now. He had other plans, and they involved him, a condom, and lots and lots of thrusting. Toward that goal, he threaded his fingers into her hair and held her immobile, pulling his dick away. She looked about to protest, but he didn't give her the chance. Instead, he pulled her to her knees, stripped her down, and finally stared at the gorgeous body he'd been dreaming about for two weeks.

"If you plan to just watch, I'll go ahead and get started." She lay back, wrapping her hands around her full breasts. She squeezed and rubbed and pinched and he was torn, because the view really was that good, but that would have to wait for another day as well. He wanted her too badly to wait.

Aaron stretched out beside her. Accepting her breasts in sacrifice, he leaned down and sucked one nipple into his mouth, grasping the other with her hand trapped between his fingers. He sucked and he squeezed and he gently scraped teeth and nails over her pert nipples. He came up for air and then kissed her mouth so hard and thoroughly that she practically purred when he pulled away.

"Where do you think you're going?" she asked huskily.

He reached for the nightstand, for the condom, and came back triumphantly brandishing it. He waggled his eyebrows.

"You goofball!" she joked.

"I don't know about a goofball, but I definitely want to get my balls involved."

She grabbed the condom from him. "Turn over."

He laid back as Shira opened and positioned the condom, pinching the tip while rolling the rest onto his very hard shaft.

Once the condom was on, he couldn't remain passive. He pushed her to her back once again and kissed her, invading her mouth even as his dick slowly glided into her opening. She raised her legs against his hips and her wetness drove him smoothly into her snug warmth. She moaned directly into his mouth, and he swallowed it up like a prize.

This was the connection he'd known they both needed, so he stayed still, fully seated inside her, allowing them both to experience it. To enjoy his fullness engulfed by her softness. "You feel incredible."

"So do you."

Being inside Shira was like coming home. It was where he wanted to return anytime. Every time. But his cock had been patient enough the last couple of weeks. He needed to move. He looked Shira directly in her eyes as his hips shifted and began a slow, easy rhythm.

They were both so, so ready. His thrusts grew faster and deeper until he drove her to the edge again. He leaned back and drew one of her hands to his mouth sucking her fingers. Getting them nice and wet. "Show me how you like it."

It was obvious she understood him, because without hesitation, she reached between them and began to rub her clit, swiping back and forth. He watched for a minute, noting she preferred a side-to-side motion instead of a more circular one, and then resumed his thrusts harder and deeper still. Her face was completely flushed, her body damp from sweat, and she had never looked more beautiful. He felt her spasms around his cock as she arched and called out his name and his control abandoned ship. Aaron lost himself in sensation, finding his own climax soon after. As he was coming down, he held her close. They were both breathing heavily, and he closed his eyes in gratitude that neither of their confessions had ruined what they'd found.

~

Saturday

Shira: *I'm banging your boss, bitch. Epic-ly so. Think you have time for a phone call now?*

Shira's phone rang.

CHAPTER 7

SHIRA THOUGHT THAT HANUKKAH WITH HER FAMILY WAS A BLAST, but they had nothing on the Sanders. Aaron's family decorated the whole house as if for Christmas, but with dreidel lights, blue and white lights, and a giant inflatable hanukkiah in the front yard. Who knew they had those?

She actually wasn't the only one from her family taking in all of the chaos as his nieces and nephews ran around. When his mom had heard that they planned to go celebrate with her family before coming over, they'd welcomed her small clan. Neither Shira nor Aaron were sure it was a great idea, but the parents had somehow gotten on the phone with each other, made all the arrangements, and conned, err…convinced them into it.

They were probably thoroughly screwed. Shira looked into the dining room and saw her mom in deep conversation with Aaron's mom. Now she had to assume they were, so she asked, "How screwed are we?"

Aaron, who was sitting next to her, whispered back, "I can't decide if it would have worried me more if they hadn't gotten along or that they're getting along so well."

"I'm leaning towards the latter myself. Think we can make a run for it?"

"No way. They'll just call and let us know they gave birth to us and we better get our butts back here."

Clearly their moms were cut from a similar cloth. She'd definitely heard lines like that before. She looked into the kitchen where both dads were putting the final touches on their dishes. She teased, "Will you be cooking for me, too?"

"Of course. My dad always taught me that a woman would do anything for a man who could cook. I took that to heart. I've even gone to some formal classes to up my game." He winked at her, and her heart wanted to skip right out of her chest and land in his hand.

Everyone started shuffling into the living room to open presents before they sat down to eat, which was apparently the Sanders' tradition. She and Aaron stood and helped in distributing gifts all around.

She was enjoying herself quite a lot. It was actually rather fun to have so much family around. She only had one brother, and he was currently studying abroad in Israel. She missed him, terribly. Maybe it wasn't a bad thing that their parents got along well? Only time would tell.

Aaron's sister, Rebecca, had already asked to join her at the gym where she taught self-defense. His divorced brother, Elijah, was hitting her up for dating advice in the modern age. And his last brother, Zach, along with his wife, Sarah, were asking Aaron and her to babysit. How had her life become so full, so fast? She wasn't totally sure.

At least she wasn't until she turned around to see if anyone else was missing a present. She found Aaron in front of her on one knee, holding a small box and looking at her with utter devotion. Yeah. That's how it happened.

She tried not to freak out too much, but she couldn't control the tears that spilled down her cheeks. She thought over the last five weeks and they were the best, most life-altering weeks of her life. The last two, in fact, they'd basically been living together minus an official move in. If someone had told her she'd be okay with what was happening, before she met Aaron, she would have laughed. Now… elation like she'd never known was the only thing she was feeling.

Her adored was saying something really profound and it had to do with how she was his Hanukkah miracle or something like that. Something about how he knew it was fast but something, something and he'd never been surer of anything.

"Yes!" was running over and over through her mind along with, "Stop talking and ask me already!" until the end of his speech, when he said, "I love you."

She was so transfixed by that last part, she forgot about her first two thoughts. She also forgot to answer. It wasn't until he raised his brows at her in expectation that she realized it was her turn to talk. She got down on her knees so they could be eye-level when she said what she had to say. She looked directly into his beloved eyes and somehow croaked out, "I love you, too. And it's a definite yes."

She barely registered the cheers and well wishes all around them, because her whole world had narrowed down to one moment, one person, and one feeling. Their time, him, and the love flowing between them was all she knew. He grabbed her hand and slipped a ring onto her finger but she still couldn't look away. He put down the box and framed her face in both of his hands and kissed her. A gentle, sweet, barely-a-press-of-their-lips kiss, and it carried the message they both felt completely.

It was perfection. Until one of Aaron's nephews loudly exclaimed, "Eeeewwwww!" Everyone laughed. The spell she'd fallen under was broken even as her connection to Aaron had never been stronger.

She wasn't a fool. They might be moving too fast, but they could always have a long engagement. Alternately, her parents had only known each other for a month before they were engaged. And despite that, they'd been together for thirty-four years and were still a very happy, affectionate couple. Sometimes, you really do know when it's right.

This was right. This was where she belonged. This was love.

And wasn't everyone a little bit foolish for love? Was there any other way to do it? She didn't think so.

Aaron leaned in and whispered in her ear, "What are you thinking about, my love? You have an interesting look on your face."

She whispered back, "I think we're very lucky to have all this love around us. I'm also lamenting having so many around us because I'm a little frisky. You think you'll have a live version well-hung gingerbread man for me later? I think I fell in love with you for that trick."

His eyes grew heated as she spoke, and he leaned in like he liked to do, brushing his cheek along hers whispering, "It's a date."

~

Later that night, Aaron looked down at his fiancé and couldn't control his stupid grin of delight. She'd wanted to eat her gingerbread man up, and she had. She had taken him in her mouth within minutes of entering his—soon to be their—home and refused to let go until he'd come, hard, down her greedy throat. She looked back at him, now, like the cat that had eaten the cream, and he knew he was one very lucky man.

"Happy now?" he asked.

"Oh yeah."

"Me too, love, but I'm far from satisfied. Come here."

She stood up, with his hand for assistance, and wrapped her arms around his neck. He kissed her deeply, enjoying the taste of himself in her mouth. When he broke away, he had to ask, just to be sure. "You positive that you like the ring? We could always exchange it."

"Would you stop? I love the ring." She held it up, as if to show it off. "I honestly hadn't expected you to remember how I felt about diamonds versus other stones, considering how many topics we covered over the course of our dates. But you did. And it's absolutely perfect."

His find sat on her ring finger. It was a delicate but decorative band with small inlaid stones of tiger's eye, onyx, and lapis lazuli—

eight bits in total that formed a colorful mosaic of a figure eight, an infinity symbol. He could have afforded something big and flashy, but he'd known instantly when he'd laid his eyes on that ring, it was the right one.

Pleased at the pleasure he heard in her voice, he was ready to get back to *their* satisfaction. "I'm still hungry myself, love. It's time for you to give me my dessert." He could actually see the shivers of anticipation that coursed through her.

"That sounds divine."

"Come. I need you to ride my face and then, I plan to give you a massage. I can't slack off just because you've said yes."

"Definitely not."

A few hot, sweaty, and intensely connected hours later, Aaron could finally claim satisfaction for them both. They lay in bed, he on his back, one arm around her, with her head pillowed on his shoulder and her arm thrown across his abdomen.

Every night. He wanted this to last every night.

EPILOGUE

Hey readers. For those of you who celebrate, Happy Hanukkah!

If you have been following along on this blog, you know that I recently used a dating app to find my Mr. Right. If you've been keeping up on our shenanigans, a.k.a., dates, you'll have watched our descent into madness, I mean love. Wink emoticon.

I have some Bold Bitch news for you all…

We got engaged last night. I hope you enjoy the picture of the ring. I forgot to look at it for thirty minutes after he slipped it on my finger. What can I say? I was distracted by my sexy fiancé. That word sounds so crazy, but it's true.

Some of you may be wondering what will happen with this blog. I know I would. Well, actually I did. Then I realized three things.

1) I have only ever scratched the surface on all my wacky dating stories. I have reserves for years, and I'll be sharing them all with you. More importantly, though…

2) People in committed relationships need to remember to keep dating each other, to allow the initial flame that brought them

206 | MICHELLE MARS

together to continue to burn throughout their lives. I plan to share tips and tricks on how to keep dating your significant other. And…

3) Self-defense and kicking ass will never go out of style, bitches.

In honor of foolish, fast, but undeniable love, my advice today is to keep your heart open and seize opportunities to try, because you never know what path brings you together with the person you could love and be loved by. And when you do find that person, hang on and enjoy the ride.

My Hanukkah miracle was finding and falling in love with my man in eight dates (not to mention getting engaged a few weeks later). But miracles can't happen if you don't put in the effort to try.

Stay Bold.

Rae

LOVE AND LATKES

JT SILVER

AUTHOR'S NOTE

Hanukkah. Time for hope. Rebecca Greenberg grieves for her mother and the promising life she left behind when her mother got sick. Now it's time to begin piecing her life back together. When she has a chance meeting with an old crush, she'll have to decide if she can be open to the light of the season or let pain and bitterness close her off forever.

Mimmo Mercurio loves the holidays. When Rebecca Greenberg walks into his store, it doesn't take him long to realize she's fighting an emotional battle this season. He'll show her that happiness can be found even in the darkest time of the year. And that even a zany family of a different faith can clear a path to happiness.

Special thanks to AJ Goodman and Michele McCoy.

For Josh. And for Edith, whose apple pancakes still inspire me. And may Mom rest in peace.

CHAPTER 1: A CHANCE ENCOUNTER

Becca

I STOPPED FOR A MINUTE OUTSIDE THE PHARMACY THAT WAS PART OF my routine. It wasn't as if I needed anything. I hadn't *needed* anything from that pharmacy in the three months since sitting *shiva* for my mother. And yet, every day I stopped in the same place and looked around, lost. The pharmacy. The bank. A Jamba Juice where I'd added a shot of protein to a smoothie that Mom wouldn't drink anyway. From ten to eleven every morning, I used those three points in time and space the way a rock climber tethers himself to a mountain: they kept me centered. Safe. Those familiar stops kept me from falling into some gray abyss where I had no purpose and where failure had become reality.

Eighteen months of routine will keep anyone grounded. In some ways, it kept her with me, like my own personal way of saying Kaddish. I knew I'd have to give up the routine soon. If anything, the winter weather in Connecticut would get in the way of my daily pilgrimage. Maybe that's why I was holding on so tightly in the too-bright days and ever-lengthening nights.

Shoppers bustled by with lists and brightly wrapped packages while I inhaled the crisp air of December and held it in my lungs. Slowly, I exhaled. Again. I did this five more times—a perfect seven —until I could open my eyes and face the sun.

I looked up to find one of my mother's best friends rapidly approaching. It wasn't as if she could walk all that quickly. But to me, it was as if she wore roller-skates and I was her destination. Immediately, my breath came faster. My palms began to sweat. I couldn't face another round of "How are you, dear?" followed by some heartrending story meant to show me what an amazing person my mother was. I got it. Really. I didn't need any reminders of what I had lost, even if my recent memories of her proved her less of a paragon and more of a pain in the butt.

So I did what any desperate person would do in my place—I bolted into a nearby storefront and flattened myself against the wall. My hand covered my pounding heart as I ran through the prime numbers from one to one hundred for the solid minute it took Mrs. Klein to meander past, completely oblivious to my distress. I took calming breaths in through my nose and out through my mouth. Slowly, I registered the crisp green smell of fresh produce, coupled with the warm aromas of baking bread and clam chowder. Someone at the deli counter complained about the price of prosciutto.

I pushed away from the wall just as the hottest hottie to ever wear a grocery apron approached.

Oh no. Not him. Not *now*.

Mimmo

"Becca? Becca Greenberg, is that you?" I squinted a bit at the woman leaning against the wall like she had just run a marathon. Despite ten years, a huge puffy coat, and an oversize scarf that hid half of her face, I could tell it was her. Her wavy hair fell over her shoulders just like in high school. Sure, it was shorter than she used to wear it. But the cold wind from the open door proved she still smelled like green apple and vanilla, exactly the same as she had in high school study hall when I sat behind her. I'd had a lot of teenage-boy thoughts associated with that smell.

Now she looked shocked, green eyes wide. I was a GLF (that's good lookin' fella), sure. But I doubted that was what had her pale and blinking like she was going to cry any second.

Crying. That wasn't good.

I shoved my hands in my pockets to stop from touching her. "Are you okay?" She pulled herself together. I could actually see her gather her wits about her and blink her tears away.

"Mimmo. Hi. I didn't expect to see you here." She sounded less than enthused. Which, of course, hurt.

So, I did what I always did in those situations and mouthed off just a little bit. "My last name *is* on the sign outside."

"Good point," she mumbled, then hid behind her curtain of hair.

I knew that look. Hell, I had seen it enough in high school when she walked down the hall. I wanted to kick myself: it had been ten years since I'd had the chance to impress her, and it had taken me ten seconds to blow it. Clearly the lady already felt lousy and being an ass to her was not going to help. So, I squared my shoulders and put on my proverbial big-boy pants. "What brings you to Mercurio's? Maybe you need something for the first night of Hanukkah?"

She jolted like I had smacked her. "Oh no, nothing like that. My brother and his family won't be here until the end of the week." She shook her head and said a little louder, "No. Nothing for Hanukkah. I would love a bran muffin, though."

"A bran muffin?" Well, that was unexpected. She smiled wistfully, a great look for her, especially given my near-sighted soft focus. A small dimple I had never noticed before materialized, and I found myself smiling back.

"Yes, a bran muffin—they're my absolute favorite. I used to come to here with my dad every weekend when I was a kid. He'd tell my mom we were running errands, then he'd get a pumpernickel bagel with cream cheese and I'd get a bran muffin. I used to pick out the raisins."

I held up a hand to stop her. "I'm sorry. I have to ask...what's wrong with raisins?"

"They *plump*. And they can explode when you bite into them directly." Her nose wrinkled. "Who wants that?"

"I don't know. Maybe someone who likes raisins?" I crossed my arms in mock outrage and raisin solidarity.

She fake-shuddered. "Psh. I'm telling you; no self-respecting person likes that texture." When I didn't respond, she continued, "I lived for those bran muffins. I used to tell myself they were healthy, but I bet they have four hundred calories each. My mother would have had a conniption fit if she knew I was off my diet."

I dropped my arms to my side. Who could be outraged on behalf of raisins when some woman had her little kid on a diet? "You were just a kid! And, if you're counting, they run about four hundred and fifty with the raisins left in. As for healthy...of course they're healthy: they have bran *in the name*."

She considered me for a moment, wearing the same soft smile. "Have you always been this funny? I don't remember you this funny."

I winked. "But you do remember me. Right? Good looks, great personality—"

"—Big ego." She rolled her eyes.

Even I knew rolled eyes weren't a good sign when you were trying to impress a lady, so I backpedaled. "I got you smiling, didn't I? Now, let's get you your bran muffin. Maybe I'll even get you to try the carrot cake ones. They're raisin-free and you still get to say they're healthy because they have a vegetable in the name." I gestured to the bakery display in the middle of the store.

As Becca walked to the display and bagged one of each kind of muffin, I summoned the courage I'd lacked as a pimply-faced teen. "Hey, you want to grab a coffee sometime?"

She looked shocked. "Coffee?"

I shrugged because I'm not as attached to coffee as the rest of America. "...Or tea. Or soda. Really, it's any beverage of your choice."

I waited for her to shoot me down, based on her completely

stunned look. A tense moment passed, then another. And then…she seemed to relax. She tucked a strand of hair behind her ear, smiled softly and said, "Yes."

I asked her for her phone number before she could back out, because the minute she said yes, something that looked remarkably like terror crossed her face.

Becca

I must have fluctuated between terror and awe at least five times on the way home. Neither prime numbers nor non-Euclidian Geometry had helped calm my excitement. And it hadn't even dawned on me that my normal trip was cut short: I was a hot mess. What had I done? Emilio—Mimmo—Mercurio had been untouchable in high school. Football player, Prom King, all-around nice guy. The kind of guy that every girl sighed over. He knew everyone by name. Even now, he had a wry charm that had made me smile when I felt like that was barely possible. Of course, I had said yes. Every woman on Long Island Sound would have said yes.

By the time I was back at my mother's house, the anxious anticipation had dwindled a bit. What if he didn't text? What if he was just taking pity on me? Did he know about my mother?

My black yoga pants and Ugg boots weren't the most flattering of fashions, especially with the pear shape I was sporting after all those leftover Jambas I wouldn't let go to waste. We may not have kept kosher in my parents' house, but we certainly knew the value of food and wouldn't let it go to waste.

I walked around in a haze as I put away dishes and started my laundry. For once it wasn't just me in a too-empty house with only marathons of *Law and Order* to keep my company. I had my abject terror and anticipation to overshadow it all. When the last bit of work was done and it was just me and the ticking clock, I carefully retrieved my mother's menorah from the china cabinet. Modeled to look like a natural tree branch, it was pretty more than it was functional my Dad had complained, and he wasn't wrong. Thinking of him brought back memories of Hanukkahs from before his death and I had to pause for a second to rub at the pain in my chest.

My phone dinged with an incoming text not too long before sunset. Expecting it to be my brother's travel details, I froze when I saw who had sent it.

MIMMO M: Looking forward to coffee.

ME: Me too.

MIMMO M: Don't get cold feet, okay? I'd like to see you.

I considered the screen for a minute. How did he know I was thinking of bolting?

ME: I won't bail if you won't.

MIMMO M: Deal. Happy Hanukkah.

I stared at my phone for a long time before getting a match and lighting the first night's candle.

CHAPTER 2: COFFEE

Becca

"THANKS FOR COMING." MIMMO STOOD AND PULLED OUT A CHAIR for me at the bakery that supplied Mercurio's. He looked even better than he had a couple of days ago, his dark shirt just the right fit for his shoulders, his dark eyes twinkling.

"I didn't order you anything to drink." He rubbed the back of his neck. Was he as nervous as I was? I reversed direction before my butt hit the seat cushion, intent on getting an enormous vat of the darkest roast coffee they carried, but his hand on my arm stopped me. "I'll get it. Just tell me what you'd like."

I couldn't stop staring at where his fingers rested on my sweater. Had he played piano when we were kids? Tingles I had thought long-dead radiated from the warmth of his palm. Finally, I mumbled, "A large coffee. Black."

I had time to look around while Mimmo waited in line at the counter. The place sported an industrial vibe in stainless steel and black and white, relieved by rattan baskets that held breads of all sorts. The glass bakery display cases gleamed and were filled with all sorts of cookies and pastries. My stomach grumbled in appreciation of the tarts and Napoleons, cannoli and lemon bars. I even spied a case just for Jewish specialties like rugelach and hamentaschen, black and white cookies as large as my hand, and *sufganiyot*, strawberry-jelly-filled doughnuts. I practiced estimating the number of items in each tray to give myself something to do while I waited. And that was when I spotted Mimmo making his way back to me with a coffee, a pastry box, and a couple of plates and forks, wearing the most adorable sheepish look on his face.

"You get there are only two of us here, right?" I gestured to the large box as I relieved him of my coffee. It immediately warmed my hand and smelled like perfection.

"What's coffee without *uno spuntino*?" He placed the box in the center of our little marble table with a flourish. He must have noticed my raised brow because he translated as he placed a plate in front of me, "*Spuntino* is a snack. Like something to nosh. Would you like a hamentaschen, or maybe a lemon bar? I didn't get any brownies because I figured pastry with fruit in it is totally justifiable as a healthy breakfast."

"You mean like those carrot cake muffins are healthy?" I shook my head while eyeballing the selections.

He chuckled. "Exactly."

There was no way we were going to be able to polish off everything in that box. But I was hungry, and it was a shame to let it all go to waste. I carefully sliced an enormous lemon bar into quarters and plated one, then added a nut-and-cinnamon rugelach after careful consideration. They were Mom's favorite. It seemed the least I could do to remember her. I gently pushed the box away to let Mimmo know I was through with my selections, only to find him watching me.

"Are you a dunker?" He motioned to the rugelach with his fork before taking a bite of the scone. "That's the perfect dunking cookie. It has enough fat in it that it doesn't completely fall apart, unlike this scone, which just wouldn't hold it together. And who wants to ruin a perfectly good cup of tea with crumbs floating in it?"

I sipped my coffee. "Ah. I'm not generally into floating bits of food in my drinks, so no. My food stays safely on my plate. And, if I'm being honest, I wouldn't have expected you to be either a dunker or an imbiber of herbal tea, either." I motioned to his steaming cup.

He raised his mug and considered me over the rim for a moment while I tried not to stare at his hands. He asked, "What did you expect?"

I shrugged. It's not as if I knew him well back-in-the-day, so putting my impression into words was difficult. I grappled with what I wanted to say before I blurted out, "I expected you not to show up, honestly. This whole meet-up seems surreal. But if I had to pick what I thought you'd be doing, it's having a beer with your buddies later today, hanging out at The Grape." The Sea Grape was a small dive bar over by the beach.

He drank a bit, then broke apart a piece of scone. "That's fair, and accurate during the summer. What about you? What do you do for fun?" He popped the piece into his mouth and chewed.

I coughed, trying to clear the bite of rugelach lodged in my throat. Suddenly it tasted like ash. How was I supposed to tell him that there was no fun? That the last eighteen months had been filled with medical visits, errands, and care for a woman who needed me there much more than she wanted me there?

Mimmo

It was an innocent question. At least I thought so. I watched while she crumbled the poor cookie on her plate and kept my mouth shut. Maybe a full sixty seconds later she exhaled and said, "My mother passed away this October. She had cancer."

Ah. Damn. Now I just felt like a heel for bringing it up.

"—before that I was in grad school. I've been trying to keep up so I can defend my dissertation, but it's been slow going." She stopped pulverizing the crumbs for a moment and seemed to brighten. "I got a bunch of editing done yesterday, though. First time in a long time."

"That's great! What's your dissertation on?" Now that she was talking, I wanted to keep her on a roll. And I'm not gonna lie—the fact that she was super-smart was sexy as hell.

She looked up as if gauging my reaction. "The Role of Meromorphic Functions in Analyzing the Berry-Tabor Conjecture."

I vaguely recognized one or two of those words. While I puzzled out what all of them linked together might mean, I said the first thing that came to mind. "Your family must be proud." Perfect filler. I mean, who wouldn't be proud of something like that?

She snorted. "They would be, except I won't be the kind of doctor who helps people. My mother didn't see the point of me going for it because all I could do was be a professor." Her eyes lit with a passion that hadn't been there before. "There are other applications, though! I could work in Finance or Economics; I could do data analysis. Computer Science, Astronomy, Physics—they all have a need for complex calculations and algorithms."

I could tell she expected me to be intimidated. I was. But I wanted to know about this topic that made her so expressive more than I wanted to protect my precious manhood. "I think any kind of doctor is pretty impressive."

She cocked her head to the side, and I tried not to get distracted by that curtain of wavy hair. "Most guys freak out that I'm a math geek."

I shrugged and grinned. "What can I say? I'm not most guys. So…you'll be Doctor Greenberg someday?"

She smiled, I mean really smiled, for the first time since walking into the bakery. "Someday, yes. That's my plan."

I smiled back, so glad I had taken the chance to ask her out. "In the meantime, would you maybe want to hang out again? My family does a family dinner on Christmas Eve. It's mostly for the grandkids now, but there's a ton of food and desserts and coffee." I motioned to her plate. "Life is too short to waste it on bad pastry."

"I don't want to intrude—"

"You'll be helping me out, especially if you let my family grill you on your entire life history. They need new blood. And I'd really like to see you again."

She chewed her lip. "I'll need to say my Hanukkah prayers and light my menorah. Would it be okay to come later? And what about gifts?"

I smacked my forehead. "I'm an idiot. Of course! We eat pretty much from seven until someone passes out, so any time you want to come by would be great. And don't worry about gifts. My nieces and nephews get so much stuff from the family that they usually fall asleep before everything is even opened."

Her jaw tightened and I sensed an immediate fight: one I didn't want to have. "Alright. Look, Joey is five, Chiara is three and Junior is under a year. I don't think they'll care if you get them a gift. If you want to do something nice, bring a bottle of wine or something."

She shook her head and laughed. "You're no help, you know that?"

I threw up my hands in mock offense. "It's not like I invite people to these things all the time! And they are going to question you, probably mercilessly. The FBI could learn something from my mother and sisters. But they'll be polite about it, and I promise the food will be fantastic."

She made some sort of noise that sounded somewhere between a snort and a laugh.

I reached across the table to take her hand. The zing was still there but I ignored it because I had something important to say. I looked her square in the eye and said, "I'm sorry to hear about your mom." I squeezed her fingers to help convey my sincerity. "I'm glad you agreed to meet me for coffee. I'm even more glad you didn't stand me up and force me to eat all these baked goods by myself. So, I hope you'll take pity on me tomorrow night and rescue me from the clutches of my family."

"You've managed them for your whole life. Seems like you can handle them just fine."

I grinned, hoping I exuded the boyish charm that had worked for me on so many occasions. "True. But maybe I don't want to manage them on my own anymore. Think about it, okay?"

Becca

I thought about it all through Wednesday afternoon as I edited my dissertation and emailed my advisor to let him know I would be ready to defend in the Spring. I thought about it some more as I tidied the rooms my brother's family would use when they arrived for Shabbat on Friday. Should I go? Every time I asked myself the question, I pictured Mimmo's smile. He had seemed so sincere, like he genuinely wanted me to go. It hadn't felt like a pity ask, either, probably because he had no idea that my main companionship for longer than I cared to remember was *The View* or *The People's Court*.

Mimmo Mercurio had given me a way to break out of my grief for a little while. And as I lit the candles and said my prayers as my mother would have before the menorah that night, I was thankful for his smile and laughter. I decided I would take the night out as a gift before my own family descended on me with their expectations.

CHAPTER 3: DECK THE HALLS

Becca

THE MINUTE I WALKED THROUGH THE DOOR OF HIS FAMILY HOME, I knew I had made a mistake. Not only was it about a million degrees inside, there were people everywhere. The living room sported a Christmas tree that was at least ten feet tall and had so many lights it could likely be seen from space. Tony Bennett crooned over the general din. "I thought you said this was just family?" I whisper-yelled as Mimmo took my coat. Not only was it warm, but it was also *loud*.

"This *is* just family. Some cousins came by at the last minute." He threw my coat—literally threw it—into a dark room off the front foyer, then led me by the hand down a hallway.

The voices were quieter here, and I tried to use the time to find my center. "Wait." I tugged his hand, letting him know I wanted to stop. "I need a second."

Mimmo turned toward me. He placed the poinsettia I had been holding on the floor between us and took my hands in his. His face was as somber as I'd ever seen it. "Thank you for coming."

"What?" I asked, confused.

"I know this is a madhouse, and I'd say I'm sorry for it. But I'm glad you came. You look great, by the way." He gestured to my black tights and red and black sweater dress, then ran a hand through his hair. "God, I'm nervous," he added. It seemed like he wanting to say something more.

I had to laugh at the fact that we were both as nervous as teenagers. So, I flirted a bit to break the tension. "Maybe a kiss for luck?"

His eyes lit and he leaned in for a quick peck. If I thought there were tingles when we touched, they were nothing compared to the jolt of electricity when his soft lips touched mine.

I froze for a moment, then, before he could pull away, stepped into the kiss—into him. His arms circled me at the same time as I finally got to run my fingers through his hair. I had imagined it would be soft, but hair gel made it wiry. He smelled like garlic and oregano, and he tasted like cinnamon. I couldn't get enough. It was like I was suddenly awake; all the good nerve endings were firing at once, demanding more.

"Ma, Mimmo's kissing someone in the back hall!" A strident voice called out.

I pulled away from him as if I'd been doused in cold water. My face burned with embarrassment as I smoothed my dress, but my body screamed because it wanted more. Mimmo didn't look much better as he attempted to rearrange his hair into a style that didn't look like he'd just been mauled.

In a back hallway.

By me. I wanted to pump my fist in the air and scream. Perhaps dance a jig.

Instead, I closed my eyes and recited the first fifteen digits of pi. Feeling more grounded, I opened them again, just in time to spy an older woman turning the corner with a determined stride. Hands on hips. Dark hair teased and sprayed. Christmas apron. Dark eyes flashed anger, or maybe just reflected the light-up Christmas earrings she wore.

I swallowed hard and reached for the poinsettia at my feet. "Hello, Mrs. Mercurio. Merry Christmas."

She took the plant and I tensed in the quiet pause until she beamed. To the younger woman next to her she said, "This is lovely. See, Mary? Rebecca brought me a lovely poinsettia."

The younger woman, presumably Mary, rolled her eyes. "Ma, I told you, I forgot. And what about Mimmo? He didn't buy you any either!"

"*Zitto*! Your brother paid for tomorrow's *antipasto*. You want him to pay for meat and flowers? Then what do we need you for?" With another smile in my direction, she turned back to the kitchen. Mary, the younger woman, followed, saying something I couldn't quite catch.

I waited until I could no longer see the light of her earrings. "Well, that was a close call. How many sisters do you have?" I asked Mimmo, who had taken to leaning against the wall of the hallway with his arms crossed while his sister ratted him out.

"Three." He stretched to his full height. "Even as we speak, Mary, the youngest, is telling the entire dining room that she caught us back here. But my mother seemed to really like you."

"Well, that's good. Do you have, like, a thing for dimly lit hallways or something?" I smiled even though I was nervous about meeting the rest of his family.

"Nah. I think Mary met us back here because she was excited to meet you. I've, uh, never brought someone home for a holiday." He rubbed the back of his neck.

I blinked as his mumbled words sank in. My smile widened. "Really?"

He nodded, smiling back. "Really."

When we made it to the kitchen, Mimmo's mother was waiting and gesturing to the dishes that covered every surface of her island countertop. "Emilio, did you explain to your friend that our Christmas Eve dinner is meatless? We do the Seven Fishes," she added. I wasn't sure what that meant, exactly.

Mary chimed in, "Ma kept the eel swimming in my bathtub for two weeks! I had to take a shower in her room when I got home from school. That means there won't be a problem if she's kosher, right?"

I certainly wasn't going to point out that she had just referred to me as blessed and processed like a kosher food, and I was already used to people talking about me like I wasn't in the room. Although, to be fair, it was usually my own family. But judging by the fact that Mimmo's hands had become fists, he didn't seem thrilled with it.

I decided to come to my own defense and help him avoid fratricide in the process. "My family doesn't actually keep kosher. Although, I'll admit I'm not a big fish eater."

Mimmo relaxed a bit and leaned toward me. "We have other stuff, don't worry. We do a nice *spaghetti aglio e olio* with broccoli rabe that's very tasty." He pointed to a bowl of pasta so large that it looked like a sitcom prop.

I couldn't help but ask, "Are these your leftovers?"

Mrs. Mercurio answered that question. "We were just getting ready to put out dessert. I'm happy to make you a plate!" To Mimmo, she said, "Make her a plate. She looks hungry."

"No! No need. I'm good. I don't mean to disrupt your dessert! Just...do whatever you were doing." I had to stop this before it got out of hand.

That earned me a long, disappointed look from Mrs. Mercurio. Then she clapped her hands, earrings swaying and ordered, "Emilio, Mary...carry out the cannoli cheesecake from the refrigerator and get the cookie tray from Luigi's off the sun porch. I'll bring the coffee in a minute. Oh, and tell Ricardo to leave off the grappa." Mimmo sent me a sheepish look that said he didn't like leaving me on my own but did as he was told.

I was alone with Mimmo's mother.

She waited until Mary had left the kitchen, then turned and faced me. "Hand me that ricotta container on the dish drainer, would you?"

I crossed to give her the requested item, then watched her scoop something that looked like a cross between salsa and coleslaw from a serving bowl into the container. She answered my unasked question while concentrating on the task at hand. "This is baccala salad. Salted cod. Very tasty and light, sort of like tuna salad without any mayonnaise." She finished, put a lid onto it, and then used masking tape to label what was inside before turning to me. "Do you like my son?"

"I'm sorry. What?" I hadn't expected such a direct approach.

"Do you like my son?" Mrs. Mercurio over-enunciated. Without waiting for an answer, she waved a hand in the air. "What am I asking? Of course, you do. No one lip-locks like that if they aren't interested." She waved me over to another container and took it when I offered it. This time, the dish she spooned into it had tentacles. "But you're conflicted, aren't you? And that means you'll hurt my Emilio. He has a big heart and I don't want to see him hurt. Do you know why I asked him to make you a plate?"

I shook my head, distracted by the idea of eating those glistening tentacles sliding from plate to spoon to container. "How could you know…No. I have no idea why you asked him that."

She banged the spoon against the side of the bowl, the loud sound startling me into meeting her eyes. "To the Mercurios, food is life. We express how we feel through food. It defines our relationships, helps celebrate our milestones. You aren't vulnerable enough to let him make you something to eat, and that means you aren't open to the idea of him caring for you. And caring for you is the same as caring about you. *Capisci?* Do you understand?"

"I don't think you can read all of that into a simple 'no,'" I argued, face hot. Just because I liked her direct approach didn't mean I knew how to handle it. We did not generally confront each other head-on in my family.

The woman crossed to me and took my hand between her own. "You could have said yes and then taken just a few bites to be polite. You could have taken the plate and eaten nothing at all. Food is about creation and the essence of life. You reject the meal; you reject the person. Emilio said you recently lost your mother. A girl's relationship with her *madre* is important. Maybe that's what is making you so closed off." She rubbed my hands as if to comfort.

I was having trouble following her logic, but it wasn't polite to continue arguing. Plus, my stomach took that moment to growl.

She smiled and dropped my hands. "See? You're hungry. Time for dessert!"

Mimmo

"What did she do to you?" I used the cover of the family pouring their coffees to talk to Becca after she and my mother joined us in the dining room. She looked a little overwhelmed, like she wasn't used to families that offered an entire pie to each guest during the holidays. What I really wanted to ask her was if she looked that way because of our kiss.

And what a kiss it had been: my lips still tingled in the best of ways. I was hoping she'd let me follow her home so we could park in her driveway and neck like a couple of teenagers. Or maybe we could head over to Lake Mohegan's parking lot and pretend we were in high school all over again.

She side-eyed me and whispered back, "I'll never tell. How do you stay so fit if you all eat like this?" She motioned to the table practically groaning with food.

I poured her a cup of black coffee. "I see you've heard the first rule of Italian kitchens is 'what happens in the kitchen stays in the kitchen?'" I grinned at the truth to that statement, then added, "We like our sweets, I guess. They make the workouts worth it. What can I get you?"

She paused for long enough that I wondered what she was thinking. Then I noticed that Ma was watching us. So were all three of my sisters. And the rest of the table. Every single person not under ten was simultaneously eating and watching the two of us.

Finally, she said, "How about a piece of blueberry pie and a sugar cookie?"

"I have to warn you that my nephew helped make those cookies. They might taste like sand." I made a shooing motion at my mother who seemed to get the hint and turned away before I plated a slice of blueberry pie and a sugar cookie. Just like the lady had requested. This seemed to appease the crowd as well, so they went back to discussing sports, politics, and the Pope. For myself, I chose a slice of cannoli cheesecake.

Becca smiled when I handed her plate to her. "And life is too short to eat bad pastry? You know, your family has a lot of sayings about food." She bit into the cookie.

She wasn't wrong so there was no use arguing. "We're in the food business, sweetheart. You don't know the half of it."

Becca

After dessert, we watched Mimmo's nephews and niece open a few gifts and devour the chocolate coins I had brought for them. Food coma had set in for the rest of us by that point, so we all lounged around the living room and sipped more coffee. I sincerely hoped it was decaf, or I would be up half the night. Insomnia was already a high probability anyway, since I wanted to relive every moment of that kiss in the hallway. It gave me shivers just thinking about it.

Mimmo Mercurio. Had. Kissed. Me.

I pondered it as gift wrap was ripped to shreds and children squealed. I thought about it as I helped clear the table and put plates and cups in the dishwasher. I considered it as I said my goodbyes. By the time Mimmo walked me out, I was a tongue-tied mess.

"Thank you for inviting me tonight. I had a great time." I fidgeted with my car keys.

He shoved his hands in his pockets. "Thanks for coming."

We stood staring at each other. Did he want to kiss me or not? Finally, I leaned in, placed a hand against his chest, and brushed my lips across his. I wanted more but I wasn't sure. And until I was certain…I wasn't going to push my luck.

As I pulled back, he placed his hand over mine. I could feel his heart pounding a staccato rhythm in time with mine through his dress shirt. I took that as a sign that he was okay with my intentions and leaned back in for another brush of lips. Mimmo snaked an arm around my waist and pulled me closer, angling his head for deeper contact.

Had I ever been kissed like this? I was pretty sure that the sparks flying between us could light up the front lawn's Christmas display. I wasn't sure how I had lived my entire life and never known kissing him. I wanted to crawl inside his coat and live there, my mouth against his.

Finally, we broke apart.

"Wow." Mimmo said as he brushed his hands through his hair for the second time that evening.

I straightened my jacket. "Wow is right."

There was silence for a moment as we each pulled ourselves together.

"I really like you, Becca, and I'd like to see you again." It was a statement, not a question. Obviously, he knew I wanted it, too.

The way he looked at me, though, gave me more than tingles. I felt warm from the inside out and was sure I would for days to come. "I like you, too. But I have my brother's family coming tomorrow and Shabbat. The next couple of days are pretty crazy."

He used his thumb to gesture back to his mother's house. "I know crazy. All I'm saying is see if you can fit me in."

I nodded. "I'll see what I can do." I sat in my car and started it, then waved before pulling out of his driveway. And, as the bright Christmas lights faded to a dull glimmer in my rear-view mirror, I wondered at the glow I still felt from Mimmo's kiss.

CHAPTER 4: LATKES

Becca

"BEC, THANKS FOR MAKING DINNER AGAIN TONIGHT," MY BROTHER, Josh, said.

"You're welcome." My first thought was that it wasn't like him to say thank you, but I suppressed it. I didn't want to start an argument after such a reasonably amicable weekend. Really, it had been surprising how much in sync we had been in terms of activities to remember my mother. It had helped that I had deferred to his wife, Sharon, on the things I had been unsure of when it came to planning Hanukkah and Shabbat for a family. My brother hadn't seemed to care much about the details as long as he had final approval.

"I still can't believe she's gone. The house looks the same as it did when I was a kid. I keep expecting her to walk in and make those apple pancakes." Josh looked around the kitchen. From where he leaned against the island, he could see the breakfast nook where my mother had her coffee every morning. What he either couldn't see or chose to ignore was the pile of dirty dishes I was rinsing and placing in the dishwasher.

I half-listened to him reminisce about breakfasts long ago in this room. Most of my head was filled with my plan to go see Mimmo later. I had even found out his new address from an old high school friend. It felt a little like high school when I had driven by it to make sure I knew how to get there.

I came back to the conversation when Josh asked, "How'd you learn to make them?"

"Apple pancakes? I finally got Mom to agree to show me near the end." She had guarded that recipe and only made them when Josh and his family came to visit. She had said they were too much work to make for just the two of us. And when I made them for her to try to get some calories in her those last few months, she had asked if Josh was coming. The memory stung, so my voice came out sharper than I intended. "She mostly used the living room and guest bath. It made it easier to keep the rest of the house clean."

"Well, that will make it easier to sell." Josh glanced again at the nook and into the adjoining family room. From his expression I wondered if he was calculating the house's appraised value.

I worked at staying calm and holding my judgement. Josh required a well-thought out plan for everything. Surely, he would need some time to weigh all of the options. "When do you think that will happen?"

He seemed taken aback. "I thought we would sell right away."

I placed the last mug in the top rack and shut the dishwasher with more force than I intended. "And I'm supposed to…what? Go back to Boston and find another apartment? Pick up my life like the last year never happened?"

He frowned. "I thought you'd be happy to get back. You seemed so unhappy being here and taking care of things."

I couldn't help my snort. "I'm pretty sure the ship has sailed on my life in Boston. I gave up a TA position when I moved back here. I'm pretty much out of the academic track at this point."

"You could have kept up with it. And I'm sure it won't be hard to get back into it, if that's what you want."

My eyebrows crept into my hairline. "Kept up with it? I put my dissertation on hold to ferry Mom to appointments and to nurse her.

That was a full-time job, Josh. And one you didn't help with at all, I might add. I was too busy here doing everything her way. And I mean *everything*. From laundry, to trying to get her bathed, to meal prep. And then she wouldn't even eat it! There was no time to write research papers or even head into the city to meet with my advisor."

"You could have asked for help."

"So you could make Sharon take a day off of work instead of taking care of it yourself? Maybe you should have been the one to go to her appointments and listen to her lie to her doctors. Maybe she wouldn't have lied, if you have been with her!" I flung the dishtowel down onto the countertop, then quieted my voice as I recalled that his wife was upstairs putting my niece and nephew to sleep. "I get it. I do. You both had other priorities. But I had a life, too. I gave it up to come help thinking that you would be more involved, that you would actually care about what was happening here."

"I paid her bills." Josh thumped a fist onto the nook table. It must have hurt because he immediately rubbed his hand.

I shook my head. "You did a great job with the finances. But I mean the day-to-day. I was drowning in a million details and you never once offered to take the pressure off." My voice dropped to become even quieter. "And it shouldn't surprise me. After all, you don't help with dishes, you don't offer to put your own kids to bed. The day-to-day is for us women, right, Josh?" Oddly, a picture of Mimmo scraping plates and washing dishes at his mother's flashed to mind.

"That's not fair." Was it possible for his face to get any redder?

I shrugged, tired of this conversation and ready to take on the next part of my evening. "Maybe I should have called and asked Sharon for help. She probably would have understood the exhaustion of endless chores. But I didn't and that's on me. This, though? This isn't something I'll keep quiet about. You'll wait on selling the house until I can defend my dissertation and get a job. I'll spend the meantime cleaning it out. Maybe you guys can come down a few times and help out, but I won't bank on that. You don't get to up-end my life—without me having a say—twice." I was exhausted. "Do we have a deal? You keep the house afloat and I'll do the manual labor. Just like before."

He was quiet for a minute. I used that time to calculate the accruing interest on my deferred student loans while I got my coat.

"Wait—where are you going?" He stammered. "There's more to this conversation."

I pulled on my jacket and crossed to pick up a Tupperware container. "Not really. Not for me. I'm seeing someone." I ignored his utterly shocked face and continued, "So I'm going to take these latkes that I've put aside and see him." I wasn't precisely sure if *seeing each* other was the label I should be putting on what Mimmo and I were doing. Nevertheless, it felt amazing to say those words out loud and watch Josh's face. He looked like a fish out of water. I took pity on him and dropped a kiss on his forehead. "I love you. We'll talk more later."

And then I walked out.

Mimmo

My doorbell didn't normally ring on Monday nights unless it was Uber Eats. And since Ma had already supplied me with enough leftovers to last until New Year's, UE was not on tonight's agenda. I paused my binging of *Modern Family* to see what was going on.

Becca stood on my doorstep, holding a plastic container, wearing a puffy coat and boots. Boots. Boots were totally my kryptonite. And boots that made Becca's legs look a mile long? I said a quick prayer of thanks to Ma's favorite saint, St. Anthony, then doubled it because I was still wearing pants. Then I remembered to triple it because surprise visits from my mother and sisters ensured I kept a pretty neat house.

"Hi." I motioned for her to come in. "Everything alright?"

"Yeah." She exhaled heavily. "I hope it's okay that I popped by…I wanted to drop these off. They're better same-day." She held out the container. Inside it, I could just make out palm-sized potato cakes.

"Are those latkes? Thanks so much!" Some people might be into flowers. Me? I like gifts that involve food or beverages. I smiled at the unexpected offering, took the container, and started for the kitchen. "I can't remember the last time I had these," I said to her over my shoulder.

"You don't have any Christmas decorations." She sounded perplexed as she looked around, hands clasped together tightly.

"I think my mother's house is done up enough for both of us."

She laughed as she walked into the kitchen. I mean really laughed. The smile changed her face into something beautiful. She was both vulnerable and strong in that moment. It was a look I wanted to see more of.

I puttered around, grabbing plates and forks, and a few of those squeeze applesauce pouches that my niece and nephew loved. To Becca, I pointed to my tiny dinette and said, "Have a seat."

Instead of sitting, she tugged at her dress. "Are you sure it's okay for me to stay? I know it's late."

I stopped short. Did she not know how happy I was to see her? I placed everything on the counter with a clatter and made my way to her. Her hands felt like ice when I took them in mine, so I rubbed my thumbs across her knuckles. "Late or not, I'm glad you're here. I'm being a terrible host. Let's start with me taking your coat." I move behind her.

Becca sent me a shy look over her shoulder, then slid her gray puffy coat down her arms. If boots were my kryptonite, I didn't know what to call the sight of Becca's hourglass figure in a clingy blue wrap-dress. I swallowed. "You are beautiful." She turned to face me, and that almost brought me to my knees. Small waist, flared hips, and the barest bit of black just peeking out at her cleavage. Somehow, I fumbled her coat out of the way before threading my fingers through her hair.

"I guess you like the dress?" she asked.

"It's not the dress I like."

Becca

I may have dressed up for Mimmo in an attempt to seduce him.

Or maybe I did it to say thank you for helping me feel things I hadn't in a long time. Maybe it was in appreciation for his being a guy who would serve me coffee and pie before he took his own piece. Or maybe I just wanted to feel pretty. I wasn't sure what had made me decide to pull a dress out of my closet, but the look on his face was everything I needed to make the five minutes sitting in my parked car and working up the courage to ring his doorbell worth it.

"Was it the latkes?" I joked.

He shook his head and pulled me closer slowly, but I wanted none of that. Slowly was for later and I knew it would be fantastic.

For now, I wanted to feel his mouth on mine, so I simply halved the distance and kissed him. It was neither the same as our surprise first kiss, nor the soft and passionate second. Our mouths met this time like they were meant to be together. Like they recognized their opposite and clung out of necessity. This kiss was as essential as the air I breathed, an incendiary blend of open mouths. I immediately wanted more.

I backed him up to his refrigerator while our mouths clung together, while I learned the contours of his lean torso with greedy hands. I nipped his earlobe while he found the sensitive hollow where my neck met my shoulder. I tugged his shirt over his head and discovered chest hair as an otter-shaped Norwalk Aquarium magnet fell to the floor and skidded somewhere out of sight.

"Leave it," he growled, while he unwrapped me from my dress.

"Couch," I whispered.

He walked me back into his living room, legs brushing and guiding mine with every step. I idly wondered if this was what it would be like to dance with him. If the answer was yes, we'd have to do that soon. I flopped onto his black leather couch and tugged him down on top of me by his waistband, relishing his weight.

"Pants," I ordered while his hands explored more of me, "Get them off. I want to feel all of you."

"Are you sure?" He punctuated each word with a little nip. Chin, shoulder, breast.

"Yes!" I used my elbows to lever myself up so I could watch as he divested himself of pants and socks. He was muscular from lifting at the store, but not overly so. I loved his long lines, all the places he was curved or hard. In return, he watched me. I suppose I should have been self-conscious, but I was not.

He raised an eyebrow. "Much as I love those boots, I'm taking them off you." He tugged one, then the other. When he was finished, he held up a finger and disappeared, only to return from what must have been his bedroom with a foil packet.

"Come here, you." I crooked a finger and he came to me with open arms, and an eager mouth.

It didn't take much to finish with our clothing and meet each other skin to skin. The relief was overwhelming in that simple touch, and a part of me, the part that had such rage and hurt, quieted. As Mimmo hovered over me and looked into my eyes, as I opened for him, I saw the joy awaiting us.

Much later, Mimmo shifted me to his side and slid a throw blanket over us both. "Are you comfortable?" he murmured.

I nodded and dropped a kiss to his chest. Comfortable was an understatement. I felt warm and loved and *seen* for the first time in over a year. Tears misted my eyes. "Thank you."

He moved so he could see my face. "Hey, for what?"

I sniffed. "For letting me in the door. For…" I gestured to both of us curled together.

"Oh, honey." He wrapped his arms around me and held on tight. He cleared his throat a minute later. "You don't need to thank me. I'd love to see more of you. Do you think you could find time for a small-town guy like me on a more permanent basis?"

I smile. "Absolutely."

He pulled back slightly so I could see his grin. "Then you'll stay? Even though I'm a goy?"

I kissed him, hard. "I'm willing to figure it out."

He kissed me back. "We'll figure it out, together."

EPILOGUE

Becca

"I'm going to be sick. I never should have eaten that bran muffin." I rubbed my stomach as I paced the length of the hallway outside the room that represented my impending doom.

"You'll be fine," Josh said, impatiently looking at his watch.

I snapped at him, "Do you have somewhere better to be?" As soon as the words were out of my mouth, I regretted them. Josh had been great after our fight during Hanukkah. It wasn't his fault the bran muffin sat in my stomach like a doorstop. "I'm sorry. I'm really nervous."

"I'm just wondering where Sharon is," Josh asked.

I nodded absently. "I'm sure she'll be here."

Mimmo strode down the hallway, smiling until he saw my face. "Bran muffin not sitting well? Take small sips of this San Pellegrino." He handed me a bottle and I took a tentative sip. When it didn't seem to make the condition any worse, I followed his instructions.

"Thanks." I found myself smiling back as he beamed at me.

I would never get over it, feeling like part of something larger than myself. Every time he looked at me, I felt that flash of recognition, the flare of hope that tomorrow would be better than today. Honestly, I was pretty sure most days would be better than today.

The Door of Doom opened, and my faculty advisor smiled at me. "Rebecca? We're ready for you now."

Josh gave me a quick hug. "Knock 'em dead."

I murmured my thanks. As I met Mimmo's eyes over Josh's head, he winked. "Remember, none of us will have any idea what you're talking about, so you've got this."

I laughed, somehow knowing everything would be okay.

Mimmo

I paced. I couldn't help it. I had figured on Becca being nervous. I had even thought I might have a few butterflies on her behalf. But, when they shooed us out of the room, even though Becca seemed fine with it, I thought for sure it was a bad sign. Hence, the pacing.

"I'm sure she's fine." Josh said. "I hear this is how dissertation defenses go."

I cocked my head to the side. "If this is how they go, how come you're not in the side room they gave us, helping set up for the reception?"

Josh smiled. It was probably the first time since we'd met that I'd seen the resemblance between him and Becca. "I guess I'm nervous for her." He paused, then added, "She's a smart woman, though."

I nodded at the truth of that statement. "Smartest one I know." I let the silence sink in for a while after that.

Josh checked his watch again. "I'm going to see how set-up is going. Sharon just got there and texted to say they're done."

I waved him off. It wasn't like Josh needed my permission to go put his rubber stamp on it. I thought back, again, to that first night when Becca had stayed over. She had described her brother as someone who watches while others do the work. I could see that.

Just as I was mulling over how different she and her brother were, the door opened. Becca stood there in her black dress, pearls, and black tights, looking every inch the academic. I didn't even have time to ask the question forming in my head when she suddenly grinned.

I couldn't resist—I grabbed her and kissed her right there in the hallway, so proud and relieved and positively giddy for her. I didn't want to let her go, but I had to. We had a reception to get to and family to see. So when I backed away and saw her tears of happiness, I pulled a hanky from my pocket and wiped them away. "Dr. Greenberg, I love you."

She shed a few more tears at that. But this time, the crying was good.

Becca

My hands shook as I finished wiping away tears. "I love you, too," I tried to keep my voice from breaking, but it didn't work.

He nodded. "I know."

"Oh? How do you know?" I asked.

"You brought me latkes and you let me serve you pie. And now you're gonna let me show you off to our families and pile high a plate for you that you can't possibly eat. That's how I know. You let me take care of you and you take care of me." Mimmo stopped talking to wipe his own eyes, then took my hand and guided me into the reception room where his mother and sisters were waiting, along with Sharon and Josh. My dissertation committee was there as well.

And the food? Every table was full. There were stuffed shells and vegetable lasagna, garlic bread and salad, and a huge antipasto tray. And the desserts? It went without saying that there were enough pies and cakes and cookies for every attendee.

I didn't think anything of it when Mimmo's sister Mary engulfed me in a huge hug. We had made a lot of strides since Christmas Eve.

"Dr. Greenberg now, right?" She asked.

I nodded, looking over her head for my brother. But her next words brought me up short.

"Ma says you're not the kind of doctor that helps people. I think that's pretty cool because it means you probably won't get sued." She shrugged as I tried not to laugh.

I worked my way through the room and finally made it to my brother. "Thanks for coming, and thanks for letting me stay in the house." I hugged him. "I'll work on the job thing next."

"I know you will." He replied. Then he got this misty-eyed look and said something I never expected, "She'd have been sorry to have missed this."

I nodded jerkily, tears falling. I wasn't sure that was entirely true, but it was kind of him to say. Most importantly, I wasn't hung up on her judgment either way. She was in my heart.

Mimmo showed up wielding a handkerchief. He waited until I had wiped my eyes—again. "Come, *bella*. Let's get you a plate. You must be starving."

I smiled at this man, who had only really known me a short time. I thought about the simple things he did for me: bran muffins in the morning, making dinner when I was preparing for my defense. Asking his mother to prepare this reception. Accepting my own gifts to him. Laundry sorting, or a plate left on his stove. Simple things, all of them. They showed how much he cared. How much *we* cared.

And then I thought about how strange it was to have met him at Hanukkah, during the darkest time of my life. How he hadn't just brought light back into it but had shown me my own. Maybe, I considered as Mimmo made me a plate, *that* was love.

HANUKKAH KISSES

ERIN EISENBERG

AUTHOR'S NOTE

To me, the Hanukkah season is a time of possibility. It celebrates a miracle. The dreidel represents the phrase, "A great miracle happened there." I think about that every year, as my husband and I celebrate Hanukkah with my family and Christmas with his. Our relationship is one of those miracles. As with so many other couples, we had so much standing in our way early on. Yet we persevered. Astrid and Jake couldn't wait to share their story with me, and I am thrilled to now share it with you.

CHAPTER 1

"Well, well, well. If it isn't Astrid Feinmen."

At the low voice, Astrid spun around, dropping the box of Cheerios in her hands. "Oh crap!" she muttered, bending to pick it up. From this vantage point, all she saw were a pair of running shoes and jeans.

Standing up, she took in the owner of said jeans. She relaxed her brow and smiled. "Jake Castillo."

"It's been a while," he said. He propped one foot up on the grocery cart in front of him, resting his wrists on the handle. "What brings you here?"

Astrid tucked a stray curl behind her ear. "To Kroger? Cereal." She held up the box.

"I'm meant, what brings you back to town?"

"I could ask the same of you. Didn't you move to Wyoming or Montana or some place like that?"

"Portland, actually," he clarified.

She placed the cereal in the basket she carried. "I knew it was somewhere out west. You're home for Christmas, then?"

Jake nodded. "Every December. You know how Mom is."

Lynn Castillo liked nothing better than a full house. Growing up, Astrid and her siblings practically grew up next door at the Castillo house. Lynn would put out a veritable feast every day after school. Nothing drew hungry, latch-key kids more than a neighbor offering snacks.

"Does she still put up the seven-foot tree?"

Jake laughed, and the twinkle in his eyes told Astrid they were remembering the same event. They must have been fourteen? Fifteen? And Samuel, Jake's dad, came home with a seven-foot live tree. They'd all been recruited to try to get the monstrosity into the house, spending about two hours just trying to get it through the door without breaking the branches.

"We talked them into a fake tree a few years back. Now Dad just pulls it up from the basement and sets it up after Thanksgiving. Much easier to deal with."

They began meandering down the grocery aisle, turning aimlessly as they caught up. Surprisingly, the store wasn't busy for the Monday before Hanukkah and Christmas. Normally, the place would be packed with everyone and their brother trying to stock up. "So seriously, what brings you back? It's not like you usually come home for Hanukkah, right?" he pointed out.

"Sage had her baby in October," Astrid said. "This is my first chance to get some time off to see them, so I jumped at the chance. Most of the company I work for shuts down the last two weeks in December, anyway. So, since Hanukkah is later this year, I figured I'd combine the trip. Beats flying out for a weekend and spending half of that time traveling."

"I bet your mom is thrilled."

Astrid barked a laugh. "You have no idea. I'm pretty sure she bought out the store last week."

He indicated her basket. "Yet you're back."

"What can I say, there are a few staples I'm used to having around. If I'm going to be home for two weeks, I might as well pick them up."

"Where are you living now?" he asked as they wondered down the dairy aisle.

Astrid picked up a package of shredded cheese, then replaced it. "I'm up in Seattle."

"It's like we're neighbors again," he said with a smile.

Jake's grin transformed his face from your average guy next door, to whoa. Astrid's stomach flipped, just as it had when she was a girl watching him from the corner window, before he'd turned into another teenage asshole. Shaking off the past, she said, "Yeah, just a three-hour drive away."

"Not the same as right next door?"

"Not quite."

Jake stopped to grab a few containers of yogurt. "We should catch up while you're here," he said as they made their way to the front of the store to check out.

She couldn't move right away. Given their past, the invite surprised her. He seemed genuinely interested in catching up. Perhaps she'd finally get a chance to understand why he'd done what he'd done.

"Sure. I'm just hanging out with family," she said. "Come on by whenever."

"Why don't you give me your number?" he suggested, unloading her basket on to the belt for her. "That way I won't disrupt anything."

"What in the world would you disrupt?"

"You are here to see your family," he reminded her.

Okay, he had a point. She pulled out her cell. "What's yours? I'll just call you and you'll have it."

He rattled off the number and she typed it into her phone's keypad. Strains of Linkin Park echoed from his back pocket. He reached back, cancelling the call. "Ah, the coveted Astrid Feinmen's phone number."

"Hardly," she replied. "And it's not like you ever needed it. You just came over."

"Point taken."

"Is this all?" the checker interrupted.

"What? Oh, yes. Thank you." Astrid stuck her credit card into the reader while the checker bagged her small number of groceries.

Behind her, Jake loaded his own on to the belt. She saw the ingredients for Lynn's famous stuffing, along with several boxes of cookies.

"I see you haven't given up on that sweet tooth of yours." Not that it was hurting him at all. She covertly studied him as he finished putting items down. He had a runner's build, long and lean. The jeans were just baggy enough to be casual. The green sweater he wore with them brought out the golden flecks in his hair and the blue of his eyes.

"Sweets were put on Earth to remind mankind that food is meant to be enjoyed."

"Says the overgrown boy who once ate an entire gallon of Rocky Road in one afternoon."

He clutched his stomach in memory. "Oof! I get another stomachache just remembering."

"I remember a lot of Pepto Bismol involved."

He grimaced. "It got ugly for a couple of days. The sugar detox alone…" He shuddered.

After tucking her wallet back into her purse, she hefted up her grocery bags. "Well, Jake Castillo. I'll see you around."

"Not if I see you first," he said.

∼

Jake shook his head as he watched Astrid walk away. "Not if I see you first?" Seriously?

"That'll be $45.67."

Clearly the checker didn't care that he'd just made a fool of himself in front of his high school crush. He pulled out his wallet and flipped around for his credit card. After paying, he tucked his wallet back into his pocket, grabbed his bags, and carried them out to his dad's Corolla.

Jake and Astrid had grown up next-door to one another, best friends all the way through elementary school. Astrid had practically lived at his house in the afternoons, waiting for her Mom to come home. His mom always said she preferred having Astrid and her sister over, rather than knowing they were all alone in the house next to her. She said it lent a "feminine air" to the house for a few hours a day. In middle school, Jake and Astrid drifted apart, as boys and girls often did. He'd hung out with his friends from the basketball team, while she dove into the theater club. In high school they'd been on friendly terms to start. Jake, always too shy to ask her out, snuck peaks during Geometry class, hoping alternately that she would and wouldn't notice him. Then he'd blown it all up with one stupid comment.

He'd gone to Michigan State for college; she'd attended the University of Michigan. They'd run into one another occasionally when home on breaks, but rarely shared more than a few words. After, they'd continued to follow their separate paths. His led to him teaching high-school English in Portland. Hers led to Seattle. Doing what? He'd have to ask his mom. Maybe she'd know.

A cold wind tugged at his hair as he loaded the groceries into the trunk of the car. It lacked the bitter damp of the Pacific Northwest, but smelled of the slightest hint of snow on the horizon. Maybe they'd have a white Christmas?

From what he remembered, Astrid's mother loved Hanukkah. She always threw giant parties, inviting half the neighborhood over for latkes, bagels, and smoked salmon. There'd be chocolate gelt sprinkled on all the tables and counters for kids to grab as they ran by. The foil wrappers from those chocolate coins would be strewn on the floor, scattered every which way. He remembered running around with Astrid, swooping in and out of the adults to grab more gelt, or standing behind her as she helped her mom light the candles on the menorah. One year, Astrid came running up to him in tears because his twin brother had stolen the dreidel and wouldn't give it back. Her younger sisters used to follow them around, trying to get Astrid to sneak them more gelt from the table they couldn't quite reach.

He briefly wondered if Ms. Feinmen would throw a party this year to show off her new grandson. It'd be a great way to catch up with Astrid, though her attention would likely be spread thin. Did she still think about what he'd done? Did it still bother her?

He drove back to his folks' house on autopilot. The straight roads of suburban Detroit made it easy to tune out the drive and think more about Astrid.

Astrid of the deep amber eyes and dark brown curls... She'd worn them piled up on her head today, a few stray strands escaping the elaborate knot she'd created. He'd seen hints of a long-cream sweater playing peek-a-boo with her coat. Would it feel soft to the touch?

His phone rang just as he parked the car in his parents' garage. He looked at the display, then accepted his brother's call. "I just pulled in," he said by way of greeting.

"Hello to you, too."

"What do you want, Jeremy?"

"This is why they call me the pleasant twin," he reminded Jake.

Jake hefted the bags out of the trunk and slammed it shut. "Did you call for a reason?"

"My plane is stuck in Minneapolis."

"How stuck?"

"As in they just herded all of us back off the plane. I'm hoping to get out on the next flight. But..." His words trailed off.

Jake groaned. He tucked his phone in between his ear and shoulder, using his free hand to twist the knob on the door into the house. "So, you're going to miss Mom's famous prime rib. You know she only makes it because you love it so much."

"Think of it this way. You'll have your pick of the ladies."

"Yeah, because that's why I'm in town."

"I *am* the handsome brother."

"If by handsome you mean the one with a fat head? Sure, we can go with that."

"Just let Mom know, okay?"

"She's not going to be happy."

"Complain to the Polar Vortex, or *El Niño*, or whatever it is that sent this storm."

After dropping the bags onto the kitchen counter, Jake put the phone to his other ear. "I'll tell her." He paused. Should he say anything? "Astrid's back in town."

"She is? Where's she living now?"

"Seattle."

"You going to finally ask her out?"

"To what end?"

"Seriously? You followed her around with your tongue hanging out for years. Man up and ask her out for a drink already."

"What's the point? We're both only here until New Year's." Plus, she had finally said more than one sentence to him. No way was he going to mess this up.

"So enjoy it for a few days. No one said you had to marry the girl. Get her out of your system already. You've held every other girl up to her incomparable fantasy. Maybe she'll yell at the waiter or get spinach in her teeth. Either way, you'll work her out of your system and finally move on."

"Jeremy, you have all the class of a peanut butter cookie."

"It's not my class that helps me get a different date every weekend. It's my charm. And by my charm I mean…"

"I know what you mean. Shit, Jeremy, are you sure we're related?"

"Mom seems pretty well convinced. You can ask her about the night we were born again. I'm sure she'd love to tell you the story for the 8000th time."

"Let me know when you get a flight out," Jake said, shifting gears.

"Will do. Ask her out already," Jeremy said before he hung up.

"Who was that?" his mom asked, coming into the kitchen to unpack the groceries.

"Jeremy," Jake said. He filled her in.

"Oh," she said. Her shoulders slumped and Jake hugged her close. "You've still got me. I'll eat extra prime rib. We'll make Jeremy eat the leftovers cold," he teased, trying to get her to smile again.

She gave him a half-hearted swat on the stomach. "Here, let's get these groceries put away. Then you can go next door and invite Astrid out for a little bit."

"How did you know she was home? I just ran into her at the grocery store."

"Sandra mentioned it at book club. The whole family was always close. I guess they had to be after everything they went through, with their dad passing so suddenly."

"If Astrid is here to see Sage and her new baby, then I doubt she wants to sit down and catch up with me."

"She's always made time for you before," his mom reminded him. "Remember when you had the chicken pox? She practically broke into your bedroom to check on you. She was so worried you'd disappear."

"She was five, Mom."

"She cared about her friend. I'm sure she'd love to catch up with you."

"Not tonight, Mom. I'll catch up with her later." He slung an arm over his mother's shoulder. "Tonight, I have plans with a different woman." Then he kissed the top of her head and squeezed her shoulder. "I'll see Astrid another time, I'm sure."

CHAPTER 2

ASTRID CALLED OUT TO HER MOM AS SHE ENTERED THE HOUSE. "I'M back!"

"We're in the living room."

We? thought Astrid. She took a few moments to put the groceries away, pour herself a glass of wine from the bottle of Sauvignon Blanc on the counter, and grab a few cookies from the plate sitting next to the bottle. She bit into one on her way to the living room. Mmmmm. Homemade.

Her mom sat on the couch, feet tucked up beneath her. Few people who met Sandra Feinmen realized she was a whole lot closer to sixty-five than she was to forty-five. Her carefully dyed hair, impeccable make-up, and still-trim figure hid her age well. In the years since Astrid graduated and moved west, Sandra had taken up regular yoga and Pilates practice, along with painting. She said it "centered" her.

This new, centered Mom didn't fit the memories Astrid had from growing up. As a local Realtor, Sandra was a single, working mom, frequently coming home just before dinner with take-out from one of the local restaurants. Astrid had spent more time at Jake's house, than at her own. At least, until high school. The memory of what he'd done snuck back, teasing at the corner of her mind. Her pleasure at running into him cooled.

Sandra had retired about ten years ago, shortly after Astrid's *Bubbe* passed away. She said it was to finally enjoy all her hard work. Astrid was pretty sure it was to ensure her mom didn't die all alone in the house like *Bubbe* had.

"Oh, hello," Astrid said, when she noticed the older gentleman sitting next to her mother on the couch. Astrid hadn't seen Eric in at least a year, not since her mother brought him with her when she visited Seattle last. He had one arm thrown across the back of the couch, stretched behind Sandra, his fingers just brushing the nape of her neck. He was dressed casually in khakis and an eggplant-colored sweater.

"Nice to see you again," Astrid said to Eric. Then she turned to her mother. "I was going to go over to Sage's to make her and David dinner. Do you want to come?"

"Oh, that's so sweet. I went by yesterday, and Eric and I have tickets to the ballet tonight. We've been looking forward to this for months! And I know Sage has been waiting to seeing you."

Astrid listened politely, but her attention was more on their body language. Sandra seemed to melt into Eric's touch. Astrid's heart thudded in her chest, an ache spreading outward. She tried rubbing it away, but it lingered. When was the last time someone had touched her like that? So casually, yet so intimately.

She tried to remember. Tried to place a face or a name. Nothing. No one. *Shit! When was my last date?*

The fact that she couldn't remember answered the question easily enough. "So, where are you two going to eat before the show?"

They exchanged a look, and for the first time, Astrid felt like she was intruding in her family home. It was like they held a silent conversation just with their eyes.

"There's a new little Italian place near the theater," Sandra said after a beat.

"Sounds wonderful," she said. *You're jealous. Stop acting like a baby.* Forcing enthusiasm into her words, she added. "Have a great time."

"We will," her mom said. "We've been waiting to try this restaurant out for months." Sandra's excitement brought out a smile on Astrid. "Eric, will you be at Mom's Hanukkah party this weekend?"

He stood, offering a hand to her mom to help her to her feet. "I wouldn't miss it. I can't wait for your mother's latkes."

Something about the way he said it made Astrid think he wasn't just talking about her potato pancakes. Ewww.

"There are always plenty. We'll chat more then." She hugged her mom. "I better get over to Sage's. If I'm late, she'll get wrapped up in their evening routine and fall asleep at the table."

"Go get those baby snuggles," her mom said. "We'll catch up tomorrow."

∼

"I can fix you up with someone," Astrid's co-worker Carrie offered, when she called later that evening. Astrid was home from Sage's house, filled to the brim with baby snuggles and spaghetti. She sat, tucked in bed, with a book in her lap but no desire to read. Instead, she'd FaceTimed Carrie to share her newly realized horror.

She hadn't been on a date in over a year.

"You're going to have to. I've been working so much, the only men I'm in contact with lately are the guys on my team. And you know that wouldn't be a good idea."

"What, you don't want to become their second mother?"

Astrid snorted. "Or their second wife. All the guys on my team are either married, or still living with mommy."

"What did you expect? The good ones are hard to find."

"But not impossible, right?" she asked her friend. An image of her cheating ex, Dan, flashed in her head. Since that ass screwed her over, all her dates seemed to fall into the one and done category. She hadn't met a single one worth date #2, but perhaps there was still? "You found one."

Carrie smiled, looking up off the screen briefly. Probably ogling her husband. "I did find one. And you will, too."

"I'm holding you to it," Astrid said. "My mom can't be getting more action than I am."

"Well…"

"You're supposed to be my friend!"

"I am your friend. And as your friend, I am honor-bound to point out that you haven't dated anyone seriously in a very long time. You haven't dated anyone not seriously. You live like a hermit, only coming out of your cave to go to work. And even that you only do a few times a week."

"It's easier to work at home when I have conference calls," Astrid pointed out.

"I'm sure it is. But you're not going to meet anyone sitting in your home office, wrapped in a blanket, hoping that the people on your Skype call think it's a new poncho."

"I'm not that bad."

Carrie raised one eyebrow.

"I'm not!" Astrid gulped. "Am I?"

"What did you wear to the grocery store this afternoon?"

"Clothes."

"Well, that's good to hear. I'm glad you didn't go in a bathrobe."

"What did it matter? I only ran into my old neighbor, and I don't even live around here."

"Old neighbor?" Of course, Carrie caught on to the one part of the sentence Astrid wished she'd toss out the window. "A cute old neighbor? Old as in ninety? Or old like you grew up together."

"Jake's my age. We went to school together."

"Oh, so the neighbor has a name."

"So, what are you doing the rest of your night?"

"You are so obvious."

"I have no desire to start up anything with a man who lives in another state." *Or one who already stomped on my heart once.*

"Where does he live?"

"Portland. He's a teacher there."

Carrie stared at her so long, Astrid put a hand up to her nose. "Is there something on my face?"

"He's ugly."

"You know him?"

"No, but the only reason I can come up with for why you aren't already asking this guy out for a drink is because he's ugly. Because why else wouldn't you get to know an eligible man who likes kids."

"Who said he likes kids?" Astrid argued, still trying to piece together Carrie's logic. No, Jake definitely wasn't ugly. Far from it.

"He's a teacher, you said. Teachers like kids."

"What does that have to do with anything? It's not like I have kids."

"But you want them."

"I'm not marrying the guy!" she shouted. "We haven't even been on a date." And based on what he had once said about her, there was no chance they were going to in the future. "I'm not his type."

"You're a woman, right? I don't know any guy who's going to turn down a date with a hot woman, when the alternative is staying at home with his parents. Even if it's not going to turn into anything, he'll say yes. So ask him out."

Astrid shook her head. Her friend was going to talk her in circles. "I'll think about it."

"What's the harm?"

"I can never come home again?"

"Hardly. Worst-case scenario, you won't be able to go to Portland again. But you never go there anyway."

"I like Cannon Beach," Astrid said. "I have to go through Portland to get there."

"You don't *have* to. There are other routes. And best-case scenario, we're planning a wedding this time next year."

"You're overly optimistic. You might want to get that checked out."

"Just a drink," Carrie said. "All you need to do is ask him to get one drink. It's not like you're going to sleep with the guy."

"One drink?"

"What can it hurt?"

Astrid tried to come up with a good reason for why she couldn't ask Jake to get a drink with her. The best she could come up with was that she'd taken off her bra already. Carrie wouldn't buy that one.

"Fine."

"Call me after, and tell me all about it."

"I'll call you tomorrow."

"Tonight."

"Tomorrow," Astrid said. "Remember the time difference."

"Is that why you're in bed at five p.m.?"

"It's ten. But yes."

"Call him."

~

Carrie's suggestion followed Astrid around Tuesday morning as she drove to pick up her mother's standard weekend bagel order, doubled this week because of Astrid's visit. With the party this weekend, things would be crazy. Sage was home on maternity leave, her mother was retired, and Astrid didn't have to work, so it made sense to move their brunch to earlier in the week.

You didn't have to ask her twice. Bagels, good ones, were hard to come by in the Pacific Northwest. Good deli was even harder.

The shop was crammed with people trying to fit into the too small space. The yeasty scent of fresh bagels immediately soothed Astrid. One customer left, and another immediately filled the space, everyone trying to squeeze so the door would stay closed. Each time it opened, a fresh blast of cold air shocked the patrons. Astrid edged closer and closer to the display cases, hoping the residual heat would help keep her from turning into an ice cube.

"You're following me," a voice murmured near her ear.

Astrid whirled. "What?" Her voice felt loud in the tiny space.

Jake stepped back. "Do you greet all your friends this way?"

"Only the ones who invade my personal space like a creeper."

"I'm a gentleman," he replied.

Astrid snorted. "I'll be the judge of that."

"Have I done anything ungentlemanly?"

"Not yet, but there's time."

The couple of in front of her paid and left. "Next!" called out the kid behind the counter, wiping his hands on his apron.

Astrid raised her hand. "That's me. I have a pick up."

"Name?"

"Feinmen."

"One second." He pivoted to the shallow counter behind him and rifled through the mess of bags and containers. When he turned back around, he held two large bags.

"You've got the whitefish salad in there?"

An older man farther down the counter answered for the kid, "You tell Sandra I never forget her whitefish!"

"I'll make sure to pass the message, Mr. G," Astrid called back.

"Can you add one more dozen to that order?" Jake told the kid. "Mixed? Heavy on the pumpernickel."

"I'm not buying you bagels," Astrid said, trying not to notice how his jeans once again made the most of his long legs. What would he look like in dress slacks? She shut that thought down as soon as it entered her mind. Stop that! No thinking about him in dress slacks. Or out of dress slacks. He was a neighbor, nothing more.

"I didn't ask you to. I'm buying *you* bagels. But I have to come home with something or my mother will be very upset. She might even ground me."

She rolled her eyes at his playfulness. "Thank you for the bagels, but not the side of charm. You've always been too charming for your own good."

"Tell that to my brother."

"Is Jeremy coming in too?"

"If the weather in Minneapolis ever cooperates."

Astrid didn't even think before saying, "You should both come to Mom's Hanukkah party on Saturday."

Jake paid the bill. He tapped a finger on the counter like he used to do when thinking through a math problem. Then he grinned. "Only if you have a drink with me tomorrow night." Then, before she could answer, he added, "You know, for old time's sake."

"Old times?"

"Yeah. One neighbor keeping another neighbor company."

"So, I'm being neighborly."

"You're saving me from a night of playing Scrabble with my folks, where they will soundly beat and humiliate me," he said. He picked up the bags. "Here, let me help you carry these to the car."

Astrid arched a brow at him. This was not the boy she remembered. Nor was he the man she expected.

"I'll have a drink with you. On one condition."

"What's that?" he asked, hip-checking the door open, then holding it while she walked through.

Astrid crossed to where she'd parked her rental car and waited for him to catch up. "You tell me what really happened sophomore year."

CHAPTER 3

J<small>AKE</small> <small>STOPPED</small> <small>SHORT,</small> <small>HIS</small> <small>ARMS</small> <small>FULL</small> <small>OF</small> <small>BAGELS</small> <small>AND</small> <small>HIS</small> <small>HEART</small> <small>IN</small> his stomach. Sophomore year? She couldn't ask him about anything else? His senior prank? His first job? His last girlfriend? No, she wanted to know about the single most humiliating night of his life.

"What's there to tell?"

Astrid unlocked the car and tossed her purse into the passenger seat. Then she grabbed her bags from his arms and carefully placed them inside. "You tell me. Tomorrow night. Seven p.m.?"

He nodded, but he couldn't make his throat work. That gave him a day and a half to come up with a way to distract her.

Astrid smiled. Was it him, or did she look a bit predatory in that moment? No, it had to be his imagination getting the better of him. She ducked into the car and pulled the door closed before starting the engine. Jake stood there, unable to get his legs to move despite the freezing temperatures. After a beat, she rolled down the window. "I'll meet you outside tomorrow night."

Then she put the window up and pulled out, leaving Jake standing on the sidewalk with a bag of bagels in his hands and the realization that maybe, he'd bitten off more than he could chew. And wondering why she didn't want him coming to her door.

~

The smell of freshly baked bagels filled the car. It was all she could do not to tear into one as she drove to Sage's house. "You're almost there," she told herself. "You can wait a few more minutes to eat."

The reminder did little to settle the restless feeling she'd been trying to tamp down since her encounter with Jake. Using one hand to steer the car she used the other to dig into the paper bag, careful to keep her eyes on the road. She pulled out a sesame seed bagel, still warm from the oven. "Oh yeah, that's the stuff," she whispered after her first bite.

You sound like an addict who's getting her fix, she pointed out to herself. Good thing she was driving, or her eyes would drift shut in bliss. Instead she moaned a little. She didn't care how she sounded. The bagel was too good. She couldn't find anything close to a bagel this good out in Seattle.

A bagel can't replace a man, the little voice niggled.

"It can come close," she said out loud. Then she groaned. "Great, now you're talking to yourself. All you need is thirty cats at home and the conversion will be complete."

Telling that little voice to shut the hell up, she took another bite of the bagel. By the time she pulled into Sage's driveway, she'd finished half of it. Her mom's car was already there. She parked and loaded her arms with everything from the store. At the front door, unable to get a hand free to try the knob, she knocked with her foot.

"There you are," her mom said when she opened the door. "I thought you got lost."

"I'm only a few minutes late." She maneuvered around her mother to the kitchen, where Sage sat with the baby. "I come bearing food!" she called, placing the bags on the counter, then went over to kiss first her sister, then her nephew, on the head. "Where's your cutting board?"

"I'll get it," said David, Sage's husband, who stood at the counter, pouring half and half into a coffee mug. "They are just over here." Then he finished and pulled a cutting board from the cabinet, then carried a burp cloth over to Sage. "Want me to take him?"

"I'm good," she said, lifting her face up for a kiss. "I need to feed him in a couple of minutes. You can take him after, though."

David smoothed a gentle hand over the baby's head, clearly unaware of the goofy grin on his face.

"You've really got this worked out," Astrid said, ignoring the envy rolling through her.

"Got what worked out?"

"This!" She waved emphatically with her hands. "Admittedly, I haven't spent a lot of time around new mothers, but you and David look like a well-oiled machine."

"Babies force you to learn fast," her sister said. "It's not like doctors let you stay at the hospital until you've got it figured out."

David nodded. "Plus, this early in the game there's only so much I can help with. It seems like all Eli does is eat, sleep, and poop. I can't help feed him at this point. So…" he let his words trail off.

Astrid watched the way he casually kneaded Sage's shoulders, and her knot of envy grew ever so slowly. They'd always been so in tune with one another. Becoming parents clearly hadn't changed much.

"It's still impressive. Now," she said, changing the subject. "What kind of bagel do you want?"

She began cutting the bagels in half, putting some in a freezer bag to save for later. The rest went into a large bowl that she set in the center of the table. She loaded the cream cheese, lox, and sliced onion onto a platter. Sage nursed Eli as their mom set out plates and cutlery, and David pulled out more coffee mugs.

Astrid studied her sister as they all sat down to eat. Sage cradled Eli in her arms while he nursed. He seemed so small, so delicate. Her sister hunched over him slightly, as if preparing to protect him from the rest of the world.

"Tell me about work," Sage said, shifting Eli to her shoulder.

Those four little words said it all. Sage had this whole life. She had a husband and a son. She had a family.

Astrid had work.

The ball of envy grew yet again, and Astrid mentally yelled, "Enough!" She had a good life. Work she loved. A home she was slowly making into her own. So she didn't have a man, a family. Who cared?

"I'd rather talk about you," Astrid said. "How are you adjusting?"

~

Jake stood in the bathroom the following night, tucking the ends of his white t-shirt into his jeans. Over that, he pulled a soft crewneck sweater the color of Cabernet. He ran a brush through his hair, then turned off the light.

"See? I told you all you had to do was charm a woman a little and you'd have a date," Jeremy said from the hallway.

"Your idea of charm and mine are polar opposites."

"So whatdya do? Blackmail her?"

The question hit a little close to home. It wasn't blackmail. Technically it was bribery. "I asked nicely. You might try that some time."

Growing up with an identical twin brother, Jake was used to people expecting the two of them to have the same personality. Hell, his mom had even dressed them alike for years. She'd buy two of each outfit, just in different colors. Somewhere around kindergarten, Jake finally rebelled and insisted on picking out his own clothes.

And while Jeremy excelled in math and science, Jake preferred English and history. Jeremy played on their high school football and basketball teams, going All-State in basketball. Jake stuck with soccer all the way through. Jeremy got a scholarship to UCLA. Jake stayed closer to home and attended MSU. Jeremy went on to become a land developer, Jake a teacher. Jeremy went through girlfriends like they were tissues. Jake…well, he didn't have that kind of time.

Time to change the subject. Jake asked, "Have you talked with Dad yet?"

"Not yet. He should be home soon enough."

"Can you try not to piss him off in the first fifteen minutes this time?"

For once, Jeremy seemed to pause instead of replying with some smart-ass remark. "We'll see." he said. "Dad's the one with the problem seeing a city grow and develop."

"Cut him some slack. He hates watching those Mom and Pop shops close."

"I'll back off as long as he does."

He gave his brother a playful shove. "He loves you. And this discussion is getting old. Kind of like you." He checked his watch. "Time to go."

"I'm only ten minutes older," Jeremy said slinging a conspiratorial arm over his shoulder and walking alongside him. "Just remember a piece of advice from your older and wiser brother, buy the first round."

~

"Normally I'd drive myself," Astrid pointed out after buckling herself in.

Jake pulled the Corolla out of the driveway. "Should I feel honored?"

She didn't bother to hide the smile blooming on her face. "Maybe."

"We're driving from the same place. Seems silly to take two cars."

"Maybe you're a serial killer."

"Again, taking a separate car isn't going to prevent that," Jake said. "Plus, if I was a serial killer, don't you think you'd have seen signs by now?"

"They always say it's the quiet ones."

Jake turned down the volume of the radio. "So now I'm quiet and suspicious?"

"Or you have mommy issues."

"You've met my mom," he reminded her. "Of course I do. But

again, one car versus two cars doesn't make much of a difference here."

She paused, tapping one finger on her chin. "But later, how can I throw a drink in your face and storm out dramatically if you drove me here?"

"Finally! The lady makes a valid point."

They laughed, and a tightness Astrid had been trying to ignore since brunch at her sister's house finally released in her chest. This was Jake, the boy who'd been her best friend until…the day he wasn't. This felt right. Even if it was temporary. She had missed this feeling of ease. With others, there was always those awkward moments as they figured each other out. With Jake, it all picked back up where they'd left off. "So, what happened?"

"When?" he asked.

She should let it go, but she needed to know why he did it. Then she'd move on. She needed her friend too much. "Sophomore year. Don't get me wrong. I'm not obsessing about it, or anything. I really hardly think about it."

"But…"

"But it was a thing. One that has niggled at the back of my brain ever since. I've never understood what really happened, and I'd like to. We were friends. Then…"

"Then I was an asshole that let his brother talk him into being more of an asshole."

She shifted in the seat to face him as he drove. "What happened."

"Jeremy was giving me a hard time."

"Jeremy always gave you a hard time. That was nothing new."

"True." She couldn't be sure, but she thought she saw him blush. "He was teasing me about having not asked you out yet. And…I was an ass."

"And you told everyone I was too ugly to date." The words hung between them, much as they had on that day.

"I told Jeremy. He told everyone on the team. I regretted it immediately," he said. His cheeks pink in the glow from the stop light. "It wasn't the truth. But I didn't know how to apologize."

Her palms sweat at the memory, at his explanation. She rubbed them on her jeans, but it didn't help. "So instead you didn't."

"And ruined our friendship in the process." The regret in his voice made her want to tell him it was okay. To tell him that she forgave him. At the same time, she wasn't sure if she wanted to let him off the hook completely. High school was awkward for everyone, wasn't it? No one really had it easy back then. Did they? She needed to stand. She needed to pace, to move around, to put some space between them.

"It was a mean thing to do," she said, finally getting to say to him what she'd wanted to say all those years ago.

"It was," he admitted. "Especially since I always thought you were out of my league."

"Then why did you say it?"

"I wanted Jeremy to back off."

"Your brother was always trying to get under your skin. Why did you let him?"

He didn't answer immediately, and judging from his clenched jaw, she'd struck a nerve.

"Tell me about your students," she said, rather than continue to push him. She turned to face the road and leaned her head back on the seat while he drove. He wasn't off the hook yet. But this conversation was best finished face to face. Plus, she needed to breath, to have a moment to let her brain process.

He took the hint and proceeded to share story after story about his high school students while they drove. It wasn't until they sat down at a small table and were waiting for their drinks that he paused. "You're pretty good at getting people to open up," he said. "You've had me talking non-stop."

"I like listening to you," she said. She picked up the little cocktail napkin their waitress had left behind and began turning it around between her fingers. "I like your stories."

"They're just high school stuff."

"But you love what you do, and it comes through."

He seemed to contemplate her words for a moment. "I do love it. Especially when I get through to that one student, the one who hates history? Who hates school? When I can get that kid interested in a topic and open to learning more?" His eyes sparkled with the confession, and she fell a little deeper in like with him.

"Have you always taught at that school?"

"I've bounced around a little. I started out teaching at one of the middle schools in Detroit. Was there only a couple of years, before I decided I needed to see something more than just Michigan."

"Is that when you moved to Portland?"

Their waitress came by with their drinks, dropping off a beer for Jake and Astrid's glass of wine.

"I tried L.A. first, but I'm not fancy enough," he joked, indicating his low-key sweater and jeans combo. "Then San Francisco for another year, before finally moving up to Portland."

"Why Portland?" she asked.

He took a drink of his beer. When he finally did, it was with a sheepish smile, like he expected her to tease him. "A girl."

All the regular quips came to mind. *Did she wear a lot of flannel? Did she spend every Sunday hiking with her dog? Did she eat only vegan, soy-free, taste-free meals?* But to be fair, the same questions could be asked of anyone living in Seattle, and she'd heard them plenty herself. So instead she asked the question she really wanted to know the answer to. "What happened?"

"Your standard story. Boy meets girl. Boy and girl fall in love. Boy leaves everything for girl. Girl leaves boy."

There was more to his lighthearted story, she could see it in the shadows driving out the sparkle in his eyes. It was in his grip on his glass, his knuckles whitening with strain. In the lines now etching the corners of his mouth. Astrid resisted the urge to wrap her hand around his and try to soothe him. *Not your job,* Carrie would remind her. *You don't need to fix the world.*

After another long drink from his beer, he asked, "Have you been in Washington since you graduated?"

While she answered, he raised a finger to flag down their waitress. "Pretty much. I was lucky enough to get summer internships at Google, Microsoft, and at Paragon, a small game developer. So, when I got offered a job at Paragon just before graduation, I jumped at it."

"What are you doing for them? Something on the sales end?"

"What makes you assume that?"

"You were a Girl Scout," Jake said. "Girl entrepreneur and all that."

"Everyone always assumes that women can only be in the business end of things." It made her see red. She drained the glass she'd been slowly nursing and placed an order for a second one when the waitress stopped over. Then she took a deep breath, and gave him the benefit of the doubt. "I'm a program manager. I worked on the coding for a few big projects we put out, then moved into managing the product side of things. I decided I like having a say in the bigger picture, rather than just with my little piece of the puzzle."

"You love what you do," Jake said. "That's the dream, isn't it? I don't remember you being into computers when we were younger, is all."

"I wasn't when we were little," she said. "But by high school, I could see that it was already a growing field. College solidified it."

"I didn't realize that." And now they were back to facing the elephant in the room. "I really fucked up in high school, didn't I?"

She didn't even hesitate. To do so would have been disingenuous. They needed to finish this conversation and move on. "Yeah, you did."

"Can you forgive me?"

She pretended to think about it. "Buy me another drink, and I'll consider it."

"Done."

Jake's throaty laugh warmed her from the belly up, filling her like champagne bubbles. Had she dated anyone recently who she could talk to so easily? Joke with so easily? There had been 'Stache-guy, as Carrie had called him. He'd taken himself so seriously, always stroking his mustache as if deciding where to go to dinner was some kind of philosophical debate. Not to mention the

Professor. He'd prefaced everything with, "Well you know, Aristotle once said." Pretentious much?

Jake, she realized, didn't have a pretentious bone in his body. How could she have missed someone this much, without realizing it?

"Maybe we need to get to know each other a little better? Over dinner?" she said, the words rushing out before she could stop them.

The twinkle returned to his eyes. "I'd like that."

∼

They drove back to her mom's house in amicable silence, her hand in his. *How did we get to this point?* Astrid wondered. *And where do we go from here?* But she didn't ask the words out loud. Didn't want to break the moment they were in with the reality of...well...reality.

"She's always loved to decorate for Hanukkah," Astrid said as Jake pulled into his own parents' driveway. "I think it was her way of making it feel as special as Christmas, so I'd stop asking for a tree."

Mom had left a light on in the kitchen, and what appeared to be a television flickered in her bedroom. Otherwise, the house was dark. Not even a porch light on. The family menorah sat on the window sill. Two candles sat unlit, ready for the first night of Hanukkah.

He put the car in Park and turned to face her, his head resting on the back of the seat. "You wanted a Christmas tree?"

She turned, matching him. "When I was little? Yeah. I loved the tree you got every year, and I wanted one for us too. It took my mom years to get me to understand the beauty of *not* celebrating Christmas. I think that's why she initially started her menorah collection."

"I remember those. Every year at your party, your family would pass out matches so we could help light them all."

"I have no idea how many boxes of candles she's gone through over the years, but I love getting the picture she sends me of them gathered on the counter, all lit. They hold such possibility. Like anything can happen. Like maybe we'll have our own miracle."

"It would be the appropriate time for a miracle," Jake said.

"It would." A shiver tingled through her. "I know I asked before, but you'll come to the party this year?"

"It's been a long time," he said, hedging.

Only the soft glow from the exterior lights of his parents' house letting her see the expression on his face. "I know," she said. "But it feels right."

His gaze met hers, and he seemed to be assessing, looking for the answer to an unspoken question. Whatever it was, he nodded as if he found the answer he'd hoped for. "I wouldn't dream of missing it."

His words held weight, carrying more than just themselves into the night. A small part of her brain urged her to ask him what he meant. The larger, more rational part of her reminded her that they lived in two different states, with two jobs they loved. This wasn't the beginning of something special. This was just a dinner. It would just be a party. A renewed friendship. Nothing more.

It was never meant to be anything more.

And yet…

He opened his car door and climbed out. When she had done the same, he came around and took her hand. He said, "Let me walk you to the door."

Tingles raced down her spine. Where were they coming from? Or had it always been there? She couldn't think, couldn't speak, so she nodded. She fell into step next to him as he guided her up the walk to her mother's house.

"We never did this," she said. "Never held hands, I mean."

"I wanted to," came his quiet reply.

"So did I."

He squeezed her hand. Did he want to put his arm around her? Did she want him to? It was like being fifteen years old again, on a first date. *This is Jake*, she reminded herself. *You've known him forever. Get over yourself!*

They reached the front steps, climbing them silently. "Well, we're here," she said. He hadn't let go of her hand yet.

"So we are." He began to lean forward and her stomach flipped in anticipation.

Her eyes fluttered closed, his face so close to her own she could feel his breath on her cheek.

The front door swung open. "Oh good, you're home!" Astrid's mother said. "I was waiting up for you."

CHAPTER 4

JAKE SPRANG BACK AND STUMBLED, BARELY CATCHING HIMSELF ON the arm of a nearby chair. "Hi, Ms. Feinmen. How are you?"

Sandra Feinmen watched him with a critical gleam in her eye. "Hello Jake. I'm fine, thank you. Did you two have a nice time?"

A benign question from anyone except for Sandra. Jake remembered her asking him a question in the same tone when he was nine, that ended with him being grounded for a week. She was a stealth agent, sneaking in below the radar.

"We had a good time, Mom," Astrid said, stepping between the two of them. She turned her back on her mother for a moment and faced Jake. "I'll talk to you later. Thank you for the drink."

"You're welcome," Jake said, caressing her hand. "I'll see you later."

Behind her daughter, Ms. Feinman asked, "You're coming to our party on Saturday, yes?"

"I wouldn't miss it."

"Good. This way your parents won't feel they have to miss the party to be with you boys."

"I'll make sure I let them know that Jeremy and I are invited, too."

Ms. Feinmen nodded, then stepped back inside the dark house.

"I'm glad we've cleared things up," Astrid said.

Jake took a step toward her, but she backed up. She now stood with one foot inside and one foot outside the doorway. He took the hint. The moment was gone "I had fun."

"So did I," she said. Did he hear a note of wistfulness in her voice? He raised a hand in an abbreviated wave, and walked back to the car. He shook his head and blew out a breath of frustration. Just as she had in high school, Astrid managed to leave him wanting more, while he had no idea what had happened.

His own family's house sat almost as dark as hers. The exterior lights, on just moments ago, had gone dark. He glanced at his watch, confirming his suspicion. Almost 10:30.

Using the garage code, he let himself in. After pouring a glass of water to take with him, he climbed the stairs to his bedroom. Jeremy stood in his own bedroom's doorway.

"Hope you weren't waiting up for me," Jake said.

"Heard a noise, wanted to make sure it was you."

Jake spread his arms wide, the water in his glass splashing a little onto his hand. "It's me."

"I can see that." Jeremy turned to go back into his room.

"You okay?" Jake asked

"You didn't get enough of a heart-to-heart with Astrid?" Jeremy asked, his question mirroring Jake's thoughts, as they'd so often done when they'd been children.

"Sounds like you're the one needing one," Jake said. "I'm happy to listen."

Jeremy ignored him, and went back into his room, closing the door behind him.

People assumed that he and his twin were close, the best of friends. Maybe growing up. That had been a long time ago. They chatted once a week, but those held little real substance. Mostly they were the "Hey, how's it going? Fine, how are you?" type of talks. Never deep conversations.

Not that Jake had much energy to talk by Friday afternoons, when one of them usually called the other. Their calls were an unspoken promise to their mother, who worried about her boys living so far away. When she called them on the weekend and asked, "Have you talked to your brother recently?" They could always answer honestly, "Yes."

Now that Jake was using his nights for sleeping rather than grading, he picked up on the signs he'd missed during their weekly calls. He took a step toward his brother's room, then backed off. Jake would try to talk to his brother in the morning.

In his own room, he pulled off his sweater and T-shirt, preparing for bed. His skin felt charged, as if Astrid had put some kind of electrical field all around him before saying goodnight. The hairs on his arms stuck straight up, and a shiver ran down his spine. His mind, usually done for by now, *thank you teaching*, raced with all he wished he'd said or done differently that night so long ago.

From his back pocket, his cell buzzed.

Thanks again for tonight.

He replied before he could think too hard about it.

I wish it hadn't ended so quickly.

When her reply didn't immediately appear, his brain began its worst-case-scenario cycle. He'd overstepped. She wasn't that into him. She was that into him but dying. She was secretly engaged. She was secretly married. She was secretly married with eight kids.

What scared him, what sent that damn shiver down his spine again, wasn't all the different, and absurd, scenarios his brain could produce. No, it was that to him, none of them were deal-breakers. "Dude, slow down," he muttered to himself.

When was the last time he'd cared how long it took a woman to reply to a text? Hell, usually his phone was buried in his desk. Half the time he forgot to turn the ringer back on when he left work, causing him to miss messages all the time. Hadn't that been Molly's biggest complaint?

"You never reply to my texts," she'd yelled during their last blowout fight.

"I don't hear them come in," he'd argued. "If you didn't text me every hour on the hour, it wouldn't be an issue."

"I love you!"

"Then you would trust that just because I'm not answering, doesn't mean I'm screwing around on you."

"I've seen how that other English teacher watches you," Molly'd said between clenched teeth.

"Irene? Are you kidding me? She's happily married. Not to mention she's a good twenty years older than I. She doesn't look at me like anything."

"Yes, she does!" Molly had shrieked at him. "She's always watching me, like I'm about to poison your apple or something."

As it had turned out, Molly's jealousy was in fact not enough to get Jake to break up with her. It had taken her keying Irene's car on the last day of school for him to figure out she was loony.

But he did learn something from dating her. Women liked a man who replied promptly to texts.

So where was Astrid's reply?

~

Astrid saw his reply come in, and purposefully ignored it. Carrie would have been proud. "You can't let a man think you're sitting around waiting for his response to come back. He'll see you as one of those crazy stalker-types."

So instead, she plugged her phone in and ignored it. She readied herself for bed, and climbed in. One final glance at the screen, and his simple reply:

I wish it hadn't ended so quickly.

He lives in another state, she reminded herself. He has a job he loves. He has a life. Hell, he probably has a dog. He doesn't mean anything by it.

But she still fell asleep with a smile on her face, and dreamed about kissing him all night long.

When she woke the next morning, a weak gray light filtered in past the window shade. Would it snow? She hoped so. She missed it. Not the kind the Seattle-area got. Not the kind that shut down the city for days when a few inches fell, then froze to the streets. No, she missed Michigan snow. The blanket of white that softened the sound of the cars, and that brought all the kids in the neighborhoods out to play in their yards. The kind that piled up on lawns, but that was plowed by the morning commute. The kind that called for cozying up with a cup of hot chocolate, and a donut. The kind of that still allowed everyone to go about their daily lives.

If they wanted.

She made her way to the shower, mentally ticking through her to-do list for the day. She'd promised Sage she'd come hold baby Eli while her sister grabbed a nap later this morning. She'd told her mother she'd help Sage with laundry and grocery shopping, too, so her mother could focus on getting ready for the Hanukkah party.

In the shower, she continued. Check email and respond to anything critical. Easy enough, if she didn't let herself get sucked into her email. "I want you to take a full two weeks," her boss had said back in November. "You're heading toward burn-out."

"I'm fine," Astrid argued.

Emma, her manager, had looked her up and down. "When was the last time you logged off before nine p.m.?"

Astrid had tried to remember. Last week? The week before that? It couldn't have been more than three weeks ago. Had it?

"I'll start setting an alarm."

"Astrid, we're in a 24/7 world. But if you don't recharge soon, you'll be no good to me. Your last presentation was not your finest moment."

Astrid had forced herself to meet Emma's gaze. Emma was more than just her manager. She was also her mentor. She had the job Astrid wanted. When she gave advice, Astrid listened. When she was disappointed, Astrid wilted. "I know it wasn't my finest hour," she'd begun.

"Can I be blunt?" Emma had asked. "It was your worst. If I didn't know you so well, our conversation would be a whole lot different right now." She'd let her words hang in the air, waiting for Astrid to get her meaning.

"It wasn't that bad."

"You cost the company its number three client."

Oh shit.

"I've been really focused," Astrid had tried to explain.

"You're working yourself into a heart attack. You're too young for this, Astrid."

"Everyone else has families, people counting on them to come home and not be working."

Emma had leaned back in her chair, folding her hands in front of her. "Astrid, I didn't get here by letting others walk all over me. It's one thing to do a co-worker a favor here or there, but you don't owe them your life. That promotion you're gunning for isn't going to happen if you're a puddle on the floor. The team won't collapse if you take some time off. Everything slows down in December. Take the two weeks. Give yourself time to recharge.

And that's what really brought her back. Astrid had booked tickets to Michigan and promised she'd stay off email. She'd even removed the program from her phone, so she wouldn't feel tempted to check at random times. Doing so had also taken her calendar off, and if she thought about that too hard it would induce a panic attack. So, she forced herself not to think about it. Now, dressed in a pair of leggings, and a cream-colored cable-knit sweater, she pulled her suitcase from under her bed. She unburied her laptop and turned it on. "Just a quick check.

There were over five hundred unread emails in her inbox. *Weren't people taking time off for the holidays this year?* She closed her eyes briefly. "Okay, maybe not such a quick check," she said, and began to open and respond.

She'd managed to clean out twenty, when her phone chirped. Astrid looked over at it. A text. From Emma.

Get off your email.

Astrid grinned. Of course she'd noticed.

Just cleaning out the inbox before I head to my sister's.

Off. Now.

Astrid replied to two more, then logged off.

There. It's closed.

Send proof.

Astrid outright laughed. Emma knew her too well. So, she clicked a pic of her closed and re-stored laptop.

See? It's even put away.

After heading downstairs, she poured a cup of coffee. As she drank, she stared out the kitchen window into the front yard. Movement off to the side caught her attention.

She blinked. She couldn't be seeing that. But it was still there when she opened her eyes. She carried her coffee with her, and stepped out onto the front porch. "Mom! What are you doing?"

"Nothing," came her mother's reply.

"Is that a giant dreidel?"

"Maybe."

Her mother stood in front of a seven-foot-tall, three-foot-wide dreidel, wearing baggy sweatpants tucked into snow boots, and a thick down coat. "Oh my goodness, does that thing light up?"

"It's festive."

"Mom!"

"I'm not trying to impress anyone, Astrid."

"Are you trying to blind them?"

"It won't be that bright. I put it up last year. The kids in the neighborhood loved it."

How did she argue with that? "There's just the one, right?"

"Oh, there's one more. What's a game of dreidel without the gelt to go with it?"

"Mom, no!"

"I like it," a voice called out across the expanse of the driveway.

Astrid looked over to where Jake stood in his own parents' driveway, a giant grin on his face. "Great addition, Ms. Feinmen!"

"See? Others appreciate it."

Astrid glared at Jake. "Don't encourage her," she said to him. To her mother she said, "It's tacky."

Her mom finished plugging the dreidel into the extension cord, and brought out to the waist-high pieces of Hanukkah gelt. "I like it," her mom said.

And how could she argue with that? She threw up her empty hand in defeat. "Fine. Festive. Whatever."

"Don't be a Grinch," Jake said, walking over from his parents.

"Wrong holiday," she pointed out.

Her mom finished setting up the gelt, and went inside with a not-so subtle wink toward Astrid.

Oy.

"Same sentiment. It's fun, and it doesn't hurt anyone. Plus, it clearly makes your mom happy."

"And shows the aliens where to land."

Jake joined her on the front porch. "It'll help the good Doctor find you."

"He only ever lands in England," Astrid said, playing along. Jake wasn't the only one to know Doctor Who.

"As long as you don't wake up to it trying to kill you in your sleep, I think you'll be okay," he said.

Astrid tried. She really tried not to react. To let his comment roll on past her. She doubled over laughing.

"Remember to breathe," he said, completely straight-faced.

"I— I— I'm trying," she managed to get out between gasps for air.

He slung an arm around her shoulder, leading her back inside, modeling deep breaths to her. She only laughed harder.

"You aren't helping!" she finally got out.

"Only because you have the giggles," he pointed out, his grin in no way apologizing. "Let's get you some more coffee."

"You want some?" she asked, leading him to the kitchen.

"I'd love a mug. Mom's gone on a health kick. All she has is decaffeinated green tea in the house. I think Jeremy is going to lose his mind."

"Caffeine addict?"

"Something like that. Between the lack of coffee and my dad, he may not last until Christmas."

"What's going on with your dad?"

"Dad doesn't agree with his, ahem, more mercenary money tactics."

"Is Jeremy bankrupting little old ladies?" She handed him a mug of coffee.

Jake breathed in the steam before answering. "That's the stuff. No, nothing as bad as that. He's a developer. He buys up property in desirable locations and sells it to developers building condominiums and subdivisions. But Dad can't help himself. He has to pipe up and tell Jeremy all the ways he's messing up and screwing over the little guy, and how he can do it all better. He hasn't learned that the only way to get Jeremy to change is to make him think it was his idea in the first place."

"So, it's a showdown."

"Something like that," he said, sipping.

∼

When was the last time a woman had laughed so hard in his presence? Jake wondered, tired of thinking about Jeremy, Dad, and all their drama. *Hell, when was the last time a woman had gotten one of his Doctor Who references?* Astrid looked like she should be curled up on a couch in front of a fire, with blanket wrapped around her feet and a stack of books off to one side.

And he wanted to be curled up on that couch with her.

Whoa. Where had that come from? This was Astrid. His childhood friend. Not some random woman he'd met through the latest dating app or fix up. But he couldn't tear his mind away from sitting on that couch with her, curling up to the latest Netflix binge or Doctor Who episode. The image morphed, and now she wasn't leaning against the couch arm, but against him. He had an arm thrown over her shoulder, pulling her close. Maybe playing with a loose curl.

She'd lay her head on his chest while they watched the show, tracing random patterns on his thigh. He'd draw a finger down her arm, and she'd turn to him, turn to his kiss. And now the image was morphing into something definitely more R-rated.

"You here?" she asked, waving a hand in front of his face.

Shit. "Yeah, yeah. Sorry. I zoned out there for a minute." Where the hell had all that come from? They'd been on one pseudo-date. They hadn't even kissed.

"What were you thinking about?"

"Nothing."

The side of her mouth quirked up in a teasing smile. "Really? Cause from here it looked pretty interesting."

He groaned inwardly. She could not know where his brain was going. Clearly Jeremy was on to something when he told Jake he'd waited too long to get laid. Now he was picturing every remotely available female in his bed.

Well, on his couch.

And it wasn't every female. It was Astrid. Only Astrid.

Shit.

"Okay, keep your secrets," she said. "I have to get over to Sage's anyway. I promised her I'd come help with the baby."

"Want to go out with me after?"

"Again?" she blurted out. Then covered her mouth. "That came out wrong."

Was that overkill? Too soon? "Yeah, why not? I'll be ready to get out of the house by then. It's not like this neighborhood is particularly exciting."

"I think we're having a family dinner tonight."

"No problem. We can grab a drink, or find some music or something."

"You do remember where we are, right? Live music isn't exactly a thing here in the 'burbs."

"You let me worry about that," he told her. "I'll find something."

She didn't answer him right away, and he figured this was it. She was about to firmly plant him in the friend-zone.

Then she smiled and his heart flipped over. "Okay, why not?" she agreed.

He felt a slow grin split his face. "Okay then." He placed the coffee mug down on the table and stood up. "I'll let you get to your sister's place. Call me when you're finishing up dinner?"

Her eyes sparkled and without thinking, he stepped closer, putting one hand on her waist and the other at the nape of her neck. He stared into her eyes, daring her to tell him no, to stop him in his tracks. Instead, she placed her own two hands right on his face and pulled him in closer.

His lips met hers and he sank his hand into her hair, holding her closer.

"Come look at the final display!" her mother shouted from the living room.

Astrid jumped back slightly, and Jake had to let go, or risk tearing her hair out. He watched as one of her hands drifted up to lightly touch her lips. The simple action stole his heart. "Be right there, Mom!"

Jake stepped closer once again, and instead of pulling her close like he wanted to, placed a chaste peck on her cheek. "I'll see you later."

CHAPTER 5

As Sage napped, Astrid rocked Eli in her arms. "What's so funny about that?" she asked Carrie, but her friend didn't get it. Astrid was trying to get Eli to fall asleep, but apparently he had serious FOMO and her love life was way too exciting.

"I can't explain it," Astrid said. "You just had to be there."

"And then he kissed you."

"Actually, I think I kissed him. Maybe we kissed each other? I don't know."

"Because he likes that silly show?"

"It's not a silly show. It's an awesome show."

Carrie snorted, and the sound carried perfectly into Astrid's earbud. "You go ahead and keep thinking that."

"You can't take away my love for the Doctor. One of these days I'm making you sit down and watch the David Tennent seasons."

"Sure, why not." She sounded utterly unconvinced.

Astrid lowered her voice another notch. "You're missing the point."

"What was the point again?"

"We kissed. And it was good."

"So? A kiss doesn't mean wedding bells."

"It means something."

"It doesn't have to."

Eli fussed in her arms, so she tried shifting him onto her shoulder. He seemed to like that position better and settled slightly. She continued to rock back and forth. "You don't think he's going to expect…things…do you?"

"Damn, girl! What kind of kiss was this?"

"That's not what I meant and you know it."

"It was a kiss. A kiss is a kiss is a kiss. It's not a promise. It's not sex in public. We're not living in the 1800's, you know."

"He lives in Portland. Been there, done that, had the broken heart to prove it. No thank you."

"So? Dan was a dick. Jake's not Dan. It's a night out. Just enjoy yourself. Sheesh. You've really got to get over this thing where every date holds deep meaning. This could be why you're still alone."

"I'm not alone."

"You have no significant other at home on any given day of the week. Male, female, alien. I don't care what floats your boat. But you're going to hit crazy-cat lady-territory soon."

"Trust me, I'm well aware.

"Listen to me. You've let Dan's cheating turn you into a workaholic. You've moved up the ladder, but you have no one to celebrate with you."

"I have you." She held Eli a smidge closer, enjoying the soft snuffling sounds he made while she rocked. He felt heavier, and she thought maybe he'd finally fallen asleep. She eased onto the couch and he stirred, whimpering protests rising quickly. "Sh, sh, sh, sh," she said, standing back up quickly.

"Astrid, you need to get past this need to succeed, and focus on other aspects of your life. Go out. Enjoy yourself. Maybe you'll even find that you like it. You're taking the easy way out by hiding behind work."

She tried to keep her voice low, her tone sing-song, but it came out between gritted teeth. "You call this the easy way out?"

Eli fussed, her agitation clearly increasing his. And obviously she sucked at baby holding, because here was her sister. "You're supposed to be napping," Astrid said.

"Me?" Carrie asked in her ear.

"Not you," Astrid replied.

Sage said, "I'll take him."

Astrid swung away, beginning to pace the room while taking deep breaths. "I've got him. You're the one who's supposed to be resting."

"It's kind of hard to rest when my sister is having a mental breakdown in my living room."

"You're exaggerating."

"Not by much. Do I need to call mom?" she said.

"You wouldn't."

"Don't think I'm not this close,"—she pinched her fingers a hair's breadth away from each other—"from calling her anyway. You know she'd pick up."

"Sage! You can't sic Mom on me."

Carrie said, "Maybe I should let you go."

"Yeah, probably a good idea."

Astrid disconnected, then pulled her earbud out. "You're not playing fair," she told Sage.

"You're not listening to reason."

"Why? Because I don't want to give a guy who lives in another state the wrong idea?"

"No, because you don't want to give a guy who seems crazy about you the right idea."

"You're not making sense. How would you even know he's crazy about me? It's not like you've seen him yet."

Sage finally sat back down. "You've told me about each of your interactions. The Jake I remember was a total sweetheart, until he wasn't. If the way he's acting now doesn't describe a guy who can't get you out of his head, I don't know what does."

Astrid continued pacing, Eli finally settling into sleep. "We live a minimum of three hours from one another. I barely have time to eat dinner at home, let alone maintain a long-distance relationship."

"You're scared."

"And you're sleep deprived. You need to enjoy your happy little family and let the rest of us figure things out on our own."

Sage pushed off the couch and approached her sister slowly.

"Have you ever thought that maybe you need to let your defenses down a bit? It was a date. A dinner. He's not walking up to you with a ring. See what happens. Maybe it'll be nothing, but maybe it'll turn into something. You'll never know unless you give it a chance."

"I thought Mom was the one into all the woo-woo crap, now. Not you."

"She's been giving me pointers," she said, taking Eli out of Astrid's arms. She settled herself on the couch and lifted her shirt so she could nurse her son. "I only want you to be happy."

Astrid brought her sister a glass of water and began folding the laundry in the basket near the couch. "I'll find someone. But Jake's not it."

"Not if you won't give him a chance."

~

Jake kicked his feet up onto the ottoman, and leaned back to watch football with his dad. A bowl of chips sat between them and they each held a bottle of beer. The perfect evening. "When was the last time you saw the Lions play?" his dad asked.

"Last time I was home, I think. I'm more likely to catch the Seahawks while I grade, these days."

"The Lions are better this year."

"You say that every year," Jake said.

"It's true. They're finally breaking out of their slump."

"Do they realize how loyal you are?"

His dad laughed, the deep belly laugh that Jake remembered from childhood. "If they did, they'd send me season tickets."

Jake grinned back. "I should let Jeremy know we're watching."

His dad didn't respond right away, just took a long pull off the bottle in his hand. "He left hours ago."

When were these two going to let go of this ridiculous

argument? So Jeremy made his living buying up property and selling to developers. Who cared? How did this make him a horrible person?

Jake pulled out his phone, but before he could open his messages to text Jeremy, the screen lit up with an incoming message.

You're very distracting, you know that?

Astrid.

"Dad, why don't you call Jeremy? He'd probably join us," Jake said before texting back.

Not half as distracting as you are.

When was the last time he flirted with a woman over text? Hell, this past week was the first time he'd flirted with a woman in person in months. Not since he'd broken up with his Molly.

Probably not. Still.

"What's with the goofy grin?" his father finally asked at half-time.

Jake swiped a hand over his mouth, as if to wipe it away. "What are you talking about?"

"You're smiling like a damn fool and watching your phone more than this game," he said. "You missed the last two touchdowns completely."

"Those? They were for the other team."

"They were still touchdowns. Who is she?"

"Who is who?"

"The woman on the other end of your phone? Call her already."

"We're watching the game," Jake said.

"No," his dad said. "I'm watching the game. You're flirting with a lady friend."

"I'll put the phone away."

"Or you could just call her already."

Jake tapped his fingers on the arm of the couch. He and Astrid had been texting back and forth for the better part of an hour and a half. Not constantly, as she was with her sister, but pretty damn close.

"Dad," he said. "Remember when you had that job down in Toledo?"

"Longest two and a half years of my life," his dad said. "Your mom was up here with you boys, and I'd drive home every Friday evening as fast as I could. It was a miracle I didn't get more than the one speeding ticket. Then I'd wake up at three a.m. to do it all again on Monday morning in the opposite direction."

"How did you two make it work?"

His dad absent-mindedly picked up a handful of chips and munched on them. Eventually he said, "First off, your mother is a saint. She put up with the two of you and all your shenanigans, so I made sure I showed her I appreciated her. Second, we talked every night. I'd call just before you boys went to bed, to say goodnight, then she and I would talk after she'd got you both down. Sometimes it was only for twenty minutes. Other times it was for two hours. Damn long-distance charges." He popped another couple of chips in his mouth. "Communication is what did it for us. I may not have been there for the day-to-day stuff, but we talked about it all. We continued to make decisions together, as best we could. And we loved each other. Doesn't matter how close you live, if you don't really love each other."

Jake mulled his words through the second half of the game. But each announcer was superimposed with Astrid's face.

~

"We've been texting for two days, nonstop," Astrid told Carrie.

"Flirty texting, or sexy texting?"

"Carrie!"

"What? It's a legit question."

"Flirting, if you must know."

Carrie blew a raspberry at her. Thank goodness for FaceTime.

Astrid needed nothing more than to see her best friend's face to feel calmer. "What does it mean?" she asked.

"That you enjoy flirting with him? You're over-thinking everything. It's texting. Just enjoy it."

Astrid's cheeks warmed. "I am enjoying it," she admitted.

"That's my girl!" Carrie replied.

Her screen blinked, indicating a new message. "I gotta go," she told Carrie."

"Is Jake calling?"

"No," she replied, but the word practically tripped over itself.

"I see," Carrie said with a knowing wink. It felt like more than just simple flirting. Two days later, they'd blown up each other's phones with texts, gifs, and random memes. "I can't remember having this much fun just talking," she told Sage.

"Will you sit down?" Sage finally asked from her spot on the couch. Astrid paced in front of the fireplace. "You're making me nervous, and that's bad for Eli." She shifted him to prop the baby against her shoulder, his wobbly little head supported by her hand.

"I can't. I have too much energy."

"Why? It's just Mom's Hanukkah party."

"Jake is coming."

"So? You've been chatting for days. And it's not like it's his first Feinman party." Eli squawked, bobbled his head a bit, then resettled. "What are you so scared of?"

Astrid scoffed. "Who says I'm afraid?"

"Everything you say! You keep telling us it's not serious, you aren't dating, it can't go anywhere."

"You've been happily married forever. You have no idea what it's like out there anymore."

"I know I wouldn't let a thing like a different city make a difference if it was someone I truly care about."

"Sage, I've done long distance before. Don't you remember?"

"Dan? That's what this is about?"

"No, but it was a good lesson."

"He was a loser. He wouldn't make a commitment, and cheated on you. He was an asshole. You can't judge Jake against that guy."

"I'm not."

"You are. It'll take work, but if it's worth it, then it won't feel like it."

Astrid arched a brow at her sister, then continued her pacing. "It's not like he's expressed interest in this going beyond these couple of weeks. I'm probably just a diversion to him."

"Or else you're someone he genuinely likes, and he'd like to give this a chance too. You won't know unless you talk with him."

Holding the baby against her in one hand, she used the other to push herself up off the couch. Astrid hurried over to lend a hand, which Sage grasped tightly. When she was finally standing, she put her free arm around Astrid to pull her into a hug. "Go talk to him. Better yet, wait until the party tonight."

Part of her wanted to shout, "No!" and run away to protect her heart. The other side finally listened to reason. She couldn't keep running. It was time to slow down and take a chance. "You may be on to something," she said.

～

Astrid's stomach jumped around like she was on a plane waiting for the landing gears to engage. All around her, neighbors and friends crowded her mother's house. Music played in the background but could barely be heard above the din of voices. Food overflowed the dining room table, where Sandra had set up a feast of Hanukkah delights. Everything from traditional latkes with applesauce and sour cream, to homemade sufganyot. Those little jelly filled donuts were Astrid's favorite. Chocolate gelt had been strewn across the table, and the lights flickered off the metal foil wrappers. "This is ridiculous."

"What is?" a male voice asked from behind her, so close she could feel his breath on her neck.

She whirled, flinging her wine as she turned. "Shit!"

Jake stared down at the red-wine stain spreading across his oatmeal colored, cable-knit sweater. "It wasn't my favorite anyway," he quipped.

"I'm so sorry," Astrid said. She felt heat creeping up her neck, onto her cheeks. *Can the floor just swallow me whole now?*

He dabbed at the stain with a napkin, but it was hopeless. "It's okay, really."

"Do you have another one?"

"Here? I didn't exactly bring a costume change with me."

"I meant at your parents."

"Yeah."

"Then we should probably go and soak that, before the stain sets."

He didn't respond right away. Instead, he just looked at her, searching her face.

"What?" she asked.

"I'm trying to figure something out."

"What?"

"What is it about you?" As questions went, she could read that one a few ways. Either she'd just ruined his favorite sweater and he was trying to figure out where to bury the body, or else he'd fallen head over heels in love with her in the that moment and couldn't wait to spend the rest his life with her.

Reality reminded her the answer was probably neither, which left her nowhere. "I'm wicked smart and hot to boot?"

"Well, yeah, but see, you've turned my world upside down, and I didn't see it coming."

She couldn't have heard him correctly. "This room is getting pretty loud. What did you say?" He stood directly in front of her, so close she had to place her hands on his shoulders to keep from falling over.

"I met this amazingly clumsy woman on my trip home."

"Oh yeah?"

"Yeah." He stepped even closer, until they were pressed against one another. They stood together in a room full of people, and he didn't seem to give a damn.

And for what might be the first time in her adult life, neither did she. Astrid licked her lips. All she could see was his face. "Tell me about her."

"She's smart, she's funny, and she's absolutely convinced that we don't have a future together."

"Is she wrong?"

"I have no idea," he replied honestly. "We live in two different cities. And I hurt her a long time ago. But we used to be friends, and I think we're friends again. And I'd like to take a chance and see where this thing leads."

"She doesn't have a great track record with long distance relationships."

"She meant something to me once." He paused and stared her straight in the eyes. Then took her by the elbow and lead her into a quieter corner at the back of the room. "You. You meant something to me once, and I'm realizing that you still do. I don't want to waste my second shot at something amazing."

"What if it is disastrous?"

"What if?" he challenged her. "What if it's a miracle?"

Around them, the lights dimmed and she heard her mother calling out for her.

"We need to finish this," she said to Jake.

"After you help your mom with the candles," he said. "I'm not going anywhere."

～

Jake watched her go to stand with her mother and sister. She was as skittish as a bunny, but he was starting to understand how her mind worked. He needed to give her space and let her decide if they were worth it.

Sandra struck a match, then lit one candle before passing it to her daughters. Astrid and Sage, held the tiny flame to the unlit wick of the waiting candle. They began to pray, *"Baruch atah…"* Those in the room who knew the words joined in, their voices carrying throughout the house. The light from the candles illuminated the dim room.

The flickering light danced off Astrid's curls, which she'd pulled back from her face with some kind of clip or comb. All he wanted to do was run his fingers through those curls. She turned, as the people in the room began to sing another song he didn't know the words to, but could remember from all those parties long ago. She caught his gaze from across the room, and a warm smile spread across her lips. A smile only for him. The candlelight danced around them as she took a step toward him, then he toward her.

It didn't seem to matter that they were in a room full of her mother's closest friends and neighbors, or that their families were both looking on. Like magnets, they pulled toward one another until they stood less than a breath apart. Jake placed a hand at the small of her back and led her just outside the room, where there'd be fewer eyes on them.

"You know everything in the world says this is a terrible idea," she told him.

"It's the season of miracles," he reminded her. "I can't think of a better time to try a terrible idea with an amazing woman."

"And if it doesn't work out?"

"We'll pick ourselves up and dust ourselves off," he said. Then he gave into the urge and ran his fingers through her curls, dislodging the comb-things. "But I'm not worried."

"You're not?"

"Nope. Because I know something you don't know."

"What?"

With one arm, he tugged her those last inches, until they stood pressed against one another. "We were meant to be."

Astrid reached up, cupping his jaw in her hand. She smiled gently, then went up on her tiptoes, bringing their faces in line. "It certainly seems that way. Thank goodness for Hanukkah miracles."

Then she kissed him, and in that moment, there was only Astrid. The rest of the world fell away.

BUBBE LINDA'S MENORAH

LAVINIA KLEIN

AUTHOR'S NOTE

I CONVERTED TO JUDAISM TWENTY-SIX YEARS AGO AND OVER THOSE years I've raised three children, enjoying each holiday and custom. I've had the fun of adopting my husband's traditions, but also creating some new ones. I've hunted down the best *sufganiyot*, learned how to bake a great cholent, and enjoyed lighting multiple menorahs each Hanukkah. Writing this novella was extra special as it let me share the traditions my family has put into practice and also to learn about some new ones. I'd never heard of giving gifts on the fifth night, but I think I'll try it this year.

THE FIRST NIGHT

Baruch atah Adonai, Eloheinu, melekh ha'olam asher kidishanu b'mitz'votav
v'tzivanu l'had'lik neir shel Hanukkah. Amein.

Blessed are you, Lord, our God, sovereign of the universe, who
has sanctified us with His commandments and commanded us to
light the lights of Hanukkah. Amen.

THE MATCH FLICKERED AS THE TAPER LIT AND CAME TO LIFE. LIFTING
the *shamash*, the servant candle, Tamara used it to light the first
night's candle in the menorah. Tears formed in her eyes. It was the
first Hanukkah she had ever spent alone. The first time she had lit
the candles herself. For as long as she could remember her *bubbe* had
been the one holding the match, even last year when her heavily
veined hands had been trembling. Her grandmother would have
scolded her for lighting the candles so late in the evening, but she'd
worked a long day at the law firm and there'd been nothing to draw
her home. And then she'd been starved, and fixing something fast
had been the only thing on her mind. In fact, she'd almost decided
to skip the whole thing, but something had prevented her from
taking that step.

LAVINIA KLEIN
304 |

With great care, she lifted the old silver menorah and carried it to the window, setting it on the sill so its light could shine out at the quiet city, the city that until this moment had always felt like home. Now she felt nothing except alone, so alone.

She knew it was her own fault. Her brother, Tom, and his wife, Carol, had invited her to join their family, but she had refused. The thought of being out of place among his wife's bustling kin had been too much for her. Tamara had known that their intentions were the best, but it had been one thing too many. She would make the trip to the suburbs on Friday for their party on the fourth night. It was only two weeks since Bubbe Linda had died, two weeks that had seemed endless.

Sitting on the couch, Tamara curled her feet up under her and stared at the flickering light in the window. The menorah had been her grandmother's, brought by her parents from Russia when they emigrated. It had always been a connection to the past, a reminder of the heritage her own mother had so largely ignored. Another tear welled in her eye and she blinked it away. Bubbe Linda would not have wanted tears. She had shed far too many of them in her life and wanted something far different for Tamara.

She should have gone to her brother's. If his children had been a year or two older, she would have. There was something about watching small children celebrate the holidays that would make anyone smile. But, her brother's children, at six and eighteen months, were too young—and their mother too frazzled. Tamara's presence wouldn't have added any joy to their holiday and...

It was time to quit being so morbid. Perhaps she should open one gift of the small pile her grandmother had left for her, already purchased and wrapped weeks before her death. They hadn't been labeled or numbered or given any indication of who or when they were for, but Tamara had known what they were the second she'd seen them sitting on a shelf in her grandmother's closet. Now, they sat on her kitchen table, a lonely pile.

Standing, she went over and lifted an amazingly well-wrapped ball. Even with no markings she knew what it was. A pair of socks, probably cashmere in some fabulous color. It had been their joke. As a girl, Bubbe Linda had always gotten socks, and she'd chosen to continue the tradition with her daughter and grandchildren. Tamara's mother had considered it silly. "It made sense when Mom was young, but now we have more than enough. Who wants socks?"

Tamara wanted socks. Her grandmother chose far nicer ones than she would ever have chosen herself. And she loved tradition. A line from the song echoed through her mind. *Yes, tradition.*

Grandma Linda had said it was time for Tamara to start her own traditions. When she'd told Tamara that the menorah would be hers, she'd said that lighting it would always bring her luck and that, almost like birthday candles, she should dream of what she wanted as she lit it.

And what were her new traditions? She turned to the kitchen. She'd heated hash brown patties in the toaster, fast and easy, but she had eaten them with applesauce. She'd do better when she went to her brother's this weekend. There was a kosher bakery a few blocks away that made the best *sufganiyot*, jelly donuts made just for Hanukkah. Hmm, maybe she'd stop by on the way to work in the morning and treat herself to one. Donuts twice in one week couldn't be a bad thing.

Leaving the menorah burning, she went to the bathroom and brushed her teeth, then slipped into an extra-large T-shirt and prepared for bed. She had a momentary debate about whether to blow out the menorah. Her grandmother had always insisted on letting the candles gut themselves.

The narrow candles were more than half burned already, and with only the smallest twinge Tamara left them alone and crawled into bed, leaving the bedroom door open so that she could enjoy their glow.

For about ten minutes she stared at the moving shadows on the ceiling, letting her mind drift, thinking about the good memories instead of the sad ones of recent days. Laughing with Tom as they spun the dreidel, eating too much gelt even though the chocolate was never good—and just being a family. She should have gone to Tom's. Maybe she'd call him and go tomorrow. Bubbe Linda would have liked that.

306 | LAVINIA KLEIN

She let her eyes slip closed and this time her mind drifted toward the future instead of the past, to the many things she could do, the traditions she could keep. If she didn't go to Tom's she could make her own latkes and play holiday songs. Tonight had only felt sad because she'd let it. The best way to keep someone's memory alive was to live the life they'd have wanted for you. With that thought in mind, Tamara let herself drift off to sleep.

She awoke some time later to the smell of smoke or charred wood. She bolted up, only to realize the candles had sputtered out. Releasing a long sigh, she resettled as her thoughts returned to a handsome face with smiling clear green eyes and a smile that…

Her own eyes opened. The face that filled her thoughts was so familiar, someone she felt she'd known forever, but she couldn't think why. She certainly didn't know anybody who looked like that. Did she? A light smile traced her lips as she let herself slide off to sleep.

THE SECOND NIGHT

Struggling with her keys, Tamara juggled the bags of goodies she'd brought home from her brother's. Driving out had been a good decision, but now she was overloaded with food and presents. And she'd have to go shopping again. She'd only planned on exchanging gifts once with Tom's family, but that clearly was not their tradition. If she was going to go again, she'd need more presents, at least for the little ones. Well, she didn't need to worry about tomorrow. Tom and the kids were going to his in-laws and she wasn't quite prepared for that.

Damn. Where were her keys? Why did they always fall to the bottom of her bag? They'd been on the top only moments ago when she'd dropped them in after locking her car. A long stream of slow curses echoed through her mind as she searched.

"Can I help you with something?"

She jumped, dropping several Tupperware containers.

"Oh, I'm sorry. I didn't mean to startle you. I thought you'd heard the elevator and realized I was here." A deep voice continued from behind her.

She turned. There shouldn't be anybody else on her floor. Two of the other apartments were empty, and Mrs. Green, the elderly woman who owned the fourth, never had visitors after dark. Maybe he'd gotten off on the wrong floor.

The first thing she saw were the eyes—smiling green eyes. Eyes just like the ones she'd dreamed about. And the face. She couldn't picture it clearly, but there was no mistaking that smile. She'd only half remembered it, but as she gazed at it, at him, she knew it was exactly the one she had dreamed about.

"I hope I didn't really frighten you."

She kept staring. Who the hell was he and why was he here? Did she know him? No, she was sure she didn't, and yet she felt like she'd known him forever. She examined him more closely, letting her eyes run up long, jean-clad legs, over narrow hips, a grey T-shirt and a black—no, navy—hoodie. His shoulders were broad and the hoodie hung loosely off them, but there was no mistaking the power of the body beneath. This was not a man who carried any extra weight.

She stepped back, brushing against her door.

He withdrew, giving her more space. "I did frighten you. I'm so sorry. I'm new and…"

"Do I know you?" She finally found her voice.

His eyes narrowed slightly, examining her face. "I don't think so. I'm new to the city and the building. I just moved in yesterday."

"Oh," she said—and wasn't that a brilliant thing to say. "Did you come and look at the building earlier?"

Now he looked puzzled, those emerald eyes drawing together. "Well, yes, a month ago, when I knew I was coming here, when I got offered a job."

Another "Oh." She knew she knew him. "Are you an actor—a model?" That could explain why she found him so familiar.

He laughed, the sound echoing in the small hallway. "Hardly."

"Are you sure?" She had to know him from somewhere.

"I am actually." He stared at her, clearly wondering if she was a little crazy.

She felt a blush on her cheeks. "I guess you would be."

He didn't answer, but his eyes focused on her mouth.

Did she have something on her teeth? Her tongue swept over

them. She couldn't feel anything, but that wasn't always reliable. There'd been spinach in the salad and...

"I think your gravy is starting to leak."

She glanced down. "Damn." One of the Tupperware lids wasn't quite sealed, and she could see a small stain starting to spread. She bent down—just as he did the same. Their heads bumped. Blast.

Her head lifted, as a curse left her lips. He was so close. Those eyes, only inches from hers, those firm lips even closer. It was so easy to imagine... She breathed in—and smelled brisket.

Her eyes dropped again. Her hand reached out for the container. And so did his. His fingers brushed against hers, warm and strong. He pulled back.

She should be frightened, at least a little. It was late and she was alone with a strange man, an obviously very strong, strange man.

"Let me," she said.

He stood, leaving her to gaze up at those long legs. Damn, he was tall—maybe six-two.

"I'm sorry to have frightened you. I didn't feel it would be neighborly to not offer to help."

"It's fine. I just wasn't expecting anyone. Which condo did you move into?"

He nodded to the left.

Shit. She'd actually dreamed of buying that one and combining it with her own. The dream hadn't been realistic, but the condo had been empty for over six months and she'd let herself fantasize. Although if she did any fantasizing tonight it wasn't going to be about an apartment. "Welcome to the building."

He stepped back farther, although his eyes returned to her lips. "Thanks. Is there any of that I can help you with? It does smell great. Reminds me of growing up."

"No, I've got it now. My sister-in-law made it and insisted I bring a bunch home. Can I offer you some? She gave me about four times as much as I can possibly eat, but she's impossible to refuse."

"No, I couldn't." His eyes moved from her mouth to the Tupperware in her hands, but the look of lust remained.

Well, there were far worse things than being considered as

desirable as a well-cooked brisket. Bubbe Linda would probably have thought such a look would lead to marriage—although as she hadn't been the one to cook it, it might not be marriage to her. But, if he ever did get to taste her brisket… And she was not going to let that give her even more dirty thoughts. "I'd really love to give you some. I'd hate to have it go to waste and I was even thinking of cooking up one of my own this weekend. I won't be able to do that if I still have some sitting in the refrigerator."

She could sense his hesitation.

"Really, I mean it," she said.

"Fine. I don't have much food yet, so I'd be a fool to refuse. And that smells so good." It was hard to tell if the desire in his voice was for her or the brisket—although, given that she'd spilled some of it on herself when reclosing the container, it might be for both.

Her door swung open. "Come on in and I'll repackage it for you." And now she was inviting strangers into her condo—although she just couldn't think of him as a stranger.

"If you're sure . . ."

She wasn't sure if he was talking about coming in or still going on about the food. "I am sure." She stepped through the door.

He followed her. Suddenly her apartment seemed smaller, but not in a bad way. More intimate.

And what was it about him that had her mind working this way? Intimate. Jeez. He was hot, but…

Walking to the kitchen counter, she set the bags down and pulled out some smaller storage containers. She brought her lunch to work most days so she had plenty. She started to transfer the brisket.

He walked to the window and gazed out. "You have a nice view."

"I imagine yours is the same."

"True. It's one of the reasons I bought the place. And I should add that your condo is lovely. I like the light gray you've painted the walls."

"I wanted to keep it bright, but I was bored with white."

"I'm always a coward about color. I'm not sure I've ever lived anyplace that wasn't white. Well, I think my childhood bedroom had train wallpaper,"

That made her smile. "I had unicorns. I can still remember it when I close my eyes. I used to fall asleep thinking about which one I would choose."

"I did the same—with the trains, not unicorns."

They were quiet for a moment and he picked up the menorah off the window sill, rubbing softly at the silver, fingering the remains of wax left by the first candle. "You haven't lit it tonight."

He knew it was the second night of Hanukkah. She didn't know why she found that surprising; he had recognized the smell of a good brisket. "I celebrated at my brother's. I was debating whether to light it when I got home. It seems too late, and yet I almost feel like it wants to be lit."

"You should do it then."

Sealing up his packages of food she considered. "Why not? It's not like there are Hanukkah police."

He smiled. "I don't know. I think there might be and they steal all the gelt if you haven't been good."

"Is that something like Santa's list, they determine if you've been naughty or nice?"

"I am sure you're always nice."

"You don't think I could be a bit naughty?" Holding out three candles, she watched him set them in the menorah. Then with a quick flick, the match was burning and she lit the *shamash*. Her voice cracked only a little as she began the prayer, relief filling her when he began to chant along. She hadn't been prepared for a solo performance.

Both candles came to life with ease. It was so much easier on the first few nights than the last few when she always felt it was a game to finish lighting all the candles before the prayer was done.

It was nice not to be alone again. She glanced over at him and found him watching her, his eyes again focused on her mouth. In response, her gaze dropped to his lips. What would they feel like against her own? She imagined them hard and firm, but the skin smooth and soft. She could almost feel them parting beneath the pressure of her mouth...

He stepped back suddenly. "Let me grab that container and I'll be going. I'm sure you have to be up for work in the morning." He grabbed the brisket off the counter.

She blinked. Was he afraid she was going to attack him?

"I'll see you around. Thanks for the food." And he was gone.

That had been strange. Maybe he'd just realized the time. It was late. Or maybe he really had thought she was going to kiss him. And hell, she might have. There was just something about him...

And double hell, she didn't even know his name.

THE THIRD NIGHT

WHAT A DAY. VERONICA, HER BOSS, HAD KEPT TAMARA RUNNING from the moment she'd gotten to work until almost eight that evening. Veronica had offered to send out for dinner, but Tamara's mind had been on the brisket in her fridge—and she'd just wanted to get home, wanted to see if...

Nope, she wasn't going to think about him. She was going to heat her dinner, light the candles, have a glass of wine, and then have an early evening. She slipped a plate of leftovers into the microwave and then strolled to her bedroom to change. Pushing off her heels with her toes, she started to unbutton her blouse, longing to be free of her bra and confinement.

The bell rang.

Damn.

Hurriedly redoing the buttons on the navy silk, she scurried barefoot to the door. She wasn't expecting anyone, but sometimes the UPS guy came late this time of year. Once one neighbor buzzed him in, he made all his deliveries in one fell swoop. It was probably her mother's annual box from Harry & David's. She always seemed to think pears were the perfect Hanukkah gift. That is, if she remembered to send one at all.

With that thought in mind, Tamara opened the door—and stopped. Green eyes. Did she really not know his name?

"Hi," he said.

"Hi," she replied.

His eyes dropped to her chest, popped back up, down again.

She glanced down. Shit. She'd misbuttoned her shirt, leaving it gaping. Her teal and silver bra was clearly visible.

Did she rebutton it or pretend not to notice? She glanced up. He was staring at her face now, noticing her noticing. Well, that solved that. She quickly undid and redid the buttons.

He looked away, clearly unsure what to do. There wasn't really an appropriate comment he could make under the circumstances. "I brought back your container," he said, holding the Tupperware up, but still not looking at her.

"It's only a bra," she said, refusing to let things be awkward.

His eyes swung back to hers. "And it looks like a very nice one, quite festive, if I am allowed to say that."

Festive. Ahh, blue and silver. "Thank you, I suppose."

"I have several comments I could make about gift wrapping, but I wouldn't want them to be taken the wrong way—particularly when I don't even know your name."

So he'd realized that too—and it was a welcome break from talking about her bra. "Tamara. Tamara Stewart."

He held out his hand, the one not holding the container. "Josh Treble."

She took his hand and shook it. "Nice to meet you, Josh."

He smiled, the corners of his eyes crinkling in a way she immediately loved. "And nice to meet you, Tamara. I've always liked that name. Do they call you Tammy?"

She narrowed her eyes. "Not if they want to live."

He laughed. "Well, okay then. I'll not make that mistake, Tamara."

"Don't," she replied. "Shit, I didn't mean it that abruptly. Come in. I was just going to light the menorah again, if you want to join. There's a nice shiraz I was going to open if you want a glass."

"I'd like that. It's my first year spending the holidays alone, I've always gone back home to my parents' for at least the first night, and I'm discovering I don't like it much. My family was always very casual, but I find I miss even the few minutes we'd come together to light candles."

"I understand. My grandmother used to talk about how overdone it all is today, but she made sure that we were together when it was important. And there was always special food and music."

"Dreidel, dreidel, dreidel . . ." Josh started to sing, far too well.

"Exactly," she cut him off. "Although, it was an old album being played over and over. None of us dared to sing. I am afraid tone deafness runs in the family."

He smiled, the grin extending across his face and his eyes crinkling again. "I won't push it then. Now, where should I put these?" He held out the container.

She started to turn, offering to take it, just as he stepped toward her small kitchen. Suddenly they were inches apart. She sucked in a deep breath. He smelled of soap and citrus. He must have just showered. She shivered. His eyes dropped to hers, locked for a second, then slowly lowered to her lips, held. Another deep breath. Her gaze moved to his mouth, back to his eyes. His pupils were large, the irises the green of an angry sea—but he didn't look angry at all. Her gaze traveled back to his mouth—she could imagine it against hers, imagine...

But then she didn't have to imagine. He leaned forward, firm lips pressed against hers. Her belly contracted. His lips moved slowly, not forcing, not insisting—asking. Could a kiss ask? This one certainly did, and she answered the only way she knew. She kissed him back, letting her lips push back against his, enjoying and relishing.

His tongue skimmed the crease of her mouth.

She parted her lips in another answer, tasting the light burn of peppermint as his tongue eased in. It was all easy, all gentle—and yet the fires that began to rise within her were anything but. Her eyes closed, letting her experience the kiss fully, her mind filled with the feel of him.

His hands settled upon her hips, pulling her closer. She leaned into him, giving into the rising desire.

Their tongues danced and played, enjoyed.

Her hands crept up to his shoulders, drew his head closer.

She let her mind go, gave in.

He moved slightly, pressing her back against the wall, letting his body push hard against hers, her now-tight nipples rubbing against his chest, her hips against his—damn, could that really be him? She wanted to pull back and look, sure he couldn't actually be that...and then all thought was lost again as his lips continued to work their magic.

Minutes slipped by—if not hours.

His fingers went to the buttons of her blouse, his skin hot against her upper chest. She pressed closer. She needed this. God, she needed this. She wanted to devour him. Wanted to be devoured.

And then he was gone. Cool air hit her face, her chest.

"What?" She opened her eyes, blinking.

"I think we need to ease off." His voice was gruff with passion.

"Why?" She knew she was still blinking and could only hope she didn't look like a fish.

"We're neighbors."

"I know, but what does that have to do with anything?" she grumbled, even though thought was returning and with it understanding. It would be bad to have an awkward morning-after with somebody who lived next door. She stepped back herself.

The container was still on the counter. She clutched it to her chest and took the few steps necessary to hurriedly put it away. "No, don't say anything. I do understand. You're right. This was a stupid idea."

His hand landed on her shoulder, the fingers warm and strong. "I didn't say that, I just said we should slow down." He turned her to face him. "It's definitely not how I want to end the evening."

Her eyes dropped, even as she felt her cheeks flush. "I know. It's just hard not to feel a little unattractive when somebody steps back —I know it was the right thing—but I sort of feel like if you were into me enough you wouldn't have stopped." Fuck, why had she said that?

"Now, that was honest."

The flush grew deeper. "I know. It's a bad habit. When I'm nervous—and I am now—I tend to say whatever is on my mind."

"I think I might like that." His hand rose to stroke her cheek. "And you're wrong."

"I am?" The feel of his fingers was rapidly making her loose her train of thought.

"I stopped because I *am* into you. I don't want to have to duck into my condo because I hear you in the hallway."

"Oh."

"And I'm hoping to be invited over to light the menorah again tomorrow."

"Oh." And that was unfortunately high-pitched.

"Yes. Now if you point me to the wine, I'll pour us both a glass."

"It's over there." She pointed to the small wine rack under the counter. It held only a few bottles, but they were all good. "And, of course, you're invited. I can even make—Oh, shit. Tomorrow's Friday."

"Yes. Most people think Friday is a good thing."

"I know. It's just that I'm going to my brother's house and... I don't suppose you'd want to come with me? He's having a party so it's not like one more would matter." What was she thinking? He wouldn't want to go to some stranger's house for Hanukkah. They were hardly more than strangers themselves, even if they were strangers who kissed.

"I'd like that."

"You would?" And that was not how she'd meant to answer.

"Yes, I would, if you really mean it. I know you must have asked without really thinking about it."

"I can't deny that, but the more I think about it, the more I'd like it if you did." And that was the truth. "Although I should warn you—"

"Is your brother going to beat me up?" He shifted, and her eyes were drawn to the hard muscles of his chest.

"Hardly." She wished she could touch that chest again, slip her fingers up under his shirt, feel the heat of his skin. "No, it's just you know how we were talking about casual observance and overdone Hanukkahs? Well, my sister-in-law is all about extravagance. I gather her family's always been like that, but now that she has her own children it's incredible. She wants to be sure they never wish that they got to celebrate Christmas. And it might be a little crazy. And that's not even considering all the little cousins."

"I think I can handle it." Josh handed her a glass of the wine he'd just poured.

She took a sip, deep and fruity but not sweet. "We should light tonight's candles." She set down her glass, took the matches, and lit the *shamash*.

His deep voice began the prayer, and she let her own quieter voice echo his words as she lit the three candles. Her thoughts, however, were on tomorrow night and the hope that just maybe she'd get to kiss him again.

THE FOURTH NIGHT

As they drew up before the small suburban house, Tamara's belly tightened. What had she gotten herself into? Last night it had seemed like a brilliant idea to invite Josh. Today she wasn't so sure. What if he didn't like her brother's family? What if her brother didn't like him? On one level it didn't matter at all. She hardly knew him, but that didn't matter to her gut. She needed everybody to get along.

And Carol's family could be a lot. She loved her sister-in-law, but Carol tended to be unpredictable.

Deep breath in. Deep breath out.

"It's a cute place," Josh said.

"I can't decide if you're being genuine. Do you really like the huge inflatable menorah and that spinning dreidel that's taller than I am?"

He chuckled. "I didn't grow up with such things, but I do remember when I was a kid being jealous of all the inflatable Santas and snowmen. I never understood why we couldn't at least have a snowman. There's nothing Christian about Frosty."

"My grandmother would buy us chocolate bunnies the day after

Easter when they were on sale. She always said it was fine to eat pagan symbols."

Josh smiled. "My mother said almost the same thing. I've decided it was just an excuse to save money on candy. We were still eating those bunnies in July."

Tamara grinned back, and together they walked up the stairs to the house. The doorbell actually played *Dreidel, Dreidel, Dreidel* when pushed and Tamara found herself blushing and enjoying herself at the same time. It was impossible to take it all seriously.

Carol opened the door, and the smell of frying potatoes greeted them. There were hugs all around as Carol took their coats and welcomed them in. Almost instantly they were surround by what felt like a throng of children—the cousins—although Tamara knew there were only three of them. "Did you bring us presents? What do you have for us? Is it something good?"

Tamara turned to Josh and whispered apologetically, "Sorry, I know I warned you about the munchkins, but I probably should have said even more. At least, Carol's two are already in bed. They really are all great kids. I brought them bags of gelt last time, and I guess they remember. I dread next year when Carol's oldest will be old enough to join the parade."

He leaned toward her. "I hope you brought them something in that bag you had me carry in, or I'm not sure that we'll escape alive."

Before she could answer, Carol spoke up. "Be quiet, you heathens. You know we don't think about presents until after dinner, and it's never polite to demand. Now come along. There are still potatoes to be grated." She walked from the room.

There were quiet grumbles, but the small crowd dispersed. Jane, the youngest girl, turned back. "You know you're my favorite, Auntie Tamara."

After she left, Tamara turned to Josh again. "That one's going far. She's only met me once, but she sure knows how to charm. Did you see her flash those big blue eyes?"

"It was hard to miss. I bet you were just as effective when you flashed those chocolate browns."

Her earlier blush returned. There was something about this man that kept her constantly on edge—and yet strangely comfortable. She couldn't remember anyone making her feel this way before. "I'm not sure I ever tried. My grandmother would have given me a swat if I asked for gifts." Her mind suddenly returned to the small pile waiting at home. She would have to open one when she was home later.

"Too well-behaved, were you? I thought you said something about being naughty the other night."

She lowered her eyes. "It's a skill I'm working on."

Carol called from the next room. "Hurry up, you two. The first batch of latkes is coming out of the pan and they're best when they're hot."

Three hours later, they waddled down the hall to her condo, bellies full to bursting. "I'm not sure I'm going to survive this holiday," Tamara complained. "I don't think I've ever eaten so much for so many days in a row. Normally I have some type of store-bought latke the first night and then make them myself one weekend day. Bubbe Linda used to invite me over and we'd grate the potatoes together and then take turns frying batches. Her recipe was different than the one Carol's family uses. The potatoes were much more finely ground. I can't imagine what she'd have thought of the party tonight—although she'd have been happy the family was together. She always said that was the most important thing."

"She wasn't wrong about that. Her recipe sounds like my mother's. We'll have to compare sometime. My mother would have complained that the ones tonight weren't real latkes, more like hash browns. I'll never forget the work that went into getting the mix grated fine enough. My knuckles used to get so scraped up," Josh stopped before her door. "I never did learn to do it without taking off half a finger."

"Bubbe Linda used to insist that her recipe called for a dash of fresh finger blood or else they wouldn't taste right. My brother gave her a food processor, but she still insisted on doing them by hand."

"I think my mother would have liked her. She felt the same way." He waited as she fit her key in the lock.

322 | LAVINIA KLEIN

Did she invite him in? Would that be too overt? She'd spent the last hours gazing at his chest in the tight tee and dreaming of when she'd have her hands on him again. Still, she remembered how he'd backed off last night, how he'd been afraid to make things awkward between them. On the other hand, she would have invited him in for another glass of wine if he'd simply been a friend…

"Are you planning to light your menorah? I mean I know we just did it at your brother's, but…"

And that made it so much easier. "But I don't want it to feel left out." She smiled. They'd had this discussion the other night and come to the same conclusion. "Come on in and I'll light it."

He picked up the bag of gifts she'd received and followed her in. "You were right about your sister-in-law's family. I don't think I've ever seen Hanukkah celebrated with such—such style. I had a roommate in college whose mother was the same about Christmas, but…"

"I know. There just aren't really words."

"And I'm glad you brought gifts. It would never have occurred to me to bring more than flowers or a bottle of wine. You'll have to let me contribute."

"That's really not necessary. And you have to remember I was there Tuesday, so I knew what was coming."

"I insist on giving my share for the gifts. I mean, they even had something for me. If you let me pay my part, then I won't feel so strange about near strangers buying me an expensive belt."

"No. I was happy to—they're my family. And I have to confess the belt was probably a regift if I know my family."

He smiled. "And if I insist?"

"Are you going to go all dominant on me?" Her voice was quiet as her mouth grew dry. It was all too easy to imagine Josh acting quite dominant.

"Would you like me to?"

Her breathing stopped as their eyes met. It was clear that his mind was flowing in exactly the same direction as hers. "I—"

And before she could get another word out, his lips were on hers, his hands sliding behind her to pull her tight against his chest.

The lace of her bra abraded her nipples and she found the ache almost unbearable. Her fingers tangled in his hair, drawing his head down, letting her mouth devour his.

His hands slipped over her ass, sliding under the soft wool of her sweater, pushing it up. "I need to see you," he whispered. "I need to see all of you. I've been dreaming of that blue and silver bra, of unwrapping you like a gift." He stepped back and yanked—pulled was far too gentle a word—her sweater over her head. It shouldn't have been sexy, but it made her feel the heat of his desire, and her insides began to melt.

As her sweater fell to the floor, his eyes locked on her. There was definite focus on her breasts, but still she felt as if he saw all of her. His pupils grew until his eyes looked almost black. His Adam's apple bobbed as he swallowed—hard.

She glanced down at herself. She was wearing her light blue lace bra. It was one of her favorites, the lace slightly translucent so that her nipples showed through clearly. Lifting one arm, she let her fingers slowly caress and lift her left breast, the thumb rubbing over the rigid peak. She shivered.

He moaned—or was that a growl?

Their eyes met, and she could see just how much he wanted, needed.

She stepped toward him, her hands moving to the bottom of his tee. "My turn." She started to lift and he bent slightly so that she could pull the shirt over his head. And then it was her turn to stare. The man was beautiful, a classical statue come to life, the chest wide and defined, the slow taper to a narrow waist, the ripple of muscle across his stomach. She'd always heard about the true six-pack, had seen them in pictures, but never before had she been this close to one. With one trembling index finger she reached out, letting first the nail and then the tip of the finger brush his warm flesh. His muscles strained against his skin, hard and firm, so different from her own soft belly.

When her whole hand was flat against him, she stroked up, relishing the satin of his skin, enjoying the soft tickle of the smattering of hairs. She ran her hand back down. Up.

He caught hold of her as she headed down again. "Stop. I don't want to embarrass myself."

"I don't think you have anything to be embarrassed about." Her eyes dropped, focusing on the bulge behind his zipper. If she'd been curious about what his chest looked like, then her mind could only boggle with...

His chest expanded beneath her touch as he drew in a massive breath. "You know what I mean."

She stepped closer, letting the tips of her breasts rub against his chest and instantly wishing she could press herself tight. She felt the need for pressure, the need to feel his flesh against her own. She looked deep into his eyes, trying to let him see all that she was feeling, all that she wanted, desired.

He slipped one of his hands up, flicking his thumb over her nipple, again, and then again. Her insides grew tight. It felt so good and yet it made her want more—more—more. A soft moan left her lips.

He pulled back slightly and bent forward until his lips could close around one lace-clad nipple. He sucked hard. She gave a small cry, her whole body moving toward him. He sucked deeper.

"More, more," she heard her own voice pant. It was unbelievable. She was ready to come and he'd barely touched her.

His lips widened, taking more of her in. One hand slid over her back while the other slipped lower, working up her skirt until it could slide under, could graze the damp fabric of her panties. His fingers brushed over her clit and her whole body shuddered. His lips pulled tighter, his tongue rubbing hard against her nipple. Her body was one endless sensation, a sensation that coiled tighter. He stroked between her legs again and she moaned, loud and clear, her head falling back. A fingertip slipped into her panties, stroked her skin to skin—and she lost it. Her body clenched and released, an endless spasm of pleasure. She cried his name even as color swirled before her eyes.

She fell back limp against the wall, might have fallen to the floor if he had not still held her.

"And you were saying you'd embarrass yourself," she breathed once the world began to right itself.

"That was magnificent. Perfect," he said, pulling her toward him again to lay an unbelievably soft kiss against her lips. He let her skirt fall, smoothing the fabric, then pulled away, bending to retrieve her sweater. He handed it to her. "Let's light the menorah."

What? She could only blink at him. "But..." Her gaze dropped to the erection that still tented the front of his pants.

He caught her hands, brought them to his lips and kissed them. "My family always opens the biggest gift on the fifth night."

"The fifth night?" None of this was making sense.

"Yes, the fifth night is the first night that the majority of the candles are lit. It symbolizes light overcoming darkness. It is a moment to be celebrated—and don't worry, I want to celebrate. I'm just a believer in delayed gratification. It's why I never wanted to open more than a token gift on the first night."

"Then why?" She gestured to herself as she began to pull on her sweater.

His hand stopped her, his eyes moving again to her breasts, to the damp nipple trying to poke through the lace. Her thighs clenched as she felt desire rise again.

He pulled his hand away, letting her finish putting on the sweater. "Just because I want to wait doesn't mean I want you to. Plus, watching you come was the best gift I could have gotten tonight."

"Better than a hundred-dollar belt?" She laughed, trying to bring her emotions under control.

"Much better," he answered. And he handed her the box of matches from the windowsill.

With shaking hands, she lit the candles, letting his warm voice surround her, trying to concentrate on the moment, but wishing she had a few seconds of peace to try and understand what was happening between them. She could have really used Bubbe Linda's advice right about now.

THE FIFTH NIGHT

SHE SHOULD HAVE MADE MORE DEFINITE PLANS WITH JOSH. THEY
hadn't set a time or said if they would have dinner together—and
she didn't have his phone number or email. It would be easy enough
to walk the fifteen steps to knock on his door—maybe he'd offer to
show her his condo—but something held her back. She knew she'd
do it soon if she didn't hear from him, but for the moment she'd
make herself wait.

She paced back and forth a few times and then forced herself to
sit down. Should she make tea? That would be relaxing. What about
a bath—with lots of bubbles? She could shave her legs again. That
would probably be good, given where she was hoping this evening
would end.

She glanced out the window. The sun was still relatively high in
the sky. Josh probably wouldn't show up until it was time to light the
menorah. Why was she so bloody impatient?

She stood and began to pace again. Hell, she didn't even want
him to come now. She wasn't ready. Glancing down at her grubby
long-sleeved tee, she grimaced. Her jeans weren't even cute ones
that hugged her butt. She definitely needed to change, but first she'd
make the tea and take that bath.

Then if she still hadn't heard from him, she'd go knock on his door. It wasn't like he had another way to contact her. Not having a phone number went both ways.

Why the hell hadn't they traded numbers? It was almost unbelievable that they hadn't. What if he hadn't been able to make it to her brother's yesterday or had been running late? Who didn't trade numbers?

She filled a mug with water and a teabag and shoved it in the microwave. Normally she was a strong believer in doing things right, rinsing a pot with boiling water, measuring out the tea leaves, letting it steep for just the right amount of time—but sometimes fast was best.

She waited for the beep and went to fill the tub.

It was hard to be patient. She'd had a wonderful time with him last night and her brother had called today to say how much he and Carol liked him. Josh had been a perfectly charming companion and—she squeezed her thighs together—showed every indication of being an incredible lover. He'd certainly found her clit on the first try. That was not something to be undervalued. If only she could relax, feel more at ease.

And yet, it wasn't the sex that had her nervous. It was the feeling that this could be something special. She couldn't remember a man ever making her feel so comfortable and so nervous at the same time. And the respect that he showed her... She really was beginning to believe that he kept backing off because he wanted this to mean something.

A fifth-night gift. She liked the idea. Could he be the light that would overcome the sadness that had held her since Bubbe Linda's passing?

There was a knock at the door.

Shit. Why did that always happen when she took a bath—or a shower for that matter. UPS and FedEx must have a sensor that let them know when the worst time to ring the bell would be.

Only it probably wasn't UPS. It was very probably Josh. She quickly stood and grabbed her fluffy robe. Maybe, this was how it was supposed to be. Maybe he'd just be there and without any awkwardness they could proceed to the next step. What man could refuse a wet, willing woman in a soft white bathrobe?

She rushed from the bathroom and toward her door, just as a thick blue envelope slid under it. Josh must think she wasn't home. It would be so much better to just talk to him in person—and to ask him for a phone number, although maybe that was in the note.

Without further thought she opened the door—and stood staring at the teenager who stood there, gaping at the bare flesh at the neckline of her robe. Quickly she gathered the edges together, grasping them high on her chest. "Can I help you?"

"No—ahhh—maybe—yes," the boy stumbled. "It's all in the card."

"Card?" she asked, a moment before she realized that she knew exactly what card.

"I slipped it under the door."

She turned and, careful not to flash the poor boy, lifted the envelope. "What is it?"

"I don't really know, but when I delivered Mr. Treble his lunch, he asked me if I could drop it off. He tipped me extra to do it."

Mr. Treble. Josh. "He couldn't just carry it down one door?"

The boy's brows drew together. "I don't know what you mean. He's at the hospital. I was delivering his late lunch from the bodega down the street, Emile's."

Hospital. Hospital. Her heart missed a beat.

No, she was going to stay calm. Not jump to assumptions, use her brain.

The bodega. She knew the place well, although she didn't recognize the kid. "What's Josh doing in the hospital?" The worry would not let go.

The kid shrugged.

Could he have been injured? Or somebody he knew? It couldn't be too bad if he was having lunch delivered. Still . . . She needed to know more.

The kid started to turn away.

"Hold on," she said. "Let me get you a little something."

The kid smiled. "No, that's okay. Mr. Treble was very generous."
He gave a little wave and walked to the elevator.

She let him go.

Deep breath. Josh wouldn't be giving generous tips if there was
a problem.

Holding the card in her hand, Tamara closed her door and
walked to the light of the window. How did she know so little about
Josh? Last night might only be the third night she'd known him, but
surely she should know more, know what he was doing at a hospital.
Did he work there? He'd kept her talking about herself and her
family and somehow, she hadn't asked him the most basic of
questions—or had he told her when she wasn't fully listening? That
was something that would have to change.

She ripped open the envelope and stared at the card. A smiling
menorah met her gaze. It looked remarkably like the one on Carol's
front lawn. She opened the card.

Tamara,

    *I saw this in a gift shop this morning and couldn't resist. I should have
something cute to say, but I'll have to let the smile speak for itself. I was hoping
to give it to you tonight, but something's come up. And I am scheduled to work
tomorrow night, too. Is it selfish to hope you're as disappointed as I am? You
can give me a call and leave a message.*

    Miss you and sorry,

    Josh

And yes, disappointment filled her. She'd really been looking
forward to tonight in so many different ways. She hoped somebody
wasn't hurt, but surely he would have told her if that was the case.
And it was a pity they'd never had time to discuss their schedules. It
would have been nice if she'd known he wouldn't be free tomorrow.

No, that wasn't quite fair. He'd probably been intending to tell
her tonight. She shoved the card back in its envelope and strode to
the bathroom. Dropping her robe and sinking into the not quite hot
water, she slapped a hand down, sending water splashing.

It probably wasn't fair to be angry, but she couldn't quite help it.

She was as angry at herself as at him. There were so many questions she should have asked. Damn.

A few hours later, as she heated a plate of Carol's leftovers, she had come to peace with Josh's absence. It would have been nice if he had given her a little more information—and even nicer if he'd actually given her his phone number!—but she'd realized that maybe she needed these couple of days to not get too swept up. It had been easy to be overcome by passion and to not take the time to realize how much she didn't know about him—and it wasn't just his phone number.

She didn't know exactly what he did for a living. She knew he'd gone to business school and had worked as a consultant right after, but somehow their conversation had never made it as far as what he actually did for a living now and what had brought him to the city. And how did he have the money to buy a condo? Her grandmother had given her the down-payment for hers, and she'd chosen to live frugally for several years to afford the mortgage.

They'd talked for hours and yet somehow not covered some of the very basics. She knew about his family, had heard stories of his youth, and had discussed music and literature. They'd even talked about who their favorite Harry Potter characters were. How could she not know what he did for a living?

Going to the window, she picked up the matches and lit the *shamash*. She'd actually debated not lighting the menorah when she learned Josh wasn't coming, but had quickly realized how foolish and wrong that was. Lighting the menorah was about far more than a relationship. It was a symbol of freedom and standing up for one's beliefs.

Trying to concentrate on that, she lit the five candles with her thoughts only straying slightly to what could have happened this evening and the hope that Josh might actually be all that he seemed.

THE SIXTH NIGHT

THERE WAS A BOX OUTSIDE HER DOOR. HMM. SHE WASN'T expecting anything? A Hannukah gift?

Josh? She couldn't help the little bit of hope that rose in her chest. Had he left her something?

She picked up the box and opened the door to her condo. Walking in, she set her purse on the counter. She'd spent a lazy day touring museums with friends, followed by a stop at the corner wine bar. It had been a lovely day, and she'd planned a lovely night. Instead of being lonely she intended to celebrate—all by herself. She'd play Hanukkah music. She'd eat a big salad—she needed a break from meat and fried potatoes. And then after she'd lit the menorah, she'd pull out her old photo albums and remember all the good times. Bubbe's small pile of gifts was also calling her, and she planned to open several.

Lifting the box up, she examined it. Simple white cardboard. Ahh, there was something stuck in the side, a small note card. She pulled it out, dislodging the top of the box slightly. A most delectable scent wafted up. She knew exactly what was in the box.

She looked at the note.

Hi, I hope you're not mad at me. You haven't called or texted. I brought these over as a peace offering to share, but you weren't here. Gotta go to work. Text me.

Josh

Only, of course, he still hadn't given her his number. Idiot, she thought with a smile.

Still, she opened the box. Just as she'd thought—*sufganiyot,* the traditional Hanukkah jelly donuts. There were only two of them, but that was perfect. If he'd given her a whole dozen, she'd probably have eaten half of them. She breathed in their delicious sugar and vanilla smell. So good. Almost better than sex. And her mind was right back there.

She wished he was here.

She was glad he wasn't. It was good to have time to decide her priorities.

Who was she kidding? She missed him. Maybe she should save the donuts to eat with him? They'd make a great breakfast. It was so sweet that he'd brought them. But no, they were never as good the second day, and she really didn't know his schedule.

Still, she could write her own note and slip it under his door. If he thought she had his number then he'd assume she was ghosting him if she didn't do anything.

But dinner and candles first. He evidently wasn't going to be home any time soon.

She asked Spotify to play Hanukkah music and sang along as she fixed her salad—something she would never have done if anyone else had been there to hear. A nice glass of wine and dinner was complete—except for a donut. That she would save until the candles were lit.

Finishing up, she moved to the window and whispered the blessing as she lit the candles, gazing out at the city below and hoping that they gave hope and comfort to someone walking in the dark. Of course, her mind also turned to Josh and her hopes for what tomorrow night would bring, good conversation and sex—

although maybe it would be sex and then good conversation. She found herself most impatient.

With the last candle lit, she walked to her Bubbe's small pile of gifts. There were three of them. She knew that the small, long thin box would contain Gelt for Grownups, dark chocolate with a sprinkling of salt. Since they'd discovered it a few years ago, it had become an annual tradition. Her mouth watered at the thought of the taste.

She ripped open the paper and took the clear box of chocolates to the couch along with her wine and the donuts. She'd already pulled out all the photo albums. She might still wish Josh was here, but it was not at all a bad way to spend an evening.

THE SEVENTH NIGHT

THE PHONE BEEPED. INSTANTLY, TAMARA WAS WIDE AWAKE. HER fingers shook slightly as she reached toward the bedside table—and not just because her brain was not waking as fast as the rest of her.

Hi. Sending you a text because I don't want to wake you. I was so glad to get your note. I put my business card with all my numbers in the envelope. Didn't you get it? Sorry. See you tonight. 7:00. Let me know if that doesn't work, otherwise I'll assume it does.

A smile spread across her face. He wanted to see her. She hadn't really had any doubt, but it was nice to be able to plan. And a business card? Who did that? Could she have missed it? She had to admit that she might have. A brief wave of regret washed through her. She'd been so eager to read his card that she hadn't looked—and she'd thrown the envelope away right after. Well, she had his number now, and that's what was important.

Her fingers moved to text him back, but she stopped. He hadn't wanted to wake her. He was probably curling up to sleep now himself. She let herself picture that for a moment. If he'd been working all night, she didn't want to wake him. And besides she still had an hour to sleep before she had to get up and get ready for work. It would be foolish not to take advantage of that—and it would give her a few more minutes to dream about his sleeping face.

~

Her head was killing her. She'd taken a couple of ibuprofen before she left the law firm, but they hadn't kicked in yet. Her boss, Veronica, was normally fairly easy-going, but today she'd been on a tear. Briefs in one of her cases had been due, and it had been an all-day affair trying to be sure that every I was dotted and every T crossed. Luckily, one of the other legal assistants had been on call to stay late or Tamara would have had to—well not quite *had to*, but she would have stayed. Normally she loved her job. Loved her boss. Today had not been one of those days.

But it was going to be one of those nights. She was determined to make it so. She glanced at the clock. 6:30. Did she have time to make something? She'd planned to buy some salmon on the way home, but she'd been running so late she hadn't wanted to risk it. She opened the refrigerator. There were still some leftovers, but she had to admit they held little appeal. She had ice cream and fudge sauce. They could do dessert for dinner.

Instantly her mind was filled with all the things she could do with that fudge sauce. It would be a shame to waste it on ice cream.

So not leftovers, not ice cream, not tomato soup or ramen, not the hot dog that had been there almost as long as she could remember.

She picked up her phone.

Tamara: *I know it's not Christmas, but how do you feel about Chinese?*

Josh: *Did your family really do that?*

No. LOL.

Mine didn't either. But Chinese is great.

Any likes or dislikes?

No jellyfish or chicken's feet.

I think I can handle that. Dumplings?

Always.

See you in a bit.

See you.

Deep breath in. Deep breath out. There hadn't been a bit of flirting in that conversation, but still she was hot and bothered—and having vaguely erotic thoughts about Chinese food. It was one thing to fantasize about hot fudge, it was something else when your thoughts turned to hot and sour soup.

She placed the order and then changed quickly, followed by a mirror check. Oversize, soft, white cashmere sweater that gave her skin the appearance of a little more color than it actually had at this time of year. Tight black jeans. Were they too tight? She didn't want them to be hard to get out off—or to make her look like she was trying too hard. Maybe faded boyfriend jeans that just slipped on and off? She was overthinking this. No shoes, but comfy dark socks. Nothing would be less romantic than having gray bottoms. Her apartment was clean, but... Yep, completely overthinking.

Her makeup looked great, soft and natural with just a hint of cherry flavor to her gloss. That made her smile. Some tricks she'd learned in high school were still valuable. What else? Tiny gold hoops that were comfortable to sleep in because you never knew.

Well, that settled it for her. What about the condo? Everything was clean and tidy. The sheets were fresh. She had bagels in the freezer and coffee and cream cheese. She didn't know if he'd stay over on a weeknight, but she wanted to be prepared.

What else? What else?

She really was a nervous wreck.

Deep breath in. Deep breath out. It was only Josh. They'd always had a good time together and nothing was going to happen that she didn't want to happen. Granted she wanted it *all* to happen.

There was a knock at the door.

It had to be Josh. It was too soon to be the food.

One more quick look.

She opened the door.

For a moment they just stared at each other. A slow smile spread across his cheeks and she felt a matching one on her own face. "Hi," she said.

"Hi."

More staring. Damn, he looked good—light blue button-down and khakis. Slightly more formal than the jeans and tee he usually wore, but not too much so. His hair was still slightly damp and a barely-there scent of soap wafted from him. Reaching out, she brushed a tiny fleck of shaving cream from in front of his ear.

He turned into her touch, kissing her palm. Heat ran up her arm and settled in her chest—and lower.

She didn't want to move. This was one of those silly moments she wished would last forever.

"Are you going to ask me in?" he asked.

Her cheeks heated as she stepped back, gesturing him in. "Of course. I'm sorry. It's just—"

"I do understand," he cut her off. "I could spend a couple of hours just looking at you, but I have a feeling that someone is watching."

A small chuckle. "That would be Mrs. Green. She likes to know what's going on, but she's good-hearted and I actually like knowing somebody is keeping an eye on things."

"I have to admit, there are some things I don't want anyone keeping an eye on."

"I can't disagree with that."

"Oh, these are for you." He held out a bunch of white roses tied with a silver bow.

"Thank you. They're beautiful."

"I wanted to get you something and I wasn't sure if a real gift was appropriate. I thought about more donuts, but . . ."

Another chuckle. "I'll never say no to donuts, but I love flowers, particularly at this time of year when the world can be so gray." And she could only be glad that he hadn't brought her a "real" gift. She hadn't gotten him anything. She'd thought of it, but nothing had struck her as quite right.

"Oh, should I have bought something with color?"

"These are lovely. I actually love white blossoms. They're so pure."

"I have to confess that, as a guy, if I have flowers in the house, I really like white. I'm not sure why, but they don't seem as girly—not that there's anything wrong with girly—but... There's no good way to end this."

"No, there's not, but I understand. I'm surprised that you have flowers at all."

"I don't all that often, but I admit that's more of a time thing than anything else. I tried plants, but I have a black thumb. At least with flowers you know they're supposed to die and then you buy new ones."

She laughed. "That's kind of a dismal statement."

"I don't know. I see it as a chance for renewal every now and then."

"I guess so. Can I get you some wine or a beer?"

"If we're having Chinese I'll go for a beer."

"Me too." She grabbed bottles from the bottom of the fridge and took hers to the living room, sitting down on the couch.

Josh sat beside her and reached out to draw her legs into his lap. He started to knead her feet through the socks.

"Oh my God, that feels good. How did you know that was just what I needed? I think it's helping the slight headache I had. Does that make any sense?"

He dug his thumbs in deeper.

"Forgive me, but I think this may be better than sex."

"I hope you're not saying that in a couple of hours."

Was she ever going to stop blushing? Before she could respond further there was a knock at the door. "The food's here."

"I'll get it," he said.

She should protest, but she wanted another minute to relish the party going on in her feet. "It's already paid for, including the tip. I put plates and utensils out on the counter."

"Just a minute then."

There was a brief murmur of voices at the door and then he rejoined her. "You're right about Mrs. Green. I saw her peeking out."

Tamara only smiled in response.

He started to open the packages. "This all looks great. You'll have to give me the number for the place."

"I'm sure there's a menu in one of the bags."

"Can I serve you?"

"Please." Her mind filled briefly with an image of him on his knees offering to serve her in a very different way. She snorted.

He looked up.

"I'm sorry. I just had a strange thought."

"If it's anything like the one I was having, I'm not sure strange is the right word." His gaze had suddenly become hot and heavy.

She swallowed. "You know we can just reheat the containers later."

He froze halfway to placing a spoonful of cashew chicken on her plate. "Don't tempt me."

"Why not?" She let her eyes move over him, making it very clear just how serious she was.

He put the spoon back in the container. "I was determined to be good. I'm like Carol with the kids. I normally wait until after dinner and candle lighting to open my gifts."

"And what if I want to open them now? I let you have your way the last time. I think this time I should get to decide."

"It wouldn't be very polite to overrule a lady."

"And what if I don't want to be a lady?" She rose on her knees and in one swift gesture pulled her sweater over her head.

He froze, eyes wide, staring. "And I was wondering what your bra would look like, given how cute the last ones have been." He sounded half strangled.

She grinned, a wide Cheshire Cat smile. "Well aren't you glad I made it easy for you by not wearing one, then?"

The look in his eyes as they moved over her... The inner muscles of her thighs tightened, and her breath quickened. His gaze trailed down and then back up. She didn't have large breasts, but she'd always thought they had a very pretty shape. And judging by the fixation of his stare, he agreed. She shivered slightly. A few moments ago, she'd been thinking about Chinese food and conversation, but now she had only one desire. "I think I'd like to unwrap my gift now. I was never the patient child you were. I always swore that as soon as I was on my own, I'd open my gifts right away —and this seems like a good chance to start."

For the briefest of moments, his eyes darted from her to the pile of Bubbe's remaining gifts, before coming back to her breasts. "I see that."

At any other time, she would have been distracted, wondered why she was so slow to open the rest of the presents. But not now. Now she had only one thought.

She moved forward, raising a hand to run a finger over the hard muscles of his chest, hard and firm beneath his thin, cotton shirt. She traced small circles until she reached the top button of his shirt. He started to reach for one of her breasts, but she pushed his hand away. "My turn. You had yours the other day."

His lips tightened, but his arm fell back to his side.

She played with the button for a moment before releasing it. Repeating the gesture with each button, she moved down his shirt until it was half undone. The she pushed the fabric wide and pressed tiny kisses upon his chest, savoring the slight roughness of his scattering of hairs. She pulled in a breath, relishing the smell of soap and man.

His hands twitched at his sides, curling and uncurling.

She smiled inwardly at the sign that he was not quite as patient as he would like to appear. She slowed her kisses and felt his chest vibrate as she moved to circle one hard brown nipple with her tongue.

"You're killing me," he groaned.

"I know," she answered, moving to the other nipple before allowing her fingers to rise up and play with his buttons again. When she reached the last one, she spread his shirt wide and used both her hands to push him back on the couch. Once she had him positioned, she straddled him and stared down at the perfection of his hard chest. "You're not a fireman or something are you? Some job that forces you to stay in shape?"

He chuckled, and she could feel it deep in her core as her thighs pressed tight into him. "No. I have to thank genetics for most of it. Although I do run when I have time, and there's a gym at the hospital."

Hospital again? She must follow up on that. She assumed it was where he worked, but now wasn't the time for questions. "Well, thank your genetics then." With both hands, she began to trace patterns again, secretly branding him with her initials. She began to raise and lower her hips, moving as if she were riding, each time lingering a little longer when she rubbed against his more than ample erection.

"Seriously, are you trying to kill me?"

"Just a little payback for the other night."

"I hardly think this is equal."

She smiled. "I do promise it won't end in the same fashion. But you are proving that you're just as patient as you pretended, so perhaps a little treat." She leaned forward until her breasts hovered above his mouth like ripe peaches. "Which do you prefer? The left or the right?"

"Is there a correct answer to that question?" He licked his lips, his eyes absolutely fixed on her swollen nipples.

She debated for the briefest of seconds. "No, I don't think there is."

"Then I'll go left. For some reason she seems more needy."

She shifted slightly in answer and then almost rose in the air as his lips fastened on her, pulling hard. The sensation was unbelievable. She'd expected something soft and tentative, but he was all business. She started to pull back, wanting to regain control, but his hands came up on either side of her and with a sudden twist she was underneath him, his hips sliding down between her legs as his mouth kept its possession of her breast.

Once he was braced, his right hand rose to cup her other breast, the thumb and forefinger closing on her rigid nipple, pulling and releasing in rhythm to his lips on the other side. She had the slightest urge to fight him, to retake the power, but his mouth felt too damn good. Almost against her will, a long, slow moan escaped from her lips.

He scraped his teeth over one nipple while abrading the other with his nails. Her breathing began to speed and the moans that left her now were anything but slow.

"Can you come just from someone playing with your tits?" He breathed against her chest.

If she hadn't already been so flushed, she was sure that heat would have risen at the question. "It's happened."

"You are so perfect." His lips closed, and he began to suck harder.

Damn. She could feel the tightness growing between her legs, feel the spring coiling. Her head began to turn from side to side. Her thighs pressed tighter and tighter against the sides of his legs as she tried to work herself closer to his groin, wanting, needing to rub against him, to feel his fullness against her softness.

A wave of pleasure began to rise within her, and she pulled back. "No. I don't want to until you're in me. I want to feel you, all of you."

"You can always come a second time." He closed his lips again, sucking harder.

She pushed against him, insistent.

He hesitated and then pulled back, hurriedly moving to stand beside the couch. His hands went to his waistband even as he toed off his shoes. Her hands went to her own zipper and then hesitated. Instead she reached over, pushing his aside. She could tell he wanted to just hurry and finish the job himself, but he dropped his hands. She slid off the couch to kneel before him. Her fingers were surprisingly sure as they undid the button and slid down his zipper. Her mouth might be dry, her eyes wide, but her hands were eager.

One hard pull, and his pants were down.

"You have dreidels on your boxers," she said with a little laugh.

"They seemed appropriate."

"I guess we *have* been talking about wrapping. I should warn you I normally just rip the paper off." She placed a hand on either side of his hips.

"Go for it."

And she did. If her eyes had been wide before, now they must be huge. She only barely managed to hold back her whisper of "Holy Fuck." She'd always laughed at books where the heroine didn't believe he would fit. Hell, babies came out of vaginas—and even this dick was far smaller than a baby's head—but Holy Fuck.

She glanced up at him and found him staring down at her. Slowly and deliberately she licked her lips. It would be like sucking on the best popsicle ever.

"It's my turn to say no. You wanted me in you and that's how this is going to happen. Besides, it's my turn to rip off the wrapping."

"You're actually turning down a blow job?" She'd never known a man to do that before.

"Let's say I am postponing. I've been dreaming of this for almost a week and I'm not going to mess it up."

He held out a hand and helped her to her feet.

She pursed her lips but made sure he could see the humor in her eyes. Once she was standing, he pulled her close for one endless, devouring kiss, their tongues moving in practice of what was to come.

His hands slid over her ass, gripping her, and it was impossible not to be aware of the full erection pressed tight against her belly. Again, she was tempted to drop to her knees. She really did want to taste and tease, but his grip held her in place.

At last the kiss ended, and for a long moment he just stood staring down at her. Then his hands slipped around to the front of her pants, tugging at the button.

"I'm afraid there won't be much ripping action here," she said. "These jeans are more of a slide and wiggle and slide again type."

He stepped back. "Then I'll be happy to watch you wiggle."

She complied and the look in his eyes made her shimmy a little extra.

When her pants slid past her hips, he gave a little laugh. "You have a dreidel on the front of your panties—and it's smiling."

"I guess great minds think alike and all that."

His gaze swept over her. "I certainly hope we're thinking alike right now."

She stepped back and sat on the couch, spreading her legs wide. She hadn't been quite brave enough to remove her panties.

He stepped between her legs and his gaze moved from her breasts to her undies and then back again. "You are the best type of gift. I don't know where to begin."

"Your choice," she said.

His gaze moved back to her panties and he dropped his head. His mouth landed on the damp silk. His tongue moved hard against the fabric, rubbing it against her. Was there anything this man didn't know how to do perfectly? His fingers slid beneath the hem, slipping between her folds even as his tongue continued its task. For a moment she let herself enjoy, but as she again felt her pleasure being to grow, she pushed him away. She still wanted him in her.

His gaze lifted, and he looked deep in her eyes. There was a message there, but she wasn't quite sure what it was. She could see his question, see his searching to be sure she really was ready, but there was more emotion, more to his inquiry than that. Her body was giving him more than enough clues about how ready she was, whatever it was he was looking for was beyond that.

It should have frightened her, at least a little—that he was clearly searching for emotions she wasn't yet ready to describe. She'd never been one to move into an emotional relationship quickly—and yet with him, she felt that they'd been together for so much longer than they actually had. Holding his gaze, she nodded.

He stood, sliding her panties down her legs until they lay on the floor. Holding one of her calves in each hand, he spread her legs, looking directly at the core of her. The look of desire on his face was so strong that all she could do was bask in his pleasure, forgetting any possible embarrassment.

He moved slowly, far more slowly than her body demanded, but she forced herself to be as patient as he had been. There was a quick shifting and the soft tear of foil and then he worked his way slowly up her legs, bending forward, positioning his penis against her outer folds. Her breath caught as he supported himself with one hand, using the other to open her fully. He shifted position slightly until the head of penis was exactly right. He flexed his hips forward, entering her just the slightest bit.

She bit down on her lip. Normally she enjoyed this part in a more mental than physical way. It was the later movement that truly got her body revved. With him, each tiny movement was exquisite. Maybe it was simply that she was sooo ready, that she was about to come merely from the slight rotation of his hips that had his dick circling the entrance to her vajayjay.

"More," she whispered.

He hesitated, but then with one fluid motion pushed himself all the way in. "Like that?" he asked between gritted teeth.

It was good to know he was not as in control as he appeared. She clenched her inner muscles tight. His face grew tense. She relaxed, tightened again.

"You are a minx," he whispered as he placed a hand on either side of her head and began to move.

Almost instantly, her pleasure began to build. She tried to relax, to take deep breaths, to hold off as long as she could—but it was useless. He was relentless, and her body was eager.

Her head moved from side to side. Her hips rose and fell in rhythm with his thrusts—and she gave in, letting her orgasm roll over her in waves of blinding delight and joy. And it *was* joy.

As her body clenched one last time and then fell back, that was the sole thought that remained. Joy. Waves of joy.

And then he thrust one last time, his whole body stiff and tight. Her name left his lips—then echoed again.

And all was quiet and sweet.

For a few moments they just lay there, half on, half off her couch.

Finally, she rolled toward him. "So you work at the hospital?"

A deep laugh left him. "Really? That's what you ask now?"

She smiled in return. "Yes. Clearly, we needed to get that out of the way, but now I want to know all the things I should have asked about a few nights ago. Surely you have questions too?"

He rose up on one elbow. "I admit I do. Although, my big one—what is your phone number—was finally answered when you texted me early this morning. I don't know how we managed not to connect on that before. It's normally one of the first things I do when I meet a woman I like."

"And you like me?"

He grinned down at her. "I'm not even going to answer that."

"No, you're just going to avoid answering my question about the hospital. You do realize that at Carol's house you filled me in completely about school and your first job as a consultant, but somehow skipped revealing what you do now."

He leaned back on the couch and pulled her up to rest against his chest. She instantly missed being able to see into his eyes, but had to admit that this was much more comfortable.

"I haven't meant to avoid the question. I work in hospital administration. I head customer relations among other things, and I also work with the transplant team, making sure that everyone is agreement and that everything is good to go. It's amazing the amount of paperwork involved, and also how carefully you have to keep everyone... Happy isn't quite the right word... How you have to keep everyone in agreement when you're dealing with the bodies of recently departed loved ones. It's what I was called in for the other night. The family was in some disagreement about what should be done, and I've become a specialist in negotiating quickly."

"That sounds intense."

"It can be. It's definitely not what I thought I'd being doing when I studied conflict resolution in business school. I thought I'd be a big corporate player, but I'm much happier doing this."

She rolled so that she could stare up at him again. "I can see that you are."

"I'm high enough up that I don't normally have to work nights, but I like to take a shift about once a month that's just routine. That's what I was doing last night. I think it helps keep both me and my staff on our toes. So much happens at a hospital at night, but it's easy to forget when I sit in my office during the day, looking over complaints about insurance coverage or authorizations."

She rested her head, listening to his heartbeat.

"I do want to finish this conversation, to hear about you, but I'm hungry," he said after a minute. "And you said something about a headache earlier. Can I get you some ibuprofen?" He started to shift, reaching down to pull on his silly boxers.

After considering for a moment, she answered, "I'd completely forgotten about the headache. I think you may have provided just what I needed to relieve my stress." She pulled on her panties and reached for his shirt. There was nothing better than a man's button-down in these circumstances.

He smiled and stood. "I do like how you look in my shirt." His eyes focused on the single button she'd fastened between her breasts.

She twirled slightly, then picked up the forgotten containers of food and carried them to the kitchen. "How about I pop these in the microwave and we can light the menorah? Somehow—I'm not quite sure how—it's gotten late."

"Hmm, I wonder how." He came up and nuzzled the back of her neck. "We may have to experiment."

"I'm all for that, but after we eat." She put a couple of containers in the microwave and set the timer. Then she picked up the matches and walked to the menorah. Josh had already put in the new candles.

He looked so good, standing there casually, the nighttime city behind him. He looked like he belonged.

She struck the match and lit the *shamash*. Belong. It was such an important word, an important concept. That had been her problem the first night. She'd been here in own apartment, but as she'd lit the menorah she hadn't felt like she belonged. Now, here with Josh, that was all changed. Being here with him felt very right. It was a feeling she wanted to continue.

THE EIGHTH NIGHT

JOSH WOULD BE HERE SOON AND BEFORE HE ARRIVED, SHE HAD something she needed to do. She lay the two remaining Bubbe presents on the coffee table.

He'd remarked on them last night, but she hadn't wanted to open them with him there. In fact, she knew that she'd been delaying in unwrapping them altogether. Somehow as long as they remained untouched, she felt that Bubbe Linda was still with her. It had been okay to open the gifts when she knew what was in them, the socks and the chocolates. These last two unknown presents were somehow different. As long as they remained a mystery, a part of her grandmother was still there, holding on to a surprise.

Now, it was time.

She lifted the first gift, a small square box. Something inside it rattled. Holding her breath, she ripped the scrap of paper. A jewelry box. That was strange. Bubbe Linda had never cared much for jewelry except for…

No, it couldn't be.

She lifted the lid. The small gold Star of David hung on a delicate chain, a diamond at each point. It had been the first gift from her grandfather, and Bubbe Linda had never taken it off. How had Tamara not noticed she wasn't wearing it at the end? She couldn't have been, if it had already been wrapped and put away. Tamara lifted the chain and with clumsy fingers and placed it around her neck. The star settled just above her collar bone, as it had on Bubbe Linda.

Standing, she walked over to the mirror. The necklace looked good. She placed a hand over it, feeling it grow warm against her skin. She had been wrong. Bubbe Linda would always be there with her.

Sitting back down, she lifted the last present. A flat rectangle, slightly bigger than her hand and about an inch thick. It bent a little in her hand. A book? They'd often shared book recommendations. A book would be a fitting final gift.

She tore the paper. Smooth brown leather. A journal. She opened it. The first page had writing in Bubbe Linda's frail hand.

Dearest Tamara,

I hope that as you are reading this your heart is not too filled with pain. I lived a wonderful life with a wonderful man and can only hope that you will as well. I imagine that you are opening this after lighting my treasured menorah. I hope it brings you the joy that it brought me over the years. I met your grandfather the day after I first lit it and I've always believed that it brought him to me, that it has a bit of magic in it. Every time I lit it, I held in my mind what I wanted to happen and more often than not it came to be. I can only hope that the same holds true for you. I know you won't be foolish and try for something like world peace, but if you keep your dreams simple, then the menorah will work its magic. I hope you can use this journal to track those dreams and the wonderful life you will lead.

Love you always,
Bubbe Linda

For a long time, Tamara sat in quiet, her mind filled with memories of Bubbe lighting the menorah, of the expression of peace that had always come over her face in those moments. And what about the menorah's magic? She didn't really believe in such things, but she *had* met Josh the day after lighting it for the first time.

There was a knock at the door. Josh. Surely it was too early? She glanced at the clock. Her thoughts had distracted her far more than she'd realized. Hurriedly, she threw away the scraps of wrapping paper and went to the door.

Josh met her with a grin. "I stopped at the deli and got some matzoh ball soup. I know it's the wrong holiday, but I had a hankering." He held out the plastic bag, the container easy to see within it.

"Matzoh ball soup is never wrong. Come in and we'll light the menorah."

He set the bag on the counter and walked to the window with her. Tamara had to hold back tears as she lit the candles on this final night. She could almost feel Bubbe Linda's hand covering her own. As she lit the final candle, she looked at her reflection with Josh in the window. She hoped for many more Festivals of Lights just like this one.

Her serious thoughts lasted only a moment though before Josh turned to her after the final prayer and whispered, "Tell me. Have you have played Strip Dreidel?"

REDEDICATION

LYNNE SILVER

AUTHOR'S NOTE

When Jill and Evan's youngest child leaves for college, they'd expected more romantic time together. But this empty-nester couple must remember how to connect and plan to spend all eight nights of Hanukkah rekindling their marriage.

JILL ATE DINNER ALONE IN FRONT OF THE TV FOR THE THIRD NIGHT that week. The new norm. The whole point of being married was to never have to eat a meal alone unless you chose to. Eating solo had seemed a treat back in September when her youngest child, Zoe left for college and Evan took on a big client.

She'd come in from work, tug off her bra, and eat bowls of Special-K while binging on Hulu episodes of shows Evan would rather bleach his eyeballs than watch. Heaven.

No varsity games to race off to straight after work, cursing yourself because you'd forgotten to slip your ballet flats into your tote and had to hike up grassy, muddy fields in heels and dress pants.

No hungry teenage monsters bursting into the house with shouts of *"I'm starving. What's for dinner?"* Even as they saw her in the kitchen prepping a meal.

No said-starving teenagers grabbing everything edible in sight to inhale and then demurring when prepped dinner was finally ready and they were no longer hungry.

The only stomach Jill had to worry about now was her own. And maybe Evan's if he came home soon. Though he was a perfectly good cook himself and thought nothing of whipping up some fluffy scrambled eggs if she were working late or was too tired to cook.

Yep, eating alone had seemed like a treat, but the treat was getting stale.

Leaving for the train now. Ate dinner in office.

Jill glanced at her phone screen as it buzzed with a message from Evan, then glanced at the time stamp and sighed. Seven forty-five. It'd take him another thirty to forty-five minutes before he climbed the porch steps to their home in Scarsdale. By then she'd be done with dinner, showered, and likely in bed trying to call Zoe on the west coast and hopefully catch her. She'd had a text that morning but it wasn't as satisfying as hearing her only daughter's voice reassuring her that she was healthy and loving UCLA.

Suddenly Jill wasn't hungry any more. Gathering up her cereal —Honey Nut Cheerios tonight—she tossed her dirty bowl and spoon in the sink. Dishes were a problem for future Jill. She headed upstairs to shower. The big house was dark and seemed lonely, filled with vacant rooms. Not quite empty but filled with the things no longer valued by their owners and deemed fit to remain in childhood bedrooms, but not ready for the donation bin yet.

When Ben had left first for college, she and Evan had jokingly discussed turning his room into a home gym or guest room. But they'd been busy with work and Ari and Zoe and it hadn't been a priority. Ditto for when Ari had fled the coop.

They should move. It wasn't the first time she'd thought of it, but it was the first time the need to get out of the overly large house called to her heart.

Where would she go? An apartment in Manhattan? A bungalow in LA? She'd be close to Zoe. And then she realized she was fantasizing about living solo from her husband and that kept her thoughts occupied during her entire long hot shower. She wasn't seriously considering leaving Evan? Was she? They were happy. They'd had sex just last night. Good sex too. She'd had an orgasm.

Her shoulder-length brown hair was wrapped in a towel, and

she was rubbing lotion into her legs when the house phone rang. Without thinking, she dropped the lotion on the counter and dashed out of the bathroom to grab it. Had she been thinking, she would've realized Zoe didn't call the landline. "Zoe?"

"Jill?"

The older woman's voice on the other end told her *not Zoe*. "This is Jill."

"Jill, it's Aunt Esti."

With a mental groan, she perched on the edge of her bed and tucked the phone between her ear and shoulder while rubbing in the remaining lotion with her free hands. "Hi Aunt Esti. How are you?" Esti was her mother's grandmother's cousin's daughter. She'd only understood the family ties when she'd seen them mapped out on a family tree. Nevertheless, Esti was a never-married elderly woman who lived in the Scarsdale area and was thus included in all family gatherings.

"It was so good seeing you at Thanksgiving."

"Yes, it was." Jill had hosted the extended family two weeks earlier, thrilled to pieces that Zoe and Ben made it home. Ari had still been wandering in Arizona somewhere.

"It reminded me that Hanukkah is coming up next week. Are you going to host the party again?"

She opened her mouth to reply with a firm no, but the word "yes" fell off her tongue. *Shit. Why had she said yes? Now she was in it.* The annual Hanukkah family open house was something she and Evan had hosted since Ben was a baby. His birthday was in December, and his toddler birthday parties had morphed into combo birthday-slash-Hanukkah parties, including sufganiyot with birthday candles.

"I mean I..."

"Good," Aunt Esti interrupted. "I missed it last year."

Last year, they'd been out in Los Angeles during most of Hanukah, visiting the west coast schools where Zoe had been accepted.

"Me, too," she said, realizing it was true, although she missed the Hanukkah parties of the past when the kids ran around the house settling down only to play dreidel and get a sugar high on gelt. If she hosted this year, there wouldn't be any children present. How…sad.

"Great. I can already taste the latkes."

Jill grimaced with such force her towel slipped, at the reminder she'd have to peel and shred a million potatoes and the house would smell like a fast food joint for the following two weeks. Could she serve store-bought latkes from the freezer section and pass them off as hers?

Aunt Esti put a halt to that little fantasy with her next comment. "It always makes me laugh to see Evan in his dreidel apron manning the four frying pans."

She smiled, warming at the memory. Evan was her hero for his willingness to stand over a multitude of oily frying pans, enduring the spatter burns. "Yes, we *will* host. I'll send out an email letting everyone know which night and time."

"Eighth night is always prettiest with all the hanukkiahs lit."

"And, I think that falls on a Sunday this year," she said, glancing around for her cell phone to check the calendar. Her gaze caught the time on the clock instead and she realized she needed to move if she were going to catch Zoe in that sweet spot between afternoon classes and dinner. "Look for that email from me, Aunt Esti. Thanks for calling."

She clicked off quickly, swallowing back the guilt at hanging up on a lonely elderly woman. Lonely new empty-nester needing to speak to only daughter trumped great-aunt in this instance.

Without bothering to blow dry her hair, she pulled on comfortable pajamas and settled into bed with her cell phone to type a message to her daughter.

YT?

The dreaded *dot dot dot* appeared. Then nothing. Then:

HO.

Yes. Mental fist pump. No, her daughter wasn't calling her a hooker as she'd mistakenly thought a few years ago. She hung on as instructed.

When the phone finally rang, her enthusiasm was a little too much for a jaded eighteen-year-old to tolerate. "Hey, Zoe!"

"Whoa, Mom, are you okay?"

"Fine, fine. Happy to hear your voice. How was your week?" Though it went against every instinct and desire as a mother, she forced herself not to call Zoe every day. A daily text here or there and a phone call every three days. After three kids, her helicopter parental instincts were pretty well grounded, but they'd roared back into lift-off when her baby and only daughter moved to the opposite side of the country for college.

"It was good. It's getting crazy with finals coming up. I'm thinking of pledging a sorority in the spring. Is that weird?"

"I thought you didn't like sororities, and didn't they do their rush thing back in September?"

"Yeah, but, I don't know. A few of the girls I really liked joined and now I don't see them as much. They said they had some open spots and were going to have a small spring rush."

"If you think it sounds fun, go for it."

"Maybe." She didn't sound convinced and went silent for a few seconds.

"Hey, guess who just called?" Jill said.

"Who?"

"Aunt Esti. She wanted to know if we're hosting the Hanukkah party this year."

"Are you?"

"I said yes."

"Aw, Mom. Now you're making me homesick. I'm going to miss dad's latkes."

Jill bit her tongue and didn't remind her daughter that if she'd gone to the college at which she'd been accepted in Maryland, she could've come home for the weekend and attended the party. "I'll send you a Hanukkah care package."

"Like the Rosh Hashanah one?" Zoe asked. "My roommate had never seen a challah before, let alone a round one."

"Like that. I'll call the synagogue and ask if they do a Hanukkah one."

"It'll only have a dreidel and gelt. They won't be able to ship hot fried latkes across the country."

"True, but I bet LA has a restaurant that serves them." She was about to suggest Zoe call a close family friend who would likely invite her for Hanukkah, but the sound of female and male voices came over the phone.

"Mom, I gotta go. Love you. Talk later."

She hung up as Jill was saying her goodbyes. Silence descended in the house once more, but before she could get despondent, she grabbed her tablet and started typing out Hanukkah party email invites. A project was what she needed.

~

Jill was in bed when Evan got home that night. She wasn't asleep, but it was clear she was done for the day, and he wasn't sure what his next steps were. Their marriage had always been so comfortable, but now he felt like he was walking on eggshells, never knowing what to say or do, feeling completely disconnected from her.

If he had his way, he'd shower, wash off the stink of corporate law on Wall Street, then climb in bed with her and make love to his wife. After 24 years of marriage, the fresh exciting zing of when they first met was no longer there, but in its place with something better. Something more comfortable. Something real.

"Hey honey, how was your day?" He smiled at her, hoping for a return smile, which he got, but it was a dim smile, not the genuine excitement to see him.

"Good," she said. "I spoke to Zoe. She's getting ready for finals and is thinking of joining a sorority."

"I thought she hated the things."

Jill shrugged as she looked at him. "Aunt Esti called. She asked if we're hosting the Hanukkah party this year. I said yes."

Evan unknotted the tie around his neck, a gift that Jill had bought him last year because she said it matched his eyes. He had brown eyes, and the tie was green, but he didn't question Jill's taste. "Do you really want to host the Hanukkah party?"

Her arms folded on top of her breasts. "Why do you think I wouldn't want to host?"

And there it was, a landmine he'd accidentally stepped in without even knowing he was in a territory that had landmines. "Because the kids aren't here, and it would just be adults."

"What's wrong with that? It might be nice to have an adult-only party."

"True," he said, shrugging, not really caring one way or the other if they had the Hanukkah party. Only that he could figure out how to reconnect with his wife.

"Will you make the latkes?" Jill asked, giving him an opening to reach out and grab.

He turned as he pulled off his suit, and smiled overly widely at her. "Absolutely. It will be fun." He disappeared to the bathroom to finish his business there, and when he came out Jill had turned off her lamp on her nightstand and was curled up, conveying that she was done chatting for the night and was ready for sleep. Frowning, he got the message loud and clear and climbed in facing his wife's back.

With a hesitant hand, he stroked her shoulder blade, not hoping to make love but hoping for any sort of connection. She gently swatted his hand away murmuring, "Not tonight babe. I'm tired. Work was hectic."

"I…" He zipped his lips, not trying to defend himself. He knew he hadn't been hoping for anything of a sexual nature. "Good night."

He lay in the dark for a few minutes, but still hadn't shaken off the buzz of work and the commute home. He wasn't ready for sleep, so he crept out of bed and headed down to the den to maybe watch a show or play a mindless game on his tablet.

His first stop on his tablet was where he always stopped first. His middle son Ari, was hiking around the country and sporadically updated his social media post with information and photos. Finding him for a phone conversation was increasingly difficult, so catching glimpses of him on social media was the best way to see his son.

Ari hadn't posted in nearly two weeks. Presumably, he was alive and healthy, but it was always nice to get visual confirmation. Tonight he got lucky and there was a new post of Ari sitting around a campfire with a group of people. Strangers he'd met that morning, no doubt. Ari had the lucky ability of being able to make friends wherever he went.

It was a gift Evan envied, and neither he nor Jill had it, so they always joked that Ari was their changeling child. Taking a chance, he picked up his phone to dial Ari's number. He should've bought a lottery ticket, because Ari answered.

"How are you?" he asked his son.

"I'm good."

"It's great to hear your voice."

"Same." They chatted for a few minutes about Ari's adventures, but then something in his son's voice changed, getting serious.

"What's going on with you and mom?" Evan held the phone away from his ear for a minute, feeling shock. How had his son, from out in the wilderness, sensed a fissure in their marriage?

"What do you mean? What makes you think something's wrong?"

Ari cleared his throat. "She hasn't posted on social media in days. Maybe even weeks."

"I think that would be a good thing," Evan said, pretending to joke. "Studies show that people who post a lot on social media are less happy."

"Mom's always posting stuff about family and events and activities and charity things, and she's been total radio silent for weeks. I'm worried. Does it mean she's not doing anything?"

Evan reached for his tablet, wondering what he'd been missing. His only activity on social media was to follow his wife and keep up with his kids, but he hadn't checked Jill's Facebook page in a while.

Was what Ari was saying true? Had his wife sunk into a morass and he'd somehow missed it? He'd been working more, true, but he'd been home every night.

Since September, it had just been the two of them. If anything they'd had more time together in the last six months than they'd had in the last six years.

Correction. They *should've* had more time together in the last few months, and though they'd had nothing but opportunity, they hadn't been taking advantage of it. Was Jill feeling the same disconnect from him that he was feeling from her?

"Ari, I think you may be right. I'm on it now. No need to worry."

"Thanks, Dad."

"How are things with you?" Evan asked.

"Oh you know me. Boring corporate job, nothing more to say." He chuckled.

Evan laughed too. As much as he worried about Ari's decisions and his free style life, he admired his sense of adventure and knew that someday Ari would land on both feet with some exciting tales in his metaphorical scrap book.

He and his son chatted for a few more minutes, though Evan knew Ari edited a lot for public consumption. When they hung up, he scoured through his wife's Facebook page and noted the exact day the posts stopped. She'd been quiet all through September and October. There'd been a few posts in November, mostly when the kids came home, and then silence until now.

It was empty-nest syndrome, Evan realized. He hadn't had it, or maybe he had, because he'd thrown himself into work as there'd been no other obligations on his time. Error. Big mistake. He did have an obligation on his time. The most important one. His wife. And he'd effed that up. No more. He was fixing that, starting tonight.

∼

Jill woke to the smell of coffee. Weird. Lately, she'd been waking up to a cold empty house. The aroma of brewed grounds wafted tantalizingly up the stairs into her bedroom. She loved the scent of coffee, despite being more of a tea drinker.

A man appeared in the doorway to her bedroom, and her sleep-addled mind took a minute to register it was Evan looking down at her, holding a mug of the Costa Rican roast he loved. "Morning, sleepy."

She sat up and smiled back. "Morning. Did I oversleep?"

"No. It's only seven thirty."

"Seven thirty?" she echoed. Evan was usually halfway to the city by now. "Are you feeling all right?"

"I'm great. Why?"

"Because...you're here." She gestured to the room around her, illustrating her confusion. "You're not at work."

He came to sit next to her on the bed. "Thought I'd spend some time with my wife. Do you have to be at work on time or can you call in late and have breakfast with me?"

She thought about it for a hot minute. "I can be late. Are we talking instant oatmeal in our kitchen or Amaranth?" she asked, naming their favorite brunch place.

"Amaranth, obviously. We have a table at eight so move it." He yanked the covers off her, and pretended to tug her out of bed, but their fake tussle turned into a handsy game that didn't end until Jill's pajama top was off and her breasts exposed to the heated air of their bedroom. Evan's gaze grew intrigued—he was always a breast man—but he pulled away and pointed toward the bathroom. "Go, get dressed. You have fifteen minutes."

Mom of three kids, dressing in fifteen minutes? No problem. She was ready in sixteen, and only needed the extra minute because it was spent searching for the earrings Evan had bought her for their twentieth wedding anniversary. They were a little dressy for your average Thursday at work, but who cared?

"You look beautiful," he said, when she came down the stairs. He rose from the living room sofa where he'd been checking his phone. She knew he meant it, because his phone was in his pocket, and his gaze swept her from head to toe, lingering on her earrings.

"Thank you. You look nice yourself." He was dressed for the day at his law firm in a slim navy suit with pale blue tie.

They headed out the door to the family car, chatting about nothing important, and yet it was everything. When they were seated at their table, full cups of coffee and water delivered to their table, Evan reached across the table.

"This is hard," he said.

She froze, her stomach somersaulting, awaiting the next part of his sentence, but he stayed silent, and simply held her hand.

"What's hard?" she forced herself to ask.

"Us. The kids all being gone. Becoming Empty Nesters."

"Oh," she said. Her shoulders relaxed, and she reached for her water. She took a rejuvenating sip of the icy liquid and squeezed his hand. "I guess it is. I mean, I've been working, and you've been occupied with your new client…"

"That's not anything new. We've always been swamped at work, but the kids kept us from getting too busy. There was always a ticking clock before telling me I had to leave work to make a sports game, or a school meeting. Now…"

"There's no clock. No calendar," she chimed in. "Our evenings and weekends are our own."

"I always thought we'd have so much fun when the kids were grown. Go into the city for a show, travel more, go for dinner on a Tuesday…"

"Or brunch on a Thursday." They grinned at each other.

"But we haven't done it."

"No," she agreed. "We haven't."

"Why not?"

She snatched her hand back, and her spine stiffened. "I didn't realize. I'll schedule some things." She pulled out her phone, but Evan took it and flipped it screen-side down on the white tablecloth.

"I didn't mean to make you defensive. When I asked why not, it wasn't an accusation." He frowned. "But I can see how you'd take it that way. You've been the train conductor for more than two decades. You told us where to be, how to dress, and when to be ready."

"True. I shouldn't schedule some things for us to do as a couple?"

"You can, if there's something you want to do, but how about you let me take on some scheduling for a change?"

"You?"

He grinned. "Don't think I can handle it? Challenge accepted," he said before she could tell him that she thought he was perfectly capable of handling nearly anything in his path. "Hanukkah is coming up. I'll plan for that."

"Remember we're hosting the party on the eighth night."

"Yep. I'll plan around that."

"So what are we going to do?" she asked, curious as to Evan's plans.

His brows rose. "How about you give me more than eight seconds to plan something, but I do have an idea."

"Oh?"

"I'm remembering how we used to do Hanukkah when the kids were little, and I think I want to plan it like that."

"Crying over who gets to hold the shamash and trying to prevent the house from burning down?"

He laughed. "No. I'm talking about the themed nights."

"Oh, right. I'd nearly forgotten." To prevent the kids from becoming spoiled brats after getting presents for eight days straight, Jill had created a theme for every night, with most evenings not ending in presents for the kids.

They'd had a game night, with one new board game for the whole family, a craft night where they'd done a family project, a *tzedakah* night where each kid got eighteen dollars to donate to a charity of their choice, a movie night, and so on.

"I'll plan Hanukkah this year," he said. "All you have to do is show up."

She smiled. "Sounds like a great idea."

NIGHT ONE

JILL PULLED INTO THE GARAGE, NOT SURE WHAT TO EXPECT. IT WAS the first night of Hanukkah, and short of buying a new box of candles, she'd done nothing to prepare. She didn't have a gift for her husband. She hadn't even organized the photos to send out a family holiday card.

Evan had said to leave Hanukkah to him this year, and she'd decided to heed his advice. She wasn't going to be the driver of this bus. For once, she was the passenger.

A curious whisper of excitement spiraled through her as she exited her car and entered the house, hanging her thick coat on a hook in the mudroom, adjacent to the kitchen. Evan was already home, standing over the kitchen counter, pulling white and red cardboard containers out of a brown paper bag.

"Sichuan City?" she asked, walking over to inspect the takeout dinner.

"Yep." He pulled her closer to his side, and brushed his lips across her cheek. "Thought about ordering all fried things, but had second thoughts. So I got *sufganiyot*." He nudged a white cardboard bakery box on the counter next to the Chinese dinner from a local all-vegetarian restaurant.

"Good choice." She bent to grab paper plates from a low cabinet. Though she and Evan allowed non-kosher restaurant food in their home, it had to be vegetarian and that had to be eaten on paper plates.

Together they gathered up the lo mein, kung-pao tofu, plates, and flatware and headed to the cozy table in the kitchen. When all three kids were home, the nook was a tight squeeze, but sitting here with the shadows of twenty-years of family dinners surrounding them, it was the perfect spot to eat together.

The table had bench seating on one side and two chairs opposite. In a martyrdom move, Jill had forced her three kids to squish on the bench for meals, while she and Evan had taken the chairs.

Tonight, by unspoken agreement, they scooched in side-by-side on the bench, looking out over the window to their backyard. The sun was setting, and the bare winter tree branches scraped against the siding of the house.

"We need to trim," Evan observed.

"Yes," she agreed, but didn't jump up to grab her phone and call their lawn service. Nor did she make a mental note. Her brain was occupied, feeling Evan's warmth pushed against her side. She kicked off her shoes and let her toes toy with his calves.

He gave her a sideways smile, pausing with a fork full of noodles to his mouth. "Hungry?"

"Yes." But her fork remained still on her plate.

The look shared between them was not of husband and wife long married and comfortable.

It was the heated look of two people getting to know each other and wanting to know more. Naked more. Though they'd known each other decades, it was a rediscovery of each other and of themselves. Who was Jill? Still a mother, but without children at home?

She continued to ignore her food as Evan deliberately put his fork on his plate. "Should we do Hanukkah now, dinner later?" He pointed out the window. "Sun's set."

A nod, and she slid off the bench, his large hand guiding her by the hip. They headed to the front windows where he'd set up a small folding table covered in foil. In past years the table had been cluttered with a hanukkiah for each person in the household and a scattering of dreidels. Yesterday, Jill had deliberately set out only one hanukkiah. The grand-daddy of them all, a large gorgeous religious artifact, doubling as a piece of modern art. They'd picked it out ten years ago in Israel while there for Ari's bar mitzvah. A set of matches lay beside it and Jill lit one while Evan stood at her shoulder, his chest to her back.

His hand remained on her hip, massaging gently, and the hint of his aftershave had her inhaling deeply. The match wavered in her suddenly shaky hand on its way to the shamash, and then Evan's hand was there, steadying her. The tallest candle was lit, and together they lit the first night's candle while singing the three first-night prayers.

Evan would be the last to cop to it, but he had a lovely singing voice, and Jill murmured the Hebrew words, content to let him take the lead.

If the kids had been there, they would've immediately launched into a rousing chorus of *How Many Candles*, with Zoe shouting the corresponding number per night like a cheerleader. Now there was silence, the smoky burning smell of a blown-out match, and the too-bright flickering of the two candle flames in the darkened room.

They stood, fingers brushing, watching the dancing flames. Jill's skin prickled, knowing something sexual would be happening tonight. She was counting on it, and had put her money where her thoughts were, spending her lunch hour getting a quick wax and body scrub.

"Present time," Evan declared and tugged her to the sofa where a small pile of presents was stacked on the glass coffee table.

She reached for one, feeling child-like excitement at the prospect of ripping wrapping paper to get to the gifts.

"*Uh uh.*" Evan's hand landed on hers, and plucked the present she'd chosen from her hand. "There's an order."

"Then you should've numbered them." Like she had for the children.

He pointed to the number on the present. A reasonably sized black Sharpied number two was written on the blue and silver wrapping paper.

"Oh. Fine." She'd have to wait for tomorrow for that particular present. She knelt and rummaged through for the present labeled with a one. "Got it." She held it up triumphantly, hiding her disappointment that she could feel it was a book. She loved to read, but she'd hoped Evan would put a little more thought into the Hanukkah themes then grabbing whatever *Times* bestseller she hadn't read yet.

"Open it," he said. "Sit on the couch."

Raising her brows at his commands, she did as ordered, tearing open the gift paper. "*Love Poems* by Pablo Neruda." She'd heard of Neruda. Who hadn't? But she couldn't recall ever having actually read a Neruda verse.

Evan took the book from her hands, sat next to her, and pulled her back against his chest. His arms wrapped around her, caging her loosely as he opened the book to a page that had been previously marked. Now she saw, several of the pages had brightly colored little flags sticking out. He'd done his homework.

Settling back, her head against her husband's pectoral, she closed her eyes as Evan began to read.

"*My thirst, my boundless desire…*"

His voice washed over her as one of his hands held the book while the other tugged her blouse from her waistband and then deftly unfastened her pants.

"*En su llama mortal…*"

Her eyes opened. "Huh?"

Evan laughed. "The book is in a Spanish and English. Making sure you were paying attention."

"Oh I'm paying attention." She unsubtly thrust her hips toward his hand, which had stilled. "Keep going."

"We've barely begun…"

NIGHT TWO

Jill stifled another yawn. She'd been fighting them all day. Worth it. She and Evan had finished their private Hanukkah celebration then lay in bed, eating their dinner straight from the takeout cartons. More "private" celebrations had followed.

Tonight she'd promised to make dinner, so she'd swung by the market to grab potatoes, zucchini and some smoked nova lox. She'd bake a potato zucchini pancake and layer salmon on top with a small dollop of the crème fraiche, fresh dill and a side salad with citrus vinaigrette. More of a summer meal on this cold night. December had remembered it was supposed to be winter today and the gray sky was threatening sleet. But it was a Hanukkah-inspired palate, so she went with it.

Evan had promised to be home for dinner and presents, and sure enough at six-thirty, the front door opened, and he stepped into the house, dripping.

"You should've called. I would've grabbed you from the station."

He hung his coat and wiped a palm over his damp hair. "This is just from the driveway to the door. Bill gave me a ride." Bill lived three houses over, and he and Evan frequently met up during their commutes to the city.

"You must be freezing. Go grab a quick shower and dinner will be finished by the time you're done."

"All right." He tugged her close for a kiss. "Want to join me?" he asked in a low murmur against her lips.

She laughed and kissed him again. "Yes, but not at the risk of burning the house down."

"We wouldn't want that. Go manage dinner. I'll be back down in a few."

When dinner was finished, they lit the candles and once again convened on the couch where Jill opened a tiny box she was sure was jewelry.

If she had bet money on her guess, she'd be toting an empty wallet.

"What's this?" she asked, looking down at two wooden dice on the palm of her hand.

"Roll," Evan said.

With a shrug, she leaned forward and rolled the two dice onto the coffee table, where they made a tiny racket then skidded to a stop. They both leaned forward to read.

"Lips lick," Jill read aloud. She licked her lips.

Evan laughed. "Not your own. Mine."

"Oh." She felt her cheeks warm and laughed at herself. When had she become a stuffy woman of a certain age who didn't recognize a sex game when she saw one? She leaned in to her husband and gave his lips a gentle swipe with her tongue. He tasted of the oil from the dinner, with a hint of the scent of dill.

"My turn." Evan rolled the dice. "Touch ear."

"*Eesh.*" Jill cringed away as his finger came in brief contact with the upper fold of her ear. "What crazy person declared ears an erogenous zone?"

"You've always hated having your ears touched."

"Yep."

"I don't mind it. I'll take one for the team. You touch my ear."

"Or we move on." She reached for the dice, but Evan stayed her hand.

"Touch my ears, Jill."

It was such a ridiculous request, she started to giggle. "Fine." She reached up and tugged his lobe gently, but then pressed the upper cartilage between her thumb and forefinger and rubbed gently.

"That feels nice."

"Really?" She massaged a little more, then slid her fingers into his hair, away from his ears, and leaned in for a kiss.

He pulled back. "Uh, uh. We haven't landed on kiss lips yet."

She froze and tried to read his expression. Was he kidding? Or had it finally been revealed where Ben's intense need for rule-following in board games had come from? "My roll then." The dice skittered across the glass.

"Lick Breast," Evan read, crouching over the table to follow her dice.

"That escalated quickly." She reached for the hem of her blouse to start to tug it upward then paused. "Wait, now I'm confused. Who does the licking and who is the lickee?"

"You rolled, so it's your action." He pulled his worn white t-shirt over his head, revealing his flat dark pink nipples, surrounded by wiry brown hair with some greys sprinkled in.

She leaned over and gave a quick swipe to his right nipple with the flat of her tongue. The soap he'd recently used filled her nose along with the indefinable familiar taste of his skin. She moved to the left pectoral, giving it more love than she had the right. Her tongue circled until it was a hard point.

Last night had worn her out, but arousal was popping its head up, announcing it was in the room. Her fingertips grazed over the pads of his pectorals, fondling the crisp hairs on his chest. "Should we keep playing? Or should we *keep playing*?" she asked in a low voice, one she almost didn't recognize.

Through the many years of their marriage, they'd had all kinds of sex—romantic, sexy, perfunctory, kinky, but the erotic burn from the first days of their dating had all but disappeared. She'd never expected to find it again at her age and at this stage in the game.

In answer, Evan sat up and reached for the dice. "Massage butt." Jill laughed and dove for the dice. "They do *not* say that."

He closed his fist around the dice. "On your belly."

"So you can rub my butt?"

"Massage."

"Fine." After a faux exasperated eye roll, she lay face down on the sofa while Evan knelt next to her and began to knead her butt with one hand, the other still hiding the dice from view. Her office day was spent mostly sitting, and she hadn't realized how tight her muscles were. A groan escaped her.

"Good?"

"Yes, don't stop. Unless you tell me one of the nights gift is a massage gift card."

"No, but that would've been a good idea." He focused on a spot below the curve near the inner thigh. His fingers began to reach places no professional massage therapist would have on the map. Jill unabashedly spread her legs and lifted her butt in the air.

The dice hit the ground and rolled on the rug toward Jill. She leaned in to look. "Kiss..." Her head swiveled to look back at her husband.

"Upstairs." He grabbed her hand and they headed up to their room, where they finished the game.

NIGHT THREE

"HERE'S YOUR DINNER." THE SECOND HER SEATBELT WAS CLICKED, Evan handed her a sub sandwich from the local deli, a bag of chips, and glass bottle of iced tea. He'd driven to work today and was picking her up with dinner. She piled her food on her lap and looked at Evan in the driver's seat, where he held the steering wheel in one hand and was polishing off the last bite of his sandwich, held in the other hand.

"Are you going to tell me where we're going?"

"You'll see. What's the fun of a surprise if it's not surprise?"

"Knowing the dress code, for one," she answered tartly as she began to unroll the thick white paper holding her tuna sub.

"You're in jeans, an old sweater, and sneakers, right?"

"Yes, but are we talking cute fashion sneakers or ones made for exercise?"

"I have no idea what that means. What are fashion sneakers?"

She rolled her eyes. Evan was hopeless when it came to fashion. He wore what was in his closet and counted on her to coordinate dress shirts with the right tie. "Never mind. You know I don't love surprises."

"Deal with it," he replied, driving away from their house. They rode in comfortable silence for ten minutes, with only the sound of her chewing her dinner.

At last, he pulled into a driveway that led to a parking lot. She glanced around. "You're taking to me to church for the third night of Hanukkah?"

Evan laughed. "Finish your sandwich, then we'll go inside."

She made short work of her dinner and grabbed a piece of minty gum from the center console. "Ok, done. Let's go in." While eating, she'd decided they were either going to an interfaith Christmas/Hanukkah dinner or a Christmas pageant to be nice to a work friend of his.

They exited the car, but Evan headed to the open trunk and pulled out two games before leading her to the entrance. "Apples to Apples and a Hot Wheels set?" she questioned. "Are we going to a game night?"

"Close," he said with a grin, and pushed the door open before gesturing for her to enter.

"Toys for Tots," she said, as she read the signs with arrows that directed them to the youth lounge down the hall. "Are we dropping those off?"

"Yes, but we're also staying."

They found the youth lounge and were greeted by the sight of fifteen or so other people ranging in ages and race, and now religion. Piles of unwrapped toys were at the center of the room and huge empty bins lined one wall.

"We're going to volunteer," Evan told her as they stood in the entrance. "We might not have kids at home anymore who want toys, but there are plenty of kids in other homes who do want them, so we're going to help them have a great Christmas."

"Fabulous," she said over the sudden lump in her throat. The room was brighter and shinier as she looked out at it with joyful, tearful eyes. Together they walked down to the pile of presents where Evan placed his offerings, and then they listened to the instructions from the organizers.

"We're sorting by toys, books, and stocking stuffers," announced a Marine who marched to the front. He pointed to a bin with each category. "I'll be monitoring and collecting data. If you have questions, ask. Thank you for your time tonight."

The room remained still for a moment, then, "Move out," the Marine barked.

A flurry of activity erupted as they moved en masse to the pile of toys and started grabbing items to bring to the correct bins.

Evan started with the two games he'd brought, obviously in the toy category. Jill peered in a paper shopping bag and frowned. "This is terrible. Someone thought it was a good idea to get rid of all the junky practically broken toys cluttering their house." She held out the open bag to Evan. "These don't even qualify as stocking stuffers."

"Toss 'em." The Marine had come up behind her and was looking over her shoulder at the contents of the bag. He too looked annoyed and made a mark on his clip board. "We get a little junk every year, but most donations are generous and quality toys." He gave her an unexpected smile, softening his face and making him look younger.

"That's good to hear." Jill grinned back at him and watched him walk off to answer someone else's question.

Evan got in her space and smirked. "Flirting with men in uniform."

"He's younger than Ari." She shrugged. "But what can I say? A man in uniform is sexy."

"Noted."

She lay a hand on his chest. "But I prefer a suit and tie."

"Also noted. Now get back to work."

She gave him a salute, then bent to grab another toy. "Legos. Remember the year Ben was obsessed?" she asked, shaking a box filled with a 720-piece set.

"How can I forget? The soles of my feet haven't recovered. It's like braille down there."

She laughed. "The pain of stepping on a Lego should be mentioned in parenting courses. That and the sleep deprivation."

They continued to reminisce as they sorted, many of the toys bringing them back to a time when their children were young enough to covet the dolls, trucks, and books. "Oh, Junie B Jones. Zoe loved this series." Jill carefully carried the stack of books to the book bin. Unfortunately the book bin was not nearly as full as the stocking stuffer and toy bins.

From experience, she could see a lot of the toys were one-hit wonders, keeping kids busy for an hour before they would lose interest. "So many battery-operated toys," she said to Evan as they carried another stack to the toy bin.

"Your least favorite thing, I know," Evan said. "I know you don't miss that."

Jill shuddered at the memory of every toy that beeped, whistled, sirened, alarmed, or made any kind of noise. She'd spent many a night while the kids were asleep, with a micro-screwdriver removing the batteries for the next day, when she'd feign surprise, wondering along with her children why in the world the toy had gone silent.

At ten o'clock, the pile was down to a tiny handful of toys that looked like the sort of plastic junk found in a birthday-party goody bag.

"Calling it a night. Thank you for your help. Merry Christmas," The Marine announced.

"Merry Christmas," Jill and Evan chimed in with the group.

They turned to each other. "Happy Hanukkah," Jill whispered and leaned up for a kiss.

NIGHT FOUR

EVAN HANDED THE WHITE RECTANGULAR ENVELOPE TO JILL WITH HIS heart pounding. The Hanukkah candles were lit on the table behind them and cast a glow over the room, giving romantic ambiance for the present opening.

Of all the themes, activities, and gifts he'd thought of for Hanukkah, this was the one he was most excited for. He couldn't wait to see her reaction. Their knees touched as they sat next to each other on the sofa, turned in facing each other. She made a production out of opening the envelope and he wanted to grab it out of her hand and rip it open, but that wasn't Jill's way, she was methodical and careful.

She pulled out the folded sheet of paper he'd printed at his office, and she scanned it. "These are plane tickets?" she said, a question in her voice. "But to where?" Her brow furrowed as she read the fine print on the paper, turning it over to see if there was more information she'd missed.

"That's the million dollar question, or rather the million mile question, isn't it? We've talked for a long time about taking a big vacation, but we haven't done it. Never just the two of us. It's time."

"That's tonight's theme? Vacation?"

"You got it. Our kids are grown. Financially we can manage it. Let's go explore."

They grinned at each other, and he continued. "I bought airline vouchers. I didn't want to dictate which days you took off work. You know your schedule better than I do. And I wanted the fun of us picking a destination together. I may have started the ball rolling with buying the vouchers, but from here on out, this vacation is a jointly planned event."

Evan wouldn't nominate himself for husband of the year or anything, but he had picked up a few things in listening to his wife over the past two decades. Every time they were invited to a surprise birthday party, Jill would attend, shaking her head the whole ride over, lamenting over the fact that she suspected the birthday girl or boy would prefer a private trip or a spa day or anything other than a surprise party.

And he'd listened the time she'd come home from work complaining that a colleague had to suddenly miss an important work event because her husband had surprised the family with tickets to Disney. "*It's like he doesn't know his wife at all,*" Jill had said at the time. "*Didn't he know how hard she'd worked on this project, and now everyone else will get the credit.*" Yes, Evan had made mental notes that his wife didn't like surprises, nor did she appreciate someone else managing her time. Hence, the vouchers good for airline tickets at a time and destination of their choosing.

"It's perfect," she said. "Let's go grab an atlas and some darts."

He laughed. "I don't want to end up in Siberia in January. And Dubai in July also sounds unpleasant. I was thinking we should plan it for this coming fall. The high holidays don't start until October, so we have the whole month of September free to travel."

"Zoe will be back in school by then," she said. "The timing sounds perfect to me." Jill pulled out her phone and opened up a map app. "Do we want city or beach?"

"Is there someplace we can do both? Like a city, and but one that has a nearby beach?"

"Barcelona, maybe," she suggested.

"We've been there with the kids before. I want to go someplace new, someplace we've never imagined a chance to go."

"India? Vietnam? Japan?"

"Those all sound amazing. How do we choose?"

"Darts," Jill suggested again.

"Crowdsourcing," he said. "You can ask your social media friends."

"I could."

"Or we could pick by amazing hotels. Aren't there travel sites with top ten places to go lists? Let's look at those."

She laughed. "Or better yet, let's quit our jobs, sell the house and backpack around the world. Let's see it all."

Before Evan could respond to that bit of whimsy, his phone rang, and Caller ID showed it was Ari, their middle son who was king of the whimsical vagabond lifestyle. "Perfect timing, kid. We need your help."

He switched the phone to speaker.

"Hi Honey. Happy Hanukkah," Jill said.

"Hi Mom. That's right, it is Hanukkah. What night is it?"

Evan exchanged an exasperated look with his wife. Religion, or calendars, had never been Ari's strong suit.

"Fourth night," Jill answered. "If you tell us where in the world you are, maybe we know a family or synagogue nearby where you could go celebrate."

"Mom, you know Hanukkah isn't that important. I promise I'll be davening in a shul for Kol Nidre."

They both knew better than to hold Ari to that promise, but they also knew they'd be wasting their breath to force religion on him.

Evan jumped in before Jill could say another word about Ari's religious practice. His wife and son had a wonderful relationship and were close, but Ari's experimentation and embracing of most world religions was a source of contention between the two and had led to some historic arguments. "Ari, we need your opinion on something important."

"How can I help?" Ari asked.

"I bought your mom airline tickets for tonight's Hanukkah gift. We're trying to pick a destination. With all the passport stamps under your belt, where do you think we should go?"

Ari had taken his junior year of college to travel abroad, and after a semester in a Hong Kong university, he'd backpacked all over Asia. And the year after he'd graduated college, he'd had a foray into a traditional job by taking a job in Madrid teaching English. He'd spent every free moment on trains and buses to other countries.

"Man, that's a good question. How do I choose?" Ari's voice had a thread of thoughtful excitement. Travel and world exploration was Ari's *raison d'etre*. "How adventurous do you want to be?"

He looked at Jill, and knew they'd be on the same page. "We're up for some excitement, but at the end of the day, we want to sleep in a safe and nice hotel. Doesn't have to have to be five stars, but we want to feel pampered."

For the next hour, the three of them discussed all the possibilities and finally settled on a luxury guided tour of Vietnam, Cambodia, and Thailand. Just as they finished the discussion, the *shamash* candle sputtered out, a fitting conclusion to night four.

NIGHT FIVE

"*FIDDLER ON THE ROOF?*" JILL GRINNED AT EVAN AS HE HANDED HER a ticket in front a theater on 44th Street. She was all dressed up and Manhattan, one of her favorite things to do. Something she didn't do nearly enough.

For Evan, going into the city was commonplace; literally an everyday activity for him. For her it was something she'd said she'd do a lot when they moved out to Scarsdale twenty years ago. But like so many goals and promises of a naïve young mother, she tended to stay in Scarsdale rather than make the train adventure into the big bad city.

So when Evan had told her that tonight's Hanukkah activity was going to theater, she leaped at the chance. He'd told her they were seeing a play, but not which one. The idea that they were seeing *Fiddler on the Roof* made her laugh, because it was a ubiquitous Jewish experience, and yet, "I don't think I've ever actually seen the musical performed live," she said.

"Me either," Evan said. "This is the perfect night. How much more thematic could we get than *Fiddler on the Roof?*"

"Well, you won't succeed on Broadway if you don't have any Jews," Jill said, quoting a line from the musical *Spamalot.*

He laughed. "True. The only other Jewish-themed play was a holocaust drama, and that seems a little heavy for tonight."

They found their row and shuffled into two excellent seats in the center, halfway up from the stage. "Agreed. Thank you for not doing that to me tonight. I'm feeling way too happy to want to sit through that." Jewish guilt and the ghosts of distant relatives who'd not survived the 1940s made her say, "Another night we should come into the city to see it."

Saying that out loud made her realize that over the course of the past four nights, she'd become used to spending every night with her husband, and she liked it. She didn't wanted it to end. She turned to Evan and said, "Promise me something."

He turned to her. "Promise what? You sound serious all of a sudden."

"This *is* serious. Before Hanukkah started, it felt like we were drifting. Drifting through our life, drifting through our marriage. And these past five days have been...really good. It's like we're a new couple all over again."

He took hold of her hand and gave it a nice squeeze. "That was my goal. I realized I was taking you for granted and maybe you were taking me for granted, too. We're not gonna let that happen. We're not going to be one of those couples who stays together out of habit, and not because we truly like each other."

Jill swallowed hard over the joyous lump in her throat as her eyes filled with happy tears.

Evan kissed the tip of her nose, then leaned back. "No tears. Tonight is for fun. What did you want me to promise you?"

She leaned into his side, inhaling his familiar aftershave. "Exactly that. You nailed it. I don't ever want us to take each other for granted. I want us to continue to do things as a couple and plan activities with each other. Maybe not for eight days in a row again, but at least once a week, we need to make a point of spending time together."

"I can promise that. And remember, we already have big plans for September. I called the travel agency today. We are officially on the list as part of the Southeast Asia tour."

Jill bounced in her seat a little, but before she could respond, the iconic and haunting melody of a fiddle wafted over the audience, the chatter ceased immediately, and the curtain went up.

NIGHT SIX

THE SIXTH NIGHT WAS NOT AS MONUMENTAL AS THE PREVIOUS DAYS.
After a long work week, they came home on Friday, ate a light
supper and made a plan for to get ready for the Hanukkah party.

They straightened the house, and hung up all the Hanukkah
decorations to make it feel more festive. They pulled out all the
hanukkiot, which elicited lots of reminiscing and conversation about
their children. They hashed out the topic of Ben's mystery girlfriend
in great detail.

By the time they finished, neither was in the mood to celebrate
Hanukkah much, so they lit the candles, and settled in on the couch
to catch up on their favorite streaming show. They were nearly a
season behind. Around ten, Jill was yawning and thinking
about bed.

She got up to head to their bedroom but was waylaid. "Wait! We
forgot to do presents tonight," Evan said. There was one remaining
package on the coffee table, so tiny Jill had almost overlooked it. He
handed it to her and she opened it, laughing a little when she saw
what it was.

"A dreidel," she said, holding the tiny blue and green Venetian
glass dreidel in her hand. "It's beautiful." She rose to add it to the

table where a display of dreidels was already laid out in preparation for Sunday's party.

"Hang on, let's play."

She turned to him, "Are you serious?"

"Yes, but let's make it more interesting."

"How?"

"How about some strip dreidel?"

She laughed, thinking he was kidding. Did her fifty-year-old husband really want to play strip dreidel? "Oh, you're serious?" she asked, chagrined at his hurt look.

"I just thought it'd be fun. We've been having a lot of fun all week, haven't we?"

She walked back to him and sank on the sofa. "We really have."

"And I don't just mean the sex, though that's been really great too."

"I know what you mean. It felt like we were in a rut, and now it feels like we're connected more."

"I'm scared of falling into that rut again," he admitted.

"Me too. So how do we stop that from happening?"

"By having fun with each other. By making time for each other."

She picked up the dreidel and gave it an experimental spin. "By playing strip dreidel."

He laughed. "Exactly."

"Rules?"

Evan's lips pursed as he thought about it for a minute. "*Nun*, nothing comes off. *Hey*, one thing comes off."

"If you roll a *shin*, you get to put something back on, and *gimel*, it all comes off," Jill contributed.

It was a disaster. Jill kept rolling *shins*. Evan got two *nuns* in a row, and then a *shin*.

They finally gave up and headed up to bed in fits of laughter. "I think dreidel games should stick to gambling for M&Ms," she said.

"Agreed."

NIGHT SEVEN

JILL ADJUSTED HER STOCKINGS AND SUCK-IT-ALL-IN UNDERWEAR IN the passenger seat as Evan finished straightening his car in the parking spot. She exited and walked to the front of the car to meet Evan, who grabbed her hand. She glanced at him with pleased surprise. Last week, he wouldn't have grabbed her hand. Last week, they wouldn't have arrived together, if they'd bothered to attend at all.

"You look nice," he said.

"Thank you."

"Jill! Evan!" A woman's voice from behind them caught their attention, and they stopped to see Debbie Kanter and her husband, Ray, hurrying toward them. They'd known Debbie and Ray since the early days when their son was in Hebrew school with Ben. They'd gone all through the elementary school years and Bnai Mitzvot years with Debbie and Ray. "Glad we're not the last people," Debbie said, slightly out of breath.

"Traffic was surprisingly bad for a weekend," Evan said.

"Tell me about it," Ray said. "Last thing I want on a Saturday evening after a long week of work is to come to the synagogue with a thousand other people and their screaming toddlers."

Debbie gave him a light shoulder punch. "Don't complain. Let's go get seats."

As a foursome, they made their way into the large, recently-renovated synagogue and into the main sanctuary. It was already packed with people, and as Ray had predicted, lots of screaming toddlers. Families milled about greeting each other and giving holiday greetings.

"At least it's not as insane as Purim," Jill offered.

"True," Debbie said.

"Four seats together over there." Evan pointed to the right of the room.

"Go grab 'em, boys," Debbie said. Evan and Ray hurried toward the seats, knowing their wives would take double the time to get there, because they'd have to stop and greet at least a dozen people along the way.

"Happy Hanukkah," Jill repeated, kissing cheeks of women she'd know for nearly two decades. "Shabbat Shalom."

"Good Shabbas."

"Jill, you look great. Glowing even," one friend said.

"Empty nesting must agree with her," Debbie said. "She and Evan were *holding hands* as they walked in here." She poked Jill's shoulder. "Caught ya. Did you think I didn't notice?"

They giggled like their teenaged children, and Jill smiled and tried to shrug off the empty-nest compliment. This wasn't the time nor the location to dive into the complicated web that made up a long marriage.

Eventually they made their way to their husbands and squeezed into the row. "Here you go." Evan handed her a plastic electric candle that looked like Shabbat candle but turned on with a small switch at the base.

"Thanks." Jill tucked the candle next to the siddur in the small wood shelf built into the seat-back in front of her.

Debbie leaned across Ray, brandishing her candle. "This is baloney. When we were kids, we lit real candles. It was so pretty."

"It might've been pretty, but after the donations we all recently made for the renovation here, I'd prefer we didn't burn the place to the ground," Evan said.

Debbie laughed and put her candle on her lap. "Good point." She started to say something else, but the lights dimmed and the lovely voice of their cantor rose above the din.

"*Ya da dai dai da dai da da da.*" She sang a wordless melody, and everyone found their seats and joined in singing as the clergy walked up the aisle to the *bimah* in front.

For the next hour, Jill was caught up in the familiar ritual of the Shabbat evening service, though the excitement from the young families waiting for the Hanukkah portion of the service was palpable. Several toddlers had to be forcibly carried, screaming, up and down the aisles as they struggled from the unfamiliarity of being dressed up in a crowded, loud room past their bedtime.

"I don't miss that," Ray muttered as yet another exhausted dad carried a two-year old out over his shoulder, and Jill, Evan, and Debbie nodded.

"It was exhausting," Jill said, "but I miss moments of it."

"You'll get it again when Ben has grandchildren," Debbie said.

Jill gave her a startled look. "Oh, I think we're a long way off from that."

Debbie shrugged. "Not from what Joey says. He visited Ben in Philly a few weeks ago on a work trip and said Ben and his girlfriend look pretty serious."

Jill and Evan exchanged a look, and she was relieved Evan looked as bewildered as she felt. *Ben had a girlfriend? And it was serious?* Surely not that serious, or he'd have brought her home to introduce her, right? He'd said nothing about a girlfriend when he'd been home recently at Thanksgiving.

She wanted to ask Debbie more, but intercepted a dirty look from the mom of the family in front of her who'd been vigilant about keeping her tweens quiet during the non-singing parts of the service. With empathy, Jill zipped it. It didn't seem fair to model bad synagogue behavior in front of the near-bar-mitzvah-aged kids.

At last, the sun was fully set and the big moment they'd all been waiting for arrived. Twenty children wearing matching navy blue collared shirts and khaki chinos marched to the front in formation and began to hum a Hanukkah tune softly.

As they hummed, the Rabbi spoke over them, instructing everyone to take their candles, switch them on, then hold them up and join in the singing. Jill followed instructions. She rose along with the rest of the congregation as the humming gave way to singing. As the power of hundreds of twinkling lights and even more powerful voices rose, her free hand found Evan's. They swayed and sang, going through the full medley of Hanukkah songs.

"Not by might, not by power…shall we all live in peace," Jill hummed to herself, still bursting with music as the last songs and candles petered out and the masses of people headed to the big hall for food.

"Latkes," Evan said. "I'm going in." He used his size to push his way through the throngs of rabid children who were fisting lurid blue sugar cookies in the shapes of dreidels and hanukkiot.

Jill remained on the safer outskirts of the room with her older-mom posse, catching up with women she didn't see nearly enough now that school drop-offs and lacrosse games were a thing of the past. Around nine o'clock the long work week caught up with both her and Evan, and they made their goodbyes and headed home.

Once home, they climbed the stairs together to their bedroom, where she planned on showering and collapsing into bed.

"What's that?" she asked, spotting a gift-wrapped box on her pillow. "How did you sneak that in?"

"I've got my ways," Evan said, coming up behind her, putting his hands on her hips, and burying his lips in the curve of her neck.

"The Hanukkah party at synagogue was the theme tonight. You didn't need to get me a present also."

Evan grinned. "Full disclosure. This is a present for myself."

She frowned. "Oh." She handed over the box to him, but he laughed and pushed it back at her.

"Open it. You'll see what I mean."

She perched a hip on the edge of the bed and ripped apart the paper, not worrying about reusing it next year. She lifted the cardboard lid of the box to reveal a gorgeous, barely-there ivory sheer nightie.

She held it up in front of her and looked at her husband. "I see what you mean. A present for yourself, indeed."

"You used to wear stuff like that, but then after the kids…"

She got it. Once the boys reached a certain age, sexy lingerie was impractical and slightly embarrassing for all parties, so she'd worn comfortable cotton to bed for the last decade.

"Kids don't live here anymore. No reason not to wear sexy stuff anymore," Evan said, and held up the nightie with a little wiggle, teasing her.

She yanked it from his hand and tossed it on the bed in front of her, then proceeded to tug off her synagogue clothes. She unpinned the tags from the nightie then slithered it on over her head. It had been years since she'd worn something this sexy and beautiful. It made her feel as beautiful as the negligée, but what made her feel the best was the look in Evan's eyes as he watched her shimmy and preen.

"Gorgeous," he said.

"Thank you."

"Now let's go to bed."

NIGHT EIGHT

AT THREE O'CLOCK ON SUNDAY AFTERNOON, JILL TEXTED EVAN A
third time then gave up. Where was he? He knew they had to start
peeling potatoes and grating them now if they had a hope of having
hundreds of latkes ready by five. He'd left an hour and a half ago
with a flimsy excuse about picking up bags of ice and more apple
sauce.

"Dammit," she muttered and left the front hall where she'd been
standing like a creepy stalker, watching the front drive for his car.
She made her way to the kitchen where she hefted the first of
several ten-pound bags of potatoes onto the counter.

All the good feelings she'd started to have toward her husband
from the past romantic week were about to erupt in a pan of hot oil.

She was working on peeling her third potato, the pile of off-
white oblong spuds stacked in a bowl of ice water next to her, when
she heard the front door open. "About freaking time," she yelled.
"Where have you been?"

No answer for a minute.

"Eeevvan! Come help." She sounded like a shrew and she didn't
care. This party was a joint effort and she was pissed.

"You sound mad, Mom." A young man's voice from behind her

had her dropping a potato and peeler on the floor and whirling around.

"Ben!"

Another man came up behind him. "Hey Mom."

"Ari!"

Evan walked into the kitchen looking like a man who'd invented a cure for cancer, solved climate change, and gotten laid all in one afternoon. "Surprise."

She leaped toward her sons and grabbed them in a full momma-bear hug. Evan stood apart, and she uncurled a hand to tug him into the group hug, too.

They all stood together in a mash for a long minute while Jill laughed and cried her joy.

"We tried to get Zoe here, but she's taking finals. And it seemed crazy to fly her home for a night only to have her fly home again next week for winter break," Evan explained, sounding almost apologetic for only getting two out of three children home.

Jill pushed Ben and Ari aside so she could hug her husband. "This is perfect. Absolutely perfect."

"Happy Hanukkah, Jilly." He lowered his face to touch his lips to hers, and forgetting their audience for a minute, the kiss turned passionate.

"Gross. Get a room," Ari said, and they pulled apart laughing.

Jill noted that Ben didn't say a word, nor did he look disgusted at the sight of his parents making out. He looked thoughtful. Interesting. Was he making the transition to where he could see his parents as role models for his desired path in adult relationships? Was his expression related to the so-called mysterious-yet-serious girlfriend?

"Let's make latkes," Evan announced, spurring them into action. Jill handed a peeler to Ari and put Ben on food-processor duty while Evan got the frying pans prepped with oil and then lined the counter with paper towels.

The time flew by with the four of them working rapidly, and soon the guests arrived, and the party was in full swing with Aunt

Esti declaring the latkes delicious. Jill played hostess, but kept returning to Evan's side to reconnect throughout the party.

As darkness fell outside, Evan grabbed her hand and pulled her over to the table where all the hanukkiot waited to be lit. He cleared his throat, but their guests kept chattering on.

Ari let out a shrill whistle, getting everyone's attention. When all was quiet, he grinned and gestured to Evan. "All yours, Dad."

Evan smiled and held up a glass of wine. "Before we light the candles, I want to make toast. A Hanukkah toast."

Jill watched him, somewhat amazed. Evan was not a trial lawyer precisely because he wasn't one to make flashy speeches. The last speech she remembered him making was at Zoe's bat mitzvah and that had been a pre-written joint effort.

But he was up in front of all their friends and family now, clearly about to launch into something heartfelt.

"I know the meaning of Hanukkah can get a little lost sometimes, with its proximity to that other holiday." A few chuckles. "But take away the presents and fried food and remember that Hanukkah is about two things. Fighting back and holding on in the face of adversity."

Evan turned slightly and it was as though they were alone in the room, his gaze intent on hers as he continued. "Remember that when the Maccabees fought against the Hellenists it was the first time in history the Jews had fought back against their oppressors. Unfortunately it hasn't been the last time we've had to fight, but it did mark the first time Jews said 'enough. We've got something good here and we're not giving it up.'"

Jill's cheeks warmed under his gaze. It was evident he was speaking about more than ancient history.

"And remember that when the Jews rededicated the destroyed temple, they only had enough oil to light the *ner tamid* for one day, but a miracle happened and the flame lasted for eight. Bear in mind now that even when a spark goes out, miracles happen and they can be relit. It just takes a little effort."

He held up his glass. "*L'chaim.* Happy Hanukkah."

Everyone repeated the gesture and the words.

Jill held up her glass, but couldn't speak over the lump in her throat. Evan's speech had been a clear love poem to her. A nerdy, history-based love poem, but it was hers, and she adored it.

"Let's light candles!" Ari shouted nearby and everyone crowded in as Jill got it together and supervised matches and who lit which hanukkiah.

When all the candles on all six hanukkiot were lit, someone switched off the light, and they basked in the warm strong glow, silent for a powerful second before someone began to sing.

I have a little dreidel, I made it out of clay...

"Happy Hanukkah, Jill," Evan whispered.

She snuggled in close under Evan's protective arm, content that their marriage had been rekindled and the spark wouldn't die. She and Evan would fight for it. "Happy Hanukkah."

ABOUT THE AUTHORS

Lori Ann Bailey is a best-selling author and winner of the National Readers' Choice Award and Holt Medallion for Best First Book and Best Historical. Lori writes hunky highland heroes and strong-willed independent lasses finding their perfect matches in the Highlands of historic Scotland. She is active in Romance Writers of America, having served on committees on the national and local levels, and is a contributor to the weekly podcast, History, Books and Wine. When not writing or reading, Lori enjoys time with her real-life hero and four kids or spending time walking or drinking wine with her friends. Find Lori at https://loriannbailey.com/

Erin Eisenberg lives in Washington state, where she shares her love of books with the next generation. She has always been a reader, and wants nothing more than to sit and read for the rest of her days. When she's not teaching, she is exploring local parks with her son, checking out great restaurants (or watching MasterChef or the latest Marvel movie) with her husband, walking or biking local trails with her mom, relaxing with friends and family, or curled up with a good book and a mug of tea.

A classically trained singer, **Rose Grey** sang professionally before audiences of thousands, conducted choirs for fun and profit, and worked for years as a full-time *hazzan*. As a result, music, poetry and Jewish themes infuse her writing. Rose's novels range from standalone contemporary romance to romantic suspense. Her contemporary romance trilogy, beginning with award-winning *Waiting For You*, is a captivating series about the Durrell Brothers of

Demerest Cove. To learn more, visit her website:
https://rosegreybooks.com/.

USA Today bestselling author **Mindy Klasky** learned to read when
her parents shoved a book in her hands and told her she could travel
anywhere through stories. As a writer, Mindy has traveled through
various genres, including contemporary romance (such as her
Harmony Springs series), fantasy, and science fiction. In her spare
time, Mindy knits, quilts, and tries to tame her to-be-read shelf. Visit
Mindy and read free samples of all her books at www.
mindyklasky.com.

Lavinia Klein (who writes as Lavinia Kent) never knew that most
people don't make up stories in their heads to pass the time. She still
has a hard time understanding how those who don't are able
to survive the doctor's waiting room or a grocery store line, without
another world to escape into. As a soon-to-be "empty-nester,"
Lavinia is looking forward to having more time to write and to
hanging out in the backyard with Trouble, her Cavalier King
Charles Spaniel, reading romance novels. She also watches far too
much HBO and Netflix and might just have a slightly unhealthy
relationship with Bravo's reality TV. She can be found on Facebook
or reached through her website, LaviniaKent.com.

Michelle Mars has an unhealthy obsession with coffee, caramel,
and funny t-shirts. This single mom of two amazing, kind, and
creative dragons/children has naturally purple hair and loves
nothing more than talking books, kids, and living your best life. She
enjoys reading romance, traveling, and writing stories that make her
readers laugh, sweat, and swoon. Author of the paranormal, sci-fi,
rom-com Love Wars Series, including *Moving Jack* and *Taming Rory*
(coming soon.) The first book in her contemporary rom-com series
The Frisky Bean, *Frisky Intentions*, will be out the first half of 2020.
Michelle's truth: Humor is a turn-on!

JT Silver used to sneak Shirlee Busbee novels from her mother's bookshelf and stay up all night reading them. She still loves a hero who makes it impossible to sleep! She currently writes short romantic fiction. She lives with her family in San Diego, California.

Lynne Silver is the author of sexy contemporary romance such as the popular Alpha Heroes and Coded for Love series. She loves to travel and explore new cities. She has a slight (huge) addiction to donuts, fancy purses, romance novels, and video games. She lives in Washington, DC with her husband and two sons. She loves connecting with readers so please find her on social media.

CPSIA information can be obtained
at www.ICGtesting.com
Printed in the USA
LVHW111301050220
645937LV00001B/137

9 781950 184040